PRAISE FOR *OLD CITY HALL*

"It's clear that *Old City Hall* has enough hidden motives and gumshoeing to make it a hard-boiled classic." —*The Globe and Mail*

"It's about time someone put Toronto on the international crime thriller map, and . . . Robert Rotenberg does just that." —*Toronto Sun*

"The book has wowed pretty much everyone who's read it. . . . A finely paced, intricately written plot is matched by a kaleidoscope of the multicultural city's locales and characters." —*Maclean's*

"Twenty-first-century Toronto is a complicated place, rife with the kind of paradox and contradiction that lends a city depth and complexity. It's a good setting for sinuous legal machinations to unfold, steeped in that elusively desirable literary quality we call character." —*The Toronto Star*

"Rotenberg's writing style is understated and fluid, enhanced but not overwhelmed by his insider knowledge of Toronto's criminal courts and the streets surrounding 'the Hall.'" —*Quill & Quire*

"A convincing portrayal of backstage operations in the justice system . . . An enjoyable addition to the literature of urban crime."
—*The Times Literary Supplement*

"An amazing debut novel. Robert Rotenberg's *Old City Hall* has everything a legal thriller should have, and more: absolutely engaging characters; a tight, taut, and believable plot; a heart-quickening pace; and, best of all, some of the finest writing I've read in years. This one has winner written all over it." —*Nelson DeMille*

"*Old City Hall* is proof that Robert Rotenberg is one of the most striking writers on the current crime scene." —*Crime Time*

"Breathtaking . . . a tightly woven spiderweb ⬛⬛⬛⬛⬛⬛⬛⬛⬛ters make this a truly gripping read. . . . Robert R⬛⬛⬛⬛⬛⬛⬛⬛⬛⬛ an Rankin does for Edinburgh." —*Jeffery Deaver*

"Robert Rotenberg knows his Toronto courts and jails, he knows his law, and he knows his way around a legal thriller. *Old City Hall* is a splendid entertainment."
—**Andrew Pyper, author of *The Killing Circle***

A TOUCHSTONE BOOK

PUBLISHED BY SIMON & SCHUSTER

NEW YORK   LONDON   TORONTO   SYDNEY

OLD CITY HALL

ROBERT ROTENBERG

TOUCHSTONE
A Division of Simon & Schuster, Inc.
1230 Avenue of the Americas
New York, NY 10020

This Touchstone export edition October 2009
Published by arrangement with Farrar, Straus & Giroux

For information about special discounts for bulk purchases, please contact Simon & Schuster Customer Service at 1-800-268-3216 or CustomerService@simonandschuster.ca.

Designed by Jonathan D. Lippincott

Manufactured in the United States of America

1   3   5   7   9   10   8   6   4   2

ISBN 978-1-4165-9286-0

FOR VAUNE

And she shows you where to look
Among the garbage and the flowers
There are heroes in the seaweed
There are children in the morning
They are leaning out for love
And they will lean that way forever

—Leonard Cohen, "Suzanne"

PART I: DECEMBER

I

Much to the shock of his family, Mr. Singh rather enjoyed delivering newspapers. Who would have thought that Gurdial Singh, former chief engineer for Indian Railways, the largest transportation company in the world, would be dropping newspapers at people's doors commencing at 5:05 each morning. He didn't need to work. But since coming to Toronto four years earlier, he had absolutely insisted on it. No matter that he was turning seventy-four years old on Thursday next. Yes, it was a silly little job, Mr. Singh was forced to concede to his wife, Bimal, and their three daughters, but he liked it.

That's why Mr. Singh was humming an old Hindi tune to himself as he walked briskly through the early-winter darkness on a cold Monday morning, the seventeenth of December.

He entered the marble-appointed lobby of the Market Place Tower, a luxury condominium on Front Street, and gave a friendly wave to Mr. Rasheed, the night concierge. The *Globe and Mail* newspapers were neatly stacked just inside the door beside a diminutive plastic Christmas tree. How strange, in a country covered in forests, that they would use plastic trees, Mr. Singh thought as he hitched up his gray flannel pants and bent down to cut the binding cord with his pocketknife. He sorted the papers into twelve piles, one for each floor on his route. It had been easy to memorize which residents took a paper, and it was a simple matter to walk down the deserted hallways and drop one squarely at each door.

The solitude was very nice. So unlike the clutter of Delhi. When he arrived at the top floor, Mr. Singh knew he would see the one person who was always awake. Mr. Kevin something. Mr. Singh could never remember Mr. Kevin's last name, even though the gentleman was one of the most famous people in Canada. There he would be, in his shabby bathrobe, a cigarette cupped in his right hand, a mug of tea in his left, scratching his gray beard with his shoulder, anxiously awaiting his paper.

Mr. Kevin was the host of a morning radio show that was broadcast across the country. Mr. Singh had tried to listen to it a few times, but it was just a lot of chatter about fishing in Newfoundland, fiddle music in the Ottawa Valley, and farming on the prairies. These Canadians were funny people. Most of them lived in cities, but all they seemed to discuss was the countryside.

Mr. Kevin, despite his unkempt appearance, was very much a gentleman. Rather shy. Mr. Singh enjoyed the ritual conversation they had each morning.

"Good morning, Mr. Singh," Mr. Kevin always said.

"Good morning, Mr. Kevin," Mr. Singh always said in reply. "And how is your beautiful wife?"

"More beautiful than ever, Mr. Singh," Mr. Kevin would say. Putting the cigarette in his mouth, he'd open his palm and pass an orange slice over to Mr. Singh.

"Thank you," Mr. Singh would say, giving Mr. Kevin his newspaper.

"Freshly sliced," Mr. Kevin would answer.

They'd then follow up with a short discussion about gardening or cooking or tea. Despite all he must have had on his mind, Mr. Kevin never seemed rushed. It was simply courteous and respectful conversation at an ungodly hour. Quite civilized.

It took the usual twenty-five minutes for Mr. Singh to methodically work his way up to the twelfth floor. There were only two suites on the top floor. Mr. Kevin's suite, 12A, was to the left, around the bend, near the end of a long corridor. The resident to the right, an older lady who lived alone, took the other paper, which he always delivered last.

Mr. Singh arrived at Mr. Kevin's door, and as usual it was half-way open. But there was no sign of Mr. Kevin. I could just leave the newspaper here, Mr. Singh thought. Then he'd miss their daily conversation.

He waited for a moment. Of course, he could not knock, that would be highly improper. Humming louder, he shuffled his feet, hoping to make enough noise to announce his arrival. Still, no one came.

He hesitated. It was the engineer in him. He liked routine. Order. He remembered the day his eleventh-form mathematics teacher taught the class that there was no such thing as parallel lines. That because the earth was round, any two parallel lines would eventually meet. Mr. Singh didn't sleep for a week.

There was a noise from inside the apartment. An odd, hollow sound. That was strange. Then a door closed. Good, he thought as he waited. But there was silence again. Maybe he should leave.

Instead, he took Mr. Kevin's newspaper and dropped it onto the parquet floor just outside the door. It landed with a loud smack, which he hoped would signal his presence in the doorway. He'd never done anything like this before.

There was another noise inside. Distant. Were they footsteps? What should he do? He certainly could not enter.

Mr. Singh waited. For the first time, he looked down at the front page of the newspaper. There was a picture of an ice hockey player raising his arms in the air and a story about the local team, the Toronto Maple Leafs. How odd that the name was misspelled: Leafs and not Leaves. And the color of the leaf on the jersey was blue. Mr. Singh had seen lovely red and yellow maple leaves. But never a blue one.

At last he heard footsteps approaching the door. Mr. Kevin came into the hallway, wearing his usual bathrobe, and opened the door all the way. Mr. Singh heard a soft tap as it rested on the door stopper.

But where was his cigarette? His tea? Mr. Kevin was looking at his hands. Rubbing his fingers. Mr. Singh noticed something red on his fingertips.

He had a pleasant thought. Blood oranges. He so loved to eat them back home, and he'd recently found that they arrived in Canadian stores this time of year. Had Mr. Kevin been cutting one?

Mr. Kevin raised his hands to the light. Mr. Singh could see the red liquid clearly now. It was thick and heavy, not thin like juice from an orange.

Mr. Singh's heart began to race.

It was blood.

Mr. Singh opened his mouth to speak. But before he could say a word, Mr. Kevin leaned closer. "I killed her, Mr. Singh," he whispered, "I killed her."

2

Officer Daniel Kennicott was running flat out. "Where do you want me to go?" he called back to his partner, Nora Bering, who was half a step behind him.

"I'll cover the lobby," she said as they rushed into the Market Place Tower. "You go up."

A uniformed man standing behind a long wooden desk looked up from his newspaper as they hurried past. Inside, the marble walls were covered with textured sculptures, bouquets of fresh flowers seemed to be everywhere, and classical music was playing softly.

As the senior officer, it was Bering's job to assign tasks in urgent situations. As they were running, she'd called the dispatcher directly on her cell phone to avoid the scanners who picked up police calls. The key facts were that at 5:31, twelve minutes ago, Kevin Brace, the famous radio host, met his newspaper deliveryman, a Mr. Singh, at the door of his penthouse, Suite 12A. Brace said that he'd killed his wife. Singh found a body, adult female, apparently deceased, in the bathtub. He reported that the body was cold to the touch and Brace was unarmed, calm.

That the suspect was calm, almost placid, was common in domestic homicides, Kennicott thought. The passion of the moment had dissipated. Shock was setting in.

Bering pointed to the stairway door beside the elevator. "Two choices, stairs or elevator," she said.

Kennicott nodded and took a deep breath.

"If you take the elevator," Bering said, "procedure is to get off two floors below."

Kennicott nodded again. He'd learned this in basic training when he joined the force. A few years before that, two officers had answered what sounded like a routine domestic call on the twenty-fourth floor of a suburban apartment building. When the elevator door opened, they were gunned down by the father, who'd already killed his wife and only child.

"I'll take the stairs," he said.

"Remember: every word the suspect says is vital," Bering said as Kennicott gulped in more air. "Be one hundred percent accurate with your notes."

"Right."

"Enter with your gun out," she said. "But be careful with it."

Kennicott nodded. "Okay."

"Radio me just before you get to the top floor."

"Got it," Kennicott said as he plunged into the stairwell. The job of the first officer on scene at a homicide was containment. It was like trying to protect a sand castle in a windstorm, because every second, bits of evidence were blowing away. He was tempted to take the stairs three at a time, but between his bulletproof vest, his gun, and the portable hand radio, he was carrying about eight pounds of equipment. Just be steady, he told himself.

By the time he got to the third floor, taking two steps at a time, he was in a smooth rhythm. Kennicott and Bering had been on shift four nights in a row and were just an hour away from going home for four days' rest when this "hotshot" emergency call came in. They'd been across the street, strolling through the St. Lawrence Market, the city's big indoor food emporium, which was setting up for the day.

When he hit the sixth floor, a small drop of perspiration formed at the base of Kennicott's neck and began to work its way down his backbone. Up until this call, it had been a pretty quiet night. A Tamil guy over in Regent Park had bitten off part of his wife's ear—when they got there, the wife claimed she'd fallen on a piece of glass. The coach house of a gay couple in Cabbagetown had been broken into and the intruder had left a turd on their Persian rug. On Jarvis Street an under-age prostitute claimed she'd been punched in the face by the old wino who gave her a room in exchange for a nightly blow job—then she propositioned Kennicott. Run-of-the-mill stuff.

By the tenth floor he was breathing hard. It had been three and a half years since he'd joined the force, turning his back on a promising career as a young lawyer at one of the city's top firms. The reason? His older brother, Michael, had been murdered twelve months before. When the investigation seemed to be going nowhere, he'd traded in his legal robes for a badge.

This was exactly what he wanted, the chance to work on a homicide, he thought as he started to take the stairs three at a time and clicked on his radio. "Kennicott here," he said to Bering. "I'm approaching the eleventh floor."

"Ten-four. Forensics, Homicide, and lots of cars are on the way. I've disabled the elevators. No one's come down the stairs. Turn off the radio. That way you can make a silent entry."

"Ten-four. Over and out."

Kennicott burst through the door on the twelfth floor and stopped. A long hallway ran straight ahead before it turned, presumably to the elevator and the other half of the floor. Pale white wall sconces cast a gauzelike light onto muted yellow walls. There was only one apartment in this section of the hall.

Kennicott moved cautiously down to 12A. The door was half-way open. Taking a deep breath, he pushed it all the way to the wall as he unholstered his gun. Stepping forward, he found himself in a long, wide hallway that had a light-stained hardwood floor. Everything was quiet. It felt strange to barge into this calm, well-appointed suite, his gun out as if he were a little boy playing cops and robbers in his backyard.

"Toronto Police," he said in a loud voice.

"We are presently seated in the breakfast room located at the rear of the flat," an East Indian–sounding male voice called out. "The deceased lady is in the hall bathroom."

He checked behind the front door and then walked slowly down the hallway, his boots thumping on the wood floor. Midway down, a door to his right was slightly ajar. The light was on, and he could see a sliver of white tiles. He didn't have gloves on, so he elbowed the door open.

It was a small bathroom, and the door opened to the wall. He took two steps in. A raven-haired woman lay in the tub. Her eyes were wide-open. Her face was drained of all blood, making it almost as white as the tub. There was no movement.

He backed out of the room, careful not to touch anything. The sweat on his body felt sticky.

"You will find us here," the East Indian voice said again.

A few more steps down the hall and Kennicott came to a big eat-in kitchen. To his right was Kevin Brace, the famous radio host, sitting quietly in a wrought-iron chair. He was holding out a ceramic mug. He wore tattered slippers, and his frayed bathrobe was pulled up tight around his neck. His scruffy beard and his trademark old-fashioned large wire-rimmed glasses made him instantly recognizable. Brace didn't even look up.

Across the table from Brace, an elderly brown-skinned man in a suit and tie was leaning over and pouring tea into Brace's mug. Between the two men, a gaudy Tiffany lamp hovered over the table, like a large bubble in a cartoon in which dialogue was waiting to be written. Under the lamp's glow was a mostly eaten plate of sliced oranges. Kennicott could see that they were red. Blood oranges, he thought.

On the far wall, floor-to-ceiling south-facing windows looked over Lake Ontario, which stretched out like an enormous black pool. Barely illuminated by the hint of early-morning light was the chain of small islands that formed a half-moon arc across the bay.

Kennicott stopped momentarily, disoriented by the expansive view and the calm tableau in front of him. With his gun still out, he stepped onto the slick tile kitchen floor. Suddenly his right foot slid out from under him. He jammed his arm down to break his fall, and the gun skittered out of his hand and slid halfway across the floor.

What a rookie move, Kennicott thought as he pulled himself up. Great. The detective who gets this case will love this.

Over at the table, Brace was pouring honey into his mug and stirring his tea, as if nothing had happened.

Kennicott edged toward his gun, careful not to slip again. "Kevin Brace?" he asked.

Brace avoided Kennicott's eyes. His glasses were smudged. He didn't say anything, just concentrated on stirring his tea, like a Swiss watchmaker at his workbench.

Kennicott picked up his gun. "Mr. Brace, I am Officer Daniel Kennicott of the Toronto Police. Is the woman in the bathtub your wife?"

"She certainly is," the East Indian man said. "And she is most assuredly dead. I saw much death in my years as a chief engineer for Indian Railways, which is the largest transportation company in the world."

Kennicott looked over at the man. "I see, Mr.—"

The elderly man jumped to his feet so quickly that Kennicott took a step back. "Gurdial Singh," he said. "I am Mr. Brace's morning newspaper delivery person. I contacted the police service."

"Morning newspaper delivery person," "police service," Kennicott thought. The phrases sounded so odd, he had to stop himself from smiling. He reached for his hand radio.

"I arrived a minute earlier than my usual time, at five twenty-nine, and called at five thirty-one, once I had confirmed the fatality," Mr. Singh said. "Mr. Kevin and I have been having our tea, awaiting your arrival. This is our second pot. It is a special Darjeeling I bring the first of each month. Most effective for constipation."

Kennicott looked at Brace. He was studying his spoon as if it were a priceless antique. Sliding the gun into its holster, Kennicott took a step back toward the table.

He touched Brace lightly on the shoulder. "Mr. Brace, you are under arrest for murder," he said. He advised Brace of his right to counsel.

Brace didn't change his gaze. He just flicked his free hand toward Kennicott, like a magician pulling something out of his sleeve. There was a business card between his bloodied fingers: NANCY PARISH, BARRISTER AND SOLICITOR, PRACTICE RESTRICTED TO CRIMINAL LAW.

Kennicott clicked on his radio. "Kennicott here."

"What's your location?" Bering asked.

"I'm in the condo." Kennicott kept his voice low. "The suspect's here with the witness, Mr. Gurdial Singh, the newspaper . . . delivery person. The scene is calm. The victim is in the hall bathtub. Appears DOA. I've made an arrest." Reporting that a victim appeared to be deceased, dead on arrival, was the top priority.

"What's he doing?"

Kennicott looked at Brace. The gray-haired broadcaster was pouring milk into his tea. "Drinking tea," he said.

"Okay. Just watch him. Backup is on the way."

"Ten-four."

"And Kennicott. Record every word he says."

"Got it. Over and out." Kennicott put the radio into its hip holder, and he could feel the adrenaline in his system begin to slow down.

What would happen next? He studied Brace. Now his spoon was on the table and he was sipping his Darjeeling tea. Looking placidly out the window. Kennicott knew that a case like this could go in all sorts of unexpected directions, but as he looked at the little tea party in the kitchen, there was no doubt in his mind that Kevin Brace wasn't going to say a word.

3

Damn it, stop yawning," Detective Ari Greene muttered to himself as he parked his 1988 Oldsmobile in the narrow driveway of his father's split-level bungalow and grabbed a paper bag from the passenger seat. Good, he thought as he felt around inside it, the bagels from Gryfe's are still warm. He reached inside a second bag and extracted a carton of milk. He fished under his seat until he found a stash of plastic shopping bags and yanked out one from the Sobeys grocery store.

This will work, Greene thought as he plopped the milk into the bag. If his father discovered that the milk came from the bagel store, there'd be hell to pay: "You bought the milk at Gryfe's? How much? Two ninety-nine? This week, at Sobeys, milk is two forty-nine, and two fifty-one at Loblaws. I have a coupon for an extra ten cents." The words would tumble out in his dad's unique mixture of English and Yiddish.

Greene was coming off his tenth straight night shift. He'd been too tired to make a second trip to the grocery store. His father had been through enough in his life. The last thing he needed was to find out that his only surviving son was a lousy shopper.

A thin layer of snow had fallen overnight. Greene took the shovel from the metal railing and carefully cleared the concrete steps. He picked up the copy of the *Toronto Star* from in front of the door and stuck his key to his father's house into the lock.

Inside, he heard the hum of the television set coming from the living room. He sighed. Since his mother died, his father hated to sleep in their bedroom. Instead he'd watch TV in the den until he fell asleep on the plastic-covered couch.

Greene kicked off his shoes. He stacked the bagels on the counter, put the milk in the fridge—making sure to leave out the Sobeys bag—and walked noiselessly into the living room. His father was curled up under a tattered brown-and-white afghan Greene's mother had knitted for his seventieth birthday. His head had slipped off a small pillow and was hard against the thick plastic.

Moving aside the teak coffee table in front of the sofa, Greene knelt beside his sleeping father. As a homicide detective for the past five years and a cop for twenty, he'd seen some pretty tough characters. None of them could hold a candle to this little Polish Jew who, try as they might, the Nazis couldn't kill.

"It's me, Dad. Ari. I'm home."

Greene touched his father's shoulder softly, then quickly moved back. He braced himself. Nothing happened. Still keeping his distance, he squeezed harder on his father's shoulder. He continued. "Dad, I've picked up some warm bagels and milk. I'll get some denture cream for you tomorrow."

His father's eyes flew open. This was the moment Greene had dreaded every morning since he was a boy. What nightmare was Dad waking from? His father's gray-green eyes looked disoriented.

"Dad, the bagels are warm. And the milk . . ."

His father looked at his hands. Greene moved closer again and slid the fallen pillow under his father's head. With his right hand he caressed his face. His father mumbled, *"Mayn tochter."* It meant "My daughter." Then he said her name: "Hannah." The daughter he'd lost at Treblinka.

Greene lifted him into an upright position on the couch. His father seemed to gather strength, like a blow-up doll slowly being inflated.

"Where did you buy the milk?" his dad asked.

"Sobeys."

"They have any coupons?"

"They're out. You know what it's like at Christmastime."

His father rubbed his face with his hands. "Yes, I know. Christmastime you do extra shifts to help out your friends. You look tired. You work last night?"

"For a few hours," Greene lied. He was pretty sure his father knew it wasn't true.

"Today you off?"

Greene touched the beeper on his hip. "Number one in the batting order." The batting order was the "on call" list in the homicide bureau. "Maybe I'll get lucky and it'll be a peaceful day."

His father patted him on the shoulder and felt the fabric of Greene's lapel. "That fancy tailor of yours, his stitching is improving."

In his heart, Greene's father was still a tailor—the job he'd had as a young married man in his little Polish village until the morning in September 1942 when the Nazis surrounded it. In the line at Treblinka, a friend told the Ukrainian guard he was a cobbler. So that's what he became. When he came to Canada, he opened his own shoe shop in a downtown neighborhood that was a smorgasbord of European ethnic groups. It turned out that the Nazis had given him the perfect training ground. Two years of mending shoes of Jews from all over Europe meant that he recognized almost every shoe that came in.

"The stitching should be good," Greene said, unbuttoning the jacket and showing his father the inside. "It took him two months to make it."

"Two months," his father snorted. "Sit down, I'll make myself some coffee. You want some tea?"

Greene smiled. "No, I'm fine, Dad."

The only place to sit was the plastic-covered couch. He'd hated the thing ever since he was old enough to have friends over to the house—rich kids whose parents didn't have accents, whose parents knew how to ski and play tennis, whose parents didn't have numbers on their arms.

All these years later, he'd still love to burn the darn sofa. But there was no point arguing with his father. Never was. And Greene was dog-tired. He lay down and pulled the coffee table back into position so he could put his feet up on it.

"Leafs lose again?" his father called from the kitchen. "I fell asleep at the end of the second period. It was two–nothing for Detroit."

"You'll be amazed," Greene said. "They scored three goals in the last ten minutes, beat the Wings three–two."

"Unbelievable," his father said. "Maybe one game they won. Still they are terrible."

Greene maneuvered his back, trying to get comfortable. He grimaced as he heard the plastic crack and squeak under his weight. As the only Jewish guy in Homicide, he scored lots of points by taking shifts this time of year. He didn't mind.

For a rising star on the squad, with just one unsolved case, this time of year was a bonanza. The last three Decembers he'd had three homicides, but this year had been quiet.

The smell of instant coffee wafted into the living room. It was a smell Greene had disliked since he was a child. He shifted a bit on the couch. The beeper attached to the back of his belt was caught on the plastic.

"Dad, try the cream cheese I got for you on Friday."

"I'm looking for it. Maybe I didn't wrap it right. After three days it's stale," his father called from the kitchen. "You want some raspberry jam?"

"Sure, Dad," Greene said. His eyelids felt heavy. As much as he despised the sofa, right now it felt comfortable.

He reached back, unclipped the pager from his belt, and held it. That felt better. He was so tired. His eyes began to shut.

Suddenly he sat bolt upright, crinkling the hard plastic underneath him, and squeezed the pager. It was buzzing wildly.

4

A-l-i-m-o-n-y

    A-l-l-t-h-e-m-o-n-e-y

    A-l-l-f-r-o-m-A-w-o-t-w-e

    A-l-l-m-y-m-o-n-e-y

That's it: All my money, Awotwe Amankwah thought as he doodled letters onto the back of his green reporter's pad. Thanks to you, Madam Honorable Justice Heather Hillgate, you and your final divorce decree, I get access to Fatima and Abdul Wednesdays from five-thirty to nine, and Saturday afternoons from two to five, one phone call per night, between seven thirty and eight. That's it. The price of admission? Eight hundred dollars a month in support payments.

"If you want your children overnight, get a place of your own," Justice Heather the Leather, as he liked to think of her, had lectured him the last time they were in court. Claire was there. Dressed all prim and proper, like the wife on *The Bill Cosby Show*, backed up by her high-priced lawyers, who filed motions against him quicker than his ex changed lovers. Amankwah couldn't afford his lawyers anymore, so he was unrepresented.

His next move—to get the kids overnight—was going to take months, and money he didn't have, to go back to court yet again.

To keep up with the court order, Amankwah had to do this graveyard shift in the Radio Room at the *Toronto Star*, the country's largest paper, where he'd worked for almost a decade.

The Radio Room—also known as the Box, the Rubber Room, and the Panic Room—was parked at the north end of the *Star*'s enormous newsroom.

It wasn't really a room, but a small glassed-in booth filled with a staggering array of equipment. There were five scanners, but only two worked—police and ambulance. They were on constantly, as was the twenty-four-hour TV news station that, in the middle of the night, went to mind-dulling infomercials about exercise or kitchen equipment. The twenty-four-hour radio news station ran at low level, to complete the constant cacophony of sound.

He had to check all of them, plus two different news services rolling through the fat old computer screen in the corner. And there was a long list of calls to be made hourly: police headquarters not just in Toronto, but in the far-reaching suburbs and surrounding cities—Durham, Peel, Halton, Milton, York, Oakville, Aurora, Burlington.

This whole area was known as the Golden Horseshoe, the fifth-biggest urban center in North America, so there was a lot of ground to cover. All the fire, transit, ambulance, and hospital authorities also had to be contacted. As well as the Ontario Provincial Police and, never forget, the lottery people. When things slowed down, you were expected to read through the daily paid obituaries to see if a story lurked there.

At first it might look confusing, but the job was strictly entry-level, intern-journalism-student stuff. Not something a veteran reporter like Amankwah should be doing.

He kept his BlackBerry on at all times to get e-mails from reporters in the field and in case something happened with his kids. Out through the front window, looking over the sprawling near-empty newsroom, a row of clocks on the far wall displayed the current time in major cities around the world: Paris, Moscow, Hong Kong, Tokyo, Melbourne, Los Angeles. Amankwah looked at them with the dreamy eyes of a poor child watching a limousine drive past. He'd wanted to be a foreign correspondent, the first black reporter at the *Star* to be sent overseas. But now that dream was in tatters. He looked at the clock labeled LOCAL TIME. It was 5:28. Another half hour to go. Then he'd have four hours to get back to his sister's apartment in Thorncliffe, where he was living on a couch, grab a shower, and be here for his regular ten o'clock shift.

He turned his gaze to the window in front of him. It was plastered with aged instructional memos, funny news clippings, and multicolored sticky notes. The protocol was for reporters to write out humorous things they heard on the scanners in the middle of the night and post them on the window. Amankwah looked at some of the funnier ones:

Dec. 29, 2:12 a.m.: Dispatcher: "Did you say baklava?" Cop 21 Division: "Oooh . . . it's been a long shift. He was wearing a balaclava."

Cop 43 Division: "I'm not up on all the gangs in Scarborough but I'm pretty sure there isn't one called the Nipples." Dispatcher: "Regardless, they should be photographed anyway."

The Radio Room was warm. Amankwah had his jacket off and his tie loosened. Every fifteen minutes he made a detailed notebook entry in his neat script. This might be a lousy job, but he was still a good reporter. He did the work well.

It had been a quiet night. The days before Christmas were a dead zone for news stories, and earlier in the night the desk had been hounding him to find something local for the front page.

Amankwah had no good news to offer. Out in the suburbs there was an Iranian cabdriver—a former history professor—who got robbed at knifepoint by a couple of young Asians. The kids weren't too bright. A bit of snow had fallen in the suburbs last night, and the cops followed the tracks in the snow back to one of their houses. And a group of Pakistani college students downtown brought some cricket bats into a doughnut shop and took some whacks at one of their former friends. A drunk driver in the Entertainment District ran over a cop's foot. Typical stuff. None of it front-page material.

At about one in the morning it had looked like he had some action. A rich doctor in Forest Hill caught his wife in bed with his teenage son's best friend. He'd sliced the kid with a kitchen knife. At first it sounded as if he'd cut the young stud's cock off. Amankwah called the desk, and they got all excited. They were hoping the doctor was a surgeon. But an hour later it turned out the guy was just a dermatologist and he'd used a butter knife. All the teenager had was a scrape on the back of his hand.

A bloody butter knife, Amankwah thought. What a wimp.

He checked the wall clock for Toronto: 5:30. He checked the wire services for fresh news alerts. Nothing. He listened to the half-hour report on the all-news radio station. Not a thing. He turned on the cabbie dispatchers and listened for a full minute. Nada. Finally, he checked the police scanner.

There was the usual chatter. Then he heard "code red." He turned up the dial. The cops changed their codes every week, but it wasn't exactly hard to figure out that "code red" meant something urgent. Probably homicide.

He heard the address: the Market Place Tower. Number 85A Front Street, Suite 12A. Amankwah's body jerked. Holy shit. He'd been in that penthouse suite. It was the home of Kevin Brace, the famous radio host. A few years before, Amankwah and Claire were on his show and they'd been invited to the Christmas party Brace and his younger second wife hosted every year in early December. Back when Amankwah and Claire were the city's glamour couple—smart, black, and beautiful. Back when Amankwah, a hot young reporter on the city beat, was the token black face in all the newspaper promo ads.

Amankwah bit his lip. Brace's building was a few blocks away. He turned down the volume on the scanner and moved his ear closer to the speaker. He could pick up the cops on the street. They were smart enough to keep Brace's name off the airwaves.

Imagine. Kevin Brace. Mr. All-Canadian Good Guy, according to his adoring fans. The Voice of Canada, they called him. Recent j-school grads in the radio rooms of the other three newspapers in town wouldn't pick this up. Red-hot news—maybe even a murder in Kevin Brace's condo—was flying under the radar, and he was the only one who had it.

Amankwah looked out at the near-deserted newsroom. There was only one editor manning the website and another babysitting some copy. He needed to alert them right away.

But he knew what would happen once they got hold of this. They'd hand the story to one of the overnight writers who were on call. If Amankwah was lucky, all he'd get would be a nice little pat on the back and then he'd be forgotten.

He started to pace. Any minute now an urgent alert would flash on the wires, and the news would be everywhere. Keep calm, he thought as he eased his wallet out of his jacket and slipped it into his back pocket. He palmed his digital camera, which was crammed with pictures of his children, and squeezed it in his hand. Trying to look casual, he walked out of the airless room and gave an exaggerated yawn.

"Just going down to grab a coffee," he said as he sauntered past the editor closest to him, jiggling some coins in his pocket with his free hand.

The night cleaner, a large Portuguese woman, was at the bank of elevators outside the newsroom. Amankwah pushed the Down button and leaned against the wall, stifling another yawn. The cafeteria was one floor below. The Up button was already lit.

The up elevator opened with a loud ding, and the cleaner got in. Amankwah affected a look of utter disinterest. The moment the doors closed, he ran for the stairway against the glassed-in west wall. Watching the dark street, he flew down the concrete stairs two steps at a time, his footsteps echoing. Five floors down, he hit the ground and walked casually out the fire door. He waved to the man at the security desk and opened the front door onto Yonge Street. Then he raced north, bracing himself against the wind.

He had to pass through a tunnel under the Gardiner Expressway, the ugly highway built in the 1950s that cut the city off from the lake. Clearly, back then planners forgot that people knew how to walk. As a meager concession to pedestrian traffic, on the side of the road there was a thin sidewalk hemmed in by a concrete railing. Every morning it was packed with people rushing to work, many of them residents of the islands south of the city who regularly commuted by ferry. A few hours later and he'd have been stuck.

Running now at full speed, squeezing the camera in his hand like a sprinter with a baton, he rushed out of the north side of the tunnel, got to Front Street, and cut east. He was breathing hard. The cold wind ripped down the back of his shirt.

Just one block to go. He could see the sign for the Market Place Tower.

"I need this story, I need this story, I need this story," he chanted to himself, like the old train in *The Little Engine That Could*, the book he used to love to read every night to the kids. "I need this story, I need this story, I need this story."

5

The early-morning streets were empty, and Detective Ari Greene was making great time. It always amazed him how quickly he could zip through the city when there was no traffic, and he'd put his magnetic police flasher on the roof of his car, giving him carte blanche to run every red light. One more hour, and the roads would be clogged with commuters.

He got to Front Street, turned east, and drove quickly past some of the city's oldest redbrick buildings, four and five stories high, most lovingly restored. Storefronts with large, tasteful windows looked out onto unusually wide sidewalks on both sides of the street, giving Front a comfortable, almost European feel. The Market Place Tower stood tall at the end of a long, elegant block.

Greene turned south at the corner and found a parking spot on the side street behind an old truck that still had snow on its back cab. Must be a supplier coming down to the St. Lawrence Market, across the street. On winter mornings when the snow had melted on the city streets, commuters from the colder outlying suburbs and towns carried the white stuff in with them.

Greene got out of his car and headed quickly toward the condo. He passed a driveway on the side street, where a discreet sign read PARKING FOR EXCLUSIVE USE OF MARKET PLACE RESIDENTS. VISITORS PLEASE SIGN IN WITH THE CONCIERGE. He kept on walking very fast, not running. There were certain unwritten protocols about being a homicide detective. You dressed well. You didn't carry a gun. And most of all, unless it was a true emergency, you never ran.

The automatic double doors of the condo slid open. Behind a long rosewood desk, a Middle Eastern–looking man in a uniform was reading the *Toronto Sun*.

"Detective Greene, Toronto Police Homicide," he said.

"Good morning, Detective." RASHEED was sewn on his jacket above his left breast, and he spoke with a lilting accent. Probably had a Ph.D. in physics back home, Greene thought.

Up ahead a uniformed female police officer stood perfectly positioned near a bank of two elevators and a doorway, which Greene assumed led to the stairs. Sensing his presence, she turned her head.

Greene saw who it was and grinned.

Officer Nora Bering nodded, gave the elevators one last look, and walked toward him, meeting him halfway.

"Hello, Detective," Bering said, shaking his hand. She was all business. "I've disabled the elevators except for police use. My partner took the stairs up to the twelfth floor. He radioed in from the apartment, and the scene is secure. Ambulance is on scene. Victim appears DOA. Two sets of officers from the division have already taken the suspect and the witness to headquarters. Detective Ho, the forensic officer, is on his way up. My partner's on scene, maintaining continuity."

Greene nodded. Bering was one of the best street cops on the force. "Who's your partner?" he asked. Anyone who worked with Bering would be well trained.

Bering hesitated for a moment. "Officer Daniel Kennicott," she said.

Greene nodded his head slowly. He could feel Bering's eyes on him. Kennicott's brother was murdered four and a half years ago, and Greene was the detective on the case. His only unsolved file.

A year after the murder, when Kennicott quit his law practice to become a cop, the story of a hotshot young lawyer who turned his back on the towers of Bay Street proved irresistible to the press. It didn't hurt that Kennicott was handsome, single, and articulate. And clearly he didn't want all the attention, which seemed to make the story all the more compelling.

Greene had treated Kennicott like any other victim who'd had a family member murdered. After their initial flurry of meetings, things had fallen into a pattern. Every two months they got together for a case update. When Kennicott joined the force, the meetings always took place when he was off shift. Out of uniform.

To his credit, Kennicott never asked for special consideration. But over the years, as the meetings grew shorter, Kennicott's frustration became palpable. There's an inevitable tension between a homicide detective and a victim's family. Their expectations—wanting a quick arrest, a speedy trial, a conviction, and a harsh sentence—often had to be tempered by the realities of police procedure and the legal system. The Crown Attorneys intentionally stayed aloof, so as their primary contact the victims turned to the detective, at times for comfort, at times to vent their frustration.

Professionally, Greene and Kennicott had avoided each other on duty. It was unspoken, but they both knew it was best. Perhaps it was time for that to change, Greene thought. Secretly, he'd followed Kennicott's career, like a hands-off older brother. He'd been impressed by the young man's progress. There was a saying on the force: To make it to Homicide, you needed a rabbi. Someone to watch over, and promote, your career.

"Kennicott's got everything under control," Bering said.

"Not surprised," Greene said.

He turned back to Rasheed, the concierge. "How many elevators are there to the twelfth floor?"

"The two you see in front of you and a service elevator around back."

Greene leaned over the lobby desk and scanned a row of live television monitors.

"Do these cover all the exits?"

"Yes. Yes. Certainly, the main doors."

Something about the man's answer bothered him. "Are there other doors?"

Rasheed looked vaguely uncomfortable. "Just one in the basement parking lot. There's no camera on that. But it is rarely used, and it closes from the inside."

Greene looked back at Bering.

"I had all three elevators disabled, including the service," she said. "I covered the stairs until backup arrived. There was no way to cover the basement."

"Right move," Greene said. The calculation was easy. Bering was alone down here and had to watch for someone coming into or trying to leave the lobby. And, Greene knew, Bering was smart enough not to lose sight of Rasheed.

"How do you know if the basement door is opened?" he asked the concierge.

"I check it when I do my rounds."

"Did you check it this morning?"

"Not yet. The door's rarely used. This is a quiet building."

It won't be quiet for much longer, Greene thought, with Kevin Brace's wife lying dead in their bathtub. "What if someone puts a brick in the door?"

Rasheed blushed. "It happens once in a while."

Greene nodded. That was the second time Rasheed had been less than forthcoming in his answers.

He walked to the elevator bank and went through a mental check-list: Bering had covered the lobby. The suspect and the witness were already taken away, and the forensic officer was now on scene. As much as he wanted to get upstairs, first he had to check the basement. There was a stairway beside the elevator, and as he reached for the door, it swung open.

A rather short older woman, her gray hair combed elegantly back up over her head, marched straight out. She wore a long black coat, and a blazing blue scarf was tied neatly around her neck. She strode toward the front door, her posture erect.

"Morning, Rasheed," she said to the concierge, moving quickly.

Greene rushed up beside her just before she got to the outer door. A rolled-up mat was slung over her shoulder. She had two white towels under her arm and a big water bottle in her hand.

"Excuse me, ma'am," he said, flashing his badge. "Detective Ari Greene, Toronto Police. We've closed the building down for a few minutes." He didn't want to identify himself as a homicide detective.

"Closed? What do you mean, closed?" The woman had a mild British accent, the kind that sounded as if it had been modified by many years in Canada. Up close she had high cheekbones that were accentuated by her age. She wore no makeup. Her skin was still remarkably smooth. Something about the dignified way in which she carried herself made Greene smile.

"We're investigating an incident in the building," Greene said.

"What does that have to do with me?" the woman asked. "My class starts in eleven minutes."

Greene moved all the way in front of her, blocking her exit. "This is a serious matter, I'm afraid."

She nodded toward the front desk. "Rasheed can give you any information you need, I'm sure."

Greene opened a leather-bound maroon notebook and pulled out his initialed Cross pen, the one that Chief Hap Charlton had given him when he made Homicide. The woman moved slightly closer to him. Greene could smell a hint of perfume. That made him smile again.

"Could I have your name, please?" he asked.

"Edna Wingate. Will this take long? I hate to be tardy. My yoga instructor does not tolerate late arrivals."

"You live in this building, Ms. Wingate?"

"Suite 12B. It's hot yoga, Detective," she said, giving him a coquettish grin. "I always bring two towels."

"And how long have you lived here?"

"Twenty years. You should try hot yoga. Men like it."

"We've disabled the elevators," Greene said. "I apologize for forcing you to walk down the stairs."

Wingate laughed. A light, engaging chuckle. "I never take the elevator. Twelve floors up and down. My yoga instructor says I have the strongest quads he's ever seen in an eighty-three-year-old."

On his drive down, Greene had called the dispatcher. He knew there were only two suites on the top floor. "Notice anything unusual on the twelfth floor last night or this morning?" he asked.

"Absolutely," she said without missing a beat.

"And what was—"

"My newspaper. I'm concerned about Mr. Singh. Never known him to miss a day."

"Anything else?"

"No. Please, I really must go."

"Can we make a deal?" he asked. "I'll unseal the building for you now so you can make your class if you'll let me drop by and ask some questions tomorrow morning."

She took a quick look at her watch. It was a Swatch, quite stylish.

"You'll have to try some of my Christmas shortbread," she said, flashing him a charming smile. And that laugh again.

"Shall I come by before six?"

"Come at eight. Monday's my only early class. Ta," she said, putting her hand on his shoulder as she waltzed past him, her posture still picture-perfect.

He watched Wingate move swiftly to the sidewalk, cross the empty street, and disappear into the morning darkness. Greene paused for a moment, taking in the last hint of her perfume before he went upstairs to see the body of the dead woman in the bathtub.

6

Six o'clock. Perfect, Albert Fernandez thought as he toweled his face dry and combed back his deep black hair. Ten minutes to shave, clip his nails, brush his teeth, and dry off. Another fifteen to get dressed, ten if he hurried. By 6:30 the coffee machine would click on, and he'd be out the door by 6:50. Drive downtown in thirty minutes, and he'd beat the 7:30 deadline for early-bird parking by at least ten minutes.

He wrapped a lush green towel around his waist and quietly made his way out of the en suite bathroom. Marissa was asleep in their bed. He stopped. Her black hair was tousled on the white sheets, and he could see the curve of her back and shoulders.

Two years into their marriage, and it still amazed Fernandez that he got to sleep with this beautiful naked woman, night after night. It had been worth it to bring a young bride back from Chile, he thought, despite his parents' objections. They'd wanted him to marry a Canadian from a good socialist background, like the people who'd taken them in as political refugees back in the 1970s. Instead, much to their consternation, he'd gone home and found a woman from one of the country's wealthiest families. His mother and father hadn't spoken to him since.

Fernandez tossed the damp towel on a chair and entered his favorite room in the apartment—the clothes closet. He loved looking at his rack of finely tailored suits. My passports to success, he thought, fingering the gabardine sleeve of his dark blue jacket. He ran his hands over the row of shirts on hangers and picked out one of his best, off-white Egyptian cotton with French cuffs.

He held the shirt up to the light. "Tsk, tsk," he whispered to himself, shaking his head. Marissa had grown up with a houseful of servants. Now she was learning to do the ironing. He would have to talk to her about the collars. He caressed his overburdened tie rack and settled on a deep red Armani tie.

His fine clothes were an important part of Fernandez's personal business plan. He pinched pennies in every other part of his life so he could buy them. Most of the other prosecutors at the downtown Crown law office dressed like schoolteachers or salesmen, with their crepe-soled shoes, brown suits, and muted ties. Not Albert. He always dressed impeccably, the way a real lawyer should.

He selected his dark brown loafers and examined their shine. They needed buffing. That would cost him two or three minutes.

Putting on his shirt, he did up his tie, then slipped on his pants and selected one of his favorite belts. Burnished brown leather with a simple brushed-metal buckle. When Fernandez was called to the bar, he had purchased a men's fashion encyclopedia, and it counseled that a belt should be done up to the third notch. He pulled his belt on and tried to get it to the well-worn line after the third hole. But this morning it felt tight. It took him a moment to realize he had to suck in his stomach to do the belt up.

Alarmed, he lifted his shirt and examined himself in the full-length mirror. Sure enough, his thin waistline had expanded. This was unbelievable. He'd always looked askance at the other male lawyers in his office, fat bellies overhanging their leatherette belts. That was it, he swore to himself, no more cheap sandwiches, no more eating doughnuts from the inevitable pack that got passed around the Crown's office at the end of the day.

Finally dressed, he emerged into the half-light of the bedroom. The illuminated clock radio beside the bed read 6:18. Two minutes ahead of schedule. Marissa had stirred in her sleep and rolled over. The sheet slid down, exposing the top part of her right breast.

Fernandez tiptoed to the edge of the bed and bent to kiss her hair. His eyes drifted down toward the rise in the sheets. Even though he saw his wife naked all the time, he still found himself sneaking looks at her body at just about every opportunity.

A warm hand touched his thigh. "You are not happy in my ironing," Marissa said, her voice hoarse with sleep.

His tsk-tsking must have been overheard. "*With* my ironing," he corrected her. "Yes, it needs work."

Marissa's hand fell away from his leg.

Damn it, he thought. He kept making the same mistake. Hidden in his closet between two folded sweaters was a book he read on Tuesday nights when Marissa went to her English as a second language classes. It was called *Marriage Survival Guide: How to Get Past the First Years*. One of the key things it said, over and over again, was don't be too critical, support your spouse.

"But I'm sure you will get better," he said, reaching for her arm.

"I need to get the iron more hot, no?" she asked. Her hand came back up again and lightly caressed his pant leg.

"Yes, hotter," he said. "It's difficult."

Marissa's warm lips parted in a tentative smile.

"And to press more hard," she said. As she spoke she began to rub her hand up, then down, his leg.

"*Harder*. See how fast you are learning."

"Hotter and harder," she said as she pulled her other hand out from under the covers and began to rub his thigh.

Despite himself, Fernandez lifted his eyes to the digital clock radio on the far side of the bed. The time was 6:26. Now he was a minute behind schedule. Without the early-bird parking, it was another four dollars.

Marissa wet her lips with her tongue. She rolled over toward him and put her hands on his belt buckle. I wonder if she noticed the extra notch, he thought as she undid it.

He took his eyes off the clock. You deserve this, Albert, he told himself. He was always the first lawyer in the office. So what if, for one day, he was the second or third.

Marissa tugged at his pants.

After all, he could skip lunch to make up the four dollars. And that way he'd lose a bit of weight. She reached for his hand and lay back, bringing it to the top of her chest. Her hardening nipple rose to the soft skin of his palm. She kept moving his hand lower as she elevated her hips to meet his fingers.

His belt undone, his pants and then his boxer shorts brought down below his knees, she reached around his back.

For the last few months Marissa had been complaining. "Albert, you leave too early every morning," she'd said. "And home so late."

"It's important," he'd explained to her. "To get ahead in the Crown's office, I need to work harder than everyone else."

"But your wife needs you too," she'd insisted.

She does need me, Fernandez thought as her lips parted and she took him in. Their bodies began to move in rhythm, her black hair waving on the white sheet. He could smell the sweetness of her. Close your eyes, he told himself, and enjoy the moment.

It was 6:39 when he zipped up his pants, too late for sure for the early parking. In the kitchen the preset coffee had been sitting for almost ten minutes. It would be stale by now, but there wasn't time to make a fresh brew. He pulled out his old glass vacuum thermos and filled it. As bad as the coffee would taste, it would be miles better than the horrible stuff at the Crown's office.

At the front door of their apartment he picked up the *Toronto Star*. He scanned the paper for the only news he really cared about: Had there been a murder last night? A picture of Toronto hockey players raising their sticks in victory dominated the front page, and a quick flip through confirmed the bad news. No one in the whole city had been killed. It had been four weeks without a murder. What a time for a dry spell, Fernandez thought as he slammed the newspaper down.

For the last five years he had worked his way up the ladder at the Crown's office. His plan had been deliberate. Arrive first, leave last, every day. Always be perfectly prepared and well dressed. Get to know the judges—secreted in a bottom drawer of his desk was a set of index cards with the peculiarities and preferences of each judge carefully noted in his fine handwriting.

And win cases.

His hard work had paid off. A month ago, the head Crown, Jennifer Raglan, called him into her corner office.

"Albert," she said, shifting a large stack of files off her ever-crowded desk, "I know you're itching to prosecute a homicide."

"I'm happy to take whatever comes my way," he said.

Raglan smiled. "You've earned a shot. Pretty impressive for someone just five years out. Next murder has your name on it."

Now, down in the basement garage, as he waited for his old Toyota to warm up, he slid his black leather driving gloves out from their special compartment.

Just before he left the bed, Marissa had whispered to him in English, "That was second base. Tonight we will make home run."

"We will *hit* a home run," he'd whispered back.

"Hit home run. But make love?"

"That's right."

"Your English is so strange."

It will be worth running home tonight, Fernandez thought as he pulled on the gloves and slammed the car into gear. Now all I need is an overnight murder, and except for that overbrewed coffee, this will be a perfect morning.

7

They sure as fuck never taught this in law school, Nancy Parish thought as she struggled to pull on her second pair of panty hose of the morning, having ripped to shreds the first one just minutes before. Opening the door of the nearby closet, she couldn't help but catch herself in the full-length mirror, the only one in her tiny semidetached home. Now, there's a lovely sight first thing in the morning, she thought: a single woman pushing forty in nothing but panty hose.

Parish looked over at her ancient answering machine. Every night she had the calls from her office forwarded to her home number. When she was a keen young defense lawyer, she'd answered calls in the middle of the night, but a few years earlier she had started turning the volume off before she went to sleep.

The "message waiting" light flashed "7." Seven bloody calls, and I haven't even had a cup of coffee. You jerk, Henry, she thought, this is all your fault.

Last month her ex-husband, a show producer at *The Dawn Treader*, Kevin Brace's popular morning radio program, had talked her into coming on as a guest on a panel called "Single Professional Women: Are They Happy?"

Only me, she thought. What an idiot. Let your ex get you to babble to the whole country about how you're eating scrambled eggs alone for dinner on Saturday nights. Henry had warned her to watch what she said. But did she listen? She completely forgot that more than a million people were out there, and Brace was so damn charming. Finally, after the scrambled eggs, she'd blurted out: "Men are afraid to have sex with a woman who earns more money than they do."

That was it. For days her answering machine had been filled with calls from guys from all over Canada and the northern United States saying they were prepared to overcome their fears. Even a few women had called. Unbelievable.

Parish looked at the floor, where she'd tossed her new leather boots last night before she crawled into bed. Damn it, she thought. A thin white line of road salt had formed a ring about two inches above the heel. She shook her head. Last September she had finally gone to the trouble of buying boots early in the season, and she'd paid full price because *this* winter she wanted a pair that looked good. The voice of the persnickety shoe salesman who'd sold her the darn things—and then sold her all the overpriced leather conditioners—rang in her ears.

"Spray them tonight when you get home, with this," he'd said, lifting a small can that cost $19.99. "Wait twenty-four hours and do it again, then coat them with this." He held up a bottle with some brown liquid gunk in it. That cost only $12.99. "Use this once a week."

"Wait twenty-four hours, then once a week," Parish said, pointing to the two jars while she added the tax in her head. Neat, she thought. This is my ritual initiation into a secret society of people who actually know how to take care of their winter boots: SLOBS—the Salt-free Leather Only Boots Sisterhood.

"And every night, wipe them down with a cloth dipped in plain vinegar," the salesman said. "No water. Water just pushes the salt farther into the leather."

"No water," she promised.

"Shoe trees are vital. Put them in within five minutes of taking the boots off, while they're still warm."

"Five minutes," she pledged. The shoe trees cost another $33.00. Not including tax.

What a waste of money, she'd thought a month later. The weather in October and November had been warm, and she forgot about them. Then there was a cold snap and sudden snowfall at the beginning of December. By that time she couldn't remember where she'd put the stupid spray and leather conditioner, and when she finally found them, she couldn't remember which one was the twenty-four-hour and which one was the weekly thing.

Looks like my membership in SLOBS has expired, Parish thought as she tossed the boots back on the floor, making yet another mental note to remember to buy plain vinegar next time she went shopping. The only vinegar she had in the house was balsamic.

That would make a good cartoon, she thought, wondering where she'd left her sketchbook. A well-dressed couple are searching through the cupboards of their modern kitchen. "Darn it, Gwyneth," the man is saying to his wife, "the kids have got into the balsamic. Again."

With her bare elbow she hit the Play button, and the first message came on.

Beep. "Hello, Ms. Parish, you don't know me, but I'm looking for a lawyer for my son. We don't have any money, but I heard you were good and that you take legal aid . . ."

She smacked the Skip button with her fist and stared at herself in the mirror. Her hair was still wet from the shower, so she started to towel it dry while she wrote up a mental report card of her naked self.

Hair: One of her best features. Still thick and bouncy. Down to her shoulders. She could get away with the length, but for how much longer? Last winter a drunk guy at an après-ski party in Whistler told her she had great "Give me a blow job" hair. Right. That trip cost more than two thousand dollars, and she never even got kissed.

Next message: *Beep. "Hi, Nancy. It's James again. You were right, I should have stayed away from Lucy, but well, you know. I'm at 55 Division. No more Form 10s. They're holding me this time. I'll be in 101 bail court this morning at the Hall . . ."* She hit the Skip button.

Face: She had always been "attractive" but rarely beautiful. Her skin was good, but it didn't gleam the way it used to. Back when she and Henry were living the young couple high life, one night at the Symphony Opening Night Ball an older man asked her to dance. "You have such wonderful skin," he said. "You won't need to wear makeup until you're in your forties." She was turning thirty-eight next month, and she rarely ventured out without at least some blush on.

Next message: *Beep.* "*Nancy Gail, your father and I are going to be downtown on Wednesday night for the ballet, and, well, I know it's corny as heck, but we were wondering if you would like to come with us and look at the Christmas windows at the Bay . . .*" Skip.

Neck and shoulders: Her best feature. Guys are idiots, so obsessed with tits and asses. But think Audrey Hepburn, think Grace Kelly. Those long necks that go on forever, those shoulders that could cut glass.

Beep. "*Ms. Parish, this is Brenda Crawford from the Law Society of Upper Canada. We're still awaiting your response from our request for your updated accounting ledger. As you know, if you do not respond within . . .*"

"Fuck," she said, and smacked the Skip button with her fist.

Breasts: Not bad still, she thought, raising her arms in the air. Especially if you squint your eyes a bit. Nose: She hated noses. Take any woman in the world. Say, Julia Roberts. Beautiful, right? Now look at her nose. Stare at it. In a few seconds her whole face turns ugly.

Beep. "*Hi, it's me. What about the Dominican?*"

"Zelda," Parish muttered to herself, shaking her head. Zelda Evinrude, her best friend, was on a mission to improve Parish's sex life.

"*Expedia's got a special deal if we leave before Christmas. Beats going home and being bored at your parents' place. Those Dominican boy toys look awful cute.*" *Beep.*

Parish took a step closer to the mirror. From there you could see her nose had a small bump right in the middle.

Beep. "*You don't know me, but I heard you on the radio the other . . .*"

"No more," she screamed.

There was just one call left.

Beep. "*Ms. Parish, it's Detective Ari Greene, homicide squad. The time now is seven fourteen a.m., December 17. Could you please meet me at police headquarters at your earliest possible convenience? It's in regards to your client, Mr. Kevin Brace. He's given us your card."*

Homicide squad.

Kevin Brace.

Shit.

Parish took one last look in the mirror, grabbed her salt-stained boots, and dashed to her clothes closet.

8

Daniel Kennicott didn't own a car. He didn't need one, as he lived and worked downtown. And after his parents' accident, he tried to avoid driving whenever he could.

It was almost eight years ago. His mother and father were doing their regular Friday-night drive up north. Like clockwork, they left the city every week at eight p.m. They were five miles away from the family cottage when a drunk driver swerved across the two-lane highway and hit them head-on. The guy was barely hurt. Kennicott's parents died on impact.

Hard to tell what was more frustrating. A brother murdered, the case unsolved, or his parents killed by an irresponsible jerk. The guy was tossed into jail for a few years. Did it really matter? The end result was the same. His family wiped out.

Kennicott was driving Detective Greene's car, which maneuvered easily through the light early-morning Toronto traffic. It was an aging Oldsmobile, not quite in keeping with the buttoned-down image of a homicide detective. A few years back, when Greene first started working on his brother's case, Kennicott had asked the detective about his old car.

"Safest vehicle on the road," Greene had said. "Made of real steel. Wide carriage. You couldn't flip it with a bulldozer."

And the thing has a lot of power, Kennicott thought as he gunned it past a streetcar. He was in a race against time. Twenty minutes earlier Greene had come into Brace's apartment and, after a cursory look around, handed Kennicott the keys to the Olds.

"I need you to get up to King City fast," he'd said. "That's where the victim's parents live. She was an only child. Try to get there before this thing hits the news."

Telling a family that their loved one is dead was one of the hardest things about being a cop. At police college they trained you: Make eye contact to establish trust; speak with confidence, hesitation will only heighten anxiety; use simple language because people respond negatively to jargon. Don't talk too much.

Kennicott remembered when Greene gave him the news about his brother, Michael. He was in the office of Lloyd Granwell, the senior lawyer who'd recruited him to the firm. They were in a big tower on Bay Street that overlooked Old City Hall. Granwell, who knew absolutely everyone, had called Hap Charlton, the chief of police. Then they'd waited. It was excruciating. The Old City Hall clock had just finished striking nine when Granwell's secretary walked in.

"There's someone to see you in the lobby, Mr. Kennicott." From her downcast look, Kennicott knew it wasn't good. He walked out and saw a tall, well-dressed man with a maroon notebook in his hand. His heart sank.

"Hi, Mr. Kennicott, I'm Detective Greene from the Toronto Police," the man said. "Is there a quiet place where we can talk?"

Looking back now, Kennicott could see how Greene had been very professional. He'd made direct eye contact; kept his voice soft, steady; used simple, straightforward language. Never looked away. And said he was from the Toronto Police, not Toronto Homicide.

Kennicott got past the streetcar and slid over the tracks. The Olds had a comfortable solidity about it. He turned on the old-fashioned radio to see if the story was out yet. A news announcer came on, speaking in French. He changed the channel. Another French station.

After four and a half years, Kennicott didn't know much about Greene. The man was quiet about his personal life. Kennicott had no idea that the detective spoke French. Interesting. Checking the radio

stations on someone's car was like looking through his desk drawers—
it gave a peek into his private self. The third channel was 102.1, the Edge,
an up-to-date station that teenagers listened to. The next was Q107,
the main competitor of the Edge. Greene must have a teenage kid,
Kennicott thought. Funny that he'd never mentioned having a family.

Kennicott pushed the final button and heard the voice of Donald Dundas, the younger broadcaster who was the usual Monday-
morning replacement host for Kevin Brace. Dundas was doing a
promo for two stories in the upcoming show. He played some native
drum music from a band in northern Ontario that was going to Rome
to visit the pope, and a clip of a group of women from some town in
Alberta trying to get into the *Guinness Book of Records* for building
the world's largest ice sculpture. It was of a giant beaver.

"The news is next," Dundas said just before the top of the hour.
"I'm going to be sitting in as host for the rest of the week." His usually confident radio voice sounded unsure. As though he couldn't wait
to get off the air. *"See you at eight."* The syrupy theme music came up.
Dundas hadn't mentioned a word about Brace.

The hourly news said nothing about Kevin Brace being under arrest, his wife dead in their bathroom. Good. Maybe the family didn't
know. Kennicott pushed the Q107 button.

"Here's a shocker," the young announcer said. "Kevin Brace, the
host of *The Dawn Treader*, the nationally syndicated morning show,
is under arrest for first-degree murder."

"Hoo-wee," his sarcastic sidekick said. "That should help us cut
down on the competition for the overeducated market."

"Yeah, man," the first voice said, "but who really cares? The Leafs
won last night, so all is well with the Leaf Nation." They both started
to crack up, as if it were one of the funniest jokes they'd ever heard.

Kennicott flicked off the radio. He had left the highway and was
driving down into King City, which wasn't a city at all. It was an afflu-
ent small town perched north of Toronto, populated by wealthy hobby
farmers who had managed to preserve some measure of quaintness
among the surrounding urban sprawl.

Unlike in Toronto, where fresh snow quickly turned into horrible brown slush, here the sidewalks were piled high with it. Kennicott felt as if he'd just arrived in winter. In the middle of town he turned north and headed up a small country road. Immaculately plowed driveways led to garish mansions.

He drove for a mile or so until he came to a house that, unlike its well-fenced-in neighbors, was bordered by a haphazard wood railing. The long driveway had been erratically cleared of snow. A simple, hand-painted piece of plywood read: TORN.

Pulling up in front of a large garage, Kennicott got out. The air was cool, and there was a pungent smell of horse manure. The house was a rambling bungalow, with the original farmhouse in the center and helter-skelter additions that seemed to have been built on a whim. The front steps hadn't been shoveled, so Kennicott tromped through the snow up to the painted front door. He looked at his watch. It was 7:10. Let's hope they haven't heard the news, he thought. He knocked.

A torrent of barking erupted inside the house. He heard footsteps charging up the hallway, then the smack of bodies hitting the front door, howling away. Just what I need, Kennicott thought. He took a step down, away from the door. A male voice inside called out, "Place, Show, get over here." As suddenly as it had started, the barking stopped. Kennicott waited, expecting the door to open. But there was nothing.

He waited a little longer and knocked again.

No sound.

To his right he heard a large door open. A tall, white-haired man in an unbuttoned sheepskin coat emerged from the garage and walked toward him. Two big dogs were behind him, docile as sheep.

"Morning," the man said, taking long strides toward Kennicott.

"Hello," Kennicott said, coming back down the steps. "Dr. Torn?"

"Call me Arden. No one ever uses the front door." He extended a large arm to shake hands. "We always come through the garage."

"Sorry to disturb you so early in the morning," Kennicott said.

Torn smiled. His aqua-blue eyes popped out against his ruddy skin and white hair. "Been up since five. Took the tractor to the driveway. We're trailering the horses down to West Virginia for a show."

Kennicott kept his eyes fixed on Torn. "I'm Officer Daniel Kennicott from the Toronto Police."

"Don't let the dogs bother you. They're country bred, that's all. We always have two dogs, figure it's cruel to have just one on its own."

"Is your wife at home, sir?"

Torn let go of Kennicott's hand. "She's back in the barn."

"Perhaps . . ."

He nodded and turned his head. "Allie!" His voice boomed across the wide driveway. "You'd better get out here."

A moment later an older woman dressed in a bulky country coat, a large scarf tied comfortably around her neck, emerged from behind the barn door. She wore a pair of knee-high rubber boots.

Torn turned back to Kennicott as he pulled the lapels of his jacket together and held them with one hand.

"Thanks," Kennicott said.

"I was in the war," Torn said quietly, reaching down to pat the dogs with his free hand, never taking his blue eyes off Kennicott. "I know what it looks like when someone comes to deliver bad news."

9

Albert Fernandez hated listening to the radio when he was driving. It was a total waste of the half-hour commute downtown to the Crown Attorney's office at Old City Hall. Instead, he listened to tapes. Self-improvement tapes, books on tape, and speeches by famous politicians and world leaders. This month he was listening to the wartime speeches of Winston Churchill.

Fernandez was eleven years old when his left-wing parents fled Chile and brought their family to Canada. None of them spoke English. His little sister Palmira had learned quickly, but for Albert the new language was a struggle. Why were there so many words for the same thing—pig and hog, street and road, dinner and supper? No one who spoke English appeared to be fazed by this. But for Fernandez it was torture. He always seemed to choose the wrong word.

His most painful memory of that first year in Canada was the day in November when his class went on a field trip to a conservation area north of the city. Just after lunch the weather suddenly turned wet and cold. Fernandez, wearing entirely inappropriate dress shoes, slid down a riverbank into a stream. When he turned to look up at the other boys on the bank, who were all wearing boots and running shoes, they were smiling.

"Aid me," he called back to them, reaching out his hand.

The kids all burst out laughing. "Aid me?" they said. "Albert wants help and he says 'Aid me.'"

For the next three years, everyone at school called him Aid Me Albert.

It wasn't until he took a linguistics course at university that he solved the language riddle. At his very first class, the professor, a thin young man with stringy blond hair and wire-rimmed glasses, strode into the crowded lecture hall, drew a line down the middle of the blackboard, and wrote the heading "Anglo-Saxon" on one side and "Norman" on the other.

He listed words with the exact same meaning on either side of the ledger: go in—enter; meet—rendezvous; help—aid. English, he explained, was not a language, but a car crash. All sorts of languages—Germanic, Latin, Nordic, even some Celtic—smashed together, but thanks to the French invasion of England in 1066, the two main ones, Anglo-Saxon and Norman, ran parallel throughout.

Fernandez sat up in class. All the confusion of this strange language suddenly became clear.

That's where Churchill came in. A great student of English history and language, Churchill understood the power of the simple Anglo-Saxon words. He preferred them to the flowery, foreign Norman words.

His most famous speech, "We will fight them on the beaches . . . ," was the greatest example. Every word was Anglo-Saxon, except for the very last one: ". . . and we will never *surrender*." "Surrender," the only three-syllable word in the whole speech, was a flowery French word instead of the simpler, Anglo-Saxon "give up." In this way, Churchill underscored how the very idea of surrender was a foreign concept to his British audience.

Years later, Fernandez was sitting in court listening to a witness. At first the man seemed totally believable. But when he came to the tough part of his story, his whole tone changed. Fernandez knew immediately that the man was lying, but he wasn't sure why. Until later, when he read the transcript and found himself circling the Norman words.

Sure enough, when the witness used simple, direct Anglo-Saxon words, he was telling the truth: "I walked into the kitchen. I saw

Tamara. She was cooking supper." But when he switched to Norman words, he became evasive: "To the best of my recollection . . . she maneuvered the frying pan . . . to be perfectly honest . . . I thought she intended to hurl it toward me . . . I was considering contacting the police for assistance . . ." He was lying.

Fernandez smiled as he flipped the tape into the car radio and roared out of the underground garage. Over the years he was amazed how many times this simple analysis of witnesses' statements had proved correct.

Thirty-five minutes later he pulled into a parking lot northwest of the Old City Hall courthouse. Thanks to the traffic, which was snarled because he'd left so late, it was just before eight. Even worse than missing the early-bird parking, he saw three cars that belonged to other Crown Attorneys parked on the south side right beside each other.

Darn. For months, Fernandez had been in the lot by 7:25, before everyone else in the office. The one day he stays home for a little extra fun, look what happens. He grabbed the nearest parking spot.

To get to Old City Hall, he first had to walk through the large square in front of the New City Hall. Even at this early hour it was busy with people crisscrossing the vast space, rushing to work. Down at the south part, on the big open-air rink, skaters were gliding across the ice, some of them dressed in business suits, others in figure-skating outfits.

When he was a kid, Fernandez's parents scraped together enough money to buy him used skates, and on Sunday afternoons they'd dragged him down to this rink with all the other immigrant families. Try as he might, he could never get his ankles to stop from bending over, never understood the effortless way young Canadian kids could propel themselves across the big white surface.

He sprinted across Bay Street and into the back entrance of Old City Hall. Waving his credentials at the young cop on duty, he raced up an old metal staircase and ran his pass card over the pad for the back-door entrance to the Crown's office.

The Downtown Toronto Crown Attorney's office was one enormous room, stuffed full of warrenlike offices that ran crazy-quilt in all directions—the legacy of government planners who'd jammed thirty-five offices into a space built for twelve. Most offices were filled with stacks of paper and books, piles of white cardboard storage boxes with words like R.V. SUNDRILINGHAM—MURDER II—VOIR DIRE—RIGHT TO COUNSEL hand-printed in black Magic Marker on the side. Fernandez was the exception. He kept his little office tidy.

Most days, when he was the first lawyer to arrive, he would open the door to the pungent smell of cold pizza and stale microwave popcorn. But this morning the air was filled with the aroma of coffee brewing, bagels toasting, and fresh-peeled mandarin oranges.

Ignoring the murmuring of voices farther down the hall, he headed straight to his office. It wasn't his style to mingle. Besides, this way his later-arriving colleagues would see him hard at work as they passed by.

Pulling a robbery file he was working on from the only filing cabinet in his office, he sat down at his desk. By eight o'clock, usually an hour when he was the only one there, the voices down the hall were building. Someone had a radio on, and the announcer's voice mingled with the sound of many people talking.

Finally, Fernandez couldn't take it. He repacked the robbery file, picked up a yellow legal-sized pad, and walked through the hallway, past the photocopy machine parked halfway down, to Jennifer Raglan's corner office.

Raglan, the head Crown Attorney for the Toronto region, was behind her paper-strewn desk, half seated, half leaning forward. Across from her, to her left, pacing back and forth, was Phil Cutter, the most aggressive prosecutor on the whole downtown team. Bald, in his late forties, he wore an old suit and a pair of crepe-soled shoes, well worn on the outside heels. To Raglan's right, sitting on a wooden chair, was Barb Gild, a willowy brunette who was the best legal researcher in the office. A typical absentminded genius type, she famously left her papers and files all over the office and on every photocopy machine. The three were involved in an intense conversation. Fernandez cleared his throat. No one heard him. He took a few steps inside. Still no one noticed him. He was almost on top of her desk when Raglan finally looked up.

"Albert, I was wondering when you'd get in," she said.

"I've been here for a while." Damn it, he thought. "Working in my office."

"We're just mapping out our preliminary strategy—there's no time to waste," Raglan said, seeming to ignore his comment. "Looks like your number came up big. Hope you've done your Christmas shopping. You'll be in bail court on this by Wednesday."

What was going on? It was as if Fernandez had walked into a movie halfway through and everyone else knew what was happening.

"Just goes to show you never can tell," Cutter said. His voice was so loud it was more of a bark than a normal speaking voice. Judges had been known to ask him to move to the back of the court before he addressed them. His bald head gleamed under the fluorescent light. "He'll probably claim she fell on the knife. Kind of tough, though, with her dead in the bathtub." Cutter started to laugh, a hard, choking cackle.

"What a bastard," Gild said. "What a total hypocrite."

Raglan peered up from her desk, tortoiseshell glasses perched on her aquiline nose. Her skin had the tattered look of too many late nights and cold cups of coffee, and her hair was mousy brown. But her eyes were a magical hazel and her mouth was wide. There was an appealing confidence about her.

"When did you hear about it?" Raglan asked Fernandez.

Fernandez shrugged. He couldn't fake it anymore. "I hate to tell you, but I haven't heard anything."

All eyes in the room turned to him.

"You haven't heard?" Raglan said.

"No."

"Kevin Brace has been charged with first-degree murder," Raglan said. "Early this morning his wife was found dead in the bathtub of their downtown penthouse condominium. One stab wound to the stomach. Albert, what an amazing draw for your first homicide."

Fernandez just nodded.

"Unbelievable," Gild said. "And people called Brace the first feminist man in Canada. Sure sucked me in good."

"The press is going to have a fucking field day with this," Cutter growled. "Albert, you lucky dog."

Fernandez kept nodding. There was another cheap chair in the corner of the room. He pulled it over, raised his pad of paper, and clicked his pen. "Let's get going," he said, trying his best to sound upbeat. He had to make everyone think he was ready—which was close to the truth.

There was just one question he needed answered but didn't dare to ask: Who the hell was Kevin Brace?

10

Just what was the Toronto police force coming to, Nancy Parish asked herself as she surveyed the bevy of food and beverage choices on offer at the spanking new police cafeteria: cappuccinos, lattes, mint teas, yogurt smoothies, fruit salads, granola bars, croissants, and mini-brioches. Mini-brioches. This was no cop shop, it was a café. Where was the weak coffee, the glazed doughnuts?

After some determined foraging, Parish managed to find a butter tart without any fancy pecans or walnuts in it and a cup of dark roast coffee that looked as if it had been brewed a few hours ago. It was a start.

Jet fuel, she told herself as she took a seat on a sleekly designed chair in the half-empty cafeteria. Sometimes you need some pure, un-adulterated crap to power you through difficult situations, she thought, eagerly digging in.

The damn tart was so big, part of the filling squished out across her cheek. Just as she reached for a napkin, a tall man wearing a beau-tifully tailored suit, a well-pressed shirt, and gleaming black loafers approached her table. He was handsome in a rugged kind of way.

"Ms. Parish, Detective Greene," he said, extending his hand.

"Hello, Detective," she managed to mumble, grabbing for the napkin. It felt as though it took forever for her to wipe her face and reach for his outstretched hand.

"Mind if I have a seat?" Greene asked.

Parish gulped down a big slurp of coffee to try to clear her throat. "Please do," she said. The coffee was burning hot, and it singed her tongue.

"Once you're done with your breakfast, I'll take you upstairs to see Mr. Brace," Greene said.

"Hardly breakfast," Parish said, wishing there was a hole in the table where she could ditch the rest of the butter tart. "Let's go."

Inside the elevator the floor numbers were written in English, French, Chinese, Arabic, and Braille. There were three other people in the car, and Greene didn't say a word. As they rose through the plant-filled atrium, a mechanical voice said "Ground floor, floor number one, floor number two . . ." in about ten different languages. I'd go mad listening to this every day, Parish thought.

Looking down, she saw that the pants she'd put on didn't quite cover the salt stains on her boots. Get your priorities straight, Nancy Gail, she thought, imitating her mother's voice in her head. First white vinegar, then Kevin Brace.

When they got off the elevator, Greene led her down an empty hallway and plunged into his narrative. "We received notification of this incident by way of a 911 phone call from a Mr. Gurdial Singh at five thirty-one a.m. Our information at this moment is that Mr. Singh delivers newspapers at Mr. Brace's condominium each morning at this time. *The Globe and Mail*. Mr. Singh reports that Mr. Brace came to the doorway in his bathrobe with blood on his hands and stated he'd murdered his wife. Mr. Singh found the body of the victim, Ms. Katherine Torn, the common-law wife of Mr. Brace, in the bathtub. There's no known relationship between Mr. Singh and Brace or Torn, except for Mr. Singh's delivering newspapers. Mr. Singh is seventy-three years old. He immigrated to Canada four years ago. Canadian citizen, married, with four children and eighteen grandchildren, no criminal record and no previous police contacts."

Greene spoke with the precision of a veteran actor performing the same part for the hundredth time. He walked at a rapid, sure pace. Yet there was nothing mechanical about him—in fact, he was quite warm amid all the highly professional polish. As constant as a metronome, Parish thought, a fine wood metronome.

"Mr. Singh informs us that he's a former engineer with Indian Railways. We've been able to confirm this independently. He has extensive first-aid experience. Before he called 911, he checked the body for vital signs, and they were absent. It was cold to the touch. Mr. Brace was arrested without incident by P.C. Daniel Kennicott at five fifty-three a.m. He's been informed of his right to remain silent and his right to counsel. He's made no statement to the police at this time. We have charged him with first-degree murder."

Greene stopped. They'd arrived at a nondescript white door.

"Any questions so far?" he asked.

Parish wanted to ask, "How about another cup of coffee? How do you get your shoes to be so shiny? At what precise moment did Ms. Katherine Torn, common-law wife to Mr. Kevin Brace, cease to be a 'she' and become an 'it'?"

Instead she just asked, "Is he handcuffed?"

"Absolutely not. Mr. Brace was cuffed at the time of his arrest and throughout transport. We removed the cuffs as soon as he was secure in this building."

Keep it simple, she told herself.

"The apartment is on the twelfth floor. No balcony. It looks south over the lake," Greene said, the metronome staying on beat. "There's only one front door. At this stage of the investigation there's no evidence of forced entry, and all exterior windows appear to be intact. There are no signs of a robbery having taken place. There are only two units on the twelfth floor—12A and 12B. Suite 12B is occupied by an eighty-three-year-old widow. I trust that's clear."

Parish nodded. Greene was deliberately showing her how strong his case was right from the get-go. Don't react to this barrage of bad news, she told herself. Just listen. Think. How many times have you seen this? The police always present the evidence as if it's an open-and-shut case. They want you to think your case is hopeless. Remember, it's not what they say that matters, but what they don't say.

What's Greene not telling you? Parish thought, rubbing her burnt tongue along the top of her mouth. What's missing?

"I'm afraid we'll have to lock you in the room, Ms. Parish," Greene said. "I'll post a police constable at the door, stationed across the hallway to ensure that your conversation is entirely confidential. If you need anything, simply knock, and she'll assist you. Please take all the time you need. We're still scrambling for transport, so he'll be here for a while. I hope that's sufficient."

Parish nodded again. It was seductive to be treated in such a courteous, professional manner. Most of her twelve-year career had been spent clawing for every ounce of cooperation she could get from the authorities. This was her first murder case. Just an hour or so in, and she could see why defense lawyers liked homicides. Sure, the stakes were impossibly high and the hours brutal, but at least you were treated with respect.

"That's fine," she said. Brace has the right to counsel, she told herself. You have the right to be here. Greene's not doing you any favors.

Where's the hole? Come on, Nancy, quit being distracted by this nice-guy detective in the fancy suit. Think.

Then it came to her. Don't overplay it, she told herself. She waited until Greene turned back toward the elevator. "One quick question, Detective."

"Of course, Ms. Parish." Greene pivoted precisely, like a skater doing a tight turn, the smile still on his face.

"A murder weapon. Did you find one?"

For just an instant Greene's smile slipped.

"Not yet, Ms. Parish," he said. "A few hours from now, when the forensic officers are ready to release the scene, I'll head back to the condominium for my final walk-through. Tell you what. I'll keep my eyes open for it."

That smile again. The detective was nothing if not charming. He turned around and waved with his back to her.

Parish looked at the closed door. She took a deep breath and opened it.

Kevin Brace, perhaps the best-known broadcaster in the country, who often joked that he was the most famous face on radio, sat in the far corner of an empty, large white-walled room. The only furniture was two wooden chairs. Brace sat on the far chair, huddled up, turned into himself, an old man returning to the fetal position.

Parish closed the door quickly. "Mr. Brace," she said, putting her hands out straight in front of her, "listen and do not say a word."

He looked up. She got to the empty chair fast and pulled it close. "Mr. Brace, this room is not monitored for sound, but there's a camera keeping constant video surveillance on you." She turned and pointed to the camera mounted conspicuously on the far wall. "I'd prefer you say nothing right now in case someone decides to lip-read the tape one day. Or—well, you never know."

Brace looked slowly up at the video camera, then back at her.

"Can you just shake or nod your head?"

Brace nodded his head.

"Do you need anything? Water? The washroom?"

He shook his head.

"You know you've been charged with first-degree murder?"

He looked her straight in the eye. For a moment she thought he was going to say something. But he stiffened his back and nodded again.

"This is very awkward," she said. "I'll see you tonight in the jail, and we can talk."

Again he nodded.

"The police will try to get you to talk. I prefer that my clients say absolutely nothing. That way no words can get put into your mouth. You okay with that?"

He let his eyes rest on her for quite a while. She remembered those deep, comfortable brown eyes from the time he'd interviewed her on the radio. Eyes that just made you trust him. Made you want to cuddle up and be his best friend.

Then Brace broke into a smile.

"Good," she said, reaching for her binder. She turned to a fresh piece of paper and narrated as she wrote.

My name is Mr. Kevin Brace. I understand that I have been charged with first-degree murder. I also understand that I have the right to remain silent. I wish to assert that right and do not wish to say anything at this time. Dated at Toronto this Monday, the 17th day of December.

She drew a line below the text. Under the line she wrote his name in capital letters.

"Here," she said, turning the binder toward him. "Sign this and keep it with you at all times. Just show it to the police when anyone tries to ask you anything. Good idea to do the same thing at the jail until I get there to see you tonight."

Brace reached out and examined her pen. It was a cheap Bic. Thankfully, it was only slightly chewed. She'd long ago given up on buying pricey pens with her name engraved on the side, which, like leather winter gloves, prescription sunglasses, and expensive lipstick, she inevitably lost within a week.

He signed his name with a flowing, neat script. Then, without waiting, he opened the rings of the binder and removed the piece of paper. He took it out and folded it neatly in half, then half again.

He gave her a sly grin.

Parish was impressed. Despite all that had happened to him in the last few hours, he seemed unfazed. Perhaps it was all those years of living on deadline, but clearly Kevin Brace was cool under pressure.

11

It took Daniel Kennicott a long time to drive back downtown, battling traffic. There was nowhere to park on Front Street, but he got lucky and found a spot on the side street where Greene's car had been parked originally. He stifled a yawn as he walked down the hallway to 12A. This will be it for me on this case, he thought. They called it the "first cop in, first cop out," rule, and he'd learned it last year.

In December, he and his partner, Nora Bering, had received a domestic call from a big house in Rosedale. They were the first officers on scene. In a fit of pre-Christmas rage, Mrs. Frances Boudreau, soon to be labeled by the press as "the not-so-sober socialite," had flung a laptop at her wayward husband. It clipped him on the temple, and he bled to death under the family Christmas tree. Kennicott and Bering were forced to arrest her right in front of her twin boys and the Filipino nanny.

Once backup arrived and the scene was under control, everything changed. Two lordly homicide detectives—perfectly dressed, with their hand-stitched suits, initialed French-cuffed shirts, and highly buffed shoes—ambled in, writing in their special-issue notebooks with their expensive handcrafted pens. On their way out the door they had a terse interview with Kennicott and Bering and dismissed them from the investigation—first cop in, first cop out—without so much as a word of thanks.

Now, inside apartment 12A, the daylight was streaming in the big windows, and Kennicott put his hand over his eyes for a moment as he walked carefully across the tiled kitchen floor. Detective Greene was huddled over the kitchen counter with a tall man. Kennicott recognized him from behind. As always, an old briefcase and a tattered canvas backpack were at the man's feet.

"Hey, Officer Kennicott, I'd say you made pretty good time," Detective Wayne Ho said as he turned toward Kennicott, his big hand outstretched in an enthusiastic greeting. Ho, the forensic identification officer responsible for securing the scene and collecting evidence, was an unusually tall Chinese man, at least six feet five. Though probably in his late fifties, Ho was as fit as a new recruit, with energy to spare. His high-pitched voice was a jarring counterpoint to his massive presence.

"Good deal, isn't it, being the Voice of Canada?" Ho said, his keen eyes boring in on Kennicott. "Just roll out of bed every morning and talk on the radio for a few hours. Imagine that, getting paid to talk. Maybe Brace can broadcast from jail. They get them up early in the joint, just like the British Army. Fight in the morning."

Kennicott laughed. Ho had been the forensic officer on his brother's case, and since Kennicott had joined the force, they'd worked together many times. Ho's motormouth was like a kid's windup toy on a gigantic spring, and nothing was going to stop it. There was no point in trying to join the conversation, at least not yet.

"Hey. You see this? Poor man's a Maple Leafs fan," Ho said, pointing with his metal pencil at the row of various blue-and-white mugs and glasses on the windowsill. He tapped them one by one, getting a different note with each. "Tragic, really. They'll never win the Stanley Cup. I blame the media. So much darn coverage, the players are nervous all the time. Look at how they win more games on the road than at home."

Kennicott looked at Greene, who gave him a bemused smile. "You going to print all those glasses?" Kennicott asked, finally getting into the conversation.

"No point," Ho said. "Prints on glass can last for months, years, unless"—with great drama he tapped his pencil against the dishwasher four times, singing a Beethoven-like "Ba ba ba ba"—"they are washed here. Dishwashers are evidence killers. Run it once, and every scrap of fingerprint and DNA, poof. Gone forever."

"I'll be with you in a minute," Greene said, looking up briefly from his notebook. Kennicott walked toward the big windows and looked out onto the lake. The inner harbor was already dotted with slabs of bobbing ice. In the summer three bulky white ferries brought overheated city residents across to the bucolic parkland and beaches there. But in the winter, service shrank to just one boat to handle the clutch of year-round residents who lived in a small community of renovated cottages.

Kennicott watched the big boat churn through the cold waters. The rest of the surface of the harbor remained spookily still. Beyond the islands, the open lake was wavy, turbulent, making it look even colder. On the horizon the sun was low in its brief mid-December arc in the sky. He moved closer to the window to feel the light.

"How did it go?" Greene asked, coming up beside him, his hand reaching for his car keys.

Kennicott shrugged. It was the universal shrug of police officers tasked to do a difficult job. He turned to leave. It would feel good to get home, take a shower, and sleep.

"Everyone at Homicide is out Christmas shopping," Greene said. "I need someone to do Detective Ho's walk-through with me. You in?"

"Sure," Kennicott said, his fatigue suddenly gone.

"Hey, perfect," Ho said as he led the way up the wide hallway to the front door, clipboard in hand. "Hey, the doorframe's intact. The door is solid steel, no signs of forced entry, peephole. There's a two-lock system, no signs of stress to either one. I've photographed and videotaped everything."

For the next twenty minutes Detective Ho led them through the whole apartment. Starting at the front door, they then went into the hall bathroom, the living room, the master bedroom and bathroom, the study. Ho kept up his running narrative, sometimes making astute observations—"Brace has more books on playing bridge than any other topic"—sometimes ridiculous ones: "Would you look at that? A penthouse suite, and the hall bathroom doesn't even have a soap dish."

At last they arrived back in the kitchen-dining area. Some clouds had moved in across the sun, darkening the room. Ho flicked on the overhead lights and worked his way around, narrating as he went.

Kennicott stopped at the table where he'd first seen Brace and Singh. He looked at the honey jar, the clay mugs, and the porcelain teapot. Nothing. He looked behind the table at the stove and kitchen counters. What was he looking for?

He scanned the dark tile floor. There was a narrow gap between the stove and the counter. It was hard to see inside the shadowed space, so he waited for his eyes to adjust to the light.

Then he saw it. He froze.

Until now the object had been camouflaged on the dark floor. He looked back at the table to the spot where he'd first seen Brace.

"Kennicott?" Greene asked, sensing something in his stillness.

"I think you should come here," Kennicott said, folding his arms in front of him.

"Hey, what's up?" Ho asked.

Kennicott focused on the narrow gap, the object becoming clearer as he stared at it. Greene stood by him, shoulder to shoulder, following his gaze to the spot on the floor.

It took a few seconds, and then Greene let out a low whistle.

"I'm not going to touch it, are you?" Greene asked, folding his arms as well.

"Absolutely not," Kennicott said, allowing himself a half smile.

"Detective Ho, keep your gloves on," Greene said.

"Hey," Ho said as he rushed over, "what've you got?"

"Good work, Kennicott," Greene said under his breath.

Kennicott nodded. I should say "Thanks, Detective," he thought, but instead he just kept staring back and forth, from Brace's mug on the breakfast table to the space between the gap, where he'd spotted the black handle of a knife.

12

Albert Fernandez cleared the last piece of paper from his desk. He put the little plastic box where he held his handwritten cue cards back in its hiding place in the bottom drawer. He checked his watch. It was 4:25. Detective Greene had left a message that they'd be there at 4:30.

Fernandez looked around his tidy 125-square-foot office. He knew it was 125 feet, because government regulations stated that an assistant Crown Attorney's office could not be one inch larger. There was enough room for a desk, a chair, a filing cabinet, and a few piles of evidence boxes. The door swung in, taking up about a fifth of the space.

The unwritten rule of the downtown Crown law office was that you worked with your door open. Prosecutors liked to drift into one another's offices at the end of the day and swap war stories about grumpy judges, sneaky defense lawyers, and difficult witnesses.

Fernandez hated all the chitchat, and his colleagues knew it. His first-year review stated that he was a good Crown but a poor team player. His peer job review suggested that Fernandez leave his door open more often and get a gumball machine to make his office a friendlier place for his colleagues to drop in.

The unspoken message was clear: Look, Albert, you're a bit of an odd duck around here, with your fancy clothes, your fastidious manners, and, well, your Spanishness. To get ahead, you're going to have to fit in . . .

The next day, Fernandez wasted his lunch hour at the Eaton Center and returned with a bubble-gum machine under his arm. Like bees to honey, Crowns sensed his new open-door policy. Soon after court, precious minutes, even hours, were wasted with useless banter as his colleagues, craving late-day sugar, quickly ate their way through the gum.

One day a senior Crown asked him about cross-examining a witness on an unsigned statement to a police officer. Fernandez knew of a recent case in point, and for the next half hour he educated his older colleague. Soon others stopped in not just for bitching and bubble gum, but to get Fernandez's opinion about complex legal issues. The door stayed open, the bubble-gum dispenser kept getting replenished, and Fernandez's star in the office rose.

Still, he resented wasting the precious time. As the years went by, he shut the door more often. One day the bubble-gum machine ran out and he didn't bother to refill it. Eventually he moved it behind the door, where it sat in a strange purgatory. Fernandez was unable to throw it out but unwilling to refill it. More often than not, it doubled as a coat hanger.

There was a knock on the door. Fernandez popped to his feet. Detective Ari Greene and Officer Daniel Kennicott stood side by side, more than filling the meager doorframe. Greene had an envelope in his hand.

"Come in," Fernandez said. "Sorry there's only one chair."

Both men looked at each other. Neither wanted to sit. "We'll stand," Greene said after they all shook hands.

There was another knock on the door, and Jennifer Raglan, the head Crown, walked in.

"Hi, everyone," she said, crossing her hands in front of her. She stood beside Greene. Clearly, she wasn't sitting down either.

Fernandez went back behind his desk. As he sat, the old chair squeaked.

"Before we listen to the CD," Greene said, lifting the package, "I'll want to go through my TTBD list." Everyone else nodded. Fernandez stared at Greene, trying not to look confused.

Greene caught Fernandez's eye and smiled. "Things-to-be-done list," he said, opening his leather-bound maroon notebook.

"Start with Katherine Torn. Age forty-seven. Lived with Brace common-law for fifteen years. No criminal record, no previous police contacts. Only child. Seems to have spent most of her free time horseback riding. Grew up in King City, where her family still lives. Father's a World War II vet and retired doctor. Mother's a housewife who was a big-time rider in her day. Kevin Brace, as you know, is the famous radio broadcaster. He's sixty-three. No record. No police contacts."

Fernandez was writing swiftly on his clean notepad.

"Officer Kennicott informed the family this morning, and they seemed to take it quite well. You never know. I've put the Torns in touch with Victim Services and will try to get them down to see you, maybe even tomorrow." Even though he had his notebook open, Greene didn't bother to look at it. "Tonight Kennicott will go through all the tapes from the lobby of the condo, Torn's and Brace's diaries, et cetera. He'll chart their movements for the last week. I've got a team going door-to-door through the apartment building and the surrounding stores and restaurants. Kennicott's partner, Nora Bering, will interview Torn's riding instructor. Tomorrow we're talking to the employees at the radio station."

Fernandez nodded. So this is what it's like when you work a homicide, he thought. A detective who's a real pro. "Talk to anyone else on the twelfth floor?" he asked.

Greene flipped back a few pages. "The only other unit on the floor is suite 12B. Resident Edna Wingate, British war bride. Eighty-three years old. Widowed three times. Came to Canada back in 1946. Parents were killed in the Blitz. I caught her in the lobby on her way out to an early-morning yoga class. She didn't notice anything unusual last night. I'm going to see her tomorrow morning."

Fernandez nodded. He looked at Greene and Kennicott. They were just twelve hours into this, and sleep was nowhere on their agenda. Both were calm. Around the eyes they looked tired but refusing to show it. "Let's hear the disc from the jail," he said.

The CD was marked DON JAIL, KEVIN BRACE, PRISONER PHONE CALLS DEC. 17, 13:00–17:00 HOURS. Fernandez was always amazed at how even the most experienced criminals talked when they were first incarcerated. They would quickly shut up, so you had to get them while they were in the shock-and-anger stage.

Brace's lawyer, Nancy Parish, had gotten there quickly and completely shut him up. Fernandez was hoping he would say something on the phone that would help at the trial and maybe even at the bail hearing.

Fernandez slipped the disc into his computer. The tinny voice of a Bell operator came on: "You have a collect call from . . . Kevin Brace. Press one if you accept, two to . . ."

There was a hard beep sound.

"*Hello,*" a male voice said.

"*Daddy? Is that you?*" a woman's voice asked. She sounded fairly young. Her voice deep, throaty. Near panicked.

Fernandez turned to a new page and wrote the date in the top right-hand corner.

"*Is this Amanda?*" The voice was deep, accented, probably Caribbean. Fernandez had never heard Brace's voice before, but he knew this wasn't it.

"*Who's this?*" Amanda demanded.

"*I'm here with your father. He's asked me to call and tell you that he's all right.*" The man spoke very slowly, as if he was reading something.

"*I don't understand.*"

"*He does not want you to come visit him yet.*"

Fernandez could hear Amanda's voice rise. "*What? Let me talk to my father right now.*"

"*He wants you to pass on this same message to everyone in your family.*"

"*But . . .*"

"I have to go now." There was a loud click.

"Wait . . . ," Amanda yelled before her voice was overrun by a loud telephone buzz.

Fernandez lifted his pen. He hadn't written a word.

"Amanda Brace is the oldest daughter from the first marriage," Greene said. "Twenty-eight years old. Married. Production coordinator for Roots," Greene said. Roots was a popular Canadian clothing chain. "No record. No police contacts. We're going to wait a day or two before we talk to her."

The detective seemed totally nonplussed by what he'd just heard. Fernandez felt like grinding his teeth in frustration.

They all listened to the blank silence of the CD and waited for the next call. Fernandez twirled his pen in anticipation. Nothing. He turned up the volume on the CD player. The empty buzz grew louder in the small office.

"A second daughter, Beatrice, lives out in Alberta," Greene said. "Married too. No record. No police contact."

After another minute Fernandez clicked the Fast Forward button, held it for a few seconds, and released it. He hit Play. Still there was no sound. He did the same thing two more times. Nothing. The machine that recorded the conversation was voice activated. The rest of the CD would be empty.

"Nada," he said. "Looks like we drew a blank." He looked at Greene, who was rolling his Cross pen in his fingers. He could almost see the wheels turning.

"Brace is keeping his mouth shut," Greene said.

"It's the 'never-ever' rule," Kennicott said. It was the first time the younger officer had spoken. Everyone turned to look at him.

"When I was a lawyer, I was trained to never, ever sign an affidavit unless all the pages were stapled together," Kennicott said. "That way, if I was ever questioned about some documents I'd put together years ago, I was protected."

"You could swear you never, ever signed an unstapled affidavit," Greene said, "the way Brace will be able to swear he never, ever spoke to anyone in jail. Protects him in case someone says Brace talked to him behind bars."

"Very good, Kennicott," Raglan said.

Greene turned to Raglan, who stood close to him in the small room. "I think you want Brace to get bail, don't you?"

She nodded. "He'll talk if he's out."

All three of them looked at Fernandez.

"Put up a good show on this bail hearing so Parish and Brace think we want to keep him inside," Raglan said, unfolding her arms. "But it's much better if you lose."

Raglan looked back at Greene. Clearly these two had worked together before.

"Just in case," Greene said, "I'll find Kevin Brace a cell mate. Someone who plays bridge."

"Why bridge?" Fernandez asked.

Everyone looked back at Fernandez.

"He talks about it all the time on his radio show," Raglan said.

"His study was filled with bridge books," Kennicott added.

Fernandez nodded. I better stop listening to all my tapes, he thought, and start listening to the radio.

"By the way," Raglan said as she and Greene headed out the door, "you've got Judge Summers. Should be interesting."

Fernandez waited until the door clicked shut, then reached into the back of the lower desk drawer and fished out his box marked JUDGES. He flipped through the alphabetically labeled cards to "Summers." He pretty much knew what it was going to say. There were three different entries. The first was from his early days in the Crown office:

Older judge, tough on new lawyers, loves ice hockey: won ice hockey scholarship to Cornell, played in a minor league. Triple A? Family has had Maple Leafs season tickets? for > 50 years, yells a lot, called me Mr. Fernando. Was in the Navy. Captain of a ship. Has bell ringer outside his court. Never be late.

Fernandez marveled at his own naïveté five years ago. The question marks denoted all the things he didn't understand back then. He'd never call hockey "ice hockey" now.

The second card was from three years ago:

Made senior judge at the Hall . . . major case of judgitis . . . pushing the hell out of everyone to settle cases, shorten the trial lists . . . trades stock online . . . likes to listen to the BBC news at 9:00 . . . bad on domestics . . . always talks hockey at JPTs, even in the summer. Works into every conversation that he went to Cornell. Loves talking about his boat. Is Jo's father.

"Judgitis" was the term both Crowns and defense lawyers used to describe judges who'd let the job go to their heads and become pompous and rude. Summers was a classic case. He was a big-time bully, if you let him be. The notation "bad on domestics" meant that Summers tended to acquit men charged with assaults on their spouses. Not a great sign for the Brace case. Jo was Jo Summers, a new Crown at the office who'd left a big job on Bay Street. She was hardworking and conscientious and, of course, never appeared in her father's courtroom.

The third entry was from last year:

Jugged a black kid who committed suicide . . . Kid was N.G. . . . Suicide note blamed the judge. Rumor—he was rushing off to a hockey tournament for the weekend. Now he's soft on bail. Crown was Cutter.

Fernandez well remembered making this entry. The case was horrible. Kalito Martin was a skinny black eighteen-year-old from a housing project in Scarborough. He was charged with a vicious rape. Cutter was the prosecutor and got Summers to deny the kid bail even though he had no record of any kind and was a top student. The first night, Martin hung himself using some pillowcases he tied together. The DNA test the next week showed he was innocent.

Every Crown Attorney's nightmare, Fernandez thought as he read through his cards again, his usually steady hands shaking ever so slightly. To convict someone who was innocent of a crime.

13

Is there any bloody sadder place in the world than a jail just before Christmas? Nancy Parish wondered as she trudged up the long concrete ramp to the front door of the Don Jail. And is there a more pathetic way for a single woman to spend a night the week before Christmas, she thought, especially when everyone else in the world is out partying? Except, of course, the prisoners.

A heavyset woman was coming down the ramp holding the hand of a little girl who looked as if she'd gotten all dressed up to visit the jail. Her hair was braided in symmetrical cornrows, and her coat was nicely pressed. The girl held a children's book in one hand, and with the other she was trailing a stick through the metal railing on the side of the ramp, making a *clickety-clack, clickety-clack* sound.

Parish smiled. She remembered when she was about five years old and discovered the magic of putting her drawing pencils through the fence railing as she walked down the street holding her father's hand, on her way to art class.

Suddenly the mother stopped halfway down the ramp. "Here, give me that, Clara." She reached across and snatched the stick from the child's hand. "Enough of that racket."

Parish caught the girl's eyes, and it was all she could do not to grab the stick from the mother. Welcome to the Don Jail, Clara, she thought as the little girl and her mother passed. You deserve better.

The Don Jail—known by everyone as the Don—was built in the early 1860s. It was a significant presence in the young city of Toronto. Perched on a hill overlooking the Don River and gazing down on the citizenry below, its fearsome stone entrance and heavy Gothic architecture cast a cold Victorian shadow on the growing port town. Subsequent attempts to clean it up and a utilitarian modern entrance added in the 1950s only deepened the sense of foreboding about the place.

At the top of the ramp, there was an intercom grid beside the metal front door. Parish pushed the small button.

"Yes," a bored woman's voice said, crackling over the bad connection.

"Counsel visit," she said.

"And I thought you were Santa. Come on in."

Parish heard a deep buzzing sound and yanked the heavy door. Inside, three green garbage bags sat in the corner of the tiny reception room, filling the small space with the stench of grease. She shoved her coat into a broken-down locker and turned to the thick glass window to speak to the guard on the other side.

"I'm here to see Kevin Brace," she said, slipping her lawyer's card under the small metal pass-through panel.

"Brace. Oh, the bathtub guy. He's on the third floor," the guard said, consulting her list. "You'll have to sign in."

Parish took out a fresh Bic pen. The sign-in sheet for lawyers was dated December 17, and even though it was seven at night, there wasn't one signature on it.

"Looks like I'm going to be the only lawyer here tonight," she said as she signed her name.

"Aren't you supposed to be at some office party?" the guard asked.

If I'd become an entertainment lawyer, Nancy Parish thought, I'd be at a catered affair at a four-star restaurant, mingling with television producers and directors and actors. Smelling roses on the white linen tablecloths. Instead I'm here with the smell of garbage.

"I would be, but my boss won't let me go," she said.

"Why not?" the guard asked.

"When you work for yourself," Parish said, picking up the pass the guard slid through to her, "your boss is an asshole."

She heard the guard laugh behind her as she went to yet another large metal door and waited for the familiar buzzing sound. A creaky old elevator took her up to the third floor, and in a small room at the end of the hall she found a tall man with a John Glenn–style crew cut. He was squeezed into a short chair facing an oversize metal desk, his knees up near his shoulders, like a basketball player on an airplane. A gray metal dinner plate, the remains of a turkey meal, with mashed potatoes and gravy and green peas, sat to one side, a plastic knife and fork tossed on top. The man was reading his *Toronto Sun*. The headline, in big black text, read LEAFS SCORE 3 IN THIRD—CLIP WINGS!

The guard was a fixture at the Don. Friendly to everyone. Always willing to bend the rules a little to help out. His haircut never varied an inch, earning him the nickname everyone used.

"Hi, Mr. Buzz," Parish said.

"Evening, Counselor," Mr. Buzz said, looking up from his newspaper and giving her jail pass card a cursory glance. He ran his hand over his brush cut as he spoke in a deep Slavic accent. "What's that name?"

"Brace. Kevin Brace," Parish said evenly.

"Oh, yeah. The radio guy."

Congratulations, Mr. Brace, Parish thought. You've graduated from the bathtub guy to the radio guy. Some kind of a comeback.

"He won't give you any trouble," Parish said.

The guard stood up. "None of the old guys do. Don't worry, I'll keep an eye on him for you. Take a seat in room 301. I'll bring him over."

Room 301 was a small cubicle with a steel table bolted to the floor and two facing plastic chairs. They were bolted down too. Parish sat on the seat closest to the door. She'd been taught early in her career always to have an escape route when she was meeting her clients in jail.

Parish opened her briefcase and took out a pad of paper and her pen. Then she waited.

This was the part she hated most about prison visits. She wasn't bothered by the fetid air, the institutional paint, or the loud slam of

metal doors closing. Even the lascivious looks she got from the men—
guards as well as inmates—rolled off her back. It was the waiting. The
feeling of helplessness. That was the thing that got to her.

"Here you go, my lady," Mr. Buzz said as he opened the door to
301. Parish quickly flipped her pad over as Kevin Brace walked in slowly.
He wore a standard one-piece, prison-orange jumpsuit. It looked about
two sizes too large, coming up over his neck and covering half his
beard. He didn't make eye contact.

"Closing time is eight thirty," Mr. Buzz said, "but I can probably
get you an extra fifteen if you need it. It's not exactly busy tonight."

"Thanks," Parish said, keeping her eyes on Brace.

He sat down across from her and waited patiently. When the
guard was out of sight, he reached inside his jumpsuit and pulled out
the piece of paper she'd given him at police headquarters. He had
written something on the back.

He flattened it out on the cold table and turned it toward her. She
leaned and read:

Ms. Parish, I wish to retain you as my lawyer on the following
conditions:
1. I do not wish to speak with you;
2. All of my instructions to you will be in writing; and,
3. You must never mention my silence to anyone.

She looked up at Brace, and for a moment he made eye contact.

"Solicitor-client privilege covers all forms of communication between a lawyer and her client," she said quietly. "Even noncommuni-
cation. I'm happy to take instructions from you in any form. None of
what you communicate to me, or how you communicate with me, will
ever be revealed."

Brace reached for Parish's pen. She gave it to him. He turned the
paper back his way and wrote:

What will happen tomorrow morning?

She took back her pen and wrote at the top of the page:

Confidential Solicitor-Client Communication Between Mr. Kevin Brace and His Lawyer, Ms. Nancy Parish

"Please remember, Mr. Brace," she said as she handed the pen back to him, "if you're going to write to me, you must put this heading about solicitor-client communication at the top of each page."

Brace pointed to his handwritten question.

"Not much happens tomorrow. The law says you must be brought to court within twenty-four hours. Habeas corpus. Bring forward the body. But because you're charged with murder, you also need a special hearing before a judge. I've already called the court. We are set for the day after tomorrow. I'll try to get you out before Christmas.

Brace folded his hands in front of him and nodded. He stared off into space.

Parish swallowed hard. None of this was what she'd expected. The only two times she'd met Brace, at the radio station and then a few weeks later, when he'd had a year-ender party at his condo, he'd been so warm, affable, wonderful to talk to. Ever since the phone call from Detective Greene early this morning, she'd been trying to figure out why Kevin Brace, a man who could have his choice of any lawyer in the country, had given the police her name.

The only reason she could think of was that he had her card at hand. She'd been asked to bring her business card to his party. Everyone's card had been put into one of Brace's many Toronto Maple Leafs beer mugs, and at the end of the night he had picked one out. The winner got to cohost the show with him the following year, and everyone threw in ten dollars toward an education fund he sponsored.

That was the funny thing. Brace had pulled out her card, and she'd been looking forward to doing the show with him. Instead here she was as his defense lawyer.

"I've called your daughters, and they've started to put together a list of witnesses we can call to support your bail."

Brace barely nodded his head.

"A lot of people want to come to court for you. I interviewed a few of them this afternoon, and tonight I'll draft some affidavits and work on your bail application."

None of this appeared to move Brace. He kept looking away, totally uninterested. Parish was shocked. The man sitting across from her seemed a million miles away from the gregarious radio-show host who'd interviewed her, and who was beloved by so many people.

What did you expect, Nancy? she scolded herself. The man's in shock. He doesn't even want to talk out loud yet. Secretly she'd thought that they might have a laugh about all the men who called to offer their sexual services after she'd appeared on his show, or that they'd talk about her cohosting with him once this nightmare was over.

She felt ridiculous. Never forget, she told herself, Kevin Brace is a client like any other client. Full stop.

"I'll see you tomorrow morning in the cells in the basement of Old City Hall before court. Okay?"

Brace unfolded his arms. He nodded and quickly stood up. Their meeting was over.

Parish collected her papers, making sure to keep her pad down so Brace wouldn't see the little cartoon she'd drawn earlier.

Brace stopped and motioned for her to give him her pen and the back of her pad.

She handed them over, and he wrote:

Do you mind if I keep this pen? And can you please get me a notebook I can write in?

"Of course," Parish said, thankful that there were no chew marks on the end of the Bic. "I'll bring one tomorrow."

He made eye contact with her and smiled.

She kicked on the door, and Mr. Buzz reappeared in the hallway. "Ready to go back to the party, Mr. Brace?" he said.

Brace simply put his hands behind his back and trudged away with the guard. Conditioned response, Parish thought as he left her alone in room 301. Already Kevin Brace was acting like a prisoner. It was remarkable how in just a few hours his whole personality seemed to have been stripped away. From national icon to the bathtub guy to just another prisoner on the third-floor range at the Don—in less than twenty-four hours.

14

Lower Jarvis Street was one of Ari Greene's favorite parts of Toronto. A strange mix of old mansions and magnificent churches intermingled with flophouses and pawnshops, the streets were filled with shoppers and office workers during the day, but at night they were left to the hardened people who made the city core their home—hookers, addicts, and a smattering of suburban wannabes.

It sure made it easy to get a free parking spot at night, Greene thought as he pulled his Olds into a vacant Goodwill lot. Whistling softly to himself, he hefted his guitar out of the backseat, locked up the car, and walked a short block north to the Salvation Army hostel.

"Good evening, Detective," a young man said as Greene opened the security door. "We're just setting up."

"Great," Greene said as he headed up the back stairs, taking them two at a time. He strolled into a dimly lit second-floor lounge. There was a small stage at the far end of the room, where a tall black man was plugging his guitar into an amplifier.

"Just in time, buddy," the man called out to Greene.

Greene made his way across the room, dodging plywood tables populated by vacant-looking residents. Each table had a paper plate on it filled with popcorn and chips.

"Folks, this is Detective Greene," the man said as Greene climbed up next to him. "He comes by a few times a year to play on our open-mike nights, so please give him a hand."

There was a smattering of halfhearted applause. Greene smiled as he took a seat on the stage and looked out over the room. There were about twenty men and a few women, seated at the tables or slouched on a broken-down sofa at the back.

Greene unpacked his guitar and quickly tuned up. "Devon, how about this?" he said as he strummed a few bar chords.

Devon nodded. "I got it," he said as he started strumming, joining in with the song. Back in the corner of the stage a drummer began to keep the beat. An old lady wandered up from the audience and sat at the piano by the side of the stage. Much to Greene's surprise, she picked up the tune.

Greene started to sing:

> "I went down to the crossroads
> Fell down on my knees . . ."

As he hit the second verse of the old blues tune, Greene looked around the room of blank faces. It's as quiet as a courtroom during a jury address, he thought as he finished up the song to a round of faint applause.

Next they played an old Lennon and McCartney song, one by Creedence Clearwater, and an early Dylan tune. Then Devon took the mike.

"Anyone want to come up and play?" he asked.

A doughy white guy, probably in his late thirties, put up his hand, as timid as a first grader.

"Tommy, come on up," Devon said.

"Yeah, play something, Tommy," someone called out from the sofa.

Tommy sauntered up to the piano. He adjusted his wire-rimmed glasses. "Well, I kind of wrote this," he said as he began to play a basic blues chord progression—G7, C7, G7, D7—and repeated it three times.

Greene gave Devon a wink. He improvised a simple melody over the top of the tune. Devon picked it up, and the drummer kicked in. They kept the song rolling for a few minutes.

"Thanks a lot, Tommy," Devon said, taking the mike again. A remarkably thin woman came up and sang an old English dance-hall number. A fat East Indian guy sang "(Sittin' on) the Dock of the Bay."

"Anyone else?" Devon asked when the Otis Redding song was done. Greene saw a head bobbing at the back of the room. "How about you, sir?" he called out.

The man stood up. He had a clownlike appearance. Bald on top, his hair too long about the sides, he wore a multicolored jacket made of an eclectic blend of cloth patches. Greene knew most of the faces in the room, from either the streets, the courts, or the times he'd come to play here, but this guy was new. Greene put him in his early fifties, but then reconsidered. He was probably younger. The street ages people fast, he thought as the man ambled awkwardly over to the piano.

"I play a little," the man said. He kept his head down, not making any eye contact. "I like to play this in G, but I'll transpose it down to C sharp." He settled onto the piano bench, rubbed his hands on his face and then put them on the keys. His wrists were high, his fingers curled in perfect position. His whole body seemed to relax.

"Why not?" Greene gripped the neck of his guitar. "What're we playing?"

"You know the 'Walking Blues'?" the man asked.

Greene moved his fingers to a minor chord and smiled. "Let's roll."

Greene and Devon played the standard blues intro. The man hit the piano keys, and a shudder went through the somnolent room.

Devon looked at Greene and nodded. "Wow," he whooped. "We got a player!"

They rolled through the "Walking Blues," then three other standard blues numbers.

"We only got time for one more," Devon said. "It's lights-out in twenty minutes. You got one last request?" he asked the piano player.

"Let's try 'Crossroads' again," he whispered.

The man started to play, and for the first time, he sang. He ended with the lyrics

> *"I'm standing at the crossroads*
> *I believe I'm sinking down . . ."*

The audience was listening, transfixed.

"Where'd you learn to play like that?" Greene asked the man a few minutes later as he packed up his guitar. The room was emptying out fast.

"I just picked it up," the man said, still averting his eyes.

"Studied music, didn't you?" Greene said.

The man finally looked up. His eyes were a remarkably light blue. Almost translucent. Greene tried to imagine him as a young boy, curly blond hair, fine white skin, gleaming eyes.

The man looked down again. "For a few years." His voice was weak.

"Let me guess—piano, grade eight, Royal Conservatory?"

The man gave a sheepish grin. "Went further, actually. Got a teacher's certificate."

He didn't say another word, and Greene let the silence sit. He knew it was best to leave the man's story untold. How he'd ended up on this sad path.

"I'm Detective Ari Greene, from Homicide," Greene said at last, extending his hand.

"Fraser Dent," the man said, giving Greene a weak handshake. "Strange way for a cop to spend his free time."

Greene shrugged. "I've been doing it for years."

"Nice of you," Dent said.

"It's also good police work. Every once in a while I find someone who can help me out. Then I can do them a favor or two."

Dent looked over his shoulder to check that no one was around. The room was empty. He looked back at Greene.

"Don't worry, Mr. Dent," Greene said. "I'm very careful."

Dent nodded. Rubbed his hands over his face again. "What kind of favors?"

"A few more questions first. You play bridge?"

"Yeah."

"Good at it?"

Dent paused for a moment. "Not bad."

"Let me guess—you got a university degree or two?"

"Two or three," Dent said.

Greene laughed. The door at the far end of the room clicked open, and Devon ducked his head back inside. Greene gave him a nod and turned back to Dent. "How bad's your record?" he asked Dent quietly.

Dent narrowed his eyes. "I've done some time."

Devon slipped back out, closing the door behind him.

"Good," Greene said. "Let's go for a walk."

"Walk? It's curfew, man."

"Curfew," Greene said, hoisting his guitar on his shoulders, "won't be a problem."

15

It was a small room, with sickeningly beige walls, a pine desk, a black chair, a television and DVD/VCR player, and a few cardboard boxes stacked neatly in the corner. No windows. No molding. No art on the walls.

That meant no distractions, a good thing when you are doing this kind of important but boring work, Daniel Kennicott thought as he looked at the chart he'd compiled over the last twelve hours. The only problem was, at four in the morning it was a struggle to keep awake. Especially when he'd been in the same room for so long and hadn't slept for days. But it had been his choice to take the assignment, and he wasn't about to complain. Even to himself.

It was Detective Greene's idea. Late on Monday morning, after Kennicott spotted the knife on their walk-through of Kevin Brace's apartment, Greene brought him back to the homicide bureau and set him up in this office. His job: systematically go through the minutiae of Katherine Torn and Kevin Brace's life, using every piece of relevant evidence Detective Ho could find.

He'd spent the first few hours watching videotapes taken in the lobby of the Market Place Tower. The cameras covered most of the ground floor. Each time Torn or Brace appeared, Kennicott carefully noted their movements on a color-coded chart. He also had a column for Mr. Singh, the newspaper deliveryman; Rasheed, the concierge;

and Ms. Wingate, the neighbor down the hall. Greene had told him to pay particular attention to the morning of the murder.

There was only one thing. At 2:01 yesterday morning the lobby video showed Rasheed getting up from his desk, going over to the elevator, and pushing the button. Then he went back to his desk and called someone. Kennicott checked the video of the parking lot and saw that Katherine Torn's car had driven in at 1:59. Obviously the concierge was sending the elevator down for her and calling upstairs to let Brace know that his wife was home.

After he finished with the tapes, Kennicott spent an hour poring over the concierge's logbook, adding each relevant entry to his chart. Throughout the night, officers delivered copies of witness statements they'd taken from the residents. Almost everyone said they didn't know much about Brace and Torn, except that the couple always seemed to be holding hands when they were together.

About midnight he started going through Brace and Torn's property. There wasn't much from Brace. The guy didn't have a diary or a cell phone or an address book. There was a box of papers taken from his desk, and Kennicott spent an hour reading through them. Half of them were notes about playing bridge.

He went through Torn's laptop, her Palm Pilot, her handwritten diary, her cell phone records, her Visa receipts, and every other scrap of paper, including notes stuck to the fridge, her mail, and the trash, each of which Ho had meticulously collected and cataloged.

Kennicott's chart grew, and a picture of their life emerged. It was remarkably patterned. Every weekday started at precisely 5:05, when Mr. Singh could be seen on the video arriving at the Market Place Tower. In his statement Singh said that at 5:29 he'd meet Brace in the doorway of 12A. Brace always left the door halfway open and always came to meet Singh with his mug in hand. Torn was never up at that time.

Brace called the radio station every day at 5:45 to confirm that he was awake and to talk to the show producer about any breaking stories. At 6:15 the lobby camera caught Brace walking out the front door. He arrived at the studio by 6:30 and was on the air by 8:00. The show finished at 10:00, and Brace would spend an hour in story meetings for the next day's show. He could be seen walking back into the lobby at the Market Place Tower every day at about 12:30.

Torn's mornings were equally predictable. The underground video showed her getting into her car on Tuesdays, Wednesdays, and Fridays just after 10:00. On Thursdays she left at eight. Her diary showed that she had an 11:30 or 12:30 riding lesson most days at King City Stables, which would be just under an hour's drive. At about 2:00 she came back to the apartment. The lobby video showed her leaving again, by foot, every day at about 2:30, always casually dressed. Her Visa receipts showed her shopping at various neighborhood clothing boutiques or houseware stores. Her library card showed her going there twice in the final week of her life. She returned through the lobby daily between 5:00 and 6:00.

Brace must have slept in the afternoon, because he wouldn't leave again until about eight at night, when he and Torn would walk through the lobby hand in hand. It was the first time all day that they were on video together. They would come back at about ten. Kennicott cross-referenced Torn's Visa accounts and traced their dining habits—always at one of the local restaurants, always someplace that was moderately priced. They were certainly not living the high life.

There was only one day of the week where the pattern was broken. Mondays. Torn wasn't seen leaving the building in the morning, and she came home about four o'clock in the afternoon. It wasn't difficult to figure out why.

Kennicott's partner, Nora Bering, had interviewed Torn's riding instructor. He read the statement of Gwen Harden, the owner of King City Stables:

Kate was a very good student, a natural rider. Great balance. Tremendous competitor. Kevin was very supportive. Loved to watch her ride. Never missed once when she was in competition. She rode every day except Saturday. Sundays she'd do an all-day cross-country ride and stay up with her parents. They live just down the road. Mondays she'd take a double class.

When she didn't show up this morning, I was surprised. It wasn't like her not to call in if she was going to miss a class.

This was the last thing Bering would do on the case. She had a six-month leave coming, and she was going back home to the Yukon to visit her dad. "Only me," she'd joke with him, "taking my holidays in the Arctic in the winter."

The only exception to this pattern Kennicott could find for the whole month was the Wednesday before, December 12. Torn appeared on the video that day at 1:15, in the lobby, not the parking garage. She was dressed in a business suit and high heels, and she carried a long envelope in her hand. She spoke briefly to Rasheed and then waited for about five minutes in one of the overstuffed lobby chairs, looking out the front window. When something caught her eye, she jumped up and rushed outside. Rasheed went out with her, as if, Kennicott thought, he was putting her in a taxi. Kennicott checked the logbook and read the entry: "Taxi for Mrs. Brace, 1:20, Rasheed."

Earlier that morning, Brace had left the condominium at the regular time. The people at the radio station said he followed his usual routine. But that afternoon he didn't come back home.

Just before five o'clock Brace and Torn walked back into the lobby. Clearly they'd met up somewhere. Kennicott ran the tape back and confirmed that Brace was wearing the same clothes he had on earlier, when he'd left for work. Neither Torn's diary nor her Palm Pilot had anything listed for that afternoon. That night the couple didn't go out. Where, Kennicott wondered, had they gone?

It was about four in the morning when Kennicott got to Katherine Torn's wallet. He'd intentionally left it to the end. The wallet would be more meaningful if he knew as much as possible about her life before he looked at it.

This wasn't the first time he had examined the wallet of a dead person. Four and a half years ago he'd pulled apart his brother Michael's wallet and every other possession he could find. Credit card receipts, phone bills, bank records, electronic calendar, computer hard drive, desk drawers, and even Mike's garbage. It was amazing how much you could learn about a dead person—and disturbingly intrusive. He'd found a plane ticket to Florence, a car-rental receipt, hotel reservations, and a raft of brochures about an Italian hill town named Gubbio. There was an annual summer crossbow contest scheduled for the following week. He still hadn't figured out why his brother was going there.

Poor Katherine Torn. Clearly she was a very private person. Now she lay dead on a slab in the morgue, a complete stranger wearing surgical gloves combing through her life. Kennicott had asked forensics to copy all of the wallet's contents and to put each item back exactly as they'd found them. It wasn't just what was in a wallet that was important, but how the things were arranged. The location, the order, the feel.

He began at the change purse. He counted out $2.23 in change, three subway tokens, and a laundry pickup slip for three men's shirts. The first compartment held forty-five dollars in bills and six different coupons for things like breakfast cereal, laundry soap, and kitchen cleaner. There was a dog-eared frequent-user's card from the Lettieri Espresso Bar and Café on Front Street. Three of the ten squares were stamped.

Looks like she was a penny-pincher, Kennicott thought as he opened the next compartment. It was filled with plastic cards. She had a Visa and a MasterCard, a library card, a Royal Ontario Museum card, and cards from five different department stores. The store cards struck him right away. Department stores were notorious for charging outrageously high interest rates, usually preying upon the poor and, in Toronto, the teeming immigrant population. Kennicott had seen this when he was a lawyer. Clients who appeared to be wealthy, but in fact were desperately trying to keep up with their monthly payments. They'd spread their debt around like this, digging deeper and deeper holes for themselves.

The third compartment held a fistful of receipts and Torn's checkbook. Kennicott worked his way through each item. She had carefully recorded the date and spending category on each slip of paper: household, entertainment, personal. Her handwriting was jagged, forced. He looked through her check stubs. Mostly small purchases. Her only extravagance seemed to be personal-care items from a very chic store in Yorkville, the city's upscale boutique area. Kennicott had been there too many times. When his ex-girlfriend Andrea got into modeling, she had become a regular customer, and like Torn, she'd bought a seemingly endless supply of products: sponges, herbal shampoos, organic soaps, body lotions, hand-ground makeup, imported facial masks, specialty eye creams, and moisturizers.

Andrea liked to drag Kennicott to the shop. He found the place overwhelmingly boring. "Oh, stop complaining, Daniel," she'd say. "You like beautiful women, and it's a lot of work staying gorgeous."

There was only one item in the last compartment—a finely printed and embossed business card. Kennicott examined it carefully: HOWARD PEEL, PRESIDENT, PARALLEL BROADCASTING.

Kennicott paused. He went back to his long list of all the items they'd found in the apartment. The connection was easy to make. In the top drawer of Kevin Brace's desk they'd found an unsigned contract between Brace and Parallel Broadcasting. Kennicott fished out the contract and read through it.

When he finished, he looked at Peel's card again. In contrast to everything else in Torn's well-ordered wallet, and every other scrap of paper that was carefully folded and neatly stored, all four corners of Peel's card were cracked and bent over. It was as if Torn had worried the edges of the fine paper, the way a nervous suitor pulls the label off a wine bottle at a good restaurant.

He looked back at the contract. It was dated December 12. Kennicott riffled through the videos from the lobby and played the tape from that day. It was the day Torn had skipped her riding lesson. He fast-forwarded to the part where she and Brace came back into the lobby late in the afternoon. Something about it had seemed off the first time he'd watched it. What was it?

He had to play it three times before it struck him. This was the only tape in which Brace and Torn walked into the lobby together and they were not holding hands.

16

Just to the west of the Market Place Tower, Ari Greene watched a group of mothers pushing strollers and sipping their midmorning lattes. Maybe I should start drinking coffee, he thought, yawning, as he fell into line behind them. It was his third covert pass by the condominium in the last half hour. This time the lobby was empty.

The concierge, Rasheed, was alone. He was reading the front page of the *Toronto Star*, which featured a big picture of Kevin Brace being led out of the condo in handcuffs by two young police officers, Mr. Singh in the background. A banner headline read CAPTAIN CANADA CHARGED WITH MURDER, and the subtitle said STAR REPORTER'S EXCLUSIVE PHOTOS OF ARREST.

"Good morning, Detective," Rasheed said. He had a ballpoint pen in his hand, which he clicked a few times. "Going up?"

Greene stopped and lifted a thin leather briefcase onto the reception desk. "Not yet," he said. "First I want to ask you a few questions. Routine stuff." Greene unzipped the case. The cool metallic sound of the zipper crackled in the marble foyer.

Rasheed clicked the pen in his hand and ticked off something in his logbook. "I made a statement and gave all the videos and the logbook to Officer Kennicott."

Greene nodded. He opened the notebook he'd pulled from his case. He wanted to take this slowly. "You know how we police are, always asking more questions."

Greene had been up all night, overseeing the investigation. Reading the various witness statements and police reports as they came in. At eight in the morning he'd gone and had tea with Edna Wingate, the neighbor in suite 12B. Her apartment was a mirror image of Brace's suite, but unlike his place, it was filled with plants and was extremely neat. Everything seemed to have little labels, right down to the place for her winter gloves. She'd reminded him again that her yoga instructor said she had the best quads he'd ever seen in an eighty-three-year-old.

Rasheed stopped clicking the pen and met Greene's eyes. For a moment his eyes flickered toward Greene's briefcase. Good, Greene thought.

Greene opened his notebook. "What's your full legal name, sir?"

"Rasheed, Mubarak, Rasman, Sarry."

Greene began to write. "Date of birth?"

"The fifth of the second, nineteen hundred and forty-nine."

"Place of birth?"

"Iran."

"Education?"

"I'm a civil engineer, graduate from the University of Tehran."

"You came to Canada when?"

"September 24, 1982, as a refugee claimant. I became a Canadian citizen the first day I was eligible to do so."

"At a ceremony in the Etobicoke Civic Centre," Greene said, raising his voice a notch and closing his book with a hard snap. "Correct?"

Rasheed looked taken aback by Greene's sudden change in tone. "That is correct," he said. The man seemed a bit shaken. Exactly what Greene wanted.

"After the fall of the shah, you were captured and held in captivity for nine and a half months. Your wife's family bribed an official, and you walked to freedom. It took you twenty-five days. In March of 1980 you ended up in Italy, went to Switzerland, then France, and from there came to Canada."

Greene spoke quickly, never taking his eyes off Rasheed.

Rasheed held Greene's gaze. He looked trapped. Finally he glanced down at Greene's briefcase. "I see, Detective, that you have read my refugee claim file."

"It's right here." Greene pulled out a white file. There were five fresh yellow tabs marking off various points.

Rasheed's pen started to click again.

"You come from a prominent family," Greene said as he zipped his bag closed. "At your hearing, you told the Refugee Board that in the early days of the revolution your younger brother and your father were killed."

Rasheed looked back at Greene. "The murder of one's family is a terrible thing."

Greene thought of the numbers on his father's arm, but he resisted the urge to nod his head. Instead he told a story. "Sir, in the late 1970s I spent a month in Paris."

"A most beautiful city."

"But for a foreigner, in January, cold. One day I stumbled into a tea shop on the rue de Malte. There were warm pillows on the floor, lovely tea brewing, soft incense burning. The owners were Iranians. Recent refugees from the ayatollah. We became close friends."

Rasheed smiled, a plastic, pasted-on smile. He's been wearing that facade for years, Greene thought, and it's not going to crack easily. "Many of my new friends had walked through the mountains to Turkey," Greene said softly.

The concierge's smile seemed to slip.

"I must have heard twenty such stories," Greene said. "And it never took anyone more than four days to get across the mountains."

Rasheed's nostrils flared, and he gave a hearty laugh. "There were many mountain passes, Detective."

Let him get a bit cocky, Greene thought. He opened the file at the first yellow tab. He wanted Rasheed to see that he was reading a section with the heading CLAIMANT'S HISTORY IN HOME COUNTRY.

"Detective," Rasheed said, staring at the file, "I had a full refugee hearing—"

"At which you denied ever having been a member of the shah's notorious SAVAK guard. Denied working for Nemotallah Nassiri, the head of the agency."

"Of course—"

"Of course," Greene said, his head down, still reading the file. "Nassiri was flown to Paris by some sympathetic members of the Iranian Air Force. Wasn't he?"

"I believe I heard about that, yes," Rasheed said.

Greene flipped through some more pages. "You're a trained civil engineer."

Rasheed looked at him without saying a word.

Greene's eyes drifted back down to the file. "Came to Canada from France."

"As you said yourself, Detective, many of us ended up in Paris."

Greene stopped flipping the pages and let the file fall open at a page titled EVIDENCE OF TORTURE. "Mr. Rasheed," he said, "many of my friends in Paris were tortured. I saw horrible scars."

"It happened to all of us."

Greene looked back up at Rasheed and leaned over the desk. "But you never had any scars. Did you?"

"Detective, please." Rasheed didn't know where to look. Greene could smell him sweating. "I have never taken a penny of welfare from this country. Never been arrested or gotten a parking ticket. My wife works full-time at the bakery. My children, both in university. Two girls—"

"At the University of Toronto," Greene said, leaning in even farther. "The oldest is in dentistry, the youngest in pharmacy."

"Detective, please. I gave Officer Kennicott all the tapes, the logbook, made a statement . . ."

Greene slowly unzipped his briefcase. He slid his hand back in and pulled out a color-coded piece of paper. "Officer Kennicott went through every tape, cross-referenced them with the logbook, and cross-referenced both with the different doormen who were on duty for the last week. Here, look, your shifts are highlighted in blue."

Greene held out the paper. Rasheed looked at it reluctantly, like a man peering over the edge of a railing as he walks across a high bridge.

"It didn't take long to realize that the story you told us when we first interviewed you about Mr. Brace was not the whole truth," Greene said. "Just like it wasn't hard for me to conclude that the story you told the Refugee Board was full of lies."

Rasheed stared at Greene. The light had gone out of his eyes.

Greene leaned in closer. "Rasheed, I don't want to do this. My own father was a refugee. Had to do things to get into this country that I still don't understand." He touched the file in front of the concierge. "I'd like to put this away and forget about it."

"Detective, please," Rasheed said. "If they send me back, that would be the end—"

"This is a murder investigation. Katherine Torn is dead. Mr. Brace is looking at twenty-five years in jail. I need to know what happened." Greene put his hand on the zipper.

The concierge stared at his file, appalled. As if he were looking at a corpse that had just come back to life.

"Please, Detective. Put it away."

Instead, Greene began to slowly close the zipper, leaving the file out. The only sound in the lobby was the *click-click-click* of the teeth touching as he moved the zipper forward.

"Stop," Rasheed said when it was almost closed.

Greene tightened it one more notch before he stopped and met Rasheed's eyes.

"Trust me," Greene said. "Nothing would make me happier than to bury this file where no one will ever, ever find it."

17

Daniel Kennicott loved walking up the wide granite steps to the Gothic building that years ago was converted from Toronto's city hall into the city's main criminal courthouse, now known as Old City Hall. Known affectionately as just "the Hall" by everyone who used it—cops, criminals, Crown Attorneys, defense lawyers, court reporters, judges, interpreters, clerks, and journalists—it was the only building in the downtown core that was elevated above the street, making it stand out above the surrounding sidewalks like a judge's dais looking down on a courtroom.

The Hall covered a whole city block. Five stories high, it was a massive stone structure, asymmetrical in design, filled with curling cornices, rounded pillars, marble walls, smiling cherubs, overhanging gargoyles, and the big clock tower to the left side of the main entrance, which topped it off like a gigantic misplaced birthday candle. Above the arched front entryway, the words MUNICIPAL BUILDINGS hidden among a swirling band of curlicues and bows, denoted its initial use.

The entryway was guarded by a tall gray stone cenotaph, a monument to the city's GLORIOUS DEAD WHO FELL IN THE GREAT WAR. The names of the battlefields in France and Belgium—Ypres, Somme, Mount Sorrel, Vimy, Zeebrugge, Passchendaele, Amiens, Arras, Cambria—were chiseled into its four sides. Cold and permanent as death.

A few nervous-looking defense lawyers and their clients huddled on the front steps, finishing their cigarettes, the whiff of tobacco hanging in the air. Kennicott strode past them and yanked open one of the wide oak front doors. Inside, a long, scraggly line of people waited to pass through the security check. All the usual suspects were there: twitchy drug addicts, burned-out prostitutes, jewelry-laden young men in running shoes and baggy jeans, and the odd fellow in a business suit, in shock that suddenly, in the midst of downtown Toronto, he'd been plunked right into the middle of this third-world ghetto.

Kennicott lifted his badge high above his head, saying, "Excuse me, police, excuse me, police," and squeezed his way to the front of the line. When he finally got to the security desk, the court cop insisted on examining his badge.

"Sorry, pal," the young man said. "New regulations. Even need to check our own people."

"No problem," Kennicott said as he walked up into the big open rotunda. Facing him was a two-story-high stained-glass window, a workmanlike tableau of the founding of the city—complete with kneeling Indians bearing food offerings, muscled laborers forging steel, and stern-looking bankers doing business. In front of it was a large landing, with two broad staircases leading to the second-floor courtrooms. Two five-foot wrought-iron "grotesques"—sculptures fashioned in the shape of huge griffins—guarded the base of the staircase, like remnants from a Harry Potter movie set.

The main floor, with its tall Corinthian columns and mosaic tile floor, had the feel of a Turkish bazaar. In the early-morning pre-court rush, the air was abuzz with urgent conversations, made all the more pressing by the coming holiday. Families frantic to get their loved ones out on bail, defense lawyers trying to cut a deal and get the hell out of court, cops sipping coffee from Styrofoam cups, waiting to get their court cards stamped so they could get paid double time, and Crown Attorneys hustling into courtrooms, their arms laden with overstuffed files.

Kennicott made his way down the west corridor past a row of

columns topped with cherubic figurines. The architect, Edward James Lennox, who'd supervised building the Hall in the late nineteenth century, had filled it inside and out with these strange and eerie stone faces. Near the end of his commission, Lennox got into a fight with the city aldermen. As a parting shot, he had the lead mason sculpt caricatures of each of his enemies. Kennicott loved to pick them out—fat-faced men, men with overhanging mustaches, men wearing round spectacles or chomping on cigars, each face contorted in some strange way. These were discovered only years later, and by then it was too late to change them. And the only sculpture that wasn't humorous was the one Lennox had done of himself. He also had his name carved on the stone corbels beneath the eaves. Kennicott admired a man who could make a mark in such a subtle, and lasting, fashion.

"I'm here to see the Crown doing bails in 101," he said as he entered the Crown's office at the end of the west hall and waved his badge at the secretary who sat behind the flimsy protective glass.

"Come in," the woman said, without even looking up.

Kennicott worked his way through a narrow hallway of makeshift rooms to a tiny office where a hand-scrawled sign with "101" was taped up at an angle. A woman with a pile of blond hair tied up over her head was working her way through a stack of beige folders while curling a renegade strand of hair with an expensive-looking metal pencil.

"Excuse me," Kennicott said.

"What's up?" she said, not lifting her head.

"I'm here on the Brace murder," he said. The woman had an unusual dark wooden clip in her hair.

"Brace. Captain Canada and the pretty, younger second wife stabbed in the bath," she said, still not looking up. "The courtroom will be packed. It's 'cry me a river day' in 101 bail court. Everyone wants out for the holidays. Just seven more shoplifting days until Christmas."

Kennicott laughed at her joke.

She looked over at him, flashing a pair of stunning hazel eyes, still curling her hair with the pencil. Kennicott recognized the hair and the hair clip from his law school days. And those eyes. She looked at him for a long moment before her face warmed. "Daniel," she said. There was a slight gap between her two front teeth, and her tongue slid over it.

At law school she'd worn that same hair clip every day. One night he was working late in the library and happened upon her slouched in a deep leather chair, books stacked high on both sides, and her hair unleashed from the clip, which she clutched between her teeth.

"Oh, hi," Kennicott had said. Unlike most first-year students, who clustered together in study groups, she rarely interacted with fellow classmates.

"Hi, Daniel," she'd said, elbowing herself up to a sitting position and pulling the clip out of her mouth. "Surprised to see me with my hair not tied up?"

Kennicott had laughed a bit nervously. He was surprised she knew his name. "Surprised to see you in the library," he said.

"I got this in Tulum, Mexico," she'd said, rubbing the clip in her hands. "It's Mayan."

Back then, Kennicott and his girlfriend Andrea had just entered one of their "off-again" phases. He hovered a moment, smiled. "Good luck with your studying," he said before he walked on.

Seeing her again now, he remembered the hair clip and he remembered the hair, but he couldn't remember her name. On her desk he spotted her copy of the *Criminal Code of Canada*. The letters S-U-M-M-E-R-S were printed in black Magic Marker ink across the exposed white pages, something all Crown Attorneys did to try to keep from losing the book that was their lifeline in court.

She caught his eye, smiling. "It's Jo—Jo Summers."

Kennicott smiled back. "It's been a while, Jo, and I haven't slept for a few days. What're you doing as a Crown? I thought you were going the big-firm route?"

"Got bored saving rich people's money. Besides, it's family destiny."

Kennicott nodded, making the connection. Summers. She was the daughter of Justice Johnathan Summers, the most difficult judge in the Hall. Despised equally by defense, Crown, and cops. A navy veteran, he ran his courtroom with everything on time, in order, shipshape.

"I'm the fourth Summers generation practicing criminal law. My poor little brother, Jake, he has the wife and two kids and has made zillions with his Internet company. But he'll come up to the cottage and tell my dad about some multimillion-dollar deal he's just made in Shanghai, and my father's eyes glaze over. Then Dad will ask me about some stupid shoplifting trial I prosecuted, and he'll be enthralled for an hour."

"He must be proud of you," Kennicott said.

Her face turned serious. "Daniel, I was very sorry to hear about your brother."

Kennicott inhaled. "Thanks," he said. His eyes drifted to the window behind her and the new City Hall Square across Bay Street. People were skating in the big open rink, the early-morning sun casting long shadows.

"I meant to call you," Summers said.

"It really isn't a problem," Kennicott said. "Look, I'll see you in court."

Twenty minutes later, tiny courtroom 101, in the bowels of Old City Hall, was packed with harried young legal-aid lawyers, tense-looking families, and the so-called Gang of Four journalists who covered the courts for the city's four major newspapers: Kirt Bishop, a tall, handsome reporter from *The Globe*; Kristen Thatcher, a tough female reporter from the *National Post*; Zachary Stone, a pudgy, happy-go-lucky reporter from the *Sun*; and Awotwe Amankwah, a top reporter from the *Toronto Star* who everyone knew had fallen on hard times a few years ago when his gorgeous TV anchor wife took off with her cohost.

The door to the right of the judge's dais yanked open. The court clerk, a middle-aged man wearing a loose-fitting black robe, strode in. From up close Kennicott could see the man was wearing jeans and sneakers underneath.

"Oyez, oyez, oyez," the clerk called out in a perfunctory voice.

"This honorable court, Her Worship Madame Radden presiding, is now in session. Please be seated."

As the court clerk spoke, a well-groomed woman, easily in her fifties, strode purposefully in from a door to his left. She wore a finely pressed black robe. The click of her high heels resonated as she rushed up to her place on the bench, overlooking the riffraff.

The clerk took his seat below. "No talking in the courtroom. Turn off all cell phones and pagers, take off all hats and head coverings except those worn for legitimate religious purposes." His voice was angry. "No waving, winking, or mouthing words to the prisoners. And no talking in the body of the court."

With a loud clang, the door from the cells opened. Three scruffy-looking men in prison-issue orange jumpsuits were led into the glassed-in prisoners' dock.

"Name of the first accused?" the clerk demanded.

The man leaned down to get his mouth into the small, round opening in the glass. "Williams. Delroy Williams," he said.

"Williams. He's mine," one of the young duty counsel called out, grabbing an interview sheet from her pile. She was a tall black woman with impossibly thin legs. "Mother's here as a surety. Perhaps my friend will agree to his release?"

Jo Summers riffled through her stack of files. "Williams . . . Williams," she said, straightening her back. "He's a crack addict who stole some pizza slices from a shop on Gerrard Street. Gave the cops a wrong name. Can he live with his mother?"

The duty counsel looked back into the courtroom. A large woman stood up, clutching a cheap-looking purse. "Yes. No problem," she said.

"How bad's his record?" the justice of the peace, Radden, asked from the bench, bored already.

Summers dove back into the file. She shrugged. "Two pages, typical addict stuff. Theft, mischief, possession. A few fail to appears. No violence." She spoke directly to the mother. "You'll bring him to court."

"Yes. No problem."

"And I don't want him downtown." Summers turned back to the bench. "Boundary restriction of Bloor to the north, Spadina to the west, Sherbourne to the east, and the lake to the south."

"Fine," Radden said. "One thousand dollars, no deposit, I'll name the mother as the surety, no nonprescription drugs. Next case."

It went on like this for an hour. Summers was good. She ran the court with authority, quickly dealing with small cases. Only once, when she was looking behind her, did she catch Kennicott's eye. Her mouth crinkled just a bit, and she gave him a quick wink.

At eleven o'clock Brace's lawyer, Nancy Parish, walked in. She wore a nicely tailored conservative suit that made her stand out among the young lawyers. The officer in the prisoners' dock swung open the door behind him. "Brace," he shouted, like a bingo caller in an echo chamber. The journalists on the benches sat straight up, straining for a better look. Three sketch artists sitting in the front row took out their charcoals and began to draw.

There was a collective intake of breath as Brace was led into the narrow prisoners' dock. He wore the oversize orange jumpsuit that made it seem as though he had no neck.

"Quiet in the court," the clerk hollered.

Brace had on his trademark metal glasses. His beard was disheveled, and his gray hair was greasy—like the hair of most new prisoners, who don't get access to shampoo for at least a week and have to wash their hair with prison-issue soap and hard prison water. His shoulders were slumped, and his brown eyes seemed glazed, unfocused.

Parish approached the prisoners' box and spoke to him through the hole in the glass. Kennicott watched, hoping to catch a nod or a headshake. But Brace's head didn't even move.

"Your Worship, if it please the court, Ms. Nancy Parish, P-A-R-I-S-H, for Mr. Brace," Parish said, turning to the bench. "We'll apply for bail tomorrow. The trial coordinator has set up a special court with a sitting judge."

"Done. Adjourned until December 19, upstairs in courtroom 121," Radden said. "Next prisoner."

There was a rumble in the seats behind Kennicott. He looked back just as an attractive young woman in the second row lumbered to her feet. Off balance. She held an overcoat in one hand, and the other hand was on her belly. The woman was very pregnant.

"Daddy!" she yelled in a voice so filled with pain that even the journalists, who'd snapped their heads around to look at her, hesitated with their pens. "No, Daddy, no."

Kennicott looked back at Kevin Brace. The fog that seemed to surround him appeared to lift as he looked out at his daughter.

"Order in court!" the clerk shouted, rising to his feet.

One of the court officers put an arm around Brace and pulled him toward the prisoners' door.

Kennicott turned back to Brace's daughter. She had the same deep brown eyes as her father. The people in the second row had all moved out of the way, clearing a path for her. She waddled with great difficulty down the narrow row. Tears streamed down her face, and the black mascara under her eyes was running.

It didn't seem to bother her. Despite her public display of emotion, Kennicott's first impression was that this was a woman who could handle herself very well.

18

Most Crown Attorneys said it was the hardest part of the job, and Albert Fernandez knew he wasn't very good at it. Meeting with the family of the victim. Listening patiently. Being a shoulder to cry on. Every family was different, and you never knew what to expect.

Two years before, in his annual review, Fernandez was told that he needed to work on his empathy skills and was sent to a Dealing with Grieving Families seminar. He'd spent a whole day in a hotel conference room listening to speaker after speaker drone on, flipping through pamphlets with such horrible titles as *Closure and Contentment—Helping Families Turn the Page.*

Near the end of the afternoon, when he was on his fourth cup of watery coffee, a slight woman had taken the podium. She was well dressed in a stylish business suit, a string of pearls around her neck.

"Closure," she said, pausing a moment to make sure she had the attention of the room. It had been a long day, and people were restless. "Is bullshit."

Fernandez immediately sat up in his chair.

"We waited ten years for a DNA match to find the man who raped and killed our daughter."

The room went absolutely silent.

"There was no 'closure' the day he was convicted. It wasn't a magic pill. This isn't a Hollywood movie. Forget all that psychobabble. What we're talking about here is grief—hard-core grief. My husband and I beat the statistics—we stayed together. I think we did it because we weren't looking for easy answers. News flash, folks: There aren't any."

When the seminar was over and he was waiting in the coat-check line, Fernandez found himself standing in front of the same woman. "If I may introduce myself," he said, extending his hand. "Albert Fernandez. I'm a Crown Attorney."

The woman regarded him cautiously. "You here for empathy training?"

"My bosses say I need it," Fernandez said. "To tell you the truth, I'm not great at hand-holding."

"Good," the woman said. "I hated all the false sympathy. People talking to me in whispers. All the brochures with pictures of flowers and sunsets. We were lucky. Our Crown Attorney was a straight shooter."

"Who was it?"

"Jenn Raglan. You know her?"

"She's my boss."

"Tell her we say hello. And try to be like her, Mr. Fernandez. Don't sugarcoat anything."

If management had hoped Fernandez would come back from the one-day seminar a more touchy-feely Crown, they were sorely mistaken. In his subsequent meetings with victims' families, he was not warmer or more overtly sympathetic than he'd been before. But something had changed. And the forms that the families filled out at the end of the cases turned from negative to positive.

Crown Attorneys at Old City Hall met their families in the Victim Services office on the third floor. It featured a small waiting area and a big room inside that was once the city clerk's office. Fernandez hated everything about the place: the soft-focus photography posters on the wall, the doily-covered cookie trays displayed on the big oak side table, the soft brown chairs. The place was insipid, and the people who worked there were worse. They dressed as if they were on their way to a folk music concert and wore big smiley-face VICTIM SERVICES badges with their names on them and the slogan REMEMBER YESTERDAY, SURVIVE TODAY, LIVE FOR TOMORROW.

To make it even worse, the huge old metal radiator in the corner of the inner office was totally unregulated. Sometimes it froze overnight. In the morning the room would be at subzero temperature, and the knocking of the radiator was deafening until it warmed up. Other days it would steam out of control, making the room insanely hot. There was only one small round window at the top of the wall near the ceiling, and it had been painted shut for decades.

It was lunchtime and the inner room was still boiling. Fernandez opened the door and started yanking it back and forth in a fruitless attempt to fan some of the heat out. The things I do in this job that nobody sees, he thought to himself. He finally gave up and simply opened both the inner and outer doors and waited.

A few minutes later Detective Greene walked down the wide hallway with an elderly, fit-looking couple. It was standard procedure to meet the victim's family in the presence of the officer in charge of the case. Beside them was a large woman in a billowing dress and Birkenstock sandals. She was carrying a plastic clipboard with a sticker of a big red heart on the back, and her VICTIM SERVICES badge was pinned just above her large left breast. Her name tag said ANDY.

"Dr. and Mrs. Torn," Fernandez said, extending his hand and greeting them at the door.

"Call us Arden and Allie," Torn said, giving Fernandez a firm handshake. "We don't stand on ceremony."

Torn was taller than Fernandez had expected, and his hands were strong. He wore a bulky sweater, and a three-quarter-length leather coat with a wool lining was slung over his left arm. He looked Fernandez straight in the eye—a good sign.

Mrs. Torn was not much shorter. She carried a heavy wool coat and wore a conservative long-sleeved dress. A bright red shawl was wrapped around her shoulders and neck. Her handshake was tentative.

"Thank you for coming in to meet us," Fernandez said. "Hope the traffic wasn't too bad."

"There's always traffic," Torn said. "You'd never know it down here, but up in King City we've got tons of snow. Took us an hour on the tractor to clear the driveway."

"Please come into our room back here and sit," Fernandez said. "I'm sorry it's so hot. This is an old building, and we can't control the heat."

"Our old house is the same," Torn said. "Freezing or boiling, you never can tell." Clearly he was the talker in the family.

This was good, Fernandez thought. Simple chitchat to start the conversation. He looked at Mrs. Torn. "Can I take your scarf?"

Her eyes flicked toward her husband.

"Allie's darn shy," Torn said. "I hope you don't mind, she's asked me to do the talking today. I'm sure you understand. Kate was her only child."

"Certainly," Fernandez said. You just never knew with families. Some brought photos, letters, even videos, and wanted to talk for hours. Others were chatty, eager to discuss almost anything but the case and their lost loved ones. Still others were silent. It was the silent ones who were the hardest to deal with, the depth of their pain impossible to measure or comprehend.

One thing they all had in common: they clung to every word you said, like a patient listening to his surgeon before a major operation.

"I want to assure you that we're taking your daughter's case very seriously," Fernandez said, fixing his eyes on Torn as everyone was seated. There were two facing couches, with a wooden coffee table between them. Greene and Fernandez sat across from the Torns. Andy, the victim lady, hovered to the side. "I always start by asking victims' families the same thing: What questions do you have?"

This could be a revealing moment. People often had a prepared list. Usually they wanted to know how long the trial would take, what sentence the accused would face, whether they had to testify. Things like that.

Torn looked quickly at his wife, then back at Fernandez. He hesitated for a moment, took in a deep breath. Fernandez caught Greene's eye. At the end of the table, among a pile of law books, he'd strategically placed a box of Kleenex, not so close as to be obvious, but not far from being at hand.

Reaching into his coat pocket, Torn pulled out a piece of paper. Here it comes, Fernandez thought, probably photographs of their daughter when she was a girl. But it wasn't a picture. It was a small, rectangular piece of white paper.

"Where the hell can you park around here," Torn asked, slamming his receipt down on the coffee table in frustration, like a poker player with a losing hand, "without spending thirty bucks a day?"

19

We know you start work very early, so thanks for coming in to see us this afternoon," Ari Greene said to Donald Dundas, the radio-show host who'd replaced Kevin Brace on *The Dawn Treader*. Greene had never met the man or even seen a photograph of him, but he'd heard his voice on the radio many times over the years when Dundas was a guest host of the show. The broadcaster looked younger, thinner, than Greene had pictured him. Funny how that worked. You hear a voice on radio for a long time and you build an image of that person in your mind. One that's invariably wrong.

They were in the video room of the homicide bureau. It was a long, narrow room, with a table running down the middle and three chairs at the far end. Greene and Kennicott had been interviewing witnesses—mostly from the radio station for a few hours.

"Glad to help out," Dundas said. "I teach a class at seven tonight, so I have to be out of here by six."

Greene looked back at the clock on the wall closest to the door. It was coming up to five o'clock. "Won't be a problem," he said as he guided Dundas to the chair at the end of the table. Greene sat next to him. He'd strategically placed his chair very close, right by Dundas's side. Since the video camera was at the other end of the room, up on the wall looking down at them, it wouldn't show just how close Greene was to Dundas. But he was right there, deliberately not observing the normal social distance. The subconscious message Greene wanted to convey to every witness right from the get-go was "I'm here. I'm not going away. I can be your best friend or your worst enemy. Your choice."

Dundas wore a brown turtleneck jersey under a corduroy sport jacket, wool pants, and round tortoiseshell glasses, the kind architecture students used to wear years ago. He looked more like an aging graduate student than a radio personality. But then again, Brace, with his disheveled clothes, certainly never looked like anyone you'd think was famous. Perhaps that's what attracts people to working in radio: they don't have to worry about what they look like.

Greene sat down, squaring his shoulders to the table. That way the video camera would hit him directly from the side, minimizing his size and making him look much less intimidating on tape than he was in person.

"This room is equipped with a video recorder. You can see it up there on the far wall facing us," Greene said, keeping his voice gentle. He turned his head to indicate the camera just below the ceiling, pointed down at them. "Everything we're saying is being recorded."

Dundas nodded. The man seemed totally devoid of emotion.

"I want to confirm that you're giving this statement voluntarily," Greene said as he moved closer. "The door is closed as a matter of convenience and privacy. It's not locked. You understand, Mr. Dundas, you can leave this room at any time."

Dundas cleared his throat and looked at the closed door. Was the man nervous or, like some media people Greene had met, surprisingly quiet once he was offstage?

"Yes, I'm making this statement voluntarily," Dundas said. His voice sounded startlingly familiar, which of course it was. "I understand that I can leave whenever I want."

Kennicott handed Greene a beige file folder. The name DUNDAS was written on a black-and-white label at the top of the file and in bold black letters on the front page. Greene had instructed Kennicott to make up a folder for each person they were going to interview and to pass it across the table in front of the witness. The folders were filled with background material, and then extra blank pages were added to make sure it was nice and thick. Important-looking.

Greene had also asked Kennicott to take a few empty storage boxes labeled R.V. BRACE and stack them in the corner of the room, near the door, where the people they were interviewing would see them when they came in but so that the camera would not pick them up.

"You're only as good as your props," Greene had explained to Kennicott, when they were setting up the interviews.

Greene opened the file, pretending that he was looking at it for the first time. In fact, Kennicott had highlighted the key points and then gone over the material with him before the interview. Greene could feel Dundas's eyes on him and could see him picking at his worn-down fingernails.

"Fine," Greene said at last, snapping the file closed. "Formally, for the record, I'm Detective Ari Greene of the homicide squad. With me is Officer Daniel Kennicott. Officer Kennicott is here principally as what we call a scribe. Even though this interview is being taped, he'll take notes so we'll have a record right away and won't have to wait for this to be transcribed." Greene smiled at Dundas. "We're still a little old-fashioned. All this technology is fine, but it's real people and what they tell us that solve most crimes."

"I see," Dundas said.

"I'll ask you to identify yourself for the record, sir. Your full name and your date of birth."

Dundas coughed. "My full name is Donald Alistair Brock Noel Dundas. Date of birth is December 25, 1957."

"A Christmas baby," Greene said.

Dundas barely smiled.

Greene ran through the usual background questions to get Dundas warmed up. His education, his print-journalism career, a little personal history. Dundas was single, never married, had a small house in the Beach area of the city, with his own radio studio in the basement.

Gradually they moved through the years, how Dundas first met Brace and began to substitute for him on the program three years ago. Something about Dundas rankled just a bit. Maybe it's just people in show business, Greene thought. It always felt as if they'd rehearsed to death what they were going to say.

"Did you see Brace socially?" Greene asked.

"Not very often," Dundas said. For the first time, he seemed to hesitate before he answered. Kennicott caught Greene's eye. "To be perfectly honest, we had different circumstances. I mean he was married, and I'm single. And, well, we're kind of different generations."

"To be perfectly honest" was a classic prevarication. A ruse witnesses used to buy time to formulate their answers. Dundas had lost his smooth cadence. It was subtle, but it was real.

Greene often lectured at Police College, where he taught a course called Interviewing Techniques. He stressed that in every interview there was a turning point. "Always one moment in a good interview when the story suddenly comes to life," he'd tell his students. "Find that turning point. If you've done your homework and set up the interview properly, hit it with a direct question."

Greene waited until Kennicott stopped taking his notes. He put the file down hard on the table. It made a thwacking sound. He faced Dundas head-on, wearing his biggest smile.

"Ever been to the Brace condominium?"

"A few times."

"Kevin Brace ever been to your place?" Greene wasn't pausing anymore. He wanted these questions to come out one on top of another.

"No, I don't think so."

"I don't think so." Another prevarication. Greene didn't change his pace, but kept it constant. Perfect technique for the turning-point question.

"How about Katherine Torn?" Greene asked, keeping his voice as calm as if he were asking Dundas the time of day. "She ever been to your house?"

Dundas stole a glance at the door.

Greene and Kennicott remained silent. Dundas seemed suddenly out of sync, the rhythm of his answers in tatters. Each moment, as the silence built, he looked more uncomfortable.

"Um . . . umm . . . do I have to answer that question?" he asked at last.

Greene could feel his heart start to race, but he kept his voice neutral. Bland. Slowly, he picked up the file folder and opened it again. This time it wasn't an act. A thought had just occurred to him, and he wanted to read something. It took a few moments for him to find it. He nodded his head for a long moment before he turned to Dundas.

"Did she come over on Thursday mornings?"

Dundas crossed his arms. "I'd like to speak to my lawyer," he said.

"No need," Greene said. "You're not under arrest at this time. Like we said at the top, you're free to leave. The door isn't locked."

Greene reached inside his jacket pocket, fished out his wallet, and felt for one of his business cards. He knew Dundas wasn't going to answer any more questions. "Here," he said, passing the card over. "Have your lawyer call me." He looked back down at the file. A moment later, he heard the squeaking sound of Dundas's chair scraping against the concrete floor. After he heard the door shut, he looked up at Kennicott.

"Having fun yet?" he asked. Greene could see that Kennicott was very tired. They had been going flat out for a day and a half, and the guy was coming off the night shift.

"This is what I signed up for," Kennicott said.

"I've only had four other people walk out on me in a homicide interview," Greene said, packing up his notebook.

"What happened to them?"

Greene shrugged his shoulders. Like the way my dad would do, he thought. "They were all convicted."

"Doesn't look good on him, does it?" Kennicott said.

"Watch out for statistics," Greene said. "Usually don't prove anything."

Kennicott nodded. He was a quick study, Greene thought. And damned determined.

"The autopsy's next," Kennicott said, looking at his watch.

"Meet me at the morgue at six," Greene said. "And then I'm sending you home for some rest."

20

The odor was the thing that Daniel Kennicott remembered about the morgue. The smell of decaying flesh. Impossible to describe, impossible to forget. And the sound. Electric saw on bone as the top of the head was removed in a circular cut, like the top off a hard-boiled egg.

Kennicott had been here only once before, when he'd identified his brother's body. The memories were seared into his brain.

Today the receptionist had asked him to sit in the waiting room, and as he tried to read a year-old copy of *Newsweek*, he struggled to keep his mind firmly on the present. Greene had told him to be here at six o'clock. He'd arrived fifteen minutes early.

"Good evening, Officer Kennicott," a squat man with a squeaky, thin voice said as he walked into the room, a large plastic coffee mug in his hand. He was about five feet tall, with a rotund chest. His short arms barely met in front, making him look like a Humpty Dumpty cartoon character. "Warren Gardner, chief attendant."

Kennicott remembered the man from that other visit to the morgue. He even remembered the man's name. Funny how, at a time like that, the small details stay with you.

"I'm sure you won't remember me," Kennicott said as he shook hands with Gardner. The little man had a very firm grip. "I was here a number of years ago as a civilian. Before I joined the force."

"Older brother, bullet behind the left ear," Gardner said without missing a beat. "Summertime. Only family you had left. Lost your parents before that in a car accident. Drunk driver. How'm I doing?"

Kennicott nodded. "You were very kind. I meant to write a note to thank you."

"Not necessary," Gardner said, sipping his coffee. "Our clients have great needs and short attention spans. Want a coffee?"

"No thanks," Kennicott said.

"We might as well go in. Detective Ho from Ident's already started." Gardner guided Kennicott across a spotless tile floor past a long wall of what looked like enormous steel filing cabinets. This was where the bodies were stored. They went into the glassed-in room where Katherine Torn lay naked on a long metal table, her body startlingly white. A body bag was folded below at her feet.

Detective Ho was busy photographing a close-up shot of the wound, near the top of Torn's abdomen, just below the sternum. A gray ruler lay beside it for measurement. Kennicott spotted Ho's old briefcase and knapsack stashed away in the corner.

"Hey. Good evening, Officer Kennicott," Ho said, sounding cheerful as ever. "Ms. Torn looks even more beautiful out of the water, doesn't she?"

Though Kennicott hated to admit it, Ho was right. Strangely, Torn's face was even prettier than the first time he'd seen her, dead in the bathtub. Her mane of hair had been tied up above her head, and her body seemed strong. The small hole in her abdomen was startling against the vastness of her skin.

"Too bad about the water, isn't it?" Ho said.

"Why's that?" Kennicott asked.

"Print killer. We can pull terrific prints off skin nowadays. But the water just wipes them out."

"Who's our pathologist?" Kennicott asked.

Ho looked at Gardner, and the two men rolled their eyes.

"You're in for a treat," Gardner said as he slid on a rubber apron with the initials W.G. written in bright red on the bottom left corner.

"Dr. Roger McKilty, a.k.a. the Kiwi Boy Wonder. Once the body bag was opened, he went out for a coffee."

"Bloody New Zealander. Good luck understanding a word he says," Ho said. "He couldn't be more than thirty-five years old. Has more degrees than a thermometer."

"Sounds smart," Kennicott said.

"Just ask him," Ho said. "And fast. Guy works so quickly he's giving the morgue a bad name." Ho started to laugh at his own joke. The sound vibrated around the antiseptic room.

Gardner chuckled. "The good doctor will make eleven hundred dollars and be out of here in record time."

"That would have been a week's pay back at my parents' restaurant," Ho said. "Just think of how many egg rolls they'd have to sell to make that."

Kennicott came closer to the body. "What would cause these?" he asked, pointing to some marks on Torn's upper right arm.

Ho took a quick look. "Postmortem lividity," he said. "See it all the time. Remember, she was on her back and her heart wasn't pumping, so all the heavy red blood cells get pulled down by gravity. Causes this purplish discoloration to the top of the torso."

Kennicott took a closer look at the skin. He walked around to the other side and bent down. There were marks there too. He was about to ask Ho a question when Detective Greene walked in, accompanied by a slender, energetic-looking man with remarkably light blond hair. He could have passed for twenty-one.

"Oh, hello," Kennicott said, looking up from the body. "I was just checking out some marks on her upper arms."

Greene and the man exchanged glances, as if to say, "That's the kind of thing rookies always notice."

"Upper-body bruises are almost always forensically insignificant," the man said. His accent was a hard New Zealand twang. Ho was right. He was difficult to understand. But there was no mistaking his tone. It was condescending, bored.

Kennicott walked back around the body over to Greene.

"Officer Daniel Kennicott, meet Dr. McKilty," Greene said.

"Nice to meet you, Doctor," Kennicott said.

"Yes," McKilty said. He gave Kennicott a weak handshake and looked over at the big clock on the wall. It was exactly 6:00. "Shall we, gentlemen?" he said, his impatience palpable.

McKilty went over to the body and quickly examined it from head to toe. He looked at her hands closely and then examined her abdomen. All without paying any attention to the stab wound in the middle of her body.

"I'd guess our girl was a bit of a drinker," the doctor said in his nasal, twangy voice.

McKilty turned toward Detective Greene. "When you get the medical chart, check her platelet level." He looked at Kennicott with a bored expression. "Platelets are tiny bodies in the blood. Colorless. They've got sticky little surfaces that help the blood to clot. Without them we'd all bleed to death. Now, take a drinker. Enlarged spleen secondary to liver disease. Causes thrombocytopenia—low platelet count. If it's under twenty, she'd bruise like a ripe banana. So you see, those marks on her arms probably mean nothing."

He hovered over the body, getting remarkably close. There's no need to keep an acceptable social distance from a dead body, Kennicott thought. "Now let's see this stab wound," McKilty said. He motioned to Kennicott. "Look here," he said without moving.

Kennicott leaned in beside him.

"Almost straight vertical," McKilty said. "I'd call it eleven-thirty five-thirty." He was referring to the numbers on the clock to describe the angle of the wound. "See the difference between the two sides?" he asked Kennicott, moving slightly out of the way. "Here, get closer."

Kennicott lowered his head even more. "The top of the wound is rounded, the bottom is like a V."

"Exactly. This was caused by a single-edged knife. The blade was on the bottom. The angle of the wound tells us that the knife was being held up and down, the way you hold a knife to spear something."

Kennicott nodded. "What about the darkness on her skin around the wound?" he asked.

"Very good," McKilty said. "We call that a hilt mark. Comes from the knife handle. Tells us it went all the way up to the hilt, with lots of force. Nasty bit of work." He looked up. "Mr. Gardner, please."

Gardner passed him a narrow metal ruler. "Wound measures one and three-quarters inches wide, that's almost exactly four and a half centimeters," McKilty said. He was now talking into a tiny microphone speaker in his lapel. He slid the ruler through the open cavity. "Estimate the depth at . . ." He put his finger at the point where the ruler touched the skin, then pulled it back out, like a mechanic checking the oil level in a car. "Seven and a half inches, just a sliver over nineteen centimeters."

"Hey, that's it," Detective Ho said. "Those are almost the exact measurements of the kitchen knife we found in the apartment." He was close to shouting with excitement, like a lottery winner who'd just won a jackpot. "She got stabbed hard."

McKilty shook his head at Ho. "Don't be so sure," McKilty said. He looked at Kennicott and held both hands up in the air. "Think of an abdomen as a feather pillow, with a tough case around it. The skin. It's a difficult surface to penetrate. But once you do"—he clapped his hands together and the sound echoed hard in the tiled room—"there's really nothing to stop it. So the stab wound could have gone in seven and a half inches, but if the body was coming toward the knife, that could account for the penetration too. Even the hilt wound. Can't jump to conclusions."

Kennicott looked over at Greene, who stood a few feet back, taking the whole scene in with his usual detached, observant passivity. Kennicott had been watching Greene for years, looking for signs of what he was thinking. The man seemed to run on many different levels at the same time.

A part of Greene appeared to be totally focused on the moment. As if he was recording in his brain everything that was in front of him, always ready to testify in court about all that he heard or saw. Another part of Greene was standing back, watching as things unfolded. Still another part seemed to be somewhere else, his mind always considering different possibilities. Like water determined to run downhill, seeking out every crevice. That was Detective Greene, Kennicott realized, remarkably present yet tantalizingly detached, all at the same time.

"I fear this will be messy," McKilty said as he sliced Torn's abdomen open with a sleek scalpel, confidently cutting slightly off center to the right of the entry point. As the body cavity opened, it let out a horrible gaseous smell. "See that?" McKilty said, immune to the odor, pointing the scalpel at the clear, straw-colored fluid that was seeping out, his voice excited for the first time. "Ascites. Free fluid in the belly. Drinker for sure. Some of it probably spilled out when she got stabbed. Awful stuff."

Kennicott nodded. He thought about slipping on the kitchen floor the morning he rushed into Suite 12A.

Gardner readied a vicious-looking set of forceps, and two sides of her skin were peeled back. McKilty kept up a running commentary in his little microphone as he cut out different organs and examined them. Gardner put each one into a separate glass jar and attached a label, as if they were odd sausages and meat parts being packaged up for shipment somewhere—the two moving as in a well-choreographed dance, chef and sous-chef.

"Hmmm," McKilty said. "The knife went in under the sternum. Blood went into her mediastinum, not her abdomen." He looked over at Greene. "You said she was found in a bathtub?" he asked.

Greene nodded.

"Hmmm," McKilty said again. "If she'd been standing on dry land, there wouldn't have been a drop. Here's the culprit," he said as he pulled out a white, bulbous, spongelike piece of tissue. "Sliced thoracic aorta."

He put the mass on a clean chrome plate and motioned Kennicott over. "Look right there." He pulled both ends to the side, like a chef checking on a piece of meat. "That's all it takes. Poor girl didn't have a chance. The aorta is one of the most vulnerable parts of the human body. Our primary blood source. Blood's under pressure. Cut it, even a bit, and you're done for."

To the untrained eye it was subtle, but when McKilty pointed to the spot, Kennicott could see where the coloration was different and the white mass had been cut. It was stunning to see up close just how little it took to extinguish a life.

He tried not to think of his brother, laid out here on the same cold table, the efficient Mr. Gardner packaging up his body parts. But he couldn't avert his eyes from the naked body that had just been sliced open and gutted.

It had been forty-eight hours since he'd started his night shift with Bering and thirty-six hours straight since he'd been on this case. He could feel the fatigue all over his body.

He watched Gardner take out a needle and thread and begin to sew up Katherine Torn.

"The rest is boring medical stuff," McKilty said, looking at Greene, then Kennicott. "No need for you gents to hang around."

Finally I'll be able to get some sleep, Kennicott thought. To sleep, and hopefully not to dream.

21

Nancy Parish got a thrill every time she pounded her way up Bay Street from her King Street office, briefcase in hand, going to Old City Hall court. Especially early in the morning.

Parish's observant father had once commented to her that Toronto was a city of straight streets and square corners built by Scottish bankers to make money—not to look at the beautiful lake or the wonderful valleys and forests. He was mostly right, but Bay was a rare exception to the city's linear grid.

Heading north from her office, she could see the street going straight up a few blocks to Queen Street—like every other city in Canada, large and small, Toronto had streets named for the monarchy—where it bent to the left, sweeping around Old City Hall, its bell tower staring right down the middle of Bay like an exclamation point.

Bay Street was the financial capital of the country—the Wall Street of Canada—and the ten-minute walk on the narrow, crowded sidewalk was like a tour of the city's economic history. The lower part was dominated by sleek, modern skyscrapers, each owned by one of the country's five big banks, the names ranging from the pedantic—Bank of Nova Scotia and Bank of Montreal—to the pretentious: Toronto Dominion Bank, the Royal Bank of Canada, and the Canadian Imperial Bank of Commerce. Farther north, steel was replaced by older stone buildings, starting with the Toronto Stock Exchange and then a series of elegant art deco office towers from the city's golden years in the teens and twenties of the twentieth century. They had evocative names like the Northern Ontario Building, Sterling Tower, and the Canada Permanent Building.

Then came the construction. Donald Trump had bought a big lot on the east side, and for the last few years a large billboard had announced the impending opening of a new condominium tower. Just north of the billboard, a full city block was surrounded by a chain-link fence as huge demolition machines took down an old concrete parking garage.

A block before Queen Street was the Hudson's Bay Company Building, the grand old lady of department stores. Now its elegant name had been condensed to simply the Bay, and the building itself had been stripped down. But like those of a sophisticated older woman from another era, thinning with age, her good bones were still intact.

Parish let a streetcar rumble by, then crossed Queen, climbed the stairs to Old City Hall, and made her way quickly to the second floor. The bell tower had just begun to ring out the top of the hour. She ran down the hallway toward courtroom 121. A thin white-haired man wearing a full constable's uniform, ribbons and medals on his lapels, rang a brass bell. "Court is in session, court is in session," he called out.

"I just made it, Horace," Parish said as she rushed up.

"The captain is taking his seat at the helm," he said, his eyes smiling at her.

Parish paused for a moment to compose herself, then swung open the ornate door to 121. A few years earlier the dramatic old room—the former council chamber when the building was a real city hall—was used to film the movie *Chicago*. It was easy to see why: the courtroom had a foreboding feel, with its dark oak benches, swinging wooden gate leading to the long counsel tables, and wraparound upper balcony. And today it was filled to overflowing with the press, friends of Brace's, women's rights advocates, and court watchers. High drama indeed.

"Oyez, oyez, oyez," the court clerk bellowed as he swung open the oak door by the side of the judge's dais and strode into court. He officiously rolled up the sleeves of his black robe and took his seat below the judge. "All rise. This court is in session," he called out, his voice effortlessly filling the big room. "The Honorable Justice Johnathan Summers presiding. All persons having business before the Queen's Bench, attend now and ye shall be heard."

A thin court constable scurried to the judge's desk carrying a tall stack of books. Hot on his heels, Justice Summers, resplendent in dark robes and starched white shirt and tabs, hurried in as if he were late for a tennis match. He brushed past his constable and ran up to his chair, high above the proceedings. The constable rushed nervously behind him and neatly placed the books before the judge.

Summers reached for a notebook on top of the pile. He opened it to the first page and, with great ceremony, fished into his vest pocket and pulled out a well-worn Waterman fountain pen. He began to write.

"You may be seated," the clerk said to the audience in his booming voice.

After what seemed like an eternity, Summers lifted his head and looked out on the assembled masses, as if somehow all these people had crowded into his secret study to catch an illicit glimpse of the great scribe penning his masterwork.

Summers stared down at the two long counsel tables that faced his dais. Fernandez sat to his left, Parish to his right.

"Where's the prisoner?" he growled at them.

"He's on his way," the clerk said in a terrified half whisper, like Bob Cratchit reporting to Mr. Scrooge. "The wagon from the Don Jail is late."

Summers gave a great harrumph. He looked out at the full courtroom. "Ladies and gentlemen of the public and the press, as you can see, we're all prepared to get to work. Our government doesn't provide us with adequate resources to run these courts. If I'd run my ship like this in the navy, believe me, there would have been hell to pay."

He looked back down at Parish. Here it comes, she thought.

"Ms. Parish, I have carefully reviewed all of your bail materials as well as Mr. Fernandez's response. The affidavit of the applicant, Mr. Brace, is not sworn."

She stood up. "Yes, Your Honor. I will ask the court for a brief indulgence to have him sign it when he's brought in." Summers was just showing off to the press. This was standard procedure when a bail application was prepared on such short notice.

"Very well," Summers said.

She sat down. Sooner or later, Summers was going to get mad at one lawyer or the other. The trick was to make sure it wasn't you.

The judge returned to writing in his notebook. The phone rang on the clerk's desk. He grabbed it and spoke in hushed tones, the worry lines across his forehead growing deeper.

"He'll be here in five minutes," he half whispered again.

"We'll wait. All hands on deck," Summers said without looking up. Parish drew a little cartoon of Summers in his navy uniform hitting the clerk below him on the back of the head with a big toy gavel. It wasn't a very good sketch, and she couldn't think of a caption.

She looked around at the reporters sitting in the front row. As well as the usual Gang of Four journalists from the papers, who covered all the big trials, there were reporters from every major television and radio station. Parish easily picked out her friend Awotwe Amankwah, the only brown face in the group.

Parish had met Amankwah a few years ago while playing outdoor hockey. They would often help each other out. Amankwah would call when he needed a quote for a story or some inside, off-the-record dope on a nasty judge or wayward Crown. Parish would sometimes ask Amankwah to look into things she couldn't do herself.

Amankwah smiled back at her. He rolled his eyes and shrugged his shoulders, as if to say, "Good luck dealing with Summers."

Finally, there was a loud rap. The oak door opened again, and in stepped two guards, with Kevin Brace between them.

An audible sigh went up in the crowded courtroom. Brace was dressed in the same oversize orange jumpsuit. Now it was dirty. His arms were handcuffed behind him. His hair was even greasier, his skin more sallow, his chin down on his chest, and his eyes lifeless. He shuffled into the court like an old man.

When the guard reached for his keys, Brace automatically turned his back to him, waiting for his cuffs to be unlocked. Like some lifer who was accustomed to doing time. Her heart sank.

With so much evidence, her best hope had been Kevin Brace himself. The man's sterling reputation. Parish always worked hard to clean up her clients for court. She knew that if a jury saw Brace looking like this, they'd convict him in record time.

She stood up quickly, hoping to take some attention away from her client. "If I could have a moment, Your Honor." She lifted the affidavits in a file in front of her.

"Be quick," Summers said, waving his hand dismissively.

Parish approached Brace, keeping her eyes down.

Brace stood awkwardly. He was a tall man. She put her hand casually on his arm, something she always did in court. Let everyone know she wasn't afraid of her client. He leaned down so she could speak into his ear.

"This is a one-page affidavit. It just says who you are and that you will obey the rules of the bail. Take a moment to read it, and then sign it."

He nodded as she gave him her pen. A fresh, new Bic. Brace looked at the affidavit, turned it over, and started writing something on the blank back side. She read his brief message upside down.

"Mr. Brace, are you sure?" she asked.

"Counsel," Summers yelled at her from the bench, "there have been enough delays in my court this morning."

"Yes, Your Honor," she said, turning back to the judge. She swung back to look at Brace one more time.

He handed her the pen.

"These are your instructions, Mr. Brace?" she asked.

He nodded once and sat down.

She took a deep breath. "Okay," she said. Taking back the papers and pen, she marched to her counsel table. If you've got bad news to deliver in court, do it fast. Short and sweet. Or, in Summers's case, short and sour.

"Your Honor, the defense will consent to the detention of Mr. Brace," Parish said quickly, and sat down.

There was a stunned silence in the already quiet courtroom. Summers did a double take. "The defense consents?" he asked.

"Yes, sir. Those are my instructions."

She stole a glance at Fernandez. He looked shocked. The man had just spent the last forty-eight hours preparing for this bail hearing, trying with all his might to keep Brace in jail. And now Parish was throwing in the towel. He'd won without a fight.

Summers was apoplectic. "Your client is what?" he thundered down at Parish.

She stood up. "Mr. Brace is consenting to his detention, Your Honor," she repeated slowly. "We no longer need to have this hearing."

"Well, I never . . ." Summers's face was flushed. He turned to Fernandez. "What does the Crown say about this?"

Fernandez got to his feet, still looking dazed. "Your Honor, the Crown takes the position that Mr. Brace should be detained until his trial. If he's changed his mind and doesn't want a bail hearing, so be it." He sat down.

Summers glared at Fernandez, expecting him to say more. Clearly there was nothing else for him to say. To his credit, Parish thought, the guy was not gloating.

Grinding his teeth in frustration, Summers let out one big, all-encompassing growl, grabbed his own papers, and then, like a lion heading back to his den, stormed off the bench.

"Both counsel will see me in chambers," he shouted just before the door slammed behind him, his words reverberating through the crowded courtroom, which was erupting in noise.

The moment the judge was gone, Parish whirled back and looked at her client. She still had the pen in her hand, and she realized she'd been clenching it so hard under the table that it had left an indentation in her thumb. Right now she felt like stabbing Brace with it. He didn't even meet her eyes. Instead he stood and turned, arms behind his back, waiting for the handcuffs to come on. As if hope were gone.

22

This isn't going to be pretty, Albert Fernandez thought as he followed one of Summers's frightened clerks through the long, wood-paneled corridor to the judge's chambers. Parish was at his side. They walked in silence.

Fernandez sneaked a peek at Parish. She must be nervous, he thought. She'd just torpedoed an all-day bail hearing in front of a packed courtroom, and now the senior judge at Old City Hall was hauling her into his office.

Parish caught his eye and flashed him a smile. Under the circumstances, she seemed remarkably relaxed.

"Your Honor," the clerk announced in a ghostly voice when they arrived at the judge's doorway, "Ms. Parish and Mr. Fernandez."

Summers's chambers were part legal library, part hockey museum, but mostly a shrine to all things naval. Almost every inch of empty wall space was filled with hand-drawn sketches of battleships. A bookshelf was adorned with odd-shaped bottles, tiny sailboats captured inside. On the credenza behind him was a set of framed photos, most of them showing Summers on sailboats with different members of his family. There was one large photo on his desk of him and his daughter, Jo. His arm was around her shoulders, her magnificent hair was down—something Fernandez had never seen before. They were holding a championship cup between them. In the background were white sails and blue sky.

The nautical motif was occasionally interspersed with photos of Summers in blue or white hockey jerseys, posing with well-known players from the Toronto Maple Leafs. In the corner was a collection of hockey sticks, apparently signed by members of the team. A glass frame held an old hockey sweater with a big crest that said CORNELL, with a large C in the top left corner.

"What the hell's going on?" Summers demanded, ripping his gown off and throwing it onto a side chair. He glared at Parish. Fernandez looked at her too.

She took a breath and slowly exhaled. "What's happening, Your Honor, is that I'm acting on my client's instructions," she said, speaking in measured tones. "He's consenting to his detention."

Technically, of course, Parish was bound to do what her client told her, and she wasn't allowed to discuss their conversations with anyone. But that didn't satisfy an angry judge.

"So I just heard." Summers sat down and picked up a silver letter opener, which he twirled between his fingers. Fernandez could see that it was engraved with some initials, worn down and hard to read. Probably a family heirloom. "Ms. Parish, if 'your client' was going to 'consent to his detention,' why did we just go through that whole charade this morning?"

He thwacked the letter opener into his palm. It looked like very fine silver, Fernandez thought.

"And why did you file this stack of material?" he said, stabbing at her thick legal brief with the letter opener. "I was up all night reading this stuff."

Fernandez picked a point on Summers's desk and stared at it. It was best to be a humble winner.

"I'm bound by my client's instructions," Parish said. From her tone, it was clear that she wasn't going to say anything else. She shrugged. Fernandez had to admit that she had guts.

Summers seemed to sense her resolve. He turned his gaze on Fernandez, probing for weakness.

"Mr. Fernandez, I know you've got these women's groups tearing up your backside to make an example of Brace. And Chief Charlton wants to pad his police budget. Listen: I read all your materials and those statistics." Summers yanked out a large brief and turned to a page he'd marked with a yellow sticky tab.

"Four out of five women report they are abused by men. Give me a break."

He reached behind him and pulled out a folder. "I checked the background of these statistics of yours. The study they're based on was done in 1993, and abuse is defined as—wait, here it is—'The three largest contributors to the eighty percent number were, Did he do something to spite you? Did he insult you? and Did he accuse you of having an affair?'" Summers tossed his folder on his desk. "Look, I'm no fan of violence against women, or men or anyone. But come on. Let's not trivialize things."

"Yes, Your Honor, but the heart of my submissions was—," Fernandez said, concentrating on keeping his voice even.

"Look," Summers said. "The simple statistical fact is that a man convicted of murdering a spouse in a crime of passion is ten times less likely to re-offend than a simple shoplifter. Everyone who works in these courts knows that. Everyone except the bloody press."

Before Fernandez could get a word in, Summers turned, like a referee at a tennis match, to take in Parish. But now his face had softened. He'd finished playing bad judge; now he was playing good judge.

"Nancy, you hear about that game last weekend?" he asked. "Cornell whooped Colgate four to one."

Parish smiled back. Fernandez had heard she was a hockey player, but he hadn't known she'd gone to college in the States.

"That was the men's team, Your Honor," she said. "Let's see what happens when the women play next weekend."

"Touché," Summers said. He turned back to Fernandez and shrugged. "Excuse us, Mr. Fernandez. Old school rivalries." He returned to Parish. "You see that Leafs game a few nights ago? I was with the chief justice. Great win. Maybe they've turned the corner."

Parish shook her head emphatically. "Too many older players on the team," she said. "They're going to get tired."

As tempted as he might have been to add his two cents' worth to the conversation, Fernandez knew that anything he said about hockey would sound ridiculous. Besides, Summers didn't even consider that he might have an opinion on the subject.

"Listen," Summers said, sitting back and spreading his arms out, as if to envelop them in his embrace. "We're in chambers. You're both excellent counsel. We can speak candidly about this matter, can't we? Ship to shore?"

Fernandez saw the letter opener flash in the judge's hand. A big grin unfurled on his ruddy face. It wasn't really a question.

"Certainly, Your Honor," Fernandez said.

"Of course," Parish chimed in.

"Two brilliant young lawyers. A case like this puts the whole judicial system on trial. Every move you two make will be scrutinized."

Summers looked back at Parish. "Nancy, if you sat down with the Crown's office, I'm sure something could be worked out. The man's sixty-three years old, after all. There must be a way to get him bail. Doesn't belong in the brig."

Fernandez gripped the sides of his chair. "Young lawyers," "Crown's office." Summers was speaking in code, and his message was very clear. Classic judicial carrot and stick. The carrot: He expected Fernandez to grovel a bit. To say, "in light of Your Honor's helpful comments," he'd confer with his colleagues and reconsider the Crown's position. To try to get on his good side. The stick: If Fernandez didn't find a way to get Brace out on bail, then Summers would be very pissed off, since he thought that was the appropriate result.

If only Summers knew that there was nothing I wanted more than to see Kevin Brace out on bail, Fernandez thought, his head spinning with the sudden turn of events that had left his carefully laid plans in tatters.

"It won't be necessary for Mr. Fernandez to reconsider his position," Parish said, standing up. "I'll let him know if my instructions change. Thank you very much, Your Honor." She extended her arm to shake Summers's hand. Slightly bewildered, the judge stood and thrust out his hand. Seconds later, she was out the door.

Finding himself suddenly alone with the judge, Fernandez rose awkwardly. He proffered a quick handshake and hustled out.

Parish was already far down the hallway, well ahead of him. Further ahead than she'll ever know, Fernandez thought as he quickened his pace to catch up with her.

23

Ari Greene drove slowly up the quiet residential street. Almost every house was bedecked with Christmas lights, either on trees in the yards or in the front windows. They were small, mostly boxy little two-story homes, but every block or two, one had been knocked down to make way for new so-called monster homes, which inevitably featured garish stonework and overly wide driveways filled with basketball nets and equally oversize cars. Totally out of scale with their neighbors, the houses stood out like mismatched pieces on a chessboard.

A crossing guard dressed in a full-length bright orange raincoat was making his way across the street, his lunchtime work with the children going back to school finished.

It felt nice to be in an old-fashioned neighborhood—one of the things Greene liked the most about the city. When he was a kid, he used to sit in the front window of his family's little bungalow and wait for his dad to come home from the shop. Every day it was the same. His father would walk slowly up the street, his shoulders slumped from a long day. There was a stout birch tree on their small front lawn, and no matter what time he came home, his father would stop in front of the tree, put his hand on it, and stand still for a long moment. His daily ritual. Then he'd come inside.

One morning when he was sick at home with the chicken pox, Greene asked his father, "Daddy, why do you stop at the tree every day before you come inside?"

His father smiled like a man who'd been caught with a little secret.

"Before I come in to my family," his father said, "I want to leave all my problems outside. So I put them on the tree."

Now he understood. "Is that why the tree's so small, Daddy?"

"Maybe," his father said. "And that's why you're going to be so big and strong."

When Greene hit the six-foot mark in grade ten, it occurred to him that his father's prediction had worked.

He drove past number 37, did a U-turn, and took a moment to study the house from across the street. It was a two-story bungalow with leaded-glass Tudor windows. A slightly battered Honda was parked in the narrow driveway, and behind it a van with the words LEASIDE PLUMBING written in bold script on its side.

Good, Greene thought as he got out of his car. Looks like she's home. He walked casually up the front walk and rang the bell. Off to the right was a small wooden door that had been nailed shut. That would have been the milk box, a relic from a gentler time.

Footsteps approached rapidly and the door was flung open. A tall brunette woman with deep brown eyes, just like her father's, stood in the door. She wore an oversize sweatshirt, with the words ROOTS CANADA prominently displayed, and a pair of stretch yoga pants over her protruding belly. He could hear the sound of a hammer banging on pipes.

"You the electrician?" she said, peering behind Greene, looking for his van.

"Afraid not, Ms. Brace," Greene said. He had his badge in his hand, and he discreetly showed it to her. "Detective Ari Greene, Toronto Homicide. Could I speak with you for a few moments?"

Her face fell in a deep frown. "I need the electrician in the next hour," she said. "Do you know how hard it is to get a plumber the week before Christmas?"

"Close to impossible, I imagine," Greene said.

"Well, I've got one working downstairs. But now I need the electrician to hook up the power. They call it nesting, Detective. First child, and I'm renovating the basement. Due in a month, and my husband just *had* to go with his buddies on their annual ski trip to Mont Tremblant. And oh, there's the little matter that my father is in jail, just before his first grandchild's about to be born. So sure, I've got loads of time to speak to you."

Greene smiled. Said nothing. Always watch what witnesses do, not what they say. Or even better, what they don't do. Despite the chaos in her life, Amanda Brace had not slammed the door in his face. He thought of the call to her from the Don made on Brace's behalf. How her father had refused to talk to her. Greene was pretty sure she was as eager to ask him questions as he was to interview her.

"Come on in for a minute," she said finally, as if her own good breeding won out over all competing emotions. "I made some coffee for all the trades. Do you want some?"

"No thanks," Greene said.

"I better check that badge again," she said. "A cop who refuses free coffee."

Greene smiled and motioned to the small living room to the left of the hall. "Can we sit and talk in here?"

"Sure," she said, closing the door behind him. The small house was remarkably neat. He noticed a framed picture over the mantel—a cover from a professional-looking corporate magazine. Amanda Brace was in front of a group of stylish-looking young people, all wearing shirts with various ROOTS logos on them. In the background there were rows of perfectly stacked boxes and binders. A headline read ALL IN ORDER and the subtitle said AMANDA BRACE AND HER TEAM KEEP ROOTS ON TRACK.

Brace took a seat against the far wall, well positioned to be able to look out the little bay window for the renegade electrician. Greene took the seat facing her.

"I should tell you, Detective," she said, tying her hair back, "I already spoke to my father's lawyer. She sent me to her partner, Ted DiPaulo, who gave me what he called independent legal advice. Wouldn't charge me for his time. Let's be blunt. I don't have to talk to you at all, do I?"

Greene nodded. "That's true."

"I can just tell you to get lost, and that's the end of it."

"You can tell me to get lost," he said.

She seemed to hesitate for a minute. "Look, it's an open secret that I hated my stepmother. I was nine when she—" Brace took her eyes off Greene and looked hopefully over his shoulder at the street. Greene heard a car pass slowly.

"I did a word jumble in grade four and called her my 'pest' mother. They made me see the school psychologist and all that. It was nineteen years ago. All I can tell you is that my dad doesn't have a violent bone in his body. Never. You want to make him out to be this horrible, nasty man. Well, that's not him."

Greene nodded.

"That's all I wanted to say. Okay?"

Greene said nothing. She didn't make any move to escort him out. He heard another car approach and slow down in front of the house.

"And you want to know my whereabouts on Sunday night and Monday morning, I imagine."

Greene nodded again. Sometimes the best question was just silence.

"You know, it's funny. I had 'Kill Katherine' on my to-do list, but I just didn't get to it. Instead I was home patching the basement walls."

"When's the last time you saw your dad?" Greene asked.

"Our weekly dinner, like always," she said, lifting herself a bit out of her seat. "It's the electrician. Thank my raging hormones."

"Where?"

"He's right outside," she said, pointing to the street.

"I mean the dinner," Greene said.

"The dinner?" Brace said. "Oh." She seemed to have almost forgotten he was still there. "Our usual place. Look, I do have to ask you to leave. Sorry." She pulled herself up sideways from the chair. "If I miss this guy, we're sunk."

Greene stood up. "Thanks for your time. I know you're busy."

"Busy? I don't have a clue how we're going to fit a baby into our lifestyle."

In the hallway, just as he pulled the door open, Brace touched his arm. "Look, you can hate someone with all your might but still put up with them. That's how I handled Katherine. It was the best I could do. No one's happy she's dead. I hear her family's doing a private cremation. Nobody in the world knows my father as well as I do. There's no way he did this. No way."

"Thanks for letting me in," Greene said. "Many people wouldn't have."

"Blame my mother," she said. "Good manners."

Out of the corner of his eye he could see a man in overalls lumbering up the driveway carrying a large plastic toolbox.

"Good luck with your plumbing," he said.

She suddenly threw her head back and started to laugh. It was a loud, enchanting laugh.

"I need it. I'm peeing once an hour."

In the narrow vestibule door he turned sideways to let the electrician in.

"All the best with the baby," Greene said.

"I can handle it," Brace said.

Greene had no doubt that Amanda Brace could handle just about anything.

There was an old saying: When a husband is having an affair, the wife's always the last to know, Greene thought as he walked toward his car. But what about a father and his daughter. When Daddy's a bad guy, isn't she the last one to know? Or did Amanda Brace really know her father better than anyone else?

24

The woman at the steel reception desk had the look of a fashion model. Daniel Kennicott knew the look. Models had a studied distance about them. They never quite made eye contact. Always seeming slightly distracted, as if their conversation with you was only a small part of what was going on in their mind. This woman had long black hair, beautiful Eurasian features, and even though she was sitting down, he could tell she had fabulous long legs. The desk she sat behind was massive. Highly buffed steel. The only thing on it was a laptop computer, with the logo PARALLEL BROADCASTING on the back of the screen. A tiny headset was attached to her left ear.

"Can I help you?" she said, glancing at Kennicott with her gray eyes.

"Daniel Kennicott. I'm here to see Mr. Peel for a five o'clock appointment," he said. "I'm a few minutes early."

She touched something on her computer, her eyes now fixed at a point just over his shoulder. "Shirani, please come to reception." Even though the woman barely whispered into her mouthpiece, her voice echoed loudly over an unseen sound system. "Officer Kennicott for Mr. Peel's five o'clock."

Kennicott smiled. He was out of uniform, and he hadn't told her he was a cop.

A glass door opened, and a tall woman holding a clear plastic clipboard walked in. Her skin was deep black. She had an elegant, thin nose, high cheekbones, thin lips, and a diamond stud in her left nostril.

"Good afternoon, Officer Kennicott," she said, extending her hand. Her fingernails were painted in an intricate pattern. "Shirani Theoraja, Mr. Peel's executive assistant. Please come this way."

The offices of Parallel Broadcasting occupied the top floor of an old converted warehouse that had been stripped down to its foundation, like a carcass with every scrap of meat torn from its bones. The ceilings were high, with exposed ductwork running overhead, the walls sandblasted brick, and the floor hard concrete painted black. Kennicott followed Theoraja down the central hallway. Offices on either side had large windows and glass doors, letting in a flood of light. The desks were made of the same steel construction as the one at reception, and each had the same laptop with the Parallel logo. There didn't seem to be a piece of wood anywhere.

Theoraja walked fast, her high heels clicking on the concrete floor. The sound reverberated, but the people in the glass-door offices didn't even look up.

At the end of the long hall, there was a dark mahogany door, heavy and ornate. The name HOWARD PEEL was written in cheap-looking brass letters. Theoraja gave a confident rap.

"Yep," a gravelly voice called from inside.

"Mr. Peel, Officer Kennicott is here. He's ten minutes early for his five o'clock."

There was no sound for a few moments, and then the door swung open. A short man stood inside. His frizzy hair was a strange, almost orange color, and there were plugs in the front of his scalp, evidence of a recent transplant. He wore a button-down white shirt with the top three buttons undone—exposing a plague of graying chest hair—and a pair of cowboy boots, which seemed to make him look even smaller. His little eyes were the only attractive point on his face, an unexpected deep blue.

"Well, Officer Kennicott, how ya doing?" he said, extending a pudgy hand. "Howie Peel. I'm supposed to run this joint. Come on in."

He escorted Kennicott in as the door closed. Peel's big corner office was unlike the others on the floor. He had a large wood desk and beat-up-looking furniture. There was an old Underwood typewriter on a battered credenza. The windows were covered by dusty brown drapes.

"Can you believe that Shirani?" Peel said as he sat in one of the two chairs facing his desk and motioned Kennicott to the one beside it. "There weren't women like that in the town I grew up in on the Prairies. We had one Chinese restaurant and some native kids in rags out on the reserve. Everyone else was whiter than a farmer's field in February."

Kennicott nodded. He'd done some reading about Howard Peel, president and CEO of Parallel Broadcasting. Every article painted the same picture of the man: a master salesman, loose-lipped, said the most outrageous things, but everyone seemed to like him.

"Shirani's gorgeous but touchy," Peel said. "Ouch. She's Tamil. What did I know? I hired her, her friends. One day I hire another Sri Lankan woman named Indira. I figured she'd fit right in. The next morning Shirani and her gang are in my office. They're all going to quit. 'What's the problem?' I ask. Turns out Indira's Sinhalese; Shirani and her troupe are all Tamil. I get my history lesson. The former Tamil prime minister killed by Sinhalese rebels. The Tamils' houses and tea farms burned. Shirani—those black eyes would melt chocolate. 'All right, all right,' I say. 'No more Indira.'"

Kennicott nodded. He'd also read that Peel could talk your ear off. He decided to wait until the short man ran out of gas.

Peel seemed to finally notice Kennicott's silence and slapped him on the knee. "Enough about me and the beautiful young women who work for Parallel. What can I do for you?"

"I'm involved in the murder investigation of Ms. Katherine Torn," Kennicott said.

"You see the contract I offered that guy? A million bucks, thirty-six weeks, no Mondays. Everything he wanted. I even threw in a limo. Good thing he didn't sign, or I'd be paying him to broadcast from the Don Jail." Peel chuckled. It was a thin, reedy laugh. "Come to think of it, it might have been a good angle. Great way to take on all those damn shock jocks."

"Why didn't Brace sign the contract?" Kennicott asked.

"Why? How should I know why?"

"What about Katherine Torn? You ever meet her?"

"Yep. She was in my office with Brace just last week."

Kennicott nodded. He thought of Peel's crushed business card in Torn's wallet. "Last Wednesday afternoon?"

"Sounds right. I'll ask Shirani."

"She want him to sign it?"

"Who knows?" Peel rubbed his hands together. "What'd you think of the contract? You used to be a lawyer. Worked for Lloyd Granwell."

Suddenly the little man's friendly banter had an edge to it. He hadn't really answered the question. Clearly he wanted Kennicott to know that he'd done his homework.

Ever since he'd become a cop, Kennicott had heard quips like this. When he took the job, Chief Charlton had held a press conference. Made a big deal about Kennicott's being the first lawyer to join the force. He had tried to duck the publicity, but it followed him. The next day, his face was on the cover of all four major papers.

"I didn't want any of this," Kennicott had said to Detective Greene.

"Charlton is a master with the press," Greene had said. "You've just been encoded into the collective DNA of the city."

Of course Peel, like anyone of any influence in Toronto, knew Granwell, Kennicott's old mentor. "The contract seemed pretty straight-forward," Kennicott said, meeting Peel's eyes. "Why was Torn at the meeting?"

"My idea. I'm an old sales guy. The best way to close a deal is to bring in the spouse. I figured a million bucks would convince her it was a great deal."

"But it didn't?"

He shrugged. "He didn't sign. And look at Brace now. Waived his bail. I hear he doesn't say a word in prison."

"Who told you that?" Kennicott asked.

"Don't be fooled by this fancy fucking office," Peel said. "I started as a beat reporter for a small-town radio station. I have my sources."

Kennicott kept his face blank. What Peel was doing was very smart. Like a good journalist. Tossing out some information from a source and hoping Kennicott would confirm it. Kennicott didn't move.

"Doesn't jail sound wonderful?" Peel said, once it became clear that Kennicott wasn't going to say another word. The short man got up from his chair and began to pace. "Meals made for you. Sit around and play bridge all day. Read the sports section to your heart's content. Now Brace doesn't have to interview some housewife from St. John who's collected a thousand bottle caps to donate to the local hospital charity. Or listen to a high school band from New Liskeard play 'O Canada' with Popsicle sticks. He must be happy as a clam."

"Ever been to the Don Jail?" Kennicott asked.

Peel whipped his head around and stared with his disarming blue eyes. This was the look, Kennicott realized, that he used to seal a tough deal.

"Too many times." He let the comment hang in the air as he walked behind his oversize desk. "Bailed out all sorts of people. It's nobody's business but my own."

The jovial salesman act was over. This is the real Howard Peel, Kennicott thought. The one who turned one small-town Saskatchewan radio station into the country's second-largest media conglomerate. Peel reached over to the credenza behind him and grabbed a framed photo.

"Kennicott, you young guys don't know shit. Look. This is me, last Thursday night after the music awards." He stabbed the photo with his stubby forefinger. It was a picture of Peel, wearing a tuxedo, being hugged by a tall, beautiful brunette who towered over him.

"That's Sandra Lance. You know her, everyone knows her—number one hit single, body to die for, half the guys in North America jacking off to her album cover. Five minutes after this photo's taken, I'm in the backseat of a limo, huge bottle of champagne. Yep, Sandra Lance alone with me, a sixty-one-year-old guy with a hair fucking transplant. She's drinking like a stripper with a free tab, and then she just pulls her goddamn top right off. What a rack. A minute later she's licking me like a lollipop. Then taking it from behind, all stretched out. Moaning like a coyote. There I am, fucking the juiciest piece of tail on the whole continent, and what am I thinking about, Officer Daniel Kennicott, Mr. Lawyer Turned Cop?"

Kennicott hadn't moved.

Peel lowered his voice to just above a whisper. "What was I thinking?"

"I don't know," Kennicott finally said. "What were you thinking, Mr. Peel?"

"You don't know? Well then, how are you going to figure out Kevin Brace? Maybe he's just like me. An old guy with a young guy's cock. You've got to crawl into his head."

Kennicott had heard enough. "Thanks for your time," he said, getting out of the chair.

"I was thinking: It's Thursday night. If I hadn't been such a shmuck and bought every radio station in Saskatchewan, then Manitoba, then Alberta, and moved here, I'd still be back home."

Kennicott was halfway to the door. He turned to look at Peel. "You just told me you thought Brace wanted to be in jail."

"Thursday's cribbage night in Rosetown. At the very moment I was poking that singer, Ray and Bob and George and Reggie and even our Chinese pal Tom are all playing. My first wife Elaine's at bingo. And where am I? Stuck in a limo fucking a tart who's younger than my daughter. All I could think about was watered-down prairie coffee and cribbage and how nice it would be to have a regular life."

Kennicott had his hand on the door. Peel looked small, diminished behind his big desk.

"I don't know the guy, other than I couldn't buy him," Peel said. "But I know what happens when ambition drives a man to a place he doesn't want to be anymore."

"What?"

"I think Kevin Brace isn't worrying about what to say about a new recipe for pea soup or getting dragged to an opening-night production by some disabled theater company."

"Meaning?"

"Meaning, I think the whole damn country sucked the guy dry. Everyone wanted a piece of him. Why the hell would he want bail?"

Kennicott opened the heavy door and let it slam behind him. He walked through the trendy offices as fast as he could without running. He didn't care about the clack of his shoes on the floor, and he didn't even look at the beautiful receptionist as he barreled through the door.

The fatigue from the endless days of work was setting in, hitting him like a hammer. He needed to get out, to breathe fresh air.

Back on King Street, the late-afternoon light had faded. The sky was a menacing black. A westbound streetcar was approaching. Kennicott let it pass. He wanted to walk for a while. He pulled up his collar and started toward the light of downtown. A damp cold had descended on the city, and a fierce, angry wind was howling in from the east. Despite his efforts to block it out, the cold air chilled him down to the bone.

25

Ari Greene had a vague memory of this highway, a three-hour drive north to the town of Haliburton. The last time he'd been on it was when he was on a bus taking him to summer camp, a pimply fourteen-year-old on a partial scholarship that allowed him to stay for one month at a camp where the rich kids got to stay for two.

This morning it had taken him almost an hour to drive through the seemingly endless suburbs that surrounded Toronto, and then he spent another hour cutting through rolling farmland and scrawny small towns. At the start of the third hour, as he approached the town of Coboconk, there was the first hint of the great Canadian Shield, the granite rock that blanketed the northern half of the country.

His fondest memory of that summer at camp was the feel of the hard granite on his bare feet. There was one night when he'd sat on a rock late at night with a girl named Eleanor, holding her hand, watching the stars, kissing for the first time.

At Coboconk, he turned left on Highway 35. The wind and driving snow seemed to crank up a notch, as if to say, "Welcome to the North."

Soon the traffic ground to a halt, a long line of cars backed up because of some road construction. It took half an hour to get through, and ten minutes later he pulled into the well-plowed parking lot of a ramshackle building nestled just below a ridge of tall hills. The name

HARDSCRABBLE CAFÉ was painted in faded block letters across the front door, and the lot was less than half filled with pickup trucks, SUVs, and snowmobiles, all facing the front door, a bit like horses tied up to a hitching post outside a saloon.

Greene put his shoulder to the door of his car and stepped out. The wind tore straight down on him, wrenching the door from his hand and slamming it shut. He lowered his head and made his way inside.

The restaurant was a simple, spotlessly clean affair, a large rectangular room with a dozen square tables covered with plastic tablecloths. The walls were decorated with black-and-white photos of early settlers sitting on their farm equipment or, in one, everyone in town welcoming soldiers back from World War I. Hanging over each table were handmade Christmas decorations. Groups of men in bulky clothing filled only a few of the tables.

Everything about the place was dead normal, except the smell. The aroma of freshly baked bread permeated the restaurant, giving it an unexpected warmth. Greene found an empty table in the corner.

A few minutes later a young woman wearing a white apron appeared. "Sorry to keep yous waitin'," she said. "I've been runnin' all day. Lakes are frozen solid, and all the snowmobilers're out."

She flipped over her little order pad. "Here's our fresh special," she said, reading. "Tomato soup, made with homegrown tomatoes and other vegetables."

"The bread smells good," Greene said.

"Everyone loves our bread." The young woman smiled for the first time. Her teeth were jagged, yellowed. Greene noticed a cigarette pack bulging out of the back pocket of her jeans. "Ms. McGill makes it every morning."

Greene smiled back. "Give me the special."

He took his time eating. Gradually the restaurant emptied out. He picked up the local weekly paper, the Haliburton *Echo*. An article caught his eye. Last Friday night two teenagers went through the ice on their snowmobiles near the town bridge. The police fished them out, but on Saturday night they went through again on the other side of the bridge. This time the local constabulary didn't get them in time.

When Sarah McGill, Brace's first wife, emerged from the kitchen there was only one table left—a group of snowmobilers who'd come in soon after Greene arrived. McGill's hair had mostly grayed, and she wore no makeup, but there was an elegant beauty to the woman that time and hardship seemed to have been unable to dent. Kind of like granite, Greene thought.

Her mere presence might have been a signal to the men that it was time to leave. As if on cue, they rose up from their table.

"Food's better than ever, Ms. McGill," a man with a bushy beard and big, friendly smile said as he zipped up his oversize coat. It seemed that everyone called her Ms. McGill.

"Jared, you say the same thing every time," McGill said, letting out a deep, confident laugh. She touched him comfortably on the shoulder.

"You're going to have to stay open Mondays. Six days a week isn't enough."

McGill swept her arms around the room and pointed to some of the empty tables. "Not with that damn road construction," she said. "That crew's twelve months behind. At this rate I'll have to close more days, not less."

The men left. McGill had a dish towel slung over her shoulder, and she pulled it off as she began to work her way through the restaurant, wiping down tables with the efficiency of a woman who'd spent a lifetime cleaning up after people.

Greene thought of the notes he'd read about Sarah McGill. Born in Noranda, a small mining town up north. Her father was a mining engineer, her mother a grade-school teacher. She was an only child who studied natural sciences at university and won a scholarship to do graduate work in England. At a Canada Day celebration in London she met a young journalist, Kevin Brace. They returned home together, got married, and promptly started having children. When their youngest was six years old, Brace left.

Brace's story was more complex. His father, the child of a wealthy Toronto family, had no interest in working. Instead he spent most of his time whoring and drinking. He married Brace's mother when he was forty-three, and Kevin was also an only child. To his father he was more of an inconvenience than anything else.

One night when Kevin was twelve, his father came home drunk and angry. He tried to attack Brace's mother, and Kevin confronted him. His father cut Brace's cheek so badly Brace had a permanent scar. He grew a beard as soon as he could to cover it up, and never shaved it off.

Brace's father was hauled off to the Don Jail. The next morning he was found dead of a coronary. When his estate was probated, there was nothing left but debt. The big house Brace grew up in was sold. He and his mother moved into an apartment above a grocery store on Yonge Street, where he lived until he won a scholarship and went away to university.

Greene watched McGill work: Take the salt and pepper and put them on a seat, wipe the table, put the salt and pepper back in the middle. Pull out four forks, knives, and spoons from a metal tray she carried with her; make four place settings. Wipe the seats. Put the seats back. Grab the cutlery tray and move to the next table.

When she got to Greene's table, McGill seemed surprised that a patron was still there.

"We're closing now," she said, whisking a hair from her forehead with the back of her forearm and nodding toward the young waitress at the cash register. "Charlene will cash you out."

"The food's wonderful," Greene said. "You make everything yourself?"

For the first time since Greene had seen her, McGill stopped moving. She let out that attractive, deep laugh again.

"No one's going to come halfway across the county to eat canned soup." She promptly started wiping down the table beside Greene.

Greene didn't move.

"I've been up since before five this morning," she said. "I hope you don't mind, but we really are closing."

"Mrs. Brace, I need to talk to you," Greene said quietly.

Hearing her married name, McGill went rigid. She kept wiping the table.

"I'm Detective Ari Greene. I'm with the Toronto Police," he said quickly. "Here's my badge."

McGill flipped her towel over and wiped the clean table again. She didn't look up.

"It's about Kevin," Greene said.

McGill kept her eyes focused on the table, giving it an unnecessary third wipe. She grabbed the salt and pepper shakers and slammed them down. The salt skittered out of her hand and fell on its side, spilling a trail of white across the plastic cloth.

"Shit," McGill said as she grabbed the shaker to right it. "Shit."

26

The streetcar heading west along College Street was nearly empty when Daniel Kennicott got on it. He could have flashed his badge for a free ride, but instead he dug into his wallet and fished out the $2.75 fare. He counted four other riders, each sitting alone by a window seat, as he made his way toward the back of the car. It felt good to sit down, even if the plastic seat was hard and cold.

As the streetcar traveled out from downtown, speeding past the emptied streets, the lights of the city core faded. As soon as they crossed Bathurst Street, a cavalcade of lights suddenly illuminated the streetcar. Up ahead, the road was jammed with cars, the sidewalks teeming with people rolling in and out of bright restaurants and cafés. They'd arrived at the edge of Little Italy, one of the city's thriving nighttime entertainment spots.

Kennicott reached for the wire cord above the window and gave it a perfunctory pull, indicating he was getting off at the next stop. A block west of Clinton Street, where the tracks bent north, he got off. Music spilled out from the half-opened windows and doors of the restaurants that lined both sides of the street. He looked in the window of the Café Diplomatico, a popular spot on the north side. It was packed with excited diners and waiters in white aprons rushing about. The sound of laughter and the smell of freshly baked pizza wafted out onto the sidewalk.

He crossed Clinton and ducked into the Riviera Bakery. It was mercifully empty. The smell of moldering cheese mixed with a hint of brewing yeast. The old Italian woman behind the counter gave him a smile.

"We still have two left," she said, pointing to the standing refrigerator behind him. "Fresh."

Kennicott turned and opened the glass door. On the bottom shelf, two plastic bags of pizza dough were stacked on top of each other. He fished out the one on the bottom, selected three kinds of cheese—Romano, mozzarella, and Parmesan—a plastic container of marinated red peppers, and a package of pepperoni. Back at the counter, he picked up a jar of artichoke hearts and pointed to a white pail of olives.

"A small tub, please," he said.

The woman nodded. "We have fresh prosciutto for Christmas," she said. Without waiting for his reply, she reached up and pulled down a hanging piece of meat from a long row overhead.

"Here," she said, cutting off a slice for him. "Better on your pizza than old pepperoni."

Kennicott slid the thin slice into his mouth. The sting of the sharp meat felt good. "Twelve slices," he said, reaching for the pepperoni so he could replace it in the fridge.

The woman put her hand on his. "Is okay," she said. "I put back."

Out on the street, plastic shopping bag in hand, Kennicott found himself standing behind a man and a woman at the traffic light. Even from the back, he recognized her. He noticed they were holding hands, and looked away.

"Daniel," a female voice said.

Jo Summers, her hair, as always, tied up above her head with the same hair clip, had turned around and seen him.

"Hi, Jo," he said.

The man beside her swiveled to face him. He was dressed conservatively, his thinning blond hair neatly combed. Kennicott put him in his early forties. A big smile on his broad face.

"This is Terrance," Summers said, offering no further explanation.

Terrance disengaged his hand from Summers's and gave Kennicott a firm handshake. "Really nice to meet you," he said.

"We went to law school together," Summers said. "Daniel was smart enough to get out of practicing."

"Really. What do you do?" Terrance said. His smile somehow seemed to grow even wider. Kennicott had a sudden urge to say "I'm a bond man," just like Nick in *The Great Gatsby*.

"Nothing that interesting," Kennicott said. "Just trying something new."

Kennicott looked over at Summers. He expected her to tell Terrance he was a cop. But instead she reached out and touched his shoulder, as if to say, "Don't worry, I'm sure you're sick of telling the story."

Some people came up behind them, and Kennicott noticed that the light had turned green.

"We've got a reservation at Kalendar at eight," Terrance said, glancing down at his watch. "They've got a new chef, and you know how hard it is to get in there."

"I'm heading this way," Kennicott said, tilting his head north up Clinton Street.

"Really great to meet you, Dan," Terrance said as he turned back toward Summers. She caught Kennicott's eye for just a moment before heading across the street. Terrance put his arm around her shoulders, and Kennicott watched for a moment to see if she put her arm around him. She didn't.

PART II: FEBRUARY

27

It was not the cold that bothered Mr. Singh about the Canadian winter. After all, he'd endured many frigid months when he was stationed in the mountains of Kashmir. And he'd learned to accept the inconsistent temperature of winter in Toronto—how one week the city would be in the grip of a freezing cold spell, and the next all the outdoor natural ice rinks would melt away.

No, the winter temperature was not what bothered Mr. Singh. It was the winter darkness he found difficult to get accustomed to. In late September the light would begin to slip away from the sky, and by the middle of October he'd wake in darkness, travel through the city in darkness, and begin his day with his deliveries at the Market Place Tower in darkness. It was most somber.

But this morning, for the first time in months, as Mr. Singh left home there had been a hint of brightness in the sky. When he arrived at the Market Place Tower, the lobby was lit up with the rising sun. A welcome sight.

Tomorrow was Saint Valentine's Day, a peculiar Canadian custom. Even Mr. Singh's own family was not immune to it. Last night when the grandchildren were at the Singh home, his little granddaughter Tejgi asked him at the dinner table, "Grandpa Gurdial, what will you give Grandma Bimal for Valentine's Day?"

"It is not necessary to give Grandma a Valentine's Day present," Mr. Singh explained to the child. "She is well aware that I love her."

Tejgi thought about this for a moment. "But I never see you kiss Grandma Bimal," she said. "Don't grandmas and grandpas kiss?"

This, of course, provoked laughter around the table.

"My child," Mr. Singh said, "there is much more to love than kisses."

Mr. Singh chuckled at the thought of his granddaughter's silliness as he lifted the first bundles of newspapers from the stack in the lobby. Today's edition was heavier than usual because of all the inserts advertising foolish Valentine's Day specials. Mr. Singh removed his knife, cut the plastic cord around the top bundle, and opened the first newspaper. A few gaudily colored brochures spilled out onto the floor.

The Times of India wouldn't carry such nonsense, Mr. Singh thought as he bent down to pick up the mess. *The Globe and Mail*, which seemed to consider itself the paper of record for Canada, was an odd publication. There were many proper articles about Canadian politics—mostly the goings-on in Ottawa—and international affairs, but then there were so many pieces written by journalists about their own personal experiences: sleeping in a tent in the snow (why, Mr. Singh wondered, would one bother?), finding a babysitter so the writer and her husband could go to a restaurant for the first time since their child was born (where, Mr. Singh wondered, were the journalist's parents?), and even, to his utter shock, an article by a female journalist about purchasing a bra and the shape of her own breasts. That one Mr. Singh quickly hid in the wastebasket.

Most surprising was the coverage of the trial of Mr. Kevin. Since the gentleman's arrest in December, Mr. Singh had been astounded by the number of articles written about the case.

Mr. Singh glanced up and saw the concierge, Mr. Rasheed, stationed at the front desk. He had a copy of the *Toronto Star* spread out before him. The *Star*, which considered itself less intellectual and more of a "paper of the people" than the rather gray-looking *Globe and Mail*, had even more coverage of Mr. Kevin's matter.

"What have they written about Mr. Kevin this morning?" Mr.

Singh asked as he took off his heavy coat—the coat Bimal was still insisting he wear each day of the winter, no matter the temperature—and draped it over a chair.

"They've found Mr. Brace's first wife," Mr. Rasheed said. "She owns a restaurant up north in a small town. There's a photograph of her." He turned the paper slightly, to afford Mr. Singh a better view.

"Mr. Kevin likes to cook as well," Mr. Singh said, curling his head to look. It was a grainy photograph, obviously taken from some distance, of a handsome-looking older woman wearing a long winter coat. She was walking across a snow-covered parking lot filled with trucks and snowmobiles.

"According to this article," Mr. Rasheed said, "Mr. Brace met his first wife when he was a young journalist in England."

"England? I had no knowledge he lived there," Mr. Singh said as he studied the woman in the picture. "Perhaps that is where he learned to drink tea properly."

"It says she was a student at Oxford." The concierge moved back half a step as Mr. Singh got closer.

"And what was she reading?" Mr. Singh tilted his head to get a better look at the photo.

"Botany. Worked in the Royal Gardens for a year before she came home and started a family. Brace told a magazine interviewer years ago, 'It was love at first sight for me. I never thought she'd be interested. She was surrounded by all these geniuses.'"

"These articles are such a waste of time," Mr. Singh said, reading the caption under her picture.

Mr. Rasheed opened the paper to the middle section. There was a two-page spread about Mr. Brace and his first wife, complete with family photos and highlighted quotations.

Mr. Singh checked his watch. He was a full minute behind schedule.

"It's a large story today," Mr. Rasheed said, digging into the article with gusto.

"Idle gossip," Mr. Singh said. He shifted his weight to his back foot and lingered for one last moment, looking at a photo of the young Mrs. Brace. She was certainly attractive. Mr. Kevin, on the other hand, looked awkward.

Just then the concierge drew in a quick breath. "Oh my. One of their children was taken away."

"Let me see," Mr. Singh said, shifting his weight again.

"Their oldest," Mr. Rasheed said, reading quickly. "The only boy. He was autistic. Could not speak."

"This is most unfortunate," Mr. Singh said. In the photo Mr. Kevin was quite tall. He had his arm around his first wife, who was much shorter. Two young girls stood in front with big brown eyes just like their father's, looking right at the camera. Beside Mr. Kevin was a thin boy almost his height who had his head turned to the side, looking off into the distance.

"They split up soon after the boy was taken away," Rasheed read.

Mr. Singh nodded. "As a chief engineer on Indian Railways, I met many families. A child like this could be a great hardship," he said.

He picked up his papers and made his way across the lobby, now a full five minutes behind schedule. How difficult it must have been for Mr. Kevin, Mr. Singh thought as he stepped into the elevator, a man of so many words, to have a son who could not speak.

28

This traffic is unbelievable, Daniel Kennicott thought as yet another light turned red without his being able to make a left turn through the intersection. He shook his head in disgust. A few years earlier, when the Forensic Identification Service—FIS, as everyone called it—outgrew police headquarters, someone got the bright idea to move it way the hell out in the suburbs. So here it was, on the northern part of Jane Street, home of endless gridlock.

The reason for the traffic nightmare was frustratingly obvious. About thirty years ago, just as the immigrant population in the city was surging, the politicians of the day stopped building subways. Smart move.

While he waited for the light, Kennicott looked over at a strip mall to his left. There were seven stores reflecting as many different nationalities. He read some of the signs: TROPICAL FRUIT; EAST AND WEST INDIAN GROCERIES; GOLDEN STAR THAI AND VIETNAMESE CUISINE; MOHAMMED'S HALAL MEAT; JOSE'S HAIR STUDIO; and the inevitable $ CASH BOOTH, CHEQUE CASHING, PAYDAY LOANS, WIRE MONEY OVERSEAS. Although he was born and raised downtown, when he became a cop Kennicott found a great affection for the people he met who were stuck in these godforsaken suburbs. Making the city work almost in spite of itself.

At last he pulled into the FIS parking lot, between a roti place and a McDonald's. The roar of the highway just to the north hit him as he

got out of the unmarked Chevrolet he'd signed out from the homicide squad. Could anyone have picked an uglier location? If some TV
producers ever wanted to do a show called *CSI: Toronto*, they sure
wouldn't film it here, Kennicott thought as he walked into the workmanlike gray building.

"Hey, good morning, young man," Detective Ho said as he strolled
out to greet him at reception. "I'm all set up," he added, ushering Kennicott into the fingerprint lab. It was a rectangular room with a long
steel workbench on one side. Above it a shelf held bottles filled with
different-colored powders and a collection of feather brushes. On the
opposite wall sat a big machine that looked like an open-window
oven, with a number of racks inside. There was a cheap-looking white
kettle at the bottom, with a white extension cord dangling out. And at
the end of the counter was a smaller, boxlike machine.

Square in the center of the bench was a clear evidence bag, with
red letters marked on the outside: DECEMBER 17, KEVIN BRACE, PAR-
ALLEL BROADCASTING CONTRACT, SEVEN PAGES, DET. HO. Detective Ho's signature was in a little box.

"For fingerprints you have two choices," Ho said, snapping on a
pair of latex gloves. He pointed to the big ovenlike machine. "This is
the Ninhydrin oven. I call it my slow cooker. Takes about two hours,
and we'll be able to see the prints with the naked eye."

"What's the kettle for?"

"Steam. Keeps the oven moist. We could also hold the pages over
the steaming kettle to develop them." Ho opened a widemouthed
plastic container, poured a light yellowish liquid into a rectangular
tray, then used a pair of rubber tongs to dip each sheet into the tray.

"What's the other option?"

Ho pointed to the box at the end of the counter. "This little baby,
our DFO oven. I call it my print microwave. Takes just twelve minutes.
Bakes at exactly one hundred degrees Celsius, two twelve Fahrenheit."

"What's the drawback?"

"We need an alternate light source to view the prints," Ho said,
picking up a piece of orange plastic and holding it to his eye like a Boy

Scout leader with a magnifying glass. "I just go in there," he said, pointing to a little booth in the corner that Kennicott hadn't noticed, "flick on the orange light, photograph the prints, and download them onto the computer at my desk. Easy." Ho looked very proud of himself.

"Let's use the DFO. Faster the better," Kennicott said as he reached into his briefcase. "I brought you an extra copy of the contract." He knew Ho would be curious to read it.

Ho loaded the wet pages into the little oven, then grabbed the document from Kennicott.

"Hey—now, this is a contract I would've signed," he said as he read through it. "A million bucks, a limo, sixteen weeks' holiday. Don't have to work Mondays. And our boy Brace didn't sign? Now, there's your motive for murder."

"What would that be?" Kennicott asked. Playing the straight man to Ho's comic act was always the price of admission.

"Insanity," Ho exclaimed. "You'd have to be nuts not to take a deal like this."

Fifteen minutes later they were back out at Ho's desk. There was a computer screen on one side and a filing cabinet on the other, packed to the gills with stacks of papers. A large aquarium took up about a quarter of the desk space, with three colorful fish inside.

"Meet Zeus, Goose, and Abuse," Ho said, motioning toward the fish. "English is the world's craziest language. Three ways to spell the same sound. My poor grandfather. Paid the poll tax to come to work on the railroad, didn't see his wife for fifteen years, and could never spell a damn thing."

Kennicott smiled. He noticed that Ho's backpack and briefcase were stuffed underneath the desk.

Ho clicked on his computer; downloaded the pages, the finger-prints now clearly visible; and printed them out. He already had copies of Katherine Torn's and Kevin Brace's prints on his desk. Brace's were on the file from his arrest, and Torn's from the autopsy. He found a round, stand-up magnifying glass among the mess and peered over Brace's prints.

"Hey, take a look at this, young man," he said, moving to the side so Kennicott could look into the glass. "See that line through Brace's left thumb? It's an old scar. Notice how the skin has puckered up around it."

Kennicott looked through the glass. He could see the old injury very clearly. "When Brace was about twelve years old, his father slashed him in the face with a knife," he said. "Could it be that old?"

Ho's usually rambunctious voice softened. "The skin never forgets. Defensive wound. Probably tried to stop the knife with his hand."

Kennicott looked up from the glass. Ho was flipping through the contract. It was seven pages long.

"Notice how there aren't many prints on the inside pages? People usually only handle the front and back pages," Ho said. He demonstrated as he flipped through the contract.

"Makes sense," Kennicott said.

"I found two other prints." He went to the last page. "Down here, beside his signature line. See the big smudge? Not a finger. We call it a writer's palm." Again he demonstrated, pretending he was holding a pen in his hand. "You often see these where people sign things. I'll bet that's Mr. Moneybags. Howard Peel. It's right beside his signature."

"That makes sense too," Kennicott said.

Ho went back to the front page. "This is a different print. It's also on page three. Near the part about the million-dollar salary. Take a look." Ho put the magnifying glass on top of it.

Kennicott leaned over. "There seem to be two semicircles, not just one," he said.

"Hey. Very good. Those circles are called whorls. When you get two together like this and going in opposite directions, it's called a double loop whorl. About five percent of the population have them."

Ho put the print on his scanner and sent it to a central database. In about a minute he got back a list of the ten most likely hits. There were no names, just numbers. He printed out the page.

"I've got to go to storage and pull these ten fingerprint files. Then

I'll come back here and check each one manually. Stay here. Just don't feed the fish."

Kennicott was glad to sit quietly for a few minutes. He watched the fish swim in slow, rhythmic circles. Around the room, identification officers were working at different desks, transfixed by their computer monitors. As they worked, many ate from colored Tupperware containers. A box of cold pizza sat on a black filing cabinet in the corner.

"Hey, hey, hey," Ho said, barging back in. "I've got a hunch I've found something. You're going to be plenty surprised. But protocol is, I check all ten before I say a word. So, lucky you, my lips are sealed."

"Promise?" Kennicott was tempted to ask. Instead he just nodded.

Ho took out each file and began going back and forth with his magnifying glass between the prints on file and the prints on the doc-ument. He worked quickly, his big body over the small magnifying glass, dropping files on the floor once he was done with them. He was mercifully silent for a few minutes, but it didn't last.

"You can have all the technology in the world," Ho said when he got to the eighth file. Kennicott noticed that he didn't drop this one on the floor, but put it on his desk. "But this is still a very human process."

He examined the last two files, and at last he lifted his head. He picked up the file from his desk with his meaty paw and waved it gleefully.

"Found a match," Ho said, passing the file over. "Hey, are you in for a surprise."

Kennicott opened it and looked at the name inside. He felt his body jerk: "Mrs. Sarah Brace, maiden name Sarah McGill."

Ho grinned and pointed to some background documents. "Back in the late 1980s she was involved in some kind of protest. Pushed a cop through a glass window. Got charged and printed."

Kennicott's mouth felt dry.

"Hey, I told you Brace had the insanity defense. His common-law wife and his ex-wife both on the same page. That's nuts."

Kennicott slammed the file shut. "Where's a phone I can use?" he said, his mind whirling. "I've got to call Greene."

29

Ari Greene put down the phone and looked around his empty kitchen. All he was wearing was a towel, which he'd wrapped loosely around his waist when he got up to answer the phone. He filled the kettle with cold water, turned it on, and then, retying the towel tight, hobbled over to the front door. Outside, he bent down to snap up the morning paper. As he walked back toward the kitchen, he opened it to read the headline. Then he paused.

There was a rustling sound coming from the bedroom. He teetered for a moment, like a waiter caught between tables. On one side was the noise in the bedroom, on the other the sound of the kettle in the kitchen as it began to boil. He tapped the bedroom door with his foot, swinging it open. "Here's *The Globe*," he said, entering the near darkness and gently tossing the newspaper on the edge of the bed.

"What time is it?" a woman's voice said from under the covers.

"Too early. I have to get going," he said.

"I heard the phone ring."

"Go back to sleep," he said, backing out of the darkened room. "I'll take a shower in the basement and you can let yourself out." There was an old bathroom downstairs, left over from the previous owner, who used to rent the basement out. It was pretty basic.

The covers began to stir, then were flung back like a wave emerging from a flat sea. Jennifer Raglan clicked on the bedside lamp and sat up, shaking her head. She wasn't wearing a top, and her breasts swayed just above the crest of the sheets. Lifting an arm, she ran her hand through her hair. She made no effort to cover herself. A younger woman might have a more sculpted body, Greene thought, but not the confidence. Raglan acted this way at work, as the head Crown in the downtown Toronto office. Confident but not cocky.

He rocked on his heels. She held his eyes. When they started their secret affair, Greene and Raglan had reached a firm yet unspoken agreement: keep their jobs out of the bedroom. He let the silence accumulate—something he was good at.

"Thanks for the paper," Raglan said finally. She reached across the bed with one hand and lifted the sheets to cover herself with the other, smiling, not pouting. That was another advantage of someone who was older, Greene thought. Maturity.

"It was Daniel Kennicott, an officer on the Brace case," Greene said. "He had a hunch about that million-dollar contract Brace didn't sign. FIS found Sarah McGill's fingerprints on the last page."

Raglan put the paper down. "Hmmm. The first wife," she said.

He nodded. "I've got to go up and see her. It's going to be a busy few days."

"I've got the kids for the rest of the week," Raglan said, picking up the paper again. Raglan had two teenage boys and a daughter who was still in the tomboy stage. She was reading the sports section. "Leafs are in trouble now. They lost their goalie, all they got left is that old guy."

"Yeah. I'm going to try to get my dad to a game," he said. "Wish me luck."

"Take a shower up here," she said, tilting her head toward the en suite bathroom. "It's much nicer than the one downstairs, and I'm not getting back to sleep."

"I'll make some tea first," Greene said.

In the kitchen the portable electric kettle had already clicked off. He poured the hot water into his porcelain teapot and refilled the kettle with cold water.

When he first made Homicide, Greene was put on the case of a professor who'd been stabbed to death by a crazy student. The man and his wife were both academics, here on a year's sabbatical from the London School of Economics. They had no children, and the wife, whose name was Margaret, stayed throughout the trial. The university extended her contract, and she ended up living in Toronto.

One afternoon, about a year after the trial was over, she happened to be walking down the street when Greene was on his way to his parking spot. Margaret tried to make it seem like a chance encounter, and Greene decided not to let on how obvious her little gambit had been.

They lived together for the next twelve months, and during that time she taught him the proper way to make a pot of tea. Eventually she got a job offer back in England, and periodically she sent him photos of her new husband and their growing daughter, and a package of assorted tea.

"First you heat the pot. Then use cold water. The hot has been sitting in the tank too long. Be careful when it boils," Margaret had said. "Stop it just when it hits the boil. You don't want to boil the oxygen out of it."

He swirled the hot water around the pot, then dumped the water into the sink and plopped two bags of white tea into the pot. He let the kettle steam up and waited until it just hit a rolling boil. Then he lifted it, tilted the teapot on an angle, and poured the water down onto its side wall.

"Never pour the water directly on the tea," she had instructed. "You need to let the bag come to the water."

Finally he put the top of the pot across the opening, not covering it completely. "And when you let the tea steep," Margaret had said, demonstrating, "give it air, room to breathe."

Leaving the tea to steep, Greene slipped into the shower. He filled his hair with shampoo and let the warm water wash over him. It felt good. He was trying to figure this out. Sarah McGill's fingerprints on the unsigned million-dollar contract.

Greene reached for the bar of soap and turned his face up to the nozzle. He bent forward and let the warm water run down his back.

He was glad to be in the upstairs bathroom. The shower stall in the basement had a narrow head, and the floor outside was cold concrete. His mind was a jumble. There was something else about Brace's condominium that had just occurred to him. What was it?

A hand slid into his fingers and took the soap from him. Raglan's skin was soft, warm. She soaped his shoulders, then his neck, then his stomach. Just go with it, Ari, he told himself. All thoughts of Brace's apartment slipped away as he arched his back gently toward her, her skin dry against his wetness, becoming wet herself.

30

Daniel Kennicott hustled out of the FIS office and battled the traffic back downtown to Old City Hall, where he swore out a subpoena for Howard Peel. Just in case the little man decided he didn't want to talk to him, Kennicott would drag him into court. Then he rushed over to Peel's office. It was always better not to call someone in advance when you wanted to serve him. It turned out that the Mini Media Mogul—as Peel liked to refer to himself—was hosting a party at his private ski club, north of the city. It was almost two o'clock by the time Kennicott hit the road. He had to hurry.

The sun was slipping over the ridge, which passed for a ski mountain in southern Ontario, when he pulled into the Osgoode Ski Club. The parking lot was massive, filled to capacity with a staggering array of expensive cars: Lexus, BMW, Acura, Mercedes, and every top-end model of SUV. There must be more money in this parking lot, Kennicott thought as he drove around hoping to find a spot, than in half the countries in sub-Saharan Africa. After five minutes he finally found a place in the farthest reaches of the lot.

Just as well. Anyone who saw him get out of the bland Chevy would know right away that he couldn't possibly be a member. After he'd picked up the subpoena, he had rushed home to change. He'd chosen his clothes carefully. A pair of corduroy pants, a cable sweater, a cashmere car coat, and a pair of handmade Australian boots. The shoes make the man, his father had taught him. He wanted to take Peel by surprise. To do that, he needed to be able to walk into the exclusive ski club and fit right in.

It was the club's annual men's day. The ski lifts had closed, and groups of men stood in clutches, holding large plastic glasses of beer and eating fresh sushi served by a bevy of tuxedoed waiters. There was an air of excited release. In the corner, the little man was holding court near a big stone fireplace. He wore a bulky ski suit that, even though he'd unzipped it, made him look even more squat, more rounded. Kennicott walked behind him, careful to keep out of Peel's sight line.

"Yep, I gotta tell ya," he was saying as he swirled ice in a highball glass filled with a clear drink, probably vodka and soda, Kennicott thought. "You guys might have big, fancy offices downtown, but you spend all your time with other guys in suits. Me, ha, come to Parallel sometime. It's just wall-to-wall gorgeous female flesh."

One of the fellows next to Peel, a tall, barrel-chested redhead, downed his beer. "And how about those female rock stars? You must get to meet some of them."

Peel put his small head back and let out a loud laugh. "Oh, man, you haven't lived until you've done some rock and roll in the back of a limo."

The redheaded man stared down at Peel, amazed. "Really?" he asked, confounded at the thought of little Howard Peel actually being in a limo with a rock-and-roll beauty.

"It's true," Kennicott said, cutting in, a big smile on his face. "Howie's told me many tales." He walked into the circle and clapped Peel heartily on the back. "But sadly for you gents, my lips are sealed."

The short man looked up. Kennicott could see that it took Peel a moment to place him.

Before Peel could react, Kennicott touched him on the shoulder, leaned over, and whispered in his ear. "Consider yourself served with a subpoena. Tomorrow morning, courtroom 121, Old City Hall. Do you want me to drop it on the floor and walk away, or can we have a little chat?"

Peel flinched only for a moment. He recovered fast. "Daniel, I didn't see you out there all day," he said, slapping Kennicott on the back as if they were old friends. "We got to talk about that deal." He took Kennicott's arm and led him out of the crowd. "This has nothing to do with rock stars in limos, believe me, guys," he called back to his audience.

Peel steered Kennicott to a staircase on the far side of the fireplace. For a small man in heavy ski boots he handled the steep stairs with surprising agility. A moment later they were standing just inside a deserted back exit door. Kennicott took out the subpoena and touched him on the shoulder with it.

"What the fuck is this all about?" Peel hissed, grabbing the paper out of Kennicott's hand. "I'll have my lawyers in court tomorrow, and we'll quash this thing in no time."

"No dice. You've got material evidence."

"Like what?"

"Like Brace and Torn went to see you the week before she was killed."

"So what?"

"You offered Brace a million bucks at the meeting."

"I already told you that."

"You didn't tell me that you saw Torn the next afternoon." It was a guess, but Kennicott was pretty sure he was right.

Peel frowned. "You didn't ask." He still had the glass in his hand. He rattled the ice around in it and put it to his lips.

"I'm asking now. Do you want to talk, or do you want to go on the stand?" Kennicott took a step closer, close enough to smell what was in the glass. He sniffed but didn't smell anything.

Peel stomped his ski boots on the metal grating in front of the door. "Why are you doing this to me now? It cost me ten thousand bucks to get all these account execs up here for the day. Every ad agency in Toronto sends someone."

Kennicott held Peel's gaze.

"Okay, okay," Peel said, his little blue eyes darting around to make sure they were still alone. "Katherine wanted me to pull the contract offer. She didn't want Brace to take the job."

"Why? You'd offered him a ton of money, a limousine every morning, sixteen weeks' vacation, Mondays off."

"I know."

"I've been looking through Torn and Brace's bank accounts and Visa statements. They could have used the money."

"I know."

"Torn was buying things on sale, going to thrift shops. Everyone says Brace never cared about money. She should have been thrilled about this deal."

Peel took a big sip from his glass, then slowly met Kennicott's gaze.

"Well?" Kennicott said.

Peel gave an exaggerated sigh. "I already told you, Officer Kennicott, she wanted out of the deal."

"And I told you it doesn't make sense."

Peel put his head back and finished his drink in one big gulp. He's drinking water, Kennicott thought. Dry pipes. He must be getting over a hangover from the night before.

"Let's go outside," Peel said. With a hard clang he opened the fire door, and seconds later they were standing in the winter dusk. With the sun down, the temperature had dropped fast. Kennicott hunched his shoulders against the cold. It was beginning to snow. The big parking lot was now dark, the herd of rich vehicles like so many sleeping cows.

"What happened?" Kennicott asked.

"Katherine was part of the deal," Peel said. He pulled a blister pack from his pocket and pushed out a piece of gum. The plastic made a hollow, crinkling sound. "We'd found a job for her as an associate producer on a weekend show. Early morning. No one is listening. Perfect way for her to get started. She was even training for it once a week. A friend of Brace's with a studio in his home."

Kennicott nodded. He knew the best thing he could do was to keep quiet. Let Peel tell his story. The comforting smell of the burning fireplace wafted through the air. He gazed across the lot and, despite himself, started to calculate in his head the value of the cars parked there.

"It was too much for Katherine," Peel said.

Kennicott thought about what he'd learned about Torn's life. The rigid regularity of it. Her abstemious spending habits.

Peel's voice turned sad. "One day she freaked out." Then, to Kennicott's astonishment, he tore open his ski jacket and pulled down the collar on his sweater. "This is what she did to me." Peel's neck had deep scratch marks. They looked quite old. "Her nails," he said, stating the obvious.

"Where were you when this happened?"

Peel flicked the gum into his mouth. "Well—"

"Where?"

"In their condo."

"That's impossible," Kennicott shot back. "I've watched all the videos from the lobby."

"I'd go in through the basement. There was a door she'd leave open. Stick a brick in it."

Peel and Torn together? Hard to imagine a more unlikely pair. "How often would you see her?" Kennicott asked. It was amazing the things people did with their lives.

"Every Tuesday morning," Peel said. His voice flat now, resigned. "Eight o'clock."

"Eight o'clock," Kennicott echoed. He remembered the chart he'd done of Torn's week. The perfect way to have an affair. "Just when the whole country knows Brace is in the studio," he said.

Peel shot Kennicott a glance. He seemed to snap out of his sadness. Suddenly, unexpectedly, he was angry.

"Kennicott, get your mind out of the gutter."

Kennicott laughed. "Peel, you should talk. You're the one who likes to brag about his conquests."

"I wasn't talking about Katherine," Peel said. He was acting genuinely upset.

Kennicott had had enough of his charade. "Peel, give me a break. You sneaked in once a week to see her when Brace was on air . . ."

"Brace knew all about it. He encouraged it."

"Encouraged it? Peel, you're too much."

Peel clawed another piece of gum out of his blister pack and jammed it into his mouth. "It's not what you think. Katherine had a problem. Not many people knew about it. I was helping her."

It was Kennicott's turn to get angry. "Peel. You were having an affair with her and Brace found out, and now you're trying to cover your—"

"Shut up, Kennicott," Peel said. "We met at AA. I was her sponsor. For the first year, I only knew her first name. I didn't have a clue who she was. Eventually she started to talk. That's how I met Brace."

Peel chewed his gum hard.

"Katherine just kept relapsing," he said. "It was very bad. We thought a job might help her self-esteem. First step." He spit his barely chewed gum into a snowbank.

Kennicott thought about how the little man had jiggled his ice-filled glass. How he'd drunk it all in one big gulp. Like a real drinker.

"How long have you been on the wagon?" he asked.

Peel glanced at him. "Five years. It was bad. I almost lost every-thing."

Kennicott nodded.

"I don't know anything about how she ended up dead. But you want to put me on the stand to bury Katherine a second time, go right ahead." He zipped up his jacket, making a cool, swishing sound. "It will be on your conscience, not mine." Peel yanked open the heavy door and disappeared into the warm chalet.

A moment later the door closed with a loud clank. Kennicott looked across the darkened millionaires' parking lot and knew it was going to be a long, cold walk back to his car.

31

The worst thing about the drive out of Toronto was the endless traffic. Here it was just past 11:30 and you'd think rush hour would be over. Especially since he was headed out of town. Instead, Ari Greene was sitting in a traffic jam on the Don Valley Parkway, heading northeast out of the city. No wonder the suburbanites who had to drive this every day referred to it as the Don Valley Parking Lot.

Forty minutes later, when he finally got to the end of the highway and turned onto a two-lane country road, everything changed. The cars thinned out, and unlike in the city, where there was only a hint of winter, the woods were filled with snow. For the next two hours, as he drove north, then east, then north again, the landscape grew even whiter. But the roads were in pristine condition. In Toronto a few inches of snow could linger on side streets for days, but up north they took good care of their roads.

The only delay was a bad patch of construction on the highway just before he got to his destination. So it was almost three o'clock when he pulled into the parking lot of the Hardscrabble Café. Huge mounds of snow were piled up on all sides, somehow making the lot feel like an enclosed bunker.

Inside, Greene smelled the now-familiar scent of fresh-baked bread. He'd read that smell is the only fully formed sense we have when we're born, and one of the last senses to go before we die. Often he asked witnesses, trying to recall an event, if they could remember the smell of a place. He found that, like a song on a car radio when something unusual happens, a scent could fix a point in time in a witness's mind. It was surprisingly effective.

Throughout his long drive north Greene had been preoccupied with the phone call he'd gotten from Kennicott about McGill's fingerprints on Brace's million-dollar contract offer from Howard Peel.

Greene replayed in his mind his first meeting with McGill at her café back in December. He remembered how he'd watched her wipe down the tables. How surprised she was to see he was still there. How she reacted when he called her Mrs. Brace and identified himself.

"Shit," she'd said. The word seemed so out of place from this proper, highly disciplined woman. She'd stopped and looked him straight in the eye. "I guess I knew someone would show up sooner or later."

"I didn't want to talk to you in front of your customers, but we couldn't find a phone number for you," he'd said, and she'd put her hand on his shoulder: "I don't have a phone, Detective Greene."

"What if someone needs to reach you?" Greene had asked.

With an easy confidence McGill replied, "You can always send me a letter, Detective. It takes just two days from Toronto."

She'd smiled a warm smile and laughed a bit more. "You get stuck in that construction on the highway?" she'd asked.

"For half an hour," he'd told her, and she'd shaken her head and said, "It's been two years. They promised us it would take nine months. Doesn't help business, I can tell you that."

"I just have some questions for you," Greene had said, and with a nod McGill pulled out a chair and sat down. She reached into her apron and extracted a pack of cigarettes, crinkling the box.

Sarah McGill swears and she smokes, he'd thought. There was something surprisingly charming about it.

McGill pulled the plastic off the cigarette pack, opened the lid, and hit the bottom corner, trying to get a cigarette out. It wouldn't come. She put the pack down.

"Everyone up here smokes, Detective. I began a few months ago. Pretty strange, don't you think, for a sixty-year-old woman to start smoking for the first time in her life."

"Doesn't look like you're very good at it," he said, pointing to the pack.

McGill grinned. She held up her left hand. "Lost the finger when I was a kid. My dad took me on a tour of the mine and I poked around where I wasn't supposed to. I was too embarrassed as a teenager to hold a cigarette, so I was probably the only kid in town who didn't smoke." She shrugged and picked up the pack again. "I'll quit soon. What do you need to know?"

They spoke for about an hour. The story seemed pretty straight-forward. When Brace and McGill's oldest child, Kevin junior, was two-and-a-half years old, he was diagnosed with severe autism. For years they struggled as their son descended into his own silent world. When puberty hit, he became big and violent. By this time their daughters Amanda and Beatrice were eight and six years old, and it was no longer safe to have him at home. Children's Aid took him into care. The stress of it all soon ended their marriage. Brace moved in with Katherine Torn, and McGill decided to come to Haliburton.

"It's a funny thing, the north," she'd said. "If you grew up here, it gets under your skin. The schools were much better in the city, so the girls stayed with Kevin for a few years. It was a hard time, but it was the right decision. Kevin was a good father. And he always paid his alimony, as they used to call it back then. I bought this café and have been running it ever since."

"And Kevin junior?"

She just shrugged her shoulders, the sadness heavy on her. "It's so hard. He's such a gentle soul now. I try to see him once a week. Take him out for dinner."

"And your girls are doing well?"

She burst into a grin. "Both pregnant. Lucky me." She yawned. "It's a long day, Detective. I start making bread at five. Every day for the last twenty years."

Greene had driven home impressed with McGill's grace and forti-tude.

Today the café was even less crowded than the last time Greene was here. He spotted a table in the far corner and made his way through the customers, mostly men wearing thick sweaters and heavy boots. The snowmobilers had their black, one-piece suits on, the tops unzipped and rolled down to their waists.

"Sorry to keep yous waitin'," Charlene, the waitress who'd served Greene before, said. "Our fresh special today is spaghetti and meat-balls, with a sauce made from our own tomatoes."

Greene was hungry. He'd driven straight through after getting Kennicott's call. "Sounds good. How do you get your own tomatoes this time of year?"

The waitress looked at Greene over her little notepad. "Ms. McGill studied botany. Bottles them fresh in the fall."

Greene ate his meal slowly and waited patiently for the restaurant to clear out. The men looked much like those who'd been there the last time. Burly. Casual. Confident. And they were all white. Living in To-ronto, Greene wasn't used to being in a restaurant where there were only Caucasians.

Both times he'd walked into the café, there'd been a slight lull in the conversation. Small towns. An outsider really had nowhere to hide.

It was almost four o'clock when McGill finally emerged from the kitchen and joked with the last of the patrons.

"We're going to miss your food on Monday," a big man said as he rose from his table. Greene remembered the gregarious fellow from the last time he'd been here. "Wish you'd stay open," he said, sounding like a petulant child who didn't want to go to bed well past his bedtime.

"Jared, I deserve one day off a week," she said as she shooed him out the door.

"You must like my food, Detective, to drive all the way up here just for lunch," McGill said as she took a seat at his table after the last customer had gone. This time she sat beside him. She looked tired but relaxed. A dish towel lay casually on her left shoulder. Greene noticed that her hands were empty.

"The food's well worth the drive, Ms. McGill," Greene said. "What happened to the cigarettes?"

"Kicked the habit. Not many sixty-year-olds can say that. The damn things were ruining my taste buds."

"And stunting your growth."

She laughed her good, hearty chuckle. Greene waited until she stopped. "We found fingerprints of yours on something in Brace's apartment," he said, watching closely for her reaction.

McGill turned her head and looked squarely at Greene. Her eyes widened.

"They were in a contract," Greene explained. "Kevin was offered a job at another radio station. For a lot of money. Can I assume you know about this?"

McGill seemed to relax. She spread her hands out in front of her, like a cat comfortably stretching, stifling another yawn.

"I knew about the contract, Detective," she said. "I told you before, Kevin always paid support. It's a miracle, because he's useless with money, always has been."

"He showed the contract to you?"

Her smile widened. "Kevin never signs anything important unless I see it. I'm the businessperson in the family."

"When did he show it to you?"

"He would have sent it to me."

"Sent it?" Greene was confused.

"Mailed it, of course. Two days for a package to come from Toronto, one day if it's sent express."

"That's right. No phone. And I assume no fax machine."

McGill smiled and started to sing. "'No phone, no pool, no pets, I ain't got no cigarettes . . .' You old enough to remember that song, 'King of the Road'?"

"Roger Miller," Greene said. "My mother loved it."

McGill kept singing. "'Short but not too big around.' Sounds like me, Detective." She burst out laughing. "Kevin and I, we're both Luddites. No credit cards. No cell phones. It took me years before I even put a dishwasher in the café."

She turned her eyes from him to the uncleared dishes on his table. Greene saw her hand go to the towel over her shoulder.

"Do you remember when he mailed the contract up to you?"

"That's easy," she said. "The first of every month he sends me my monthly check and anything else he wants me to read or help him with. I would have got it in early December and mailed it back the next day." She began to rise up from her chair. The towel was in her hand now. "I don't want to be rude, Detective, but I still have a lot of cleaning up to do."

"One last question," Greene asked as he stood up. He'd left a very good tip under the far side of his plate. "What'd you tell him about the contract?"

She laughed. Her hearty chuckle reverberated around the empty room. "Detective, I might be old-fashioned, but I'm not an idiot. I told him, 'Sign the damn thing, just skip the limo so you don't get fat.'"

32

Albert Fernandez paced back and forth in his office, which meant he took two steps, turned, and took two steps back in the other direction. It was absurd. Here he was working on the biggest case in the country and his office was no bigger than a prison cell. Smaller, probably, he thought, when you consider all the space the five evidence boxes took up, dominating the north wall.

He stopped and stared at the boxes. Each was filled with thirty or forty files. He'd handwritten the labels to each and handwritten an index for every box.

It was not that Fernandez was afraid of computers. He was very good with them. But when it came down to the final preparation of a case, he had to touch every document, organize every file, and sweat every detail by hand. That way, when he got to court, he knew exactly where everything was.

He went back to his desk, where a simple black binder sat alone. A label identified it as TRIAL BINDER—BRACE. He opened it to the first page. He'd written the heading "Key Facts," underlined it, and listed them:

- Jurisdiction—85A Front Street—City of Toronto
- Identity—Kevin Brace—Age 63
- Condo 12A—one front door—no other exits, no forced entry

- December 17, 5:29 a.m. Brace meets Mr. Singh at the door
- Blood on his hands
- Torn's body in bathtub—one stab wound
- No defensive wounds to victim
- Bloody knife hidden in kitchen
- No alibi
- No other suspects
- Confession
- Slam dunk

Fernandez smiled when he read the last phrase—slam dunk. It was uncharacteristically flippant, his own private joke. He closed the binder, got up, and started to pace again. One step, two steps, turn, one step, two steps, turn.

Ever since he'd gotten the Brace case, he'd stayed late at the office. It had been hard on Marissa. Last week, when the January phone bill arrived and Fernandez saw that she'd spent almost four hundred dollars calling her family back in Chile, they'd had their first big fight. She'd ended up in tears, saying she couldn't stand how cold it was in Canada, that she had no friends or family here, and she threatened to go home.

"Come on, Marissa," he'd said once he thought things had calmed down. "Let's go to bed and make it better."

"Bed, bed. With you it's always bed," she'd said, and slammed the bedroom door in his face.

For the next five nights he slept on the couch. The sixth day he brought home a very long, very ugly down-filled coat and a pair of equally ugly boots. "You'll like the winter much better if you stop worrying about how you look and just keep warm," he told her.

She took the coat grudgingly.

"Look in the pocket," he said.

She reached in and pulled out an airplane ticket.

"I'm sending you home for a month in March," he told her. "When you come back, the winter will be over."

Marissa grabbed the ticket from his hand and ran back into the bedroom. Fernandez heard her talking excitedly on the phone for the next half hour. At last she emerged from their bedroom wearing only a towel and a big smile.

Tomorrow was Valentine's Day, and he'd promised to be home by eight. He'd planned the whole evening. Dinner at a Mexican restaurant on Wellington Street; then he'd take her to a new gelato place down the block. It featured homemade South American flavors. Guanabana and lulo were her favorites. They'd be home by ten.

Yes. Fernandez smiled. Get to bed early with Marissa, that sounded like a very good idea.

As he sat back down at his desk, he was startled by a quiet knock on his door. The night watchman had been by ten minutes ago and Fernandez hadn't heard anyone else come in. "Who is it?"

"*Hola,*" a familiar voice whispered. The door opened slowly, and Marissa was standing in the dimly lit hall wearing the down coat and the ugly boots.

"What are you doing—"

"Shhh," she said, coming inside and closing the door behind her, lowering the light in the small room.

"How did you—"

"Don't get up. I just spoke to the guard," she said as she walked around his desk.

"What did you tell him?"

"I said, 'Excuse me, sir. I am here bringing my husband some nourishment because he work so late.'" She turned his chair toward her.

"He *works* late," Fernandez said. "And the word isn't 'nourishment,' it's 'food' . . ."

"No. Nourishment," she said as she opened her coat. Even in the near darkness, Fernandez could see that she was naked underneath. "I've been studying my nouns," she said as she straddled him and brought his head to her breast. "This is nourishment, no?"

Happy Valentine's Day one day early, Fernandez thought as he felt Marissa reach down and undo his belt, then lower his zipper. As he slid inside her, his government-issue chair began to squeak as it rolled backward.

Just then he heard an outer door open. The sound came from the side entrance the Crowns used at night.

"Here's the latest and greatest," a deep male voice said. It was Phil Cutter. What was he doing at the office so late?

Fernandez put his mouth to Marissa's ear. "Shhh . . . ," he whispered. She nodded her head, but he couldn't tell if she was saying yes or if it was just part of her rhythmic rocking on top of him.

"Let me see that." This second voice was softer, female. It was Barb Gild, Cutter's constant companion.

Marissa's rhythm was increasing as Fernandez heard Cutter and Gild's footsteps draw nearer. She lowered his head to her breast again and buried it there.

"Brace—he thinks he's so damn smart," Cutter said. His laugh pierced the empty office space. They were almost right outside the door.

Fernandez held his breath. He spread his feet wide and held tight to the floor, trying to stop the old chair from squeaking and to slow Marissa down. But she was lost in her movements.

"What's he written this time?" Gild said. The two had stopped to look at something right on his doorstep. Marissa squeezed the back of his head. He grasped her as tight as he could. Cutter and Gild must be able to hear them.

But Cutter started to laugh. "This is fantastic," he said.

Fernandez heard their footsteps start up again, moving down the hall. "Take a look, Barb . . . ," Cutter said. Their voices were quickly receding. Fernandez strained to hear, but now Marissa had her hands over his ears as she moved his mouth to her other breast.

"If Parish ever found out we had this . . ." Cutter's voice was disappearing.

Fernandez tried to pull back from Marissa to hear better, but their voices had faded, covered by the rumble of the photocopy machine across from Gild's office.

"What is wrong?" Marissa whispered, bending down to his ear.

That's what I'm wondering, he thought. What are Cutter and Gild up to?

"Poor Albert," she said, stroking his hair. "Too much working."

Marissa's touch on his face brought him back to her. Soon after they were married, it became apparent to Fernandez that although he was a virgin when they exchanged their vows, she was sexually experienced. It had been unspoken between them, but very quickly she became the teacher and he the willing pupil.

And now he'd been distracted. He'd disappointed her.

But she didn't look upset. She looked determined.

"Too much work," he said.

"No, no," she said, reaching back down to take him in her hand. "Not enough nourishment."

33

The foul odor was the first thing Ari Greene noticed as he walked past the bull pen—the big holding cell for male prisoners in the bowels of Old City Hall court. A hundred and fifty men, at least half of them who hadn't had a shower for days, most wearing orange jumpsuits, shuffling around on the cement floor. The few men in street clothes would have been picked up the night before and would have slept at whatever police division they'd been taken to before being brought to the Hall for their bail hearings. The rest would have come from the Don or one of the suburban jails.

Greene made a point of not stopping or looking in. As far as any of the prisoners inside the bull pen were concerned, he'd be just another cop walking on the free side of the bars.

There was a small, windowless room in back with a steel table and two chairs, all bolted to the floor. This was the "P.C." interview room. Protective custody was for prisoners who needed to be kept apart from the general population for their own safety—usually guys charged with sex crimes against children and, as the cops liked to joke, police constables, P.C.'s. Unlike the glassed-in gallery, where groups of prisoners met with their lawyers and had to lean down and yell through little screens to be heard, this room was private.

Greene took the seat farthest from the door and waited patiently. It took about ten minutes for Fraser Dent to be led in.

Greene had seen Dent three times in this room since the night they'd met at the Salvation Army. Dent nodded quietly at Greene. He wore his orange jumpsuit like a pair of comfortable old pajamas. On his feet he had a pair of prison-issue blue running shoes, the back stomped down for more comfort. Just like all the real cons.

The guard pulled out his keys. Hearing the jangling metal, Dent turned his back and waited patiently while his handcuffs were taken off.

After the guard left, Dent turned to Greene and shrugged his shoulders. He looked like a man who'd been in the jail for a few weeks. His stringy, clownlike hair was greasy, his face roughly shaven, and his fingernails bitten down. His light blue eyes were empty.

"Good morning, Detective," he said in a grumpy voice.

"How ya doing, Mr. Dent?" Greene said. He'd risen from his seat to greet Dent when he came in. Now he sat down and pulled out a pair of cigarettes from inside his jacket.

"Could be worse," Dent said. He sat on the facing metal seat and looked down. "I got Brace and me moved up to the fifth floor, hospital wing. Gets us away from all the punks and the noise. It's no big deal to clean out a few bedpans. They got a TV and the sports channel. The bloody Leafs, eh?"

Greene smiled. In early January, the Leafs had gone on an improbable run, beating clubs well above them in the standings and climbing back into the play-off race. The city had been energized by the team, the radio talk-show programs filled with optimistic chatter from phone-in fans who claimed they "bled blue and white." Greene's father had even made noises about actually going to a game.

Fat chance.

It didn't matter. Predictably, in mid-January the team had returned to its losing ways, causing Greene's father no end of heartburn, and all talk of going to see a live game faded. His dad's newest theory for the team's travails was that the goalie was no good, too young, and they needed to bring in a veteran.

"A team from Tampa and a team from Carolina can win the Stanley Cup," he'd said in frustration a few nights earlier after the Leafs lost for the fourth time in a row. "They don't even have skating rinks down there."

"Dad, give it up," Greene said. "The Leafs haven't won since 1967."

"I know, I know," his father had said. "I'm waiting. I know how to wait for things."

"My dad's a big-time Leafs fan," Greene said as he passed over some matches to Dent. "They're driving him nuts."

"That coach has got to go," Dent said. "You see that last night? Two minutes left in the game and he's got his third-line center out taking the face-off."

Greene passed over his Styrofoam cup for Dent to use as an ashtray. He'd intentionally left a thin layer of water on the bottom. Dent lit up and took a few deep drags. Greene waited patiently.

"Brace still hasn't said a damn thing," Dent said, blowing the smoke to the side. He looked over at the wall to his left. "Not one fucking word. At first it was spooky, but now I'm used to it. I'm not sure what I'd do if he started to talk."

"He still write notes?" Greene asked.

"Yeah. In his book. He's got us all trained. He'll write us little notes. And when we play bridge, he'll just make his hand signs."

"He ask you anything about yourself?"

"Doesn't really have to. I took your advice, Detective. I just talk about myself whenever I feel like it. It's like having my own therapist, 24/7. I'm even lying down in my bunk half the time. Like with the real live shrinks the bank used to send me to." Dent gave a deep, guttural laugh that ended when he started to cough. "Before everything went to rat shit."

"And you defrauded them of half a million bucks."

"Whatever," Dent said. He took a drag on the cigarette.

"What's he read? Newspapers?"

"Devours them. Every word on every page. Does the crosswords in bloody pen."

"Any books?"

"Whatever comes around on the cart. Mysteries, thrillers, biographies. Doesn't seem to matter to him."

"Anything else?"

"That's it, man. Easiest cell mate I've ever had."

Greene sat back in his chair and looked Dent straight in the eye. Dent kept his eyes turned to the left. Finally drawn in by the silence, he looked over at Greene but then quickly looked down. He tossed his half-smoked cigarette on the concrete floor and twisted it under the heel of his shoe. It made a squeaking noise on the cement floor.

"Dent, you're a smart guy. Why do you think he's clammed up?"

Dent picked up the cigarette butt and rubbed it flat on the bottom of his shoe. "Hard to say," he said at last.

Greene could sense Dent being protective of his cell mate. "Why don't you try?"

"I remember when he was on the radio—boy, could he talk. Maybe he got tired of talking."

"That's an original theory," Greene said.

Dent shrugged. He rolled up his left pant leg and slid the butt into his gray sock along with the other, fresh cigarette. "He seems happy enough."

"He didn't mention anything about his case?"

"He wrote that his judicial pretrial's this afternoon. That why we're talking now?"

"He tell you Summers is the judge?"

Dent's body tensed. "Fucking Summers," he said. "Mr. Naval Academy. I hate that judge. He gave me six months once for stealing some aspirin from a Shoppers Drug Mart."

Greene nodded. "That the time a young clerk followed you and you pushed him through a glass door?"

"Yeah, whatever," Dent said. "Summers is a prick."

"We know Brace's lawyer visits him. Anyone else?"

Dent shook his head.

"He communicate with anyone else?"

"Just the other two guys we play bridge with and Mr. Buzz, the best guard in the Don. He got our bridge partners moved up to the fifth for us. Now he's up there too. Says he's our bodyguard."

"Tell me about the bridge partners."

Dent shrugged. "No big deal. One's an old Jamaican guy waiting for his murder trial. The other's an old native guy. Says he was a schoolteacher—wife and kids, the whole bit, till he started drinking again."

"What do they say about Brace?"

Dent shrugged. "He's a damn good bridge player."

"The prelim will be in May," Greene said, referring to the preliminary inquiry, the judicial hearing that precedes the trial.

Dent rubbed his hands over his face. "Look, Detective, now I'm in the hospital ward, I'll stick with this gig through the play-offs. That should be about the end of May. But that's it. Once hockey is over, I'm out of the Don."

"Let's hope Brace starts talking before then." Greene reached into his pocket and passed over a packet of mints.

"Let's hope the Leafs somehow get into the play-offs," Dent said. He dug out a handful of mints and popped them into his mouth. The others disappeared up his sleeve. He stood up and kicked the door in a well-worn spot. "That guard better hitch me up quick," he said. "Guys'll start to wonder if I'm out too long."

Greene stood up. A guard opened the door, and Dent, as if on cue, turned and put his arms behind him. Greene heard the metal clicking sound of the cuffs being unlocked, then the slow crunch of the cuffs being tightened, metal teeth on metal teeth.

It was an awful noise, much worse than fingers on a blackboard. It always made Greene wince.

34

Ever since Brace's arrest, Daniel Kennicott had tuned in to the new morning show to hear how Donald Dundas handled what must have been a very touchy situation. The first few days after the arrest, the show just carried on using Dundas as the substitute host. Over the Christmas holidays it disappeared, replaced by insipid local programming from regional stations. In January the show was back with a new name—*Morning Has Broken*—with Dundas installed as the permanent host. There wasn't a word said about Kevin Brace sitting in the Don Jail, charged with first-degree murder.

It reminded Kennicott of the pigs in the book *Animal Farm*, sneaking out at night to the signs, constantly erasing the rules. Kevin Brace, like Snowball in George Orwell's novel, had been wiped clean from the history books.

Dundas was a competent host. He could speak knowledgeably with people on a number of topics, but his interviews didn't have the depth Brace had brought to the airwaves. His humor was too nice, and he lacked Brace's sharp tongue. And his voice, warm and sweet, lacked the weight, the gravitas, of Brace's smoke-seasoned baritone.

After spending almost two months tracing Brace's life, Kennicott had a good idea how Dundas would spend his day. The show ended at 10:00 a.m. Toronto time. It was broadcast live to Atlantic Canada at nine and was tape-delayed one hour as it went west across the country.

The host spent the next hour taping promo pieces for upcoming shows and attending the daily story meeting for the next day's show. He couldn't go far during that one-hour delay in case some news broke and they had to redo something live for the central region—Ontario and Quebec. By eleven, though, he was essentially done.

That's why, just before eleven in the morning, Kennicott was walking slowly around the broadcast building. There were three different exit doors, which made guessing which one Dundas would come out of a problem. The north exit gave onto Wellington Street, a busy thoroughfare. Not likely that the aesthetically minded Dundas would want to come out that door. The west door faced a less-crowded side street with a big Starbucks on the other side. Kennicott noticed a lot of the company employees trooping out this door and heading zombielike for their doses of caffeine. "Time for some four-bucks," he overheard one of them say.

He couldn't see Dundas going to Starbucks. The man was always doing nostalgic pieces about things like small-town general stores. He liked championing the "little people." On the south side of the building, there was a friendly-looking coffee shop with a collection of antique teapots in the window. That's it, Kennicott thought. He went inside and found a seat near the back. He took a *Globe and Mail* from a pile beside the condiments table and opened it, keeping an eye on the south door.

A few minutes after eleven Dundas strolled in, wearing a long, dull overcoat, big brown mittens, and what looked like a hand-sewn toque. He carried a beat-up old leather briefcase in his left hand. His round eyeglasses fogged up as soon as he came through the door, and he took them off and waved them in the air. He was alone. Kennicott watched him turn and head toward the take-out counter, still shaking his specs.

Perfect. Kennicott followed him in line, tucking *The Globe and Mail* under his arm.

"Good morning, Mrs. Nguyen," Dundas said to the short Asian woman behind the counter when he got to the front, pronouncing her Vietnamese name the proper way—with the g silent.

"Mr. Dundas. Happy Valentine Day." She pronounced the V in "Valentine" like a B. "Green tea today?"

"A pot, please," he said, lifting his briefcase. "I stay. Student essays to mark."

Kennicott stepped out of the line and backed up. He watched Dundas take a seat at a corner table, put his teapot down, open his briefcase, and pull out some papers. He waited until Dundas was hunched over reading before he walked across and sat down on the other side of the table.

"Excuse me," Dundas said without looking up. "If you don't mind, I need some privacy . . ." His voice trailed off as he lifted his head and recognized Kennicott.

"Good morning, Mr. Dundas."

"Hello, Officer Kennicott." Dundas kept his voice low. "After that first interview, my lawyer was in touch with Detective Greene. We've informed him that I don't wish to make any further statements."

"I know that," Kennicott said.

"So?"

"There's nothing to prevent us from continuing our investigation."

Dundas nodded, as if showing Kennicott that he didn't have to say anything.

"Nothing to prevent us from talking to you, even if you don't want to talk back," Kennicott said.

"I guess not," Dundas said with an exaggerated frown. He reached across his papers and picked up the small porcelain teapot and teacup and brought them near him, like a boy lining up his toy soldiers.

"I spoke to Howard Peel yesterday," Kennicott said.

Dundas eyed Kennicott. "You can talk to me about anything you want. I don't intend to respond."

"Peel didn't want to talk to me at first either. But after I told him some things I'd found out, he changed his mind."

Kennicott watched Dundas carefully. Dundas lifted the lid of the teapot to look in. A puff of steam came up and fogged his glasses again. Kennicott smelled a hint of jasmine. Dundas hadn't said anything, but that didn't matter. He'd stopped objecting to being questioned, and that was the first step.

"You knew about the contract Peel offered Brace, didn't you?" Kennicott asked.

Dundas took his glasses off and cleaned them with his sweater.

"A million dollars, thirty-six weeks' work a year, limousine service," Kennicott said. "No shows on Mondays."

"I don't want to be rude, but I have all these papers to mark." He motioned to the pile in front of him.

Kennicott didn't let up. "Peel told me that Brace wanted to sign, but Katherine was the problem. Sounds like Katherine had a lot of problems."

Dundas furrowed his brow. When he did that, he didn't look so young.

"Peel said that Katherine wanted to be a radio producer. Right?"

Dundas was done fiddling with his teapot. Now his hands were at his sides, his shoulders slumped.

Time to go in for the kill, Kennicott thought. "Peel said she was training with a 'friend' at his home studio. That's why, back in December, when Detective Greene asked you if Katherine had ever been at your house, you terminated the interview." Kennicott toughened up his voice. "Isn't it, Dundas?"

Dundas pursed his lips.

"I checked back into the archives of *The Dawn Treader*," Kennicott said. "Last April, Brace interviewed you for twenty minutes about the radio production studio you had in your house, didn't he?"

Dundas fiddled again with his teacup. "Yes," he said at last.

Good, Kennicott thought. I've got him talking.

Dundas lifted the little teapot and a teaspoon and poured the tea onto the spoon so it wouldn't spill down the spout.

"And that's how it started. First you gave Torn radio production lessons," Kennicott said.

Dundas's hand slipped, and tea spilled over the rim of the cup onto the saucer. He gave an exaggerated exhalation.

"It's no secret," Dundas said, "that I have a home studio. I take my journalism class there once a term."

Better, Kennicott thought. Dundas has progressed to whole sentences. But he'd dodged the question.

"Listen, Mr. Dundas. I've looked at the videotapes from the condominium lobby. Katherine was very patterned. Tuesdays, Wednesdays, and Fridays she left just after ten and was at the stables for her riding lesson by eleven. But Thursday mornings she went somewhere at eight."

"And so you're wondering where she went," Dundas said, unprompted.

"We both know, don't we? I checked with the radio station—Thursday was the one day you were *not* available to do backup for Brace."

Dundas dropped the metal spoon, and it clanged off the corner of the saucer.

"It's not what you think," he said.

It's not what you think. Kennicott recalled that Peel had used the exact same phrase. "And what do I think?"

"I wasn't having an affair with Katherine." Dundas met Kennicott's eyes and held them for the first time since he had sat down. Kennicott could see the subtle wrinkle lines around the man's eyes, which were usually masked by his fair complexion. He'd once read that crow's-feet around the eyes were the trick carnival hucksters used when guessing people's ages. He could see why. Up close Dundas looked older, tired, and scared.

"You know, after you walked out of our interview, Detective Greene told me that in all his years on the homicide squad, only four other people had stopped an interview during an investigation. And guess what?"

"Why don't you just tell me."

"All four were eventually charged and convicted."

"Are you saying I'm a suspect?"

"Getting pretty darn close. You were sleeping with your boss's wife and—"

"Stop it," Dundas said, straightening his backbone. "I told you I wasn't having an affair. It's the truth. Hook me up to one of those machines if you want."

"What were you two doing, drinking tea?"

"No," Dundas said. He was angry now. He closed his eyes, clearly weighing whether he should keep talking or not. Kennicott could almost hear him explaining to his lawyer hours from now: "But you don't understand, I had no choice."

Dundas reached for his teacup. He took a long sip. Kennicott waited. "Okay," he said finally, "I saw her on Thursday mornings."

"Why?"

"Katherine had problems. The biggest one was self-confidence. She needed a job."

Dundas tried to lift the teacup again, but his hands were shaking. He turned to Kennicott like a man resigned to his fate.

"I knew about the contract," Dundas said, speaking rapidly, as if by saying the words fast, he could get over his discomfort quicker. "Kevin asked me to train Katherine in radio production as a personal favor. It was his idea."

This was exactly what Peel had said. That Brace knew all about Peel's seeing his wife too. Kennicott decided to switch tactics. Be nice. Understanding. "So that's why he went along with your not being his substitute host on Thursdays."

Dundas just nodded.

Then it hit Kennicott. Dundas was telling the truth. He wasn't afraid of Brace. He was afraid for his job.

"I assume this is something management didn't know anything about," Kennicott said.

"I don't think they'd be too pleased that I was helping their star host get a job with a competitor. Kevin wanted to sign the contract. The plan was I'd train Katherine, then she'd have the confidence to take a weekend production job." He looked around the small café again to make sure they were alone. "If they found out, I'd be fired. That would be it for my career. All because I was trying to help a friend."

"Help a friend, and then get his job," Kennicott said.

Dundas whipped off his glasses and glared at Kennicott. He looked as if he wanted to hit him. Good, Kennicott thought. When people get mad, they really talk.

"I didn't know any of this was going to happen," he said through clenched teeth.

"But when it did, you were more interested in your job than in assisting a first-degree murder investigation. Katherine dead. Brace in prison facing twenty-five years. And you won't even give us a statement. All so you can protect your new job. Or should I say Brace's old job?"

Dundas wouldn't meet his eyes.

Kennicott poked his finger at the papers Dundas was marking. "Stab the guy who gave you your first job in radio right in the back. Do you teach that in Journalism Ethics 101?"

Kennicott pulled back his chair and stood.

Dundas looked up at him like a lost child.

"Kevin was desperate to get her to stop the booze. She would be clean for a while, but then . . ."

Kennicott moved to the chair beside Dundas and sat down. He was done being the man's worst nightmare. Time to be his best friend.

Dundas leaned his head, as if sheltered by Kennicott's presence. "The thing with Katherine, when she got angry, she was out of control." Dundas reached down and rolled up the left sleeve of his sweater.

Kennicott saw a wide, ugly scar on his forearm. It looked fairly fresh, and deep enough to last a long time.

"She did this to me last time we were together," Dundas said. He was whispering now. He closed his eyes. "I'll make the statement," he said. "But that's all I can tell you."

That will be more than enough, Kennicott thought as he stared at Dundas's arm. The words he'd just used, "She did this to me," were similar to the ones Howard Peel used yesterday, standing in the cold outside the ski chalet.

35

Detective Greene watched Albert Fernandez put a yellow pad on the table while Dr. Torn sipped his double espresso. It was just past eleven in the morning, and they were at a high-gloss Italian restaurant on Bay Street. Torn had come down to meet with them before the judicial pre-trial with Judge Summers, which Fernandez was attending that afternoon. Torn had made apologies for his wife, who was down in the States at some riding competition.

Torn had wanted to get away from the cloying atmosphere of the Victim Services office, so Greene had brought them here. The restaurant was his own little oasis in the downtown sea of noisy food courts and cheap fast-food places. Fernandez was also drinking espresso, and Greene was sipping white tea.

"Apologies for Detective Greene," Fernandez said, pulling out his pen. "The only homicide detective I've ever met who doesn't drink coffee."

Torn shook his head in mock disgust. "That true, Detective?"

"Only tried it once," Greene said.

"Must have been for a woman," Torn said, laughing for the first time since Greene had met him.

Greene broke out into a bit of a smile. "I was living in France at the time, so at least it was good coffee."

It was almost twenty years ago. Chief Hap Charlton had sent him on a special assignment, and when it was over Greene took a leave from the force for a year. That was pretty standard for someone who'd almost gotten killed in the line of duty.

Greene had gone to Europe. Went to all the places his school friends got to see when they were nineteen, not thirty-two. In late October he ended up in a small town in the south of France, just west of Nice. One cool night he went to the movies and left with the *ouvreuse*—the woman who tore your tickets as you walked into the theater.

Françoise was so French that she'd never left the country, except for the occasional day trip across the border to the Italian towns on the coast. Nice, she liked to remind Greene, was really an Italian city. Their second night together they went to a café, and when he ordered tea instead of coffee, she laughed. The next morning she brewed her own espresso and insisted he try it. He gagged on the dark liquid. His first and last cup of coffee.

Her day job was as a graphic artist, but her real passion was fixing cars. On the weekends the two of them would spend hours pulling engines out of old-model Peugeots and touring the hilly backcountry, away from the pretension of the Côte d'Azur.

"I had my first cup of coffee in Italy, during the war," Torn said. "Loved it."

Greene nodded. "How are your horses?" he asked.

"Frisky as hell," Torn said. "They like it good and cold."

"I understand Katherine liked to ride," Fernandez said, trying to jump into the conversation.

Torn gave Fernandez a look that seemed to say, Quit the cutesy segues into talking about my daughter. "Kate was a natural rider," he said, taking another sip. "You need two things to be good on a horse—balance and hand coordination. She was blessed with both. Like her mother."

"I know this is very difficult for your family," Fernandez said, taking a sip of his own espresso.

"Really?" Torn said. "How do you know that?"

"Surely for you and your wife the death of your only—"

Torn's hand came down on the table hard, making a loud, thumping noise that rattled around the chrome-plated table. A few young waiters turned to look.

"Don't 'surely' me, Fernandez. And quit telling me how difficult this is for my family." Torn's face was growing red with anger, making his blue eyes pop out. "I don't want someone telling us how we're surely supposed to feel about Kate dying."

Fernandez nodded. He looked over at Greene. Confused.

Torn reached into his pocket. "Look, here's my parking chit. Can you guys take care of it for me?" He stood up to leave.

Greene stood up immediately. Fernandez scrambled to his feet and reached for the receipt. "Dr. Torn," he said, taking the receipt, "I'll pay for it myself." He reached into his coat pocket and pulled out his wallet.

Torn teetered a bit on his feet, arms crossed in front of his chest. Fernandez handed over thirty dollars. Torn shook his head and sat down, stuffing the money into his front pocket.

"The judicial pretrial is this afternoon," Fernandez said, sitting. "I'll meet with the defense counsel in the judge's office. He's going to push us hard to take a plea to something less than first-degree murder. Second degree, even manslaughter. We're not going to budge."

Fernandez looked over at Greene, satisfied with himself. Usually families of victims hated it when Crowns were forced to plea-bargain their cases down to lesser charges.

"You decided without asking us?" Torn demanded. He glared at Fernandez. Then at Greene. "You want to win big, don't you?"

"The Crown doesn't win or lose," Fernandez said. "We have a very strong case."

"What's the point? The man is sixty-something years old."

"Sixty-three," Greene said, getting back into the conversation. He could see this was going off the rails. "You don't want to put your wife through a trial, I'm sure."

"If he pleads to second degree, he gets ten or so years, right?"

"Ten's the minimum. At his age, he might get eleven or twelve," Fernandez said.

"That's my point," Torn said. His voice was rising again, echoing around the empty restaurant. "We lived through this once with Kate. All the publicity. It was horrible."

Fernandez wrinkled his brow.

"When Brace and Katherine first became involved, it was big news," Greene explained to Fernandez.

"Kevin was the country's top broadcaster. His happy family, their pictures splashed over all the magazine covers," Torn said. "Then he runs off with a receptionist who worked for his book publisher. Kate's tall. Beautiful. Press made her into the home wrecker from hell."

Torn stood up. It was clear he wasn't going to sit down again.

"I refused to talk to Kevin at first," he said. "But then I learned that when their boy was taken away, he took the girls in and raised them well. That counts in my book. He was good for Kate. Gwen Harden, the old goat who was her riding instructor, said Brace was the only husband who actually watched her when she rode in competitions. Not like those other guys, who spend half the time on their cell phones."

"Doctor, we appreciate your input," Fernandez said. He was on his feet now too. So was Greene.

"She was something to watch on a horse. I saw it myself. He couldn't take his eyes off her. I don't know how she ended up dying. But you want to send Brace to jail for twenty-five years? I've seen enough death in my life. That police chief of yours wants to make Kevin his poster boy for domestic assault. Shake the taxpayers down for more money. Make a deal today, or my wife and I are taking our horses to West Virginia. I'm not putting her through all this again."

Torn whirled and walked out of the restaurant. Fernandez looked stunned.

Greene reached down and tugged the parking receipt from between his fingers. "Give it to me," he said. "I can expense it."

Fernandez slowly released the thick paper.

"Can you make a deal?" Greene asked.

"My hands are tied. Orders from on high," Fernandez said, shaking his head. "Torn's right. They want Brace delivered on a platter. Got a hunch my career prosecuting homicides depends on it."

Greene studied the young prosecutor carefully.

"Did you notice how he kept talking about his daughter dying?" Fernandez said.

"As opposed to being killed or murdered," Greene said, handing him thirty dollars.

"Dr. Torn is not what you'd expect, is he, Detective?"

"I wouldn't say that," Greene replied.

"Why not?" Fernandez asked. He looked very curious.

"Because," Greene said, slipping the parking receipt into his wallet, "the longer you do this job, the more you stop anticipating how people will react to a death in the family."

36

Good afternoon, Counsel," Judge Summers said to Fernandez and Parish as he ushered them into his chambers. It was exactly 1:30. Summers would want to be finished by 2:00. Parish had arrived about ten seconds earlier. "Time to get down to work," Summers said as he slipped on his reading glasses and picked up his initialed Waterman pen. "Let's start with all these darn forms." He opened a red file in the middle of his desk. "More paperwork these days than in the navy, for goodness' sake."

Summers went through a series of pedantic questions.

"Is the identity of the accused an issue?"

"No," Parish said.

"Is the jurisdiction of the alleged crime an issue?"

"No," Parish said again.

"Is the accused mentally competent to stand trial?"

"Yes," Parish said.

With each answer the judge carefully ticked off a box on his form. These questions were just the warm-up for the harder stuff. After a few more perfunctory questions Summers looked over his reading glasses at Fernandez.

"Is the Crown alleging motive?" he asked in a neutral tone, as if he were asking how to spell someone's name. This was the money question.

"The Crown has no obligation to prove motive," Fernandez said.

"I know the law, Mr. Fernandez." Summers took off his reading glasses. "And I know juries. They want two questions answered: how and why. One stab. How can you prove intent with just one stab? Without the why, you'll be lucky to get them to convict on manslaughter."

This must be a classic Summers pretrial, Fernandez thought. The moment he sensed a crack on either side, he pounced. Summers was known to yell, scream, cajole, and swear at even the most senior lawyers, Crown or defense, it didn't matter. Once he'd weakened you, he'd go after the other side. Then, with both of you on your knees, he'd force a deal. Anything to settle a case.

"We're still investigating the issue of motive," Fernandez said.

"Huh," Summers snorted, as if he'd just swallowed a fly. "It's a domestic homicide. Forget about this being Kevin Brace, much-beloved broadcaster. These things are a dime a dozen. Motive 101—he's sixteen years older. Maybe his machinery is no longer quite up to snuff, finds her with a younger man. O. J. Simpson. Simple. I've seen it fifty, maybe a hundred times."

"That's certainly a possibility," Fernandez said. "But we have no proof of any such motive at this time."

Summers gave a big scowl. "Anything else for motive? Think he was after her insurance money, so he stabbed her in the bathtub, hoping to make it look like an accident?"

"We are not alleging that, Your Honor," Fernandez said. When Summers was pouring it on like this, if you showed any sign of backing down you were in trouble. "And we do have Mr. Brace's confession."

"I read that, Mr. Fernandez." Summers liked to let you know that he'd done his homework. He looked over at Parish and held her gaze. "You mean the utterance he made to the old Indian newspaper guy?"

"Yes," Fernandez said.

Summers nodded, and for the first time since they'd come into his chambers, he was quiet. Finally he looked away from Parish and glanced at the clock on the wall. It was 1:50. Ten minutes to go, Fernandez thought.

Taking a deep breath, Summers turned back to Parish. Like a hungry real estate agent determined to close a big house deal, he'd go back and forth from buyer to seller, probing, until he got the concessions he needed to narrow the gap.

"Ms. Parish." Summers put his glasses on again. "I'm sure your client would plead to manslaughter in a heartbeat." He was not so much asking Parish as telling her. "No record, crime of passion, only one stab wound—sounds like about five, maybe seven years to me. He'd be a prime candidate for early remission at one-third time. So he'd do another two years—most of it at one of those farms with a golf course. Brace likes to golf, doesn't he?"

Summers was selling the deal. Trying to move the goalposts closer together.

"Didn't your client say anything about provocation? You know, a younger man, something like that?"

"I'm afraid not, Your Honor," Parish said.

Summers shook his head. "That's a damn shame."

"If the Crown made an offer for manslaughter," Parish said, "I'd be glad to take it to my client. And I emphasize the 'if.'" It was a smart move by Parish. She was throwing it back to him.

Summers looked at Fernandez. He raised an eyebrow, zeroing in.

"Mr. Fernandez, can we expect an offer? The Crown, of course, could ask for much more time. Ten, twelve years. I'm sure you'd furnish me with a compelling victim-impact statement from the family. She was an only child, was she not?"

"Yes, she was, Your Honor," Fernandez said. "But we'd never agree to manslaughter. I'd withdraw the charge before I took a plea to that." Fernandez was careful not to shut the door on a plea to second degree. It was unspoken, but he knew everyone got it.

"Uh-uh," Summers said, raising a finger at Fernandez. "There's one word a criminal lawyer must never use: 'never.' A trial is like a boat in high seas. You never know which way the currents will take it."

Fernandez smiled. "I agree, Your Honor," he said. It was always important to let Summers have the last word. "We will be proceeding with the charge of first-degree murder."

Summers seemed to take this in. Then he exploded. He slammed his fist down on the red file. "Goddamn it, you two. This is not some poker game. A woman is dead, her husband in jail. These are real people, not some political football. Mr. Fernandez, without motive, you don't have a chance for first-degree murder. First degree, I remind you, is a planned and deliberate killing. And, Ms. Parish, the poor woman is dead, naked in the bathtub. The bloody knife is hidden in his kitchen. That's no manslaughter. Manslaughter, I remind you, is a killing without intent."

The judge sat back in his chair. "This is a second-degree murder, minimum ten years without parole. A lot better than twenty-five years without parole for a first. Mr. Fernandez, you ask for twelve or thirteen years, and, Ms. Parish, you ask for the minimum ten."

Summers stood up gruffly and grabbed his file. "I want you both back here in a week, and I want this thing settled. No way am I giving up a courtroom for a month for a useless preliminary inquiry. I'll see you both in seven days."

Fernandez stood up. "Thank you very much, Your Honor," he said. It was one minute to two.

"Thank you too, sir," Parish said.

Outside in the hallway Fernandez looked at Parish. "That's about what I was expecting," he said.

Parish laughed. "I've seen him much worse."

They both knew they'd come back in a week with nothing new to report and that Summers would put on another show. It would be futile. Clearly, they were going to trial.

37

Nancy Parish rushed into her office and threw her coat onto one of the two client chairs facing her desk. Without breaking stride, she sank into the chair behind her desk, tossed her briefcase onto the floor, and with one hand tapped her phone to call her voice mail while with the other she flicked on her computer and opened her e-mail.

"You have eighteen new messages," her voice mail told her. She'd received thirty-two new e-mails.

"Would you all just fucking leave me alone," she muttered as she unhitched her cell phone and put it in its charger on the desk. There's a cartoon, she thought as she kicked her salt-stained boots under the desk. A woman in a business suit, all dressed up—string of pearls, leather briefcase, the works—is sitting in hell. Fires burn all around; a bunch of little red devils prod her with pitchforks. She's checking the voice mail on her phone. The caption reads, "You have two thousand four hundred and sixty-six messages . . . Beep."

It was ten to six, and she'd finally made it back to the office. After her pretrial with Summers, she'd had to run off to court. Yesterday the daughter of a top family lawyer, a woman who sent Parish about twenty percent of her business, had been busted selling dope at her private school. It took Parish all afternoon to get the kid bail. Meanwhile, one of her oldest clients, who'd gone AWOL while on parole a few weeks before, had been picked up by the "rope squad," and wanted to trade some information on a "murder beef" to keep from going back to "the joint." She'd dealt with that on her cell phone during the breaks at the bail hearing.

From the edge of her vision she saw something move at the entrance to her office. It was her partner, Ted DiPaulo, holding on to the doorframe and curling his head inside.

"Hi, Nancy." DiPaulo wore his usual unflappable smile. "How'd the JPT go?"

Before she could answer, the voice-mail lady, with her sickeningly sweet voice, chimed in: *"Your first unheard message."* It started to play. *"Happy Valentine's Day, Nancy Gail. Your father and I are—"* She winced at DiPaulo and hit the Skip button.

"Just the usual JPT nonsense," she said to DiPaulo. "Summers tried throwing his weight around. Fernandez is going for a first, no matter what anyone says." She waved in the direction of four storage boxes piled up in the corner of her office, the letters B-R-A-C-E handwritten in black Magic Marker. "I've just got to keep working it."

"That's the problem with high-profile cases," DiPaulo said. "All reason goes out the window in the Crown's office."

"Summers really leaned on him. Said without motive, how does he get to first?"

"Summers is an arrogant prick," DiPaulo said, "but he's right."

The second voice mail kicked in.

"It's me. Costa Rica. You wouldn't believe this deal. And they have nude beaches with these young—"

Parish hit the Off button and killed the phone. She smiled up at DiPaulo.

"Zelda?" he said, smiling back.

"My own personal social planner," she said.

DiPaulo nodded.

Neither of them said anything for a very long moment. "You all right, Nancy?" he said at last.

Parish nodded. Ever since she got this case, there'd been an unspoken pact between them. They'd discussed everything about their law practices—other cases, details about running the office, the usual gossip about Crown Attorneys and judges—everything under the sun except the one thing they were both thinking about all the time: Kevin Brace. Parish knew that DiPaulo yearned to ask her about it, to be there as her silent partner, bounce ideas around, talk strategy.

She desperately wanted to confide in him. To say, "Ted, I've never seen anything like this. My client refuses to talk to me. Completely refuses to say a word. Once a week he writes me a cryptic note with the most basic information. He's never asked for anything—except that I not tell a soul, not even you, about his silence."

"I'm fine, Ted," she said, forcing a smile.

"Listen," DiPaulo said. "Tell me to shut up whenever you want. But this case cries out for a plea to second. Ten years, Brace will be seventy-three when he gets out, for God's sake. A first would be a death sentence. Have I missed something?"

"That's what Summers said. He tried to ram a plea to second down our throats. But Fernandez wasn't biting. It's clear he's got a lot of pressure from the higher-ups."

DiPaulo nodded. "Even if Fernandez wants to make a deal, Phil Cutter and that crowd at the Crown's office won't let him. Still, how does he justify first degree without evidence of motive?"

Parish balled her hand into a fist and put it in the air. She put up one finger. "Katherine Torn was found stabbed to death in the bathtub." She put up a second finger. "The knife is found hidden in Brace's kitchen." She put up a third finger. "He confesses to the newspaper guy, Mr. Singh." She put up a fourth finger. "And we're not going to talk about it." She put up a fifth finger. "Go home and have fun cooking dinner for your kids."

DiPaulo, a former Crown, had become a defense lawyer four years earlier, when his wife got sick. They had two kids, ages fifteen and thirteen. He thought it would give him more flexibility, which it did at first. His wife died a year later. Parish had noticed recently, as the kids got older, that he was burying himself more in work.

"The Crown wants to point to Kevin Brace and say, 'See, any man at any time can snap,'" DiPaulo said.

"Ted, go cook," she said.

"Watch Summers. He's an old fart, but don't underestimate him. If he's pissed off at the Crown, he'll try to do you a favor. Did he give you any hints?"

"Not that I heard," Parish said. "What's for dinner?"

DiPaulo took a deep breath. "It's lasagna tonight, with Caesar salad, spring rolls, and hot and sour soup. Got all the cultural bases covered."

"See you tomorrow, Superdad," Parish said. DiPaulo's wife was Chinese. His kids were fashion-model gorgeous. "I've got sixteen more stupid voice messages to check."

"Don't stay too late, Nance," DiPaulo said, and gave her a final smile. "And by the way, happy Valentine's Day." He pulled his arm from behind his back and tossed her a box of very expensive chocolates.

A few seconds later there was a slam as the outer door closed. Parish stared at the phone. Then she looked at the computer screen. Finally her eyes settled on Ted's box. Suddenly she was starving.

She ripped the box open. There were a dozen handmade chocolates, each one a different shape. She popped the first one into her mouth. It was delicious. She thought to herself, Did Summers give me a hint? She ate the second one. It tasted wonderful. Something clicked in her brain. The third one. Mmmm. What was it? The fourth one. Yummy. Think, Nancy, think.

It wasn't until she got to the ninth chocolate. "Oh my God," she said as she swallowed. Each one tasted better than the last one. "How could I have missed that!" She counted off her fingers again and started to laugh. Did Ted catch it? she wondered.

I've got to call Awotwe, she thought, looking for the phone number of her friend, who was a reporter for the *Star*. Parish grabbed the last three chocolates, and as she flew out of her chair and rushed toward her wall of boxes marked B-R-A-C-E, she jammed them into her mouth.

38

When you spend two months with a guy 24/7, sharing his cell, working with him in the hospital wing, sitting beside him at meals, and playing as his bridge partner, after a while you get used to the fact that he doesn't say a word. You even begin to like it, Fraser Dent thought as he rubbed his hands over his face before dealing out a new hand to the other three players around the metal table. Besides, Dent himself was a quiet guy. He didn't mind sitting with someone and just saying nothing.

The four men were the oldest prisoners in the Don, the "four-eye" set, as a black kid had nicknamed the bespectacled quartet. Because they were quiet and old, none of the young punks really bothered them. And now that they were up on the hospital range, everything was nice and quiet. The way veteran cons liked it.

The conversation tonight was, as usual, about the Toronto Maple Leafs. Up here on the fifth floor, the four-eye gang got special privileges, one of which was getting to watch the whole game, even if it went into overtime.

"I used to blame the coach, but now I blame the general manager," Dent said as he picked up the cards to deal out the last hand of the night. "The trading deadline is past, and we're stuck with this old goalie no one's ever heard of. They say he even went to law school. We're fucked."

The previous night had been another typical disaster for the home team. Playing out on the West Coast, winning 2 to 1 late in the third period, the hated Los Angeles Kings scored a tying goal, and in overtime they scored the winner. Even worse, the goaltender, the only player on the team even worth watching, broke his hand on the final play. A thirty-eight-year-old journeyman goalie, who'd spent almost his whole career in the minor leagues, was going to have to take over in tomorrow night's game in Anaheim.

Dent finished dealing and picked up his cards. Three aces and a bunch of high spades. Looks good, he thought as he sorted his hand. "I'll start the bidding at one spade," he said.

He looked Brace straight in the eye. If his partner had the fourth ace and a few high cards in some other suits, they were in great shape. As always, Brace was impossible to read.

The bidding moved quickly. Brace was a quick study at cards. When it was his turn to bid, he'd hold up his fingers and make a signal for the suit. For spades he'd point to his hair, even though it was now more gray than black. For hearts and diamonds, he'd point to his own heart or his pinky, where, as he told them in a note a long time ago, he usually wore a diamond ring. For clubs he pointed to his right foot. In that same note he told them that as a child, he'd had a clubfoot and had worn a cast for two years.

"Three spades," Dent said when the bidding came around to him a second time, eyeing Brace hopefully. Still no reaction from the former radio host.

The guy was a closed book, Dent told himself yet again. It had been his assignment to try to pry him open. Good luck.

Dent had followed Detective Greene's instructions to a T. "You're being charged with fraud over. Just let it be known that you got caught kiting some checks at Zellers and Office Depot," Greene told him. "If Brace ever asks, tell him you needed the money for some payments, and if he pushes, then tell him it was support payments. A kid you had out of wedlock."

Greene had instructed Dent to take things slowly. "He likes smart people, but not braggarts. When the newspaper arrives, everyone will grab the sports section. He's a hockey nut. You take the business section and study the stock pages. Let your story out slowly. How you were a top money trader, started drinking, wife left, ended up on the street. That part, just tell him the truth. And when you play bridge, play smart."

The bidding came around to Brace. He passed.

He was a good player, Dent had learned. Never overbid his cards. This time his message to Dent was clear: "You may have good cards, partner, but I've got squat."

Just like what I have on you, Dent thought to himself. Squat. Nada. Nothing. In almost two months Brace hadn't said a word. And most of the notes he'd written to Dent had been totally perfunctory. "Can I borrow a pen?" "Would you like to read this book?"

The guy to his right, who was east, bid four diamonds.

We've got ya, Dent thought. "Double," he said when the bidding returned to him. Bidding went around the board one more time. Pass, pass, pass, pass.

Should be fail, fail, fail, fail, he thought as he pondered the meeting he'd had with Detective Greene this morning.

"Last game, professors," a heavily accented eastern European voice called out from over Dent's shoulder. It was Mr. Buzz. He paused at the edge of their game. "What're they in?" he asked Dent.

"Four diamonds doubled," Dent said.

"A girl's best friend," Mr. Buzz said, tapping Dent quietly on the arm as if to say, "Nice bidding." "Happy Valentine's Day, boys. I'll round up all the riffraff, and you gents pack up once you're done."

Dent and Brace easily won the final round and soon were making their way back to their shared cell.

"Sleep tight, my children," Mr. Buzz said as he sauntered by, fiddled with his oversize key chain, and locked them inside. "Tomorrow night the Leafs start that old guy in goal. Should be a slaughter."

Mr. Buzz was a Montreal Canadiens fan, and he loved to rub the Leafs' continuing failure in their faces.

"Mr. Buzz," Dent said, "one day the Leafs will have a good team."

"Yeah," Mr. Buzz said, "and one day every criminal will be reformed and I'll be out of a job."

He walked away from the cell laughing wildly at his own joke.

As he did every night, Dent turned to his cell partner: "Good night, Mr. Brace."

Dent moved over to his bunk, expecting, as always, only silence from Brace in return.

As his head hit the meager feather pillow, he heard a voice.

"My father died in this place," Brace said in a voice so hoarse Dent could hardly hear him.

Dent sat up in his bed. "Kevin?"

"That young goalie lets in too many goals late in the period," Brace said. "This older guy will be better."

"You think so?" Dent said, keeping his voice soft, echoing Brace.

There was a long silence. Dent waited. At last he heard his cell mate start to snore. He lay back on his bunk and chuckled to himself. The Leafs drive everyone in this town crazy, he thought. Everybody.

39

In the early 1960s, a group of young politicians at city hall, determined to drag their drab, functional metropolis into the modern era, held an international design competition for a new city hall. The surprise winner, an unknown Finnish architect, created a postmodern building of two facing concave towers with a bubblelike council chamber in the middle. He put it on the north end of a large open square, right across the street from the former, now the "old," city hall.

City Hall Square took up a whole block. The only open space in the increasingly crowded downtown core, it quickly became the home to civic celebrations, outdoor concerts, protest rallies, open-air markets, and the like. Its most prominent feature was a large skating rink—a perceptive addition by the designer, who understood the northern climate—on the southwest corner of the square. In winter the rink was a magnet for all kinds of skaters: couples on first dates, immigrant families eager to indoctrinate their children into Canadian rituals, rowdy teenagers, even office workers—whose skates had been tucked under their desks—on lunch break.

Late at night, when the lights in the white overhead arches were turned off and the city staff had gone home, a ragged collection of hockey players emerged. Mostly poor downtown kids, with a smattering of university students up late and suburban players in search of open ice, they walked through the darkened streets of the city, hockey sticks over their shoulders, like lonely samurai warriors on their way to do battle.

Laces tied up, sticks thrown in the middle of the ice and divided into teams, they played a chaotic yet organized game that lasted through to the early hours of the morning. The puck was lit from above by the refracted lights of the high-rises that towered across the street like tall trees next to a clearing and from below by the shimmering white of the hard ice. Every quarter of an hour, the sound of the cut of blades and the slap of sticks was punctuated by the ding-dong of the clock tower atop the Old City Hall, hovering just across the street like a watchful moon.

Nancy Parish started playing late-night hockey here when she came back to the city after going to college in the States. Most of the players were much younger. One night she found herself on a pickup team with Awotwe Amankwah, a newspaper reporter she recognized from the courts. They struck up a friendship based on what they called the three *h*'s: hockey, helping each other out, and high regard for each other as professionals.

The rink was a perfect place for them to meet, and talk, in secret during the Brace trial. They'd developed a simple code if either of them wanted to get together. Earlier in the day, Parish had left a message on Amankwah's voice mail at work.

"Mr. Amankwah," she'd said, making sure to mispronounce Awotwe's last name, "I'm calling from Dominion Life Insurance to talk about your coverage." She then left a phone number, with the last four digits 1145. Amankwah arrived at the rink just as the Old City Hall clock started playing. It sang out three parts of its tune. The time was a quarter to twelve.

"How are things going?" Parish asked. She was sitting, doing up her skates on a flat wood bench well away from the other skaters.

"My editors are going nuts because there was nothing to write about your pretrial with Summers," Amankwah said in a hushed voice as he sat down beside her and pulled off his boots. "They're on my ass to come up with another scoop. I could do a story about Brace's kindergarten teacher and they'd put it on the front page above the fold."

"Off the record," Parish said, "Summers tried to force a plea to second, but the Crown isn't budging."

"Would Brace do that?" Amankwah said as he tugged on the laces of his skates. "Plead?"

Parish finished lacing up her skates. She stood and flexed her hockey stick on the rubber padding on the ground for protecting people's skates. "You know I can't tell you that."

"Understood," Amankwah said. He was still lacing up his second skate.

Over at the rink, a game was already in progress, and the grunts and groans of the players filled the thin night air. Parish twirled her hockey stick in her hand. "I need to ask you a favor," she said.

Amankwah didn't say anything. Silence. Good interview technique, she thought.

Parish sat down beside him again. "This might be the key to my defense. It has to do with Brace's so-called confession."

"Happy to help," Amankwah said.

She exhaled, and a white plume of steam rushed out. "You're going to need to get someone on the foreign desk to assist you," she said.

"The foreign desk is where I'm going in my career. I've got great contacts there."

The Old City Hall clock tower began to play again. This time it chimed through all four parts of its tune and then drummed out twelve steady beats.

Freedom at midnight, Parish thought, turning to Amankwah and tapping his skates with her stick. "I'll tell you about it after. First, let's go get some hockey therapy."

40

Daniel, you're the last person I'd expect to see here," a familiar female voice said from the other side of the laminated Chinese menu that Daniel Kennicott was holding up and studying. He lowered it and saw Jo Summers standing in front of him. Her great mane of hair, as always, was clipped up over her head. A nearly bald man who was immensely overweight stood beside her in a floppy double-breasted blue suit.

"Hi, Jo," Kennicott said, standing up.

"Daniel, this is Roger Humphries, Mr. Everything at my old firm. Roger, this is Daniel Kennicott. We went to law school together."

Humphries reached out and gave him a firm handshake. Even firmer than Terrance's handshake on College Street, Kennicott thought. "It's just great to meet you," he said. "Any friend of Jo's is a friend of mine."

"Why don't you join us?" Summers said, tugging at Kennicott's arm.

"No, I really wouldn't want to impose."

"Oh, come on," she insisted. "Chinese food is always better with more people. We have a table in back."

"I'm telling you, man, this is going to be terrific," Humphries said, his big face beaming. "There's a bunch of us from the firm. I'm the head of the social committee."

"My old law firm," Summers explained. "It's a Valentine's Day tradition. Anyone in the office who's single, we all come here."

"Yeah, and we still make Jo come, even though she deserted us

moneygrubbing Bay Street bums for the path of truth and justice,"
Humphries said. Impossibly, the smile on his face just grew bigger.
"Need her. She can order in Chinese."

"Really?" Kennicott said, looking at Summers.

"Yep," she said, pulling the menu out of Kennicott's hand. "Can-
tonese *and* Mandarin."

They went together through a curtain of red and white hanging
beads and entered a big square room that was all fluorescent lights,
plastic tablecloths, and clattering dishes. The place was packed with
groups of hip young Chinese couples, chopsticks in one hand and cell
phones in the other, and multigenerational families, the grandparents
hovering over the babies. There was a big round table in the middle
with a number of people in business suits sitting around it. They were
the only white, black, and East Indian people in the room.

Summers led Kennicott over to the table and introduced him to the
sea of faces as she sat beside him.

"Listen, people," she said. "Everyone put down your menus. We're
ordering the daily specials." She pointed to the far wall, where rows of
colored construction-paper signs were filled with Chinese characters.
The only things Kennicott could read were the prices.

A thin waitress approached the table. "Hello, how are you?" she
said, smiling down at Summers. Her English was very poor. "We have
nice food today. Which number on menu?"

Summers pointed to the wall and started speaking in fluent Chinese. The waitress's eyes widened. Then she started nodding enthusi-
astically, writing away on a small pad of paper.

When she left, Summers turned to Kennicott and gave him a sly
smile. She shrugged her shoulders. "I grew up around the corner from
here. My father insisted that we not live a pampered suburban
lifestyle. There were only two Caucasian kids in my grade-one class.
Then, after university, I taught English in Hunan Province for two
years. It comes in handy sometimes in court, when they arrest a Chinese
gang and I hear them all talking to each other in the prisoners' box."

The people around the table were smart and friendly. Although
Kennicott hadn't liked practicing law very much, he'd almost forgot-

ten the pleasure of the companionship of working with a group of bright, energetic people.

On the police force, he was an oddity. A rookie cop in his early thirties, a former lawyer who lived downtown and wore handmade shoes. Most cops married young and, at least before they got divorced, lived in the suburbs, and in the summer they'd get together for barbecues in the backyards of their town houses. Kennicott had gone a few times when he first joined the force, and once, the wife of a young cop tried to set him up with her sister. He and Andrea were back "on" at the time. After that he'd found excuses to duck the parties, and soon the invitations petered out.

The meal seemed to fly by, and when the dishes were cleared by the waitress, who simply folded the plastic sheet at all four ends and lifted everything up with one simple pull—like a stork delivering its bundle—Summers put her hand on Kennicott's arm.

"I have a theory about Chinese food in Toronto," she said. "The closer you are to the lake, the better it is."

Kennicott nodded. "Never eat Chinese in the suburbs."

"Never go to the suburbs," she said. "I live as far south as you can go—on the Islands."

Toronto was originally chosen as a townsite by the early British settlers because a chain of islands about half a mile offshore formed a perfect natural harbor. The Islands, as they were known, had been a cottage destination for wealthy Torontonians at the start of the twentieth century, then were turned primarily into parkland in the 1940s. In the sixties a group of adventurers took over a number of the dilapidated old homes and, after years of fighting with the city council, established a freestanding community across the water from the most expensive real estate in the country.

"You like it out there?" Kennicott asked.

"Love it," Summers said.

"Does it take long to get to work?"

"Exactly forty minutes, if I don't miss the ferry. The ferry's the only real problem. It makes me into a Cinderella. The last boat leaves downtown at eleven thirty—so at night I'm always watching the clock."

"And if you miss the ferry in the morning?"

"You're stuck for half an hour, unless you steal a boat or find Walter, the water-taxi guy who's been there for a hundred years."

Just as she spoke, Kennicott heard a beeping noise coming from her waist. She reached down and turned off her cell phone alarm.

"Hey, everybody," Summers said, "Cinderella's got to say nighty-night." She got up and kissed and hugged her way around the table. When she got back to Kennicott, he'd already stood up. She stepped away from the table, and he followed her. "Thanks so much for joining us, Daniel. It was great."

He considered saying he was ready to go too and walking out with her. But under her gregarious affect, he sensed that old shyness. Something told him to stay put.

"Thanks, Jo. I don't get to socialize like normal people very often, so I really appreciate it."

"I meant what I said about your brother," she said under her breath. "You must miss him."

Kennicott forced a smile. "Everyone says you must miss your family during special times like the holidays, birthdays, and anniversaries, but it's more the everyday of it that's not there. Going to a good movie and wanting to talk about it after, coming home from a trip and reaching for the phone to call. Sometimes I'll go days and not think about him, then I'll start reading a new book or hear a funny joke, and suddenly we're having a conversation in my head."

She touched his arm. And in a moment she was gone.

"That Jo is really something," her big friend Roger Humphries said, coming up beside him. "We really miss her at the firm."

"I can imagine," Kennicott said. "Looks like she was very popular."

"Oh, yeah. Everyone loved Jo," Humphries replied. "And smart. Man, she was really going places. But it just wasn't her thing."

"I guess it wasn't," Kennicott said, still feeling the touch of her hand on his arm.

"Jo's great. But no one could quite figure her out."

"I guess not," Kennicott said, watching the beaded curtain she'd just walked through settle back into place. "I guess not."

41

The snowbanks on the little side street were piled almost two feet high, so Ari Greene had to circle the block five times until he finally found a parking spot. He flicked off the car radio and, before he turned off the engine, gave the heater one last blast. Not that it would make a difference. By the time he met his father at the synagogue and walked him back, the car would be freezing. But maybe, Greene thought, it will be a little less cold.

The snow was high on the sidewalks too, so Greene walked down the middle of the street. The falling snow was illuminated by the lampposts, creating an eerie, almost stagelike feel—as if the snow didn't exist at all until it hit the light, making its quick entrance onto the streetscape and then falling to the ground to its assigned position as part of the complex theatrical set.

It was three blocks to the little synagogue where his dad went to pray every Friday night. The parking lot, which took up almost as much land as the building itself, was full every other day of the week. Tonight it was chained off, this being the Sabbath. That meant that everyone who drove—which included most of the congregation—had to park on the side streets, much to the annoyance of the local residents.

As Greene approached the white brick building, he saw four or five other men, all about his age, walking in the same direction. He nodded at them, and each nodded back. Every Friday night he saw most of these men—or men who were obviously their brothers. They were all Shabbat chauffeurs for their fathers.

"I heard the Leafs are winning two to nothing after the second period and the new goalie stopped twenty shots," Greene's father whispered when he came out of the chapel to meet his son, after he made sure the rabbi was looking the other way. "I told you that young goalie was the problem."

Greene nodded. Despite the fact that listening to radios or watching television was strictly prohibited on the Sabbath, somehow, someway, news of the latest sports scores always magically penetrated the walls of the sanctuary. How the news arrived, Greene's father steadfastly refused to explain. "It's like the war," his father once told him. "We always knew how far away the Allies were from the camp. Don't ask."

"That older goalie was incredible," Greene whispered back. "You were right, Dad." He didn't bother to mention to his father that the "goalie was the problem" theory was the fourth or fifth solution his dad had promulgated for the Leafs' woes since the New Year.

"Where'd you park?" Greene's father asked when they got to the front door and he stuffed his *kipa* into his pocket.

"Three blocks up, on Alexis. Half the usual spots are snowed in."

"And the snowplows? Not one in sight, I bet."

"Dad," Greene said, helping his father on with his coat, "let me go get the car and drive around."

It was an unspoken but faithfully observed Shabbat rule that no one drove right to the synagogue door. Somehow it was okay to drive, just as long as you pretended you didn't. Greene's father gave him a sideways look.

"Dad. Let's just wait a few minutes until the rabbi's gone. It's minus twenty out." The synagogue owned a house on the very same block, which they rented to the rabbi, making it simple for him to get home and back. As Greene's father liked to say, "Easy for him to preach about not driving on Shabbat, when he can walk home to take a leak."

A tall younger man came up and slapped Greene's father on the back. "Good *shabbos*, Mr. Greene," he said. The man spoke with a trace of an American accent, probably New Jersey or New York, Greene thought.

Greene's father frowned toward his son. It was the new rabbi. He had been there for a year and was generally despised by the elder members of the congregation. This was not too surprising. It usually took them about five years to break in a new man.

"Good *shabbos*, Rabbi Climans," he said.

"You're blessed to have such a loyal son, Mr. Greene," the rabbi said, then strolled over to another congregant.

His father rolled his eyes in Greene's direction. "Rabbi Climans? Why is he called Rabbi Climans?" Greene's father liked to say. "They should call him Rabbi Cliché. What does he think, he's auditioning for *Fiddler on the Roof*?"

"Where do they find these boring rabbis?" Greene's father asked as they trudged silently through the white streets, their boots crunching sharply on the cold snow. There was not a trace of wind.

"I don't know, Dad," Greene said as he opened the passenger door for his father. The inside of the car was the exact same temperature as outside. So much for preheating it, Greene thought as he put the key in and pushed the reluctant engine to turn over. It finally caught, and they sat, waiting for the engine to warm up. There was no point in trying the heater yet—it would just blast out cold air. He flicked on the wipers, and the cold, dry snow flew off the windshield, which was still covered by a layer of frost.

"How's your case going?" Greene's father asked.

Greene shook his head. "Here is what I haven't worked out yet. I've arrested thirty, maybe forty people charged with murder. They all say something when we take them in. Maybe just 'Fuck off, you cop,' or 'I'm not saying anything,' but they say something. But Brace, not a word. Not one word. I put a guy in his cell, and it's been almost two months. Not a bloody word."

"Not a word?" Greene's father turned his head away. He started to scratch a small hole through the frost on the inside of his passenger-side window.

When his father grew silent, it was a sign that he was thinking deeply. They'd been discussing his cases like this for years. Greene would come to his father when he was at a crossroads or a dead end. His father's insights, often so simple, were always useful.

"Brace had his son taken away," Greene's dad finally said.

"The boy was autistic," Greene said. He bent down and flicked on the heater. Freezing-cold air flew out of the vent. He flicked it off. "Back then it was pretty brutal."

Greene's father swung his head and looked at his son. "In the camps, often men would not talk for months. Especially when they got bad news."

Greene nodded. He switched the fan setting to the windshield and cranked it up. The inside of the glass gradually defrosted, slowly opening a round hole, like a fade-in scene in a silent movie.

"He has two girls?" his father asked. "What are their names?"

Greene shrugged. "Amanda and Beatrice," he said.

His dad nodded. "Very British." He whispered, "When my first family was murdered, it took me almost a month to say a word."

Greene nodded. The times his father talked about his first, lost family were few and far between.

"Dad, the chief offered me tickets to the Washington game at the end of this month. Want to come? You've never been to the ACC." The Air Canada Center was the fancy new home of the Toronto Maple Leafs.

"Maybe."

Greene knew his father would never come. Years ago, before Greene made Homicide, Charlton had given him a pair of tickets to the old Maple Leaf Gardens. His dad had spent a lifetime in Canada watching the Leafs on TV, but he'd never seen a game live.

The evening was a disaster. Greene's mother was worried about the parking downtown, so they took the subway. At the Eglinton station they got on a crowded car, and as soon as the door closed,

Greene's father began to sweat. People started to jostle them. His father began to shake.

At the next stop, Davisville, Greene pulled his dad off the car. It was a busy Saturday night, so it took twenty minutes standing in the brutal cold to hail a cab. By the time they got to the Gardens, the first period was almost over. They had to pass through a long tunnel to get to their seats, and halfway through, Greene's father became panicked. When they emerged into the brightly lit open arena, his father seemed to shrink. At just that moment, the Leafs scored a goal and, in unison, seventeen thousand people stood and cheered. For the first time in his life, Greene saw fear on his father's face.

Somehow Greene managed to get them to their seats. His father remained glued there for two periods. Even in the intermissions he refused to budge. Halfway through the third period he leaned over and whispered, "I've got to piss."

By that time the Leafs were already losing by three goals. Greene scooped up their jackets and guided his father back through the tunnel and into the men's room across from the popcorn stand.

The washroom was surprisingly large. The floor was cold tile and the walls were a stained, lackluster green. There were no individual urinals. Instead, the room was dominated by a long, two-sided porcelain trough, where a clutch of men stood on both sides urinating, generating a foaming yellow river of piss. The stench of urine hung heavy in the air.

His father froze. He clutched Greene's hand like a child. Then he vomited all over himself.

The heater in the car was gradually beginning to warm up, and the frost on the front window was clearing. But the falling snow gathered on the windshield, blocking Greene's vision again, wrapping them in a foamy white cocoon. The air was dry, and Greene's skin felt scaly.

"A man doesn't forget his children," his father said. "Never."

PART III: MAY

42

Mr. Singh found the lengthening days at the beginning of May to be most agreeable. Especially enjoyable was the early-morning sunlight, which meant that when he rose at 4:13 a.m., he knew the light would soon be upon him. Usually this made him feel very alert. By 5:02, when he was making his way down Front Street toward the Market Place Tower to commence the day's deliveries, there was just a hint of brightness in the sky.

Still, he felt just the slightest fatigue. Last evening the grand-children had been over for Sunday dinner. He'd stayed up rather late explaining to Ramesh, his eight-year-old grandson, the principle of liquid displacement. His wife, Bimal, had made a fuss because they'd spilled some water onto the kitchen table. Why such a bother? How else was the boy to learn the principles of physics?

Ramesh was an inquisitive child. "Mommy says you saw a dead person," he said as Mr. Singh returned a large bowl to its place above the stove.

"Unfortunately, this is true," Mr. Singh said.

"Do dead people have their eyes opened or closed?" the child inquired.

"It can be either way," Mr. Singh said.

"What about the dead person you saw?"

As he walked along the south side of Front Street, Mr. Singh shook his head at the memory of their little talk. The city was very hot for May, and already it was quite warm. Nevertheless, Bimal had insisted he bring his raincoat in case it rained. And because today he was to testify at Mr. Kevin's preliminary inquiry.

"The air-conditioning might be very strong in the courthouse," his wife had said.

"That is true," he agreed. And he would feel uncomfortable going to court without a proper overcoat.

All weekend the newspapers had been filled with stories about Mr. Kevin. Even, it seemed, Mr. Singh's small grandson was aware of it. But lately the biggest story in the newspaper had been about Toronto's ice hockey team. Remarkably, they were still playing, even though it was almost summertime.

Many mornings, on the front pages of all four major newspapers were photographs of a helmeted player wearing a blue-and-white jersey, raising his hockey stick in the air, embracing other helmeted players in similar uniforms. And on many nights one could hear vehicles driving up and down the street honking their horns, with young men hanging out of car windows waving blue-and-white flags.

Mr. Singh knew that today Mr. Kevin's story would be prominent. So he was not surprised when, as he approached the Market Place Tower, he saw a group of reporters at the front door. Mr. Rasheed had kept them out of the lobby. Thank goodness.

It would be best to walk around the crowd, Mr. Singh thought. He was about halfway past them when a man called out, "There's the guy who found the body." Suddenly a horde of microphones descended on him.

"Mr. Singh, Mr. Singh, we understand you're the first witness. Correct?" This was a woman's voice.

"How does it feel to testify against your former customer?" another female voice demanded.

"I will ask you to kindly excuse me," Mr. Singh said. The sun was not yet fully up, but it was warm. The reporters were wearing inappropriate clothing for people of their profession. Many of the men wore

T-shirts, shorts, and sandals. And the women. A number had on shirts that revealed parts of their torsos.

Mr. Singh had learned that such a spell of warm weather in Toronto was labeled a heat "wave." This was in contrast to chilly winter days, which were called cold "snaps." Why heat should wave and cold should snap, Mr. Singh could not understand.

"I am already two minutes behind with my deliveries," he said as he stepped around a woman with extremely short hair and colorful glasses who had jumped in front of him.

"But Mr. Singh—," another reporter started to say.

"Did you not comprehend what I just said?" Mr. Singh asked. "Kindly allow me to pass."

That seemed to quiet the rabble, and the reporters stood aside. Mr. Singh made his way into the lobby, took out his penknife, and cut the binding off his first stack of newspapers. The papers would be heavier again this week because it was Mother's Day this weekend. What will these Canadians think of next for their holidays? Mr. Singh wondered.

The reporters were right. He would attend court this morning, and it was his understanding that he would be the very first witness.

Despite himself, he considered the other reporter's question. How will it feel to testify with Mr. Kevin in the courtroom? He imagined that the whole proceeding would be extremely uncomfortable for Mr. Kevin. Although he was a well-known radio personality who spoke to millions of people each day, Mr. Singh knew that Mr. Kevin was a very private man.

Take for example that terrible morning in December, when Mr. Kevin told Mr. Singh he had killed his wife. He could barely speak. After that, he did not say another word. When Mr. Singh asked if he would like some tea, Mr. Kevin had simply nodded.

The police detective who interviewed him that afternoon and the Crown Attorney who met with him last week had both pressed him to try to remember any other words Mr. Kevin had said. But there was nothing to remember.

Mr. Singh couldn't understand what was so complicated about this case. Mr. Kevin had said he'd killed Miss Katherine, and she was dead in the bathtub.

An unfortunate circumstance, no doubt. Poor Miss Katherine. So sad for Mr. Kevin. Yes, Mr. Singh thought, it will be most odd to see him again today and not be able to wish him good morning and ask about his beautiful wife.

43

"Boy Wonder finally delivered his toxicology report," Jennifer Raglan said to Ari Greene as he walked into her cluttered corner office. She was holding a brown legal-size envelope in her hand, the words OFFICE OF THE CORONER OF ONTARIO clearly marked on it. He had a large latte in one hand, which he'd brought for her, and a chamomile tea for himself in the other.

They'd worked out this system on mornings when she'd stayed over at his place. He'd drop her off a few blocks away from the office, and she'd walk in alone. He'd show up sometime later.

"Just-in-time delivery," Greene said as he put her coffee down on one of the few clear spaces he could find on her desk. "The Kiwi doctor is a busy man, but he always comes through."

"Thanks," she said, sipping the coffee. "Fernandez is down the hall, as always. The guy practically sleeps here."

"Keen, isn't he?" Greene said, standing across the desk from her.

Raglan exhaled loudly as she pulled a set of reports out of the envelope and began to read. "You have to watch it with young Crowns. They can get caught up. Want to win at all costs. Last thing I need is another Phil Cutter."

She flipped through the document quickly, with a practiced eye. "Shit," she said as her fingers traced a passage at the bottom of one of the pages. She tossed it across the desk to him.

Greene read the section marked "Toxicology." He let out a low whistle. "That's a lot of alcohol in her system at five in the morning. Two point five. Howard Peel, her AA sponsor, said she was back on the juice."

Raglan bit her lower lip. "This case isn't the straight shot we thought it was when it came in."

"They never are," Greene said, flipping through the medical report. "Look at this," he said, coming around the desk and standing beside her. "Hospital tests of Torn's platelet level. Ridiculously low."

Raglan leaned over to look, putting her hip against his. "Seventeen," she said. "Isn't that almost like being a hemophiliac?"

"Close. Below ten's the number. Dr. McKilty said anything under twenty and she'd bruise like a ripe banana. She had some prints on her upper arms. Could have been from anything."

"Presumably the platelet count's so low from the drinking," Raglan said. "But she was in great shape. Didn't she ride horseback almost every day?"

Greene nodded. "Often go hand in hand. Addicted to drinking, addicted to exercise."

Raglan slipped her hand behind Greene's back. "There's never a perfect victim, is there?" she said.

"When Parish sees this, she's going to push for a deal," Greene said.

She nodded as she tucked her fingers into his belt loop. "And Summers is going to go ape shit. He'll haul me into his chambers and practically demand a plea to second, if not manslaughter. But my hands are tied. Orders from on high—make no deal." She slipped her fingers in under the top of his pants. "Two more days until the kids come back," she said, turning her hip slightly toward him.

Greene nodded.

The BlackBerry she always wore on her hip began to buzz. She grabbed it and looked down.

"It's Dana," she said, turning away from Greene to take the call.

"Hi, sweetheart," she said, looking at her watch. "How come you're up so early?"

Raglan nodded.

"Oh, the zoo. That will be a great trip. I thought Daddy . . ."

There was a pause, and Greene saw Raglan clench her fist. "Isn't the form in your backpack?"

Raglan rubbed her hand over her face. "Why didn't you call me last night?"

Raglan nodded again. "Yeah, I was working late, so that's why I didn't answer the phone at home. Sweetie, I told you to always call my cell. Okay, I'm going to leave the office in a few minutes and go home and get it, and I'll drive it over to the school. Love you."

She clicked the phone off and looked at Greene. "Grade-four trip. They won't let her on the bus without the damn form."

There was a knock on the door. Fernandez walked in proudly, holding a black binder. A label squarely in the center: R.V. KEVIN BRACE—PRELIMINARY INQUIRY BINDER—ALBERT FERNANDEZ, ASSISTANT CROWN ATTORNEY.

"Albert, I was just about to call you," Raglan said. "Dr. McKilty finally got us the toxicology report. Bad news. Torn had two point five alcohol in her system. And her platelet level was pathetically low."

Fernandez reached out and took a copy of the report. He sat down in one of the chairs in front of the desk and began to read it slowly. Methodically.

Raglan looked at Greene and then back at Fernandez. She took a deep breath. "Albert, I've got a crisis with my daughter, so I have to run out."

"She okay?" he asked, looking up. He seemed genuinely concerned.

"Yeah. Just a school permission form thing. Good luck today in court."

He shrugged. "Summers is going to yell at me for not offering a deal. Especially when he sees this."

Raglan's cell phone rang again. She grabbed it and looked at the display. "Sorry, Albert, I have to take this . . . just a second."

She turned sideways. "Sweetie, I'm on my way. What? He did. Tell him thanks. I'll talk to you tonight. Love you."

She clicked the phone off and looked at Greene. "Her father got another parent to fax him over a blank form. Crisis solved."

Fernandez stood up. "Those are my marching orders, aren't they? No deal."

Greene looked closely at the prosecutor. Raglan was right about young Crowns. Young defense lawyers too, for that matter. The urge to win at all costs was so very powerful.

"For now," Raglan said, "no deal."

44

Nancy Parish put on her best smile as Justice Summers strode into court at precisely ten o'clock. She'd been a full minute early. Horace, the constable at the door with the bell, had been impressed.

She rose to her feet with everyone else in the packed courtroom and watched as Summers's clerk rushed in and placed his books beside him on his desk. An old air conditioner rattled in the window, billowing out cold jets of air into the large room. Summers took one look at the noisy machine and with a powerful wave of his hand he dispatched his clerk to turn it off.

Parish stayed on her feet after the court had been called to order and everyone but her and Fernandez had sat down. She waited until the racket from the air conditioner stopped.

"Good morning, Your Honor," she said.

"Good morning, Your Honor," Fernandez said.

"Good morning, Counsel," Summers said, acting for all the world as if this were just any day in court, not even deigning to lift his eyes to acknowledge the crowd that filled every seat on the main floor of the courtroom and every available space in the upstairs balcony.

"If it please the court, Ms. Nancy Parish—that's P-A-R-I-S-H— counsel for Mr. Kevin Brace; he's the gentleman behind me in the prisoners' dock," said Parish.

"Yes. I'm glad to see they got him here on time today," Summers said.

"As am I," she said. "Thanks to your efforts, sir, they are now bringing my client to the courthouse on the so-called early run."

"Good," Summers said, clearly pleased with himself.

He's happy with me so far, Parish thought. Just wait until I drop my first bombshell.

"Any preliminary motions, counsel?" Summers asked after Fernandez introduced himself and sat down. The judge made a show of opening a new book and dipping his pen into an ink bottle, which his faithful aide had unscrewed for him. "I assume there will be the usual exclusion of witnesses."

"I would request that," Parish said.

"As would I," Fernandez piped in, rising briefly to his feet. Summers gave him a look that seemed to say, "Relax, Fernandez, don't be such a bootlicker."

Thanks, Fernandez, Parish thought. Let Summers start the day getting pissed at you.

"And I imagine, Ms. Parish, you'll be asking for the usual ban on publication of these proceedings." Summers was already making a little note in his book. Parish had learned always to watch the judge's pen. Never start talking until he'd stopped writing.

He finished his scribbling and looked up, surprised to see that Parish still had not responded. She let the silence settle in for another moment.

"Thank you for that suggestion, Your Honor, but the defense will not be requesting a ban on publication of these proceedings." She sat down quickly.

There was a gasp from the gallery behind her. She heard a shuffling of papers and a clicking of pens in the front rows, which were filled with anxious reporters.

"Silence," Summers roared. "Members of the press will remain silent, or they will be removed from my court." Then he smiled down at Parish. A real Cheshire cat grin.

Summers is smarter than some people give him credit for, Parish thought. Clearly her move had taken him totally by surprise, so he used the opportunity of yelling at the press to give himself a few moments to absorb what she'd said. Now he'd appear to take it in stride.

"That's your option, Ms. Parish," he said coolly.

Out of the corner of her eye, Parish saw Fernandez glare at her. Just as she thought he would.

Fernandez stood up.

"Yes, Mr. Fernandez?" Summers asked.

"Your Honor, if the defense is not requesting a ban on publication, then the Crown will."

"Oh, you will, will you?" Summers said. He was starting to growl.

Parish was ready. She opened a yellow file folder on her desk as she stood. Some more informal judges didn't mind if counsel spoke to them while seated, but in Summers's court you never uttered a word unless you were on your feet.

"Your Honor, the case law is settled on this point. The defense has an absolute right to request a ban on publication at the preliminary inquiry stage; the Crown does not. For the Crown to gain a ban on publication, they will have to show extraordinary reasons, usually something in the nature of a threat to an undercover operation or national security. Surely that's not an issue in this case."

She took a blue-bound casebook from the file and handed it over to the clerk, who passed it up to Summers. She gave a second copy to Fernandez. He took it reluctantly, like a rejected suitor taking back his ring.

Summers grabbed the binder from his clerk's outstretched hand and tossed it aside—making a show of not even looking at the cases.

"Ms. Parish, the court very much appreciates your assistance. I believe that after thirty years on the bench I am well familiar with the law on this point. The leading case is De La Salle, isn't it—1993, '94, somewhere around there? Volume . . . what . . . four or five of *Supreme Court Reports*. Summers gave the case name a hefty French accent, and as he spoke, he waved his hands back and forth like a man estimating the age of a vintage wine.

Summers loved showing off like this, and Parish knew the trick was never to upstage him. Never interrupt. And if he cracked a joke, never, ever crack one back. In other words, always let Summers have the last laugh.

"Very good, Your Honor," Parish said. "It's in 1994." In fact the case was called Dagenais, not De La Salle, and it was in volume three. But there was no need to contradict His Honor on such trivialities in front of a packed courthouse. She knew that at the break he'd go back and check the citation, and then he'd be even more grateful that Parish hadn't shown him up in court.

Summers smiled. He turned his gaze to Fernandez. "Mr. Fernandez," he said, speaking slowly, "can you convince me to rewrite the *Criminal Code of Canada*?"

Parish sat down quietly and kept her eyes lowered. She didn't have to look up to feel the waves of tension emanating from Fernandez. She'd learned a long time ago never to gloat in court. Don't ever be a bad winner.

"Thank you, Your Honor." Fernandez practically spit out the words. Still keeping her eyes down, Parish could only see Fernandez's legs. Instead of his usual ramrod-straight posture, he seemed to be swaying on his feet. "I think my friend Ms. Parish makes a good point. Upon consideration, we do not request a general ban on publication."

Fernandez had regained his cool quickly and been smart enough not to fight a losing battle with Summers. Parish was impressed.

"But, Your Honor, there may be certain witnesses for whom I will ask to revisit this issue," he said. "I'm sure Your Honor will keep an open mind if certain extraordinary circumstances arise."

Parish looked at him. Something about Fernandez's tone caught her attention. "Extraordinary circumstances" was a code phrase in an open courtroom. It usually meant that there was a rat somewhere in the prison who'd claim he'd heard a jailhouse confession. Every defense lawyer's nightmare. She glanced at Summers, who was giving Fernandez a knowing nod. He'd gotten the message.

"Certainly, the bench will be prepared to revisit this issue, Mr. Fernandez," he said, all sweetness and light, "should the need arise."

Parish clenched her pen. Despite herself, she glanced quickly back at Brace in the prisoners' dock. Suddenly she didn't see him as Kevin Brace, famous broadcaster, the Voice of Canada. Now he was just another client in an orange jumpsuit. Another client she'd told a hundred times to keep his mouth shut. Another client who had probably torpedoed his own case by something stupid he'd said in jail. Shit.

"I'm sure you won't object to that, Ms. Parish?" Summers said. She could almost hear what Summers was thinking—"Nancy, for God's sake, didn't you tell your client to shut the fuck up?"

"Of course I did," she felt like standing up and screaming. "Only about a hundred goddamn times. He wouldn't say a word to me, and still he's in the bucket yakking away, like they all do!"

Instead she rose slowly to her feet. "Thank you for your ruling, Your Honor," she said. Her head was pounding. Fuck, what did Brace say? What did Fernandez have?

She smiled at Judge Summers. "The defense," she said, "is ready to proceed."

45

The first witness for the Crown will be Mr. Gurdial Singh," Albert Fernandez said as he moved to the podium at the side of the counsel table, speaking in a slow, confident voice.

Some Crown Attorneys believed that it was best to start a prelim with the police witnesses—set the scene, get the forensics out of the way. But Fernandez liked to tell the story in order—in simple Anglo-Saxon language—even if it meant pissing off a bunch of cops because they had to sit around all day waiting to be called to the stand. That's why he was starting with Singh.

Besides, Singh was just the kind of witness Crown Attorneys loved. He had no criminal record, of course, was a completely respectable citizen, and had no motive to do anything but tell the truth. Best of all, a jury would adore him. The perfect opening witness.

"Mr. Gurdial Singh!" a police officer at the door called out into the hall. A moment later Mr. Singh walked in. Despite the hot day, he wore a white shirt and tie, gray flannel pants, and thick-soled shoes. He was carrying a long raincoat over his arm, and as he walked in, he looked around for a place to put it. This simple, small act suddenly made Singh look unsure of himself. If a jury ever saw that, Fernandez realized, their first impression would be that he was a confused old man. And first impressions, Fernandez knew, counted for seventy percent of a jury's final impression.

It always amazed Fernandez how the slightest thing could change how you felt about a witness. Credibility was a fragile resource. Thankfully, this is just the prelim, he thought as he made a notation in the margin of his court notebook to be sure, before the trial, to walk Singh through the courtroom, get him fully acclimatized to the setting, and have someone take his coat well before he testified.

Just as Fernandez was about to speak to Singh, Summers jumped into the breach. "Good morning, Mr. Singh," he sang out from his perch high up on the dais.

"Oh, hello, Your Honor," Singh said, raising the coat in his arm.

"The clerk will take that for you. Just have a seat right up here beside me." Summers patted the wood railing by his side.

The clerk shot out of his seat below the judge and rushed over to relieve Singh of his coat.

"Good morning, Mr. Singh," Fernandez said after Singh had taken the stand and been sworn in as a witness.

"Good morning, Mr. Fernandez."

"Mr. Singh, I understand that you were born in India in 1933, that you're a civil engineer, and that you worked for forty years as a railway engineer in India, rising to the position of Chief Engineer for the Northern District of Indian Railways before you retired."

"It was forty-two years, to be precise," Mr. Singh said.

Fernandez smiled. He'd intentionally said forty, hoping that Singh would correct him. At the trial, this kind of little thing would let the jury know right from the start that Singh was a stickler for detail.

"And are you a Canadian citizen?" Fernandez asked. Part of the art of examining witnesses in chief is remembering that the judge and jury don't know anything about them. You had to start from the very beginning and be very curious about a story you'd already heard at least ten times.

"Most certainly," Mr. Singh said. "And my wife, Bimal, and our three daughters. At the first available date. Precisely three years after we arrived."

For the next ten minutes Fernandez led Singh through all the non-contentious parts of his evidence—his years as a railway engineer in India, his decision to bring his family to Canada, and his job for the last four and a half years delivering newspapers. "One must keep oneself busy," Singh said.

Fernandez glanced up at Summers. With that last remark, he could tell that the judge was falling for Singh, just as the jurors would at the upcoming trial.

Singh spoke about meeting Brace a few years earlier and the commencement of their daily early-morning ritual of having a brief, cordial conversation. Finally they got to the morning of December 17. Singh described in vivid detail coming to the door, no one being there, hearing a groaning sound, and then Brace coming to the door with blood on his hands.

"What, if anything, did Mr. Brace say to you at that time?" Fernandez asked, making certain he didn't lead his star witness in any way.

"'I killed her, Mr. Singh, I killed her.'"

"Those exact words."

"Yes," Mr. Singh said, "as best I could hear them."

For a moment Fernandez froze. This was a new wrinkle. He scanned his brain. Had anyone ever asked how loud Brace's voice was? Probably not. But did it matter? Fernandez had to make a strategic decision, and he had only a moment to do it. Should he ask Singh to elaborate or not?

There would be plenty of time to ask Singh about this later, he decided. He didn't want to lose the rhythm of his examination.

"Where did you go after that?" he asked.

"Directly inside."

The rest of the evidence went in perfectly. Fernandez had Singh describe following Brace into the apartment, going first to the kitchen, checking the master bedroom and bathroom, the second bedroom, and then the hall bathroom, where he found the body in the bath, determining that Torn was "most certainly dead," calling the "police service," Officer Kennicott rushing in, slipping, and dropping his gun while Singh and Brace were having tea in the kitchen, offering Kennicott some tea. The tea, Fernandez had decided, was a good place to end.

Summers looked over at Singh and smiled. This is exactly what Fernandez wanted. Rule number one in advocacy: Make the judge—or the jury—like your witness. A trial was like real life. People are more tolerant of those they're attracted to. At the trial, Fernandez wanted the jury to think of Singh as their favorite uncle and to be pissed off at Parish for cross-examining him.

Fernandez sat down and looked at Parish. Just what, he wondered, would she try to do with Singh?

"Questions, Ms. Parish?" Summers asked. He had a twinkle in his eye, which made Fernandez slightly uneasy. It was the same look he'd seen at the pretrial back in February. Just what had he been hinting at to Parish?

"Mr. Singh," Parish said, standing up slowly, taking her time. "You've tried today to answer every question to the very best of your ability. Correct?"

"Of course, ma'am."

Thanks for making my witness look good, Fernandez thought with a smile.

"And, sir, Officer Kennicott, the first officer on the scene, the one who dropped his gun, you remember him?" That was a good move, slipping in a little dig at Kennicott to start off with. Make the police look foolish right away.

Parish's manner was gentle, unlike most criminal lawyers, who went on the attack with Crown witnesses. It was, Fernandez knew, very effective.

"Of course, ma'am."

"You answered all of his questions too?"

"Of course, ma'am."

"And you remember that day clearly?"

"Ma'am, I have seen much tragedy as a chief engineer for the northern section of Indian Railways. Many people in Canada do not realize that it is the largest transportation company in the world. Each time there is a tragedy, one cannot forget."

"Of course, sir," Parish said. Perfect, Fernandez thought. Parish was echoing Singh's words. He had her eating out of the palm of his hand.

"And, sir, you not only have no criminal record, but you have never been investigated by the police for committing a crime." Parish spoke in such an easygoing manner. It was as if she and her witness were having a private conversation instead of being in a courtroom packed to the rafters.

"Of course not, ma'am."

"And you've never committed a crime?"

"Of course not, ma'am."

Fernandez clicked his pen. Where was Parish going with this?

"And you've never committed a murder."

"Of course not, ma'am."

Fernandez looked over at Parish. He could have objected that the witness had already answered the question, but what was the point? Parish, with her soft tone, was hardly badgering Mr. Singh.

"But, Mr. Singh, you have killed many people."

Fernandez bolted to his feet. Now Parish was over the line. "Objection, Your Honor," he said. "The witness has twice told this court he has not committed a crime and he has not even been the subject of a police investigation—"

"I have never been investigated for committing a crime, no—but yes, I have killed many people." It was Singh speaking.

Summers held his hand up to Singh to try to stop him. But the words were already out. Summers smiled at him. "Thank you, Mr. Singh, I imagine this is the first time you have given evidence in court."

"Oh, not at all. I've testified many times in India. As a chief engineer, I was often a witness at all sorts of trials. Murder, rape, child abandonment, illegal gambling, drug smuggling . . ."

Summers broadened his smile. "I see, sir. Perhaps this is the first time you have testified in Canada."

Mr. Singh nodded. "Certainly, Your Honor. As a newspaper delivery person, one does not see many crimes."

There was a small ripple of laughter from the crowd behind Fernandez.

"Yes," Summers said. "In our courts, when a lawyer stands up to object, the witness must wait until I make a ruling on the question. One person speaks at a time."

For the first time since he entered the court and was uncertain about where to put his raincoat, Singh looked confused. "Your Honor, in this country I often find that people speak at the same time. My grandchildren, for example, will speak to their parents well before they are spoken to."

This time the laughter from the gallery was even louder. Summers lifted his eyes to the crowd, then, smiling, turned back to Fernandez.

Parish had already sat down. Fernandez stood alone in front of the judge.

"Mr. Fernandez," Summers said, "you already asked Mr. Singh about the utterance that Mr. Brace made to him that morning. Correct?"

Summers smiled toward Parish. "Utterance." That was the term Summers had used during the JPT in February. Not "confession." That was the signal he'd sent to Parish. She'd got it. Damn. How had he missed it?

"That's correct, Your Honor," Fernandez said, trying to keep his voice firm.

"Certainly she has the right to explore this further in cross."

Fernandez saw how he'd walked right into Parish's trap. And now he understood her earlier move. This is why she hadn't wanted a ban on publication. She'd just taken his strongest piece of evidence, Brace's statement to Singh, and muddied the hell out of it. And she wanted it in the press, so any prospective juror down the road would already have some doubt. Very, very smart.

"Correct, Your Honor. I'll withdraw my objection." Fernandez made himself sit slowly. Never show fear or disappointment in court. Even if for the second time in a row you've been caught flat-footed.

Parish rose and opened an orange file folder in front of her. She pivoted and for a moment looked back at the front row, where the press was sitting.

Fernandez followed her eyes. The reporters were on the edges of their seats. He noticed Awotwe Amankwah, from the *Star*, the only brown face in the whole row, nod at Parish.

Fernandez turned back to Parish. She reached into her handbag, which was sitting on the table, and fished out a pair of reading glasses. Taking her time. I've never seen her wear reading glasses before, he thought. A nice touch.

"Mr. Singh, you have killed twelve people, correct?"

"Correct. Twelve people in forty-two years was considered very low."

"But each one you remember."

"Like today."

"The first was Mrs. Bopart, in 1965."

"Most tragic. The woman had left her village to get water, and she fainted right on the edge of the tracks. It was in the winter, early in the morning, before sunrise, and there was no way to see her. Unbeknownst to her husband, she was pregnant."

"And then there was Mr. Wahal."

"Again, most tragic . . ."

Fernandez watched Parish go through each of Mr. Singh's dozen deaths, each one more horrific than the last. He tried not to show that he was impressed by her research. It was clear as day where she was going with it, and there was nothing he could do to stop her. Like a general on a hill seeing his army being slaughtered, all he could do was watch the inevitable unfold.

Finally Parish finished with the twelfth gruesome railroad accident and closed the orange folder. "Mr. Singh, on the morning of December 17, Officer Kennicott asked you to tell him what Mr. Brace said to you," she said. "Correct?"

"Correct, ma'am," Singh said.

Now she was firmly in control of this cross-examination. She had Singh echoing her words.

"And you told Officer Kennicott exactly what Mr. Brace said to you."

"Exactly."

Parish picked up the transcript of Singh's statement. "This is what you told Officer Kennicott, and I quote: 'Mr. Brace said, "I killed her, Mr. Singh, I killed her." Those are precisely the words he used.'"

"Precisely, ma'am."

"And that *is* what Mr. Brace said to you, word for word."

"Word for word."

Parish took her glasses off and looked straight at the witness. "He never said, 'I murdered her, Mr. Singh, I murdered her.' Did he?"

For the first time in her whole cross-examination Parish's pleasant tone had just a hint of an edge to it, a dash of pepper in a bland soup. There's a rhythm that a good cross-examiner establishes with a witness, a subliminal beat that ties everything together, like a song played to a metronome. It adds quality and credibility to the words spoken.

By this time in the cross-examination, Parish had a practically singsong relationship with Singh. By changing her inflection, she was drawing attention to the importance of the question, like a jazz riff that comes in slightly behind the beat.

Singh seemed to be affected by the new tone. Naturally, Fernandez and everyone else in the court expected him to simply answer in turn. On the beat. But he didn't. He paused.

Summers, who had been writing away, stopped and lifted his pen. Parish teetered slightly on her feet. Greene, sitting beside Fernandez and taking precise notes, stopped writing. Fernandez tried to stay still so as not to heighten the moment even more. He kept his eyes fixed on Singh.

Singh lifted his head and looked for the first time at Brace.

"In the years that I have known him, Mr. Kevin Brace has always spoken to me with great courtesy and great care. He never once used the word 'murder.'"

"Thank you, Mr. Singh," Parish said, and quickly sat down.

Summers turned to Fernandez with his biggest smile of the morning. A smile that said, "Don't you dare underestimate me. I saw this from a mile away."

"Any reexamination, Mr. Fernandez?" he asked. A big, warm smile on his face.

Fernandez had the right to reexamine the witness about things that came out in cross-examination that he could not have foreseen. Singh had slipped over the line when he'd opined that Brace was someone who always spoke with great care. But what was the point? This was not the trial.

Clearly round one had gone to the defense. Fernandez's best strategy was to get back to his corner of the ring as quickly as possible and try to stanch the bleeding. Right now he just wanted Singh off the stand.

"No questions, Your Honor. The Crown's next witness is Officer Daniel Kennicott," he said. Kennicott, Fernandez thought. Great. The cop who dropped the gun. Let's hope he doesn't drop the ball.

46

"Officer Daniel Kennicott," the booming voice of the cop at the door of courtroom 121 called out.

"Here," Kennicott said, picking up his police notebook from beside him on the wooden bench and tucking it into his jacket's inside pocket.

Kennicott had testified in court many times as a police officer, and he'd cross-examined hundreds of cops as a criminal lawyer. When he joined the force, he was determined never to be a wooden witness, like so many of the cops he'd seen in court. Too often their answers were rote, their testimony overly rehearsed. Or deliberately vague, filled with phrases like "to the best of my recollection" and "that was my understanding at the time." He knew that what impressed judges and juries most was not a witness who simply read from his notebook, but one who genuinely tried to remember what it was he had seen and heard and felt.

He'd been in courtroom 121 many times, but he'd never seen it as crowded as it was today. Never even close. He made his way steadily across the carpeted floor and through the swinging wooden gate, and he went quickly up to the witness-box. After he was sworn, he turned to look at Fernandez. Some cops liked to play to the judge; others liked to eyeball the defense counsel or, when the media was there, to try to talk to the press gallery. Kennicott always kept direct eye contact with the person who was asking him the questions, and no one else.

"Officer Kennicott, you've been a member of the Toronto Police Force for three years now, is that correct?" Fernandez asked.

Kennicott had learned that, back in the 1980s, when the citywide police force was amalgamated, its name had been changed from Police Force to Police Service. Most of the older cops resented the new name. They were a force, not a service. And the older judges felt the same way.

Summers peered over his glasses at Fernandez and gave him a little smile.

"A bit more than that. On June twenty-first it will be four years since I joined," Kennicott said, thinking, And five years since Michael's murder. Most cops gave clipped answers that made them sound like "yes sir"/"no sir" automatons. Kennicott liked to engage in a conversation and steer away from words like "correct" or "right."

"And before that you were a lawyer?"

"A criminal defense lawyer, for five years."

"Now, I'd like you to take your mind back to the morning of December seventeenth of last year and the events that bring you to court today. I understand that you made notes at that time, is that correct?"

Kennicott reached into his pocket and withdrew his notebook. This, he knew, would be the first point of contention. He expected the defense lawyer, Nancy Parish, to run him through the mill on his notes before she agreed to his being able to refer to them in court.

"Yes, I did. Here they are."

"A copy of your notes has been provided to the defense. Do you wish to refer to them to refresh your memory when you testify?"

Out of the corner of his eye he could see Parish rising to her feet.

The usual dance was that he'd say he needed the notes to refresh his memory, then she'd ask him every question she could think of about how and when he made the notes, and then the judge would let him use them. A smart defense lawyer would do that not to prevent him from using the notes, but to get in an early dig at how the notes might not be entirely accurate.

Kennicott took a deep breath. "I don't think it's necessary," he said. "I remember the morning very well, and I've memorized all the relevant times. If I do need to look at them, I'll let you know."

He kept his eyes on Fernandez. Beside him he heard Judge Summers sit up in his seat. He knew he'd caught his attention. Parish was still on her feet.

"Now, that's impressive," Summers said. "Saves us having to go through all the nonsense of qualifying the notes. Good for you, Officer. Ms. Parish?"

Parish looked at Kennicott and smiled. "I'll leave any questions I have for this officer for cross-examination," she said, and sat down.

Fernandez began to lead Kennicott through his evidence. He wasn't a flashy lawyer, but Fernandez was extremely competent and well prepared. A full-scale architectural drawing of the apartment was on a nearby easel, and Fernandez asked Kennicott to come over to it and mark his movements of that morning with a felt pen.

"When you first saw Mr. Singh and Mr. Brace, where were you, Officer?"

"I was here." Kennicott marked the end of the hallway, at the entrance to the kitchen.

"And what happened next?"

"I approached Mr. Brace, and I slipped on the tile floor," Kennicott said, putting a little x on the spot. "I fell here, and my gun, which had been in my right hand, slid all the way to here." He drew a dotted line up to the kitchen counter.

He'd been back to Brace's condominium so often, he felt he knew every inch of the place. Still, seeing the layout in an architectural drawing gave him a totally different perspective on the space. He found himself staring at the easel even when he got back to the witness-box.

Fernandez had many more questions for him. About what he did the rest of the day, his review of the lobby videotapes, and all that he'd learned about Brace's and Torn's lifestyles. They'd agreed to avoid any discussion of Torn's drinking problem. All of this had been disclosed to the defense. If it was going to come out in court, let Parish bring it up. That way Dr. and Mrs. Torn wouldn't blame them for it, and perhaps they could get them back on the Crown's side.

When Fernandez was done, Parish got to her feet. She was an accomplished cross-examiner. Kennicott could see right from the start what her technique was. Ask only leading questions, limit him to answers that were either yes or no, gradually work him into a corner, like an endgame strategy in chess, when the player with the advantage slowly cuts off his opponent's avenues of escape.

As he expected, Parish started off asking about his notes.

"Taking notes is an essential part of your job. Correct, Officer Kennicott?"

"That's right, it's required," he said.

"You're trained to take notes, correct?"

"We are. They even bring in an ex–homicide detective to do a special seminar on note taking. It is very thorough."

"You're required to take notes under the Police Act. Correct?"

"That's right."

"And as a defense lawyer, you cross-examined hundreds of police officers about the accuracy of their notes. Correct?"

There was a murmur of laughter in the courtroom. Kennicott smiled. Keep it casual, he told himself, don't be stiff.

"With great pleasure," he said, and everyone laughed, even Summers.

Here it comes, Kennicott thought. He'd read his notes over a dozen times, looking for something he'd missed. He hadn't found anything. But she must have found something.

"Could I look at your book, please, Officer?" Parish asked. "I have a photocopy, but I've never seen your original notes."

"Be my guest," Kennicott said. This was strange. Was Parish looking to see if he'd somehow doctored his original notes?

She approached him on the witness stand. He watched her eyes as she slowly flipped through his notes. Taking her time. What was she looking for?

She moved back to her place behind her table. "Your notes and the photocopy you provided are exactly the same. Correct?"

"Correct." Damn it, Kennicott thought. Here he was echoing her with that damn word "correct." His first one-word answer. Now he got it. She'd done her little act looking at his notes just to try to rattle him.

"Officer, you've looked at these notes many times before you testified today."

"At least ten times."

"Is there anything you can think of that you've left out?"

It was the first question she'd asked that was not a leading question, that didn't suggest an answer of either yes or no. Parish had just broken the first rule of cross-examination: Don't ever ask a question you don't know the answer to.

But Kennicott realized it was a smart move. If he said he didn't leave anything out—and there was always something—then he was stuck with that answer and she had a free shot at him when she found something. If he said he noticed something he'd left out, then he'd have to explain his error. Either way, she'd put him on the defensive.

On top of that, she'd established a quick rhythm in her cross-examination, an underlying beat to their conversation. He knew that if he hesitated too long, it would break the pacing and make him look unsure of himself. Kennicott heard Summers's pen stop. Out of the corner of his eye he saw Fernandez and Greene look up at him.

"Of course I didn't put every minor detail in my notes," he said. "Things like the color of Mr. Singh's shoes, for example. But I can't think of anything important that I left out."

"When you first saw Mr. Brace, he was having tea with Mr. Singh. Correct?" Parish had moved off the notes and was heading into the meat of the cross. Here we go, Kennicott thought.

"I was told they were having a special tea that Mr. Singh had given Mr. Brace."

As much as he wanted to keep focused on Parish, Kennicott's eyes were drawn back to the scale rendering of the apartment. When Fer-

nandez was examining him, he'd noticed something that had never occurred to him before. How, he demanded of himself, did I miss that?

Parish lifted her copy of Kennicott's notes. "On page forty-eight
you've written, 'Brace and Singh seated at breakfast table. Brace on
the left—west side, Singh on the east. Drinking tea.' And you even
made a little drawing of the location of both people."

"I did," Kennicott said. He was staring at the full-scale drawing.
His mind slipped back. Suddenly he wasn't in courtroom 121. He was
in Brace's condominium. First man in on a murder call. He could see
it all in his mind. "Mr. Brace didn't look at me," he said. "He was
looking down at his cup, stirring his tea with a spoon and pouring in
honey. Mr. Singh said the tea was a special blend and that it was good
for constipation."

"That's not in your notes, Officer Kennicott."

Kennicott looked at Parish. It was as if he'd just come back from
a short journey.

"What's not in my notes?" he asked. "The constipation?" There
was a murmur of laughter in the audience.

"No. In fact, Mr. Singh's comment about the constipation is in
your notes, on the next page. But I'm talking about the honey and the
spoon."

"The honey and the teaspoon are not in my notes," Kennicott
agreed. "But I remember them distinctly. I simply didn't think they
were important details."

"Less important than the constipation?" Parish asked.

There was another murmur of laughter, a little louder this time.

"The constipation was part of the statement made by Mr. Singh.
It was the first thing he spoke about after he'd introduced himself.
That's why I noted it. I noted every word Mr. Singh said to me. No one
said anything about the honey and the teaspoon, it was just an obser-
vation."

"What did you observe about the honey and the teaspoon?"

Kennicott took a moment to put himself back in the breakfast
room again. He looked at the drawing. It was important as a witness

not to rush things. When he was a lawyer, he'd always told his clients to tap their feet three times before they answered a question. It was easier said than done, he'd learned once he started to testify himself.

"Brace had the teaspoon in his left hand, and he was pouring the honey with his right. I thought it looked awkward, and now that I think of it again, I guess it occurred to me that Brace must be left-handed."

"Thank you very much, Officer Kennicott. No further questions." Parish smiled. It seemed as if she couldn't wait to sit down.

Fernandez had no reexamination, and a moment later Summers was thanking Kennicott and he was climbing down from the witness-box. It had all ended so quickly. He took another look at the drawing as he walked out of the courtroom.

He could see what Parish was trying to do. The position of Torn's body in the bathtub made it clear that the obvious way to stab her was with the right hand. But even a lefty could have stabbed a naked, vulnerable woman in the bathtub using his other hand.

That was not what had distracted him while he was on the stand. It was what he'd seen looking at the scale drawing of Suite 12A. It was so obvious. As he reached for the swinging doors leading out of the counsel area, Kennicott sneaked one last look back at the drawing. It was right there in front of him all the time. And he'd missed it. They'd all missed it.

47

I realized this afternoon that I made a big mistake in your case," Nancy Parish said after Kevin Brace took his seat in interview room 301 and Mr. Buzz had closed the door. She noticed, as he walked in, that he'd stomped down the back of his prison running shoes. "We now have a serious problem."

Brace didn't look away. For once, she seemed to have gotten his attention. In fact he seemed surprised.

He brought out his notebook and reached for his pen, but Parish put up her hand to stop him.

"No," she said, her voice rising in anger. "It's my turn to talk. That's the mistake I've made. Every other client I've ever had, I tell them the same thing. I call it 'the speech.' And I've never given it to you. So here it is."

Brace took his hand off the pen. He kept his eyes on her. Well, well, we're making progress here, Parish thought. But to her chagrin, her own internal voice sounded the way her mother's did when she was angry.

"I take cases because I want to win. Straight-out. And why do I want to win? Because if I don't win, I don't sleep. And that's our problem. I like to sleep. Is that clear?"

Brace looked at his notebook.

"You don't need your notebook to answer this question," Parish said. She was mad. "Is that clear?" This could be the best cross-examination I do all day, she thought.

Brace nodded his head. That's a first, she thought. We've moved from written communication to gestures.

"And I can't win a case when my client isn't listening to me."

Brace tilted his head a bit. He looked confused.

"I've told you over and over again, don't talk to anyone in this place about your case. But that move Fernandez pulled today in court about the ban on publication, saying he might need to challenge it in 'exceptional circumstances.' I know what that means. He's got a rat in here somewhere. Any minute now I'm expecting to be told about a statement you made to some asshole that's going to torpedo our case. And then we'll lose. And then I won't sleep. Got it?"

Brace reached again for his pen. Parish didn't object. He started writing furiously. At last he passed his book over to her.

I've never said a word, with but one exception. Back in February, when the Leafs were losing, I said to my cell mate that with the older goalie, the Leafs would be better. That's it.

Parish read the note twice. Was Brace deranged? Did she literally need to get his head examined? Finally she passed the notebook back to him.

He wrote again.

Don't look at me like I'm crazy. I was right about the goalie.

Parish took the notebook back. It was true. The thirty-eight-year-old journeyman goaltender had taken over on the Leafs' West Coast trip. Much to the amazement of all the sports pundits, he caught fire. He recorded two shutouts in a row, and the team's fortunes turned on a dime. Suddenly they just couldn't lose. Now they were one game away from winning the Stanley Cup. By tomorrow night they could be world champions.

Still, what did that have to do with his case? Parish threw the notebook down. The spiral wire binding made a hard, clicking sound on the metal table. "You'll talk some gibberish with your cell mate, but you won't talk to me? What the hell's going on? Enough is enough. Will you talk to me or not?"

Brace shook his head. Parish tried to read his look. He wasn't defiant or angry or defensive, like most of her clients became when she challenged them like this.

Brace picked his notebook up and wrote:

I can't talk to you.

Parish ran her hand across her face. She was bone-tired. It was only Monday night. She had four more grueling days ahead of her before the weekend. And right now she had no idea what to do.

"Look, Mr. Brace," she said at last. "Summers will totally freak out, but tomorrow I'm going to have to go into court and tell him that I'm unable to communicate with my client or take instructions from him, and I'm going to resign from the case." This was a bluff. Parish knew there was no way that Summers would let her off the case now, short of her saying that Brace had tried to strangle her. And knowing Summers, maybe not even then. The only way off the case was for Brace to fire her.

Brace was no fool. He picked up his book and wrote:

But I *am* communicating with you.

Parish closed her eyes. "Why the hell did you hire me? You could have had any lawyer in the city. Why me?"

Brace looked genuinely taken aback by this. He wrote again.

I thought you were brilliant today. Proved I made the right choice picking you.

It was, Parish realized, the first compliment she'd ever received from him. Although she hated to admit it, it felt good. Her anger began to melt away.

"Okay, Mr. Brace, help me. I'm missing something here, and I know it. You've got to stop holding out on me."

Brace looked at her long and hard, like a man weighing his options. At last he picked up his notebook and turned his pen upside down, so the rounded side touched the page, not the ink. He pointed to a word he'd written.

Parish read the word. She furrowed her brow. What did he mean by that?

To emphasize whatever point he was making, he underlined it with the back of the pen, indenting the page. For once, he was staring right at her, his smoky brown eyes alert, knowing. He looked down at the page and underlined the word again.

She read the word again. It seemed innocuous enough. She read it a third time. Then it hit her. So hard that her breath rushed out of her lungs as if she'd been bashed in the chest full force.

"Oh my God," she whispered, leaning forward across the table toward Brace. "That never, ever occurred to me," she said.

Brace closed his notebook, looked at her, and shrugged his shoulders.

"That changes everything," Parish said. She felt a sense of vertigo, as if her feet weren't really touching the concrete floor. And for the first time since she'd taken the case, she saw the thing she needed more than anything else to keep going. More than pats on the back from her client, more than sleep, more than food itself. At last she saw the one thing that every defense lawyer lives for: hope.

48

For Albert Fernandez, the advantage of having Detective Ho as his main witness the next day was that he didn't have to do any preparation. Sure, the forensic officer would bore the hell out of everyone in the courtroom and he'd drive Summers nuts, but all Fernandez would have to do was ask, "What did you do next?" every few minutes, and Ho would fill in the narrative. So tonight Fernandez could take a bit of a breather.

Not that it was easy to do. Being involved in a big trial made a lawyer suspicious of downtime. Fear it. Fernandez knew that if he let himself lift his head and look around, he'd realize that three billion people in the world didn't care about the length of the knife that pierced Katherine Torn's abdomen or the statement Kevin Brace made to Mr. Singh. Earlier this week the Chilean soccer team had won a crucial game in the World Cup qualifying round, and Fernandez had made a point of not reading anything about it.

He was tired. He sat back in his office chair and let his eyes drift closed. Just for five minutes, he told himself, it would be nice if he could think of something other than the case. It was almost eight o'clock. Thankfully, Marissa would be here soon. He'd left a stack of papers for her to photocopy.

Ever since she'd come back from Chile, Marissa had been a different person. She'd put a big push on to learn English, insisting that they speak no Spanish when they were together, and she'd started coming down at night to help him with his work. It turned out that she was very organized, and they made a good pair. She'd even encouraged him to contact his parents, something that to date he'd resisted.

There was a light knock. His eyes flew open, and he rushed to the door. Marissa was wearing a very short black skirt and a low-cut blouse. She slipped inside, and he gave her a kiss.

"I have a lot of papers for you to photocopy," he said, turning back to his desk.

She reached out, grabbed his hand, and pulled him toward her.

"Don't be such a stick in the earth," she said, giggling as she shut the door.

He smiled. "Stick in the mud."

"Shhh," she said. "I brought you something."

"What?" he asked.

"Sit on your chair and I'll show you . . ."

"Really, we can't do it now. I've got a lot of work to do . . ."

"Sit," she purred. "And take your mind out of the ditch."

"The gutter," he said, sitting down.

Marissa sat astride him and hitched her skirt up high.

"Really, Marissa . . ."

"This is something you really desire," she said. "Here, feel."

She took his hand and placed it on her inner thigh. Instead of feeling warm flesh, Fernandez felt something cold and hard, covered in plastic.

"What the heck?" he said as he pulled the thing out.

"A refund," Marissa declared as he stared at the bag of gumballs in his hand.

"A refill," he said. They both started to laugh.

"I'll refill the machine, and you do the photocopying," he said as they got up. It felt good to laugh with his wife.

She went down the hall. He was still filling the gum machine when she came back. Not nearly enough time to do all the copying.

"Marissa," he said without looking up, "this work is important."

"This is more important," she said in a surprisingly solemn voice.

He turned and saw that she was holding a sheet of paper. Her hands were shaking a bit. "I found this on the machine."

"What is it?" he said, reaching for the paper.

"I don't think it is supposed to be there."

Fernandez took one look, and he understood as he read the hand-written heading:

Confidential Solicitor-Client Communication Between Mr. Kevin Brace and His Lawyer, Ms. Nancy Parish

Below the heading were notes clearly written by Brace.

"Albert, this is not proper, is it? For your office to have the notes from the other team?"

"No, it's not proper," Fernandez said. He didn't bother to correct her use of the word "team." She'd gotten the important word right. He looked in her dark eyes and saw a depth there he'd never noticed before.

"You said it perfectly," he said, his mind reeling. "This is not proper at all."

49

Good morning, Mr. Singh. I hope I didn't scare you," Daniel Kennicott said as the elevator opened and Mr. Singh walked out onto the twelfth floor of the Market Place Tower, holding just one newspaper under his arm. "With Mr. Brace gone, I imagine you're not accustomed to seeing anyone up here."

Singh smiled. "Most mornings there is no one."

"Would you mind if I spoke with you for a minute?" Kennicott asked.

"Of course not, once I make my final delivery," Singh said. Kennicott waited at the elevator as Singh walked around the corner and down the hallway toward Suite 12B. Kennicott heard his steady steps, the sound of the newspaper being quietly deposited at the door, and the footsteps' return. The only other sound was the whir of the air-conditioning fans. He remembered how quiet this hallway was that first morning he was here.

"I'd like to take you back to 12A, Mr. Singh," Kennicott said when he reappeared.

"That would be fine," Singh said. "I am three minutes ahead on my delivery schedule."

Without another word Singh walked ahead toward 12A. Kennicott followed. He unsealed the front door and then said, "Sir, in your initial statement you said that when you first came to this spot, the front door was halfway open."

"That is correct."

"Please, open the door to the exact position it was in that morning."

"It was like this," Singh said. Without hesitation he opened the large door. "I stood in this spot, in the center of the doorway."

Kennicott nodded. "If you'll excuse me, could I stand there?"

Singh moved out of the way, and Kennicott took his place. From this angle, the view down the wide front hallway was obstructed. You could see only a sliver of the kitchen and the windows beyond. The kitchen table was out of sight, off to the right.

"And when Mr. Brace came to the door, did it remain in the same position?"

Mr. Singh had to think about that. "No," he said finally. "Mr. Brace opened it all the way to the wall."

Kennicott nodded. Now he was seeing the apartment not through his own eyes, but through the cipher of the architectural drawing he'd seen in court. It was as if he were up in the air, looking down. "Show me where the door was after Mr. Brace moved it."

"Like this." Singh pushed the door gently. It came to rest on a rubber stopper on the floor, just in front of the wall. "Then he said, 'I killed her, Mr. Singh, I killed her.'"

"And right then, what was the first thing that you did?"

"I said, 'We must contact the authorities.' As I said in my statement."

"Yes. I know you said that. But what did you do? Here, stand back in the place where you were, and now I'll go inside and face you. I'll be Brace."

Kennicott went over the threshold and turned back to Singh, standing right in front of him. "Is this where he was?"

"Precisely. Then Mr. Brace stepped aside, and I walked in," Singh said.

"Which side did he step to?"

"The door side."

Kennicott moved to his left. "He moves, this way, toward the door. How far does he go?"

"All the way over."

Kennicott nodded. He covered the narrow gap between the door and the wall. "Here?"

"Yes."

"And he lets you in along the wall side."

"Exactly. I walked down the hallway to the kitchen, and Mr. Brace followed me. I believe I said all of this in my statement as well."

Kennicott nodded. "I'd like you to walk through it exactly as it happened. Please come in, Mr. Singh, just like you did that morning."

Singh did not hesitate. "I considered that the situation was most grave," he said as he walked past Kennicott. "I proceeded directly down the hallway." Saying that, Singh walked in at a steady pace.

"And Brace, what did he do?" Kennicott asked, not yet moving from his spot by the door.

"He followed behind," Singh said. "I came directly into the kitchen. Mr. Brace came up behind me." It had taken Singh only a few seconds to walk to the end of the hallway and enter the kitchen. Kennicott followed him, arriving a moment later.

"Did Brace walk behind you like this?"

"Yes, he followed me. I do walk quickly, and he joined me right at this spot a short time later."

Kennicott took a deep breath. "Mr. Singh, think carefully. Did you actually see Mr. Brace walk down the hallway behind you?" He expected that the older man might have trouble reconstructing such a small detail. But he was wrong.

"No. I did not look back. I was most concerned to find Mr. Brace's wife. So I walked directly here."

"Did he say anything else while you two walked down the hallway?"

Singh seemed surprised by the question. "No. I do not like to indulge in chatter."

Kennicott had watched Singh carefully a few minutes before at the elevator, when he'd asked the old man to come down to Suite 12A. Singh had just walked straight ahead, without saying a word or looking back at Kennicott.

"Mr. Singh, listen to this next question," Kennicott said. Suddenly he felt like a defense lawyer again, trying to nail down a witness on a key point in cross-examination. "At any time from the moment you walked into the doorway until you came to this spot, did you look behind the front door?"

"No, I did not."

"And now you and I are facing the kitchen, away from the front door. Did you look back down the hallway at this time?"

"No. As I said in my statement, I proceeded directly here, to the kitchen area. When I did not see Mr. Brace's wife here, I proceeded to the bedrooms." He pointed off to his right, where the master bedroom and the second bedroom were located, beyond the kitchen. "There was no one in the bedrooms or the bathroom back there. I returned to the kitchen. Mr. Brace remained right here, where we are standing now."

"Let's walk through your exact movements, Mr. Singh." Kennicott took a quick glance at his watch, then followed Singh as he walked into Brace's bedroom, the en suite bathroom, the second bedroom, which was Brace's study, and then came back to the same spot in the kitchen.

"That took just over a minute, Mr. Singh," he said. "Does that sound about right?"

"Certainly. But Mr. Brace did not follow. He remained right here, at this spot, in the kitchen."

Kennicott nodded. He turned and looked back up the hallway, where he had a clear view of the opened front door.

"I then asked, 'Mr. Brace, where is your wife located?' He pointed up the hall, and I went to the lavatory there." Without prompting by Kennicott this time, Singh walked back up the hall.

Kennicott walked behind and stopped him just before he got to the bathroom door. "Mr. Singh," he said, pointing to the front door, "when you walked back up the hall, did you look at the front door? Do you remember what position it was in?"

For the first time since he'd entered the apartment, Singh seemed a little unsure of himself. "Let me see," he said. "Mr. Brace did not move from the kitchen. He just pointed. I walked here. I must have looked back at the front door."

"Don't assume, Mr. Singh. Try to remember."

"I was most concerned about Mr. Brace's wife."

"Of course you were."

Mr. Singh closed his eyes. Kennicott could see that he was beginning to reenact things in his mind. His head started to bob, as if he were walking. Suddenly his eyes flew open. "My goodness," he said. "I hadn't thought of this before. The front door was back the way it was when I first arrived, half opened. I remember thinking it was strange, because I had been most careful not to touch it for fear of fingerprints."

Kennicott remembered the exhilaration he used to feel in court when he'd gotten a key fact from a witness in cross-examination. "Thank you very much, Mr. Singh," he said.

Singh's mouth was agape. "But that could only mean—"

"Yes, I know exactly what that means," Kennicott said, ushering Singh back out the front door. "And I'd ask you not to discuss this with anyone but myself and Detective Greene and Mr. Fernandez."

"Such a wide hallway. Such a large door," Singh said. "The possibility had never occurred to me."

"You're not the only one," Kennicott said as he walked Singh to the elevator and shook his hand. "Please excuse me, sir," he said. "I've got a few calls to make."

"Most certainly, Officer Kennicott."

Kennicott turned and walked quickly. You're working a homicide now, he told himself. You are not supposed to run. But as soon as he was around the corner, he sprinted back to the condominium. To call Greene.

50

It felt strange for Albert Fernandez not to be driving downtown on a weekday morning, but instead to be heading north to the suburban wasteland, on the way to an industrial park he once knew so well. He was surprised that before seven in the morning the traffic was as heavy as it was, a sign that the unabated urban sprawl surrounding Toronto had led to constant gridlock in all directions. It's as if my car has muscle memory, he thought after he exited the main highway and drove seamlessly through the twists and turns of the antiseptic streets of the industrial park. He stopped at the last building.

The big parking lot was packed. In a few minutes it would be shift change, the night workers would roll out, and soon half the cars would be gone. Fernandez parked on the far eastern extremity, just inside a bend in the chain-link fence, and started toward the front door. He passed through the rows of workers' cars—aging trucks, large vehicles, worn-out-looking vans—many of them adorned with blue-and-white Maple Leafs flags or GO LEAFS GO and MEMBER OF LEAF NATION bumper stickers. Tucked under the windshield of each one was a black-and-white leaflet, flapping in the wind and making a bird-like fluttering sound.

Fernandez leaned over a rust-colored Pontiac and yanked out a flyer. He recognized the bold typeface and the grainy card stock. How many thousands of similar leaflets had he tucked under windshields or tried to hand off to scoffing workers?

WORKERS—UNITE IN OUR STRUGGLE

FRIDAY—MEET TO SUPPORT THE TRANSIT WORKERS' UNION

SPECIAL SPEAKERS—PRESTON DOUGLAS—VICE PRESIDENT—TWU

190 CLINTON STREET—8:00

REFRESHMENTS SERVED

Underneath the headline, a few paragraphs in achingly small type outlined in mind-numbing detail the alleged transgressions of the "employer." Fernandez forced himself to read through the prolix prose, then folded the flyer once vertically and slipped it into his shirt pocket, where it stuck out like a flag.

He spotted the coffee truck parked near the factory entrance, and keeping his head down, he eased his way into line. He was much too well dressed to fit in, and it didn't take long until he was recognized.

"Hey, Little Alberto, that you?" It was a man carrying a helmet and goggles.

Before Fernandez could say a word, a second man chipped in. "I saw you on TV last night. It's a big trial, eh?" His accent was even stronger than the first man's.

"Not really," Fernandez said.

"You going to nail the bastard, aren't you, Alberto?" It was the first man speaking. "My daughter, Stephanie, you remember her? Now she's living with an older guy. They come for dinner on Sunday, and an hour later they're gone. Like she's his prisoner. But this Brace, he's rich. The judge will want to help him out, no?"

"Rich. Poor. It's all the same," Fernandez said.

The two men exchanged cynical glances. "But you going to win?" the second man asked.

Fernandez shrugged. "The Crown never wins and never loses," he said. "My job is to let the judge or jury decide."

"Yeah, I heard you say that on TV. Same old Little Alberto," the first man said. He clapped a meaty paw on Fernandez's shoulder. "Your dad's over there. Still with the leaflets. Every Friday another meeting."

"And his own mug of coffee," Fernandez said, giving the men a knowing smile.

They both nodded. As Fernandez began to walk away, the first man said, "Think of Stephanie, and nail that old guy, Alberto."

Fernandez approached his father from the side, just out of his line of vision. His dad's hair was still thick and matted, but significantly more gray than the last time he'd seen him.

"Meeting this Friday . . . take a leaflet . . . important meeting . . . help out the transit workers' union . . . take a leaflet . . ." His father spoke in a constant patter, like a popcorn vendor at a baseball game, working the passing crowd.

Fernandez counted as ten men walked past. Only three took a leaflet, and none even bothered to look at it.

Gradually his father felt a presence at his side. He turned with his arm out, trying to hand off a leaflet. "Here, there's an important meeting Friday night, take a . . ." His voice slowed as he recognized his son, and his arm slid back down to his side.

"Hi, Father," Fernandez said, filling the sudden silence.

"Albert," his father said, regaining his voice. "What are you doing back here?"

"I came to talk to you," he said, watching his father's jaw clench. "It's been long enough."

His father eyed him suspiciously. "What is it? You getting divorced or having a baby? Got fired and need your old job back?"

Fernandez shook his head. "I'm not getting divorced. And, no, we're not having a baby."

His father frowned. "They're firing you? Why? You're on this big case. Your mother has been following it in the newspaper for months. Okay, we'll talk. But this is the best time for the leaflets." His father turned back to the row of men passing by. Fernandez waited. About a dozen men walked past, and only a few took the leaflets.

"Here, Dad," he said. "Give me half of those."

For the next fifteen minutes they handed out leaflets together, falling back into the rhythm of Fernandez's youth. When the flyers were all gone, they sat on a nearby bench. His father pulled a battered green thermos from his old backpack.

"Coffee?" he asked.

"Sure, Dad," Fernandez said. He sat down and watched his father unscrew the lid on the thermos. Fernandez smelled the deep aroma of the coffee. He was just eleven years old when his parents moved from Chile, and he still remembered them complaining about Canadian coffee. Even when money was desperately low, they always bought their own espresso beans to grind. This smell had been with him all his life.

"All these years with the workers, you still can't drink their coffee," Fernandez said.

His father shook his head. "It's not coffee they drink. It's just brown hot water. Albert, there are some things even a committed worker like me can't do for the cause."

He took a sip from his detachable cup and handed it over to Fernandez. The taste was as familiar as the smell of the pillow in his old bedroom.

"Have they really fired you?" his father asked.

"Not yet. But I think they will, next week."

"Albert, I don't agree with what you do. Working for the state to prosecute the poor—"

"Dad, I didn't come here to have a political—"

"But I know you work hard. And I know you're honest."

Fernandez clasped the cup firmly.

"Your mother's been cutting clippings of the trial from the paper," his father said. "Yesterday she told me this Sunday was Mother's Day."

"Disgusting capitalist institution," Fernandez said, doing a pretty good imitation of his father's voice.

They looked at each other, and both chuckled.

"I might need some help," Fernandez found himself saying, not really sure how to talk to his father like this. How to ask for guidance.

51

DAY TWO = BORING!" Nancy Parish wrote in big, dark print in her trial book, then used her yellow highlighter to magnify the point. She couldn't even think of anything to draw.

For the last six hours Fernandez had been questioning Detective Ho. The man loved to hear himself talk. He'd gone over everything he'd examined in Brace's condominium in minute detail, right down to the fact that the bathtub Katherine's body was found in didn't have a soap dish. It was almost 4:30, and Parish was hungry and tired and sick to death of Ho, who looked like he could happily talk for another century.

"And finally, to wrap up your evidence for today," Fernandez said, approaching the railing in front of the court clerk, "I want to ask you about the knife you found."

"Certainly," Ho said, as eager as a dog at its dish at feeding time.

There was a box on the counter. Fernandez reached in and pulled out two pairs of thin plastic gloves. He passed one set over to Ho, and then, with meticulous care, he slid on the gloves and opened the rectangular box that held the knife.

The court grew silent, still. The court reporter pulled the recording mask from her face and looked over. Summers pushed up his eyeglasses and stared down. Fernandez knew he had everyone's attention, and he took his time. This was only a prelim, and there was no jury, but Parish could see that he was playing to Summers and the press. His strategy was clear. End the day on a high note. Give the onlookers a memorable image they'd carry with them for the next eighteen hours. The murder weapon.

"Do you recognize this, Detective Ho?" Fernandez asked, gingerly lifting up a big black kitchen knife.

These are the moments at trial that defense lawyers dread—when a key piece of physical evidence is presented. It is one thing to hear about a knife or to look at photographs of a knife, but the moment when you actually see it has its own natural drama. Even from where she sat, Parish spotted specks of dried blood on the silver blade. She'd spent hours studying the pictures of the knife that had been provided to her as part of the disclosure of the Crown case, but actually seeing it for the first time sent a chill down her back.

At law school her professor had told them about the cigar trick of the famous defense lawyer Clarence Darrow. He'd take one of his wife's hairpins and insert it into the head of a cigar. The wire prevented the ash from falling, even as it grew precariously in length. Darrow timed it so that just when the worst piece of evidence was coming out, the ashes at the end of his cigar would be impossibly long. The jury would be distracted. Transfixed, they'd watch his cigar and ignore the prosecution.

Parish did the only thing she could. Looked right at the knife and tried to pretend she was completely bored.

"Yes, I recognize that knife," Ho said.

"Where was it found?" Fernandez asked as the clock ticked past 4:30.

Ho pointed to the floor plan sketch. "On the floor in the space between the counter and the stove."

"And did you find it during your initial search of the condominium?"

This was a smart question by Fernandez. A subtle way to underscore that the knife appeared to have been hidden.

"I didn't actually find it. After my initial review of the scene, Officer Kennicott and Detective Greene did a more detailed search, and they discovered this knife."

"Can you describe this knife for us?" Fernandez said, nicely dove-tailing his question with the last answer.

"It's a black Henckels kitchen knife," Ho said, picking it up and running his fingers just over top of the blade. "It's ten point eight inches in total length. The handle's three point four inches long, and the blade's seven point four inches in length. The blade tapers to a fine point, the width going from one point seven five inches to the tip."

He managed to describe the knife for a full ten minutes. When he finally finished, it was 4:45. Ho looked pleased with himself. Summers looked as if he wanted to kill him. The reporters looked like a bunch of children who had to go to the bathroom, so anxious were they to get out of there and file their stories in time for their deadlines. And somehow the drama of the moment seemed to have dissipated.

"This court will resume tomorrow at ten in the morning," the clerk finally said, dismissing the court at ten to five. Everyone rose. Judge Summers gave Fernandez an aggrieved look and flew off the bench. As Parish started packing up her books, she saw a folded piece of paper on her desk with the name "Nancy" written in Fernandez's neat script.

She looked over at him. He was looking away, toward Greene. He must have just passed it to her when he sat down. She opened the note. It said, "Nancy, can I talk to you after court in my office? Thanks, Albert."

When a Crown wants to talk to a defense lawyer, it means one of two things. Either he wants to make a deal or he has some new— inevitably bad—evidence to hand over. She clicked her pen and wrote, "Hey, Al, glad to see we're on a first-name basis. See you in ten. Nance," and slipped it back to him.

A jailhouse rat must have spilled the beans, she thought as she took a seat in Fernandez's tiny office ten minutes later. Just what I need after a day like this.

Fernandez sat behind his desk. Detective Greene stood to one side, nattily dressed as ever, his pants perfectly creased. Why can't I get my clothes to look like that? she wondered.

"A glass of water, a juice, anything else?" Fernandez asked.

"I'm fine, Albert," she said, even though her throat was completely parched. "I could use a gag to stuff in Ho's motormouth."

They laughed. Making fun of witnesses who drove both sides crazy was part of the game.

No one spoke. Fernandez straightened papers on his desk that didn't need straightening. Greene flattened out his tie. Beautiful, silk. Probably Armani.

"Albert," she said finally, thinking, Okay, hit me with your best shot. "You called this meeting. What's up?" She stared straight at Fernandez. His eyes, she noticed for the first time, were not quite as black as she'd thought. They had a hint of greeny brown.

Fernandez flicked a look at Greene. "What I'm going to tell you today is extremely vague. I apologize in advance. In the last twenty-four hours I've become aware of a possible development in this case that might affect the Crown's position. I wish I could be more specific, but right now I can't tell you anything else. I wanted to give you a heads-up."

Parish nodded, expecting Fernandez to explain further. But he just looked at her and shrugged.

"That's it?" she asked at last.

"That's all I can tell you right now. Of course, the moment I get more information, *if* I get new information, I'll give it to you immediately."

Parish breathed a heavy sigh. "You guys the CIA or something, with all these secrets? Why didn't you tell me this earlier, whatever *this* is."

"I knew I'd have Ho on the stand all day, so I thought it best to wait until after court," Fernandez said. "I'm telling you now because if I get this information tomorrow morning, I'll probably ask for an adjournment before you're forced to cross-examine another witness."

Fernandez looked at Greene again and nodded.

Parish's first reaction was relief. At least he's not telling me about a confession by Brace. Not yet.

"Come on, Albert. What's going on?"

Fernandez shrugged. Parish looked at Greene for a moment. He didn't give anything away.

She felt like an upset kid with no place to put her frustration. "What do you want me to do?"

"Tell Brace I might have to adjourn this sucker. He's the one sitting in the bucket," Fernandez said. "Summers will be pissed off at me. But so what."

"I'll talk to him," she said, thinking, I'll talk to him, but he won't talk to me. Who knows how he'll react to this news?

"Tell him I'll agree to his bail," Fernandez said.

Parish nodded. Fernandez must have been wondering why Brace had pulled the plug on his bail hearing back in December. They'd probably love to have Brace out of jail, since he was keeping his mouth shut on the inside. At home they could tap his phone, follow him around. So that was their angle. Fernandez's offer of bail meant that their case was not as strong as they wanted it to be. They were hunting for more evidence. Stay cool, she told herself.

She shrugged. "Thanks. I'll talk to him."

After shaking hands with both of them, she grabbed her briefcase and headed for the door. Back to the Don I go, she thought. While the rest of the city is yelling and screaming at TV screens during the final game of the Stanley Cup, I get to spend another evening in the jail. With my silent client.

52

Ari Greene had never seen the city explode like this. When Italy won the World Cup in 1982, Little Italy and all of St. Clair Avenue had turned into a magnificent all-day party. In 1992 and 1993, when the Blue Jays won the World Series, all the city's main streets were packed with what was later estimated to be up to a million revelers. But this was pure madness everywhere. A gigantic collective euphoria, after more than forty years of waiting for the Leafs to win the Stanley Cup.

Greene had gone to his dad's to watch the game. With five seconds left, the Leafs' goaltender made a miraculous save, and when the final buzzer went and he threw his stick and gloves into the air in celebration, Greene clutched his father.

Except for the day of his mother's funeral, it was the only time he'd seen a tear in his father's eyes. Greene's father pulled out a sealed bottle of Chivas Regal, and they toasted the great win. Then they heard it. The roar, from Bathurst Street, ten blocks away. Horns honking, people yelling, music blaring. One big sound wave of joy.

Greene got into his car and spent almost two hours picking his way through the side streets to get back downtown to the Market Place Tower. Quite a contrast to that first morning when he'd zipped through the empty streets in no time.

It was a warm night, and he kept his windows open. The air was moist, comfortable. He found a parking spot just north of Front Street. There was a small park across the street, and a broad lilac tree was in full bloom. Greene smelled its soft fragrance from the sidewalk. He slipped behind the black metal gate and twisted off two twigs from a low-hanging branch. The only light was the faint glow of a streetlamp well up the street, but still the rich purple color stood out. Up close, the smell was almost overpowering. As he made his way down to Front Street, the city lights grew brighter. Front was packed with people—tourists spilled out from clusters of restaurants on the north side, groups of young women, dressed to the nines, walked in close formation searching for a bar, guys in open shirts leaned on their expensive cars, strategically and illegally parked in prime locations. Up and down the street, car after car, their horns blaring, drove by, with hordes of young men and women waving blue-and-white flags out the windows and screaming "Go, Leafs, go!" "Leaf Nation rules!"

Greene crossed to the south side, unnoticed.

As he walked down Market Lane, the side street to the east of the condominium, the lights and the noise began to fade. A row of broad forsythias stood guard at the entrance to the private driveway, and even in the diminished light Greene could see that their yellow leaves of spring had mostly turned to summer green. He took one last look around to be sure that no one saw him, and then he slipped behind the shrubbery and along the walkway leading to the white metal door beside the garage entrance. At first the door appeared to be closed, but up close he saw a red brick sitting on end, holding it just open.

Greene nodded to himself. It was just as the concierge, Rasheed, had promised it would be when Greene called him a few hours ago.

"Leave the brick in the door," Greene had told him, "and I'll lose your immigration file forever."

He pulled the door open, slipped inside, and gently nestled it back into position. There was a tiny tick sound as the steel settled on the brick.

The artificial lighting inside the parking garage gave off a cold white glow. The air was musty. The only sounds were the low rumble of a large fan at the far end of the garage and Greene's shoes on the hard concrete.

He walked carefully along the south wall, keeping outside of the line of the security cameras, just as Rasheed had instructed, until he found his hiding spot behind a supporting wall near the stairwell. He put the two lilac twigs at his feet. Purple sentries, he thought as he checked his watch. Ten minutes after midnight. Greene's best guess was that he'd have to wait about two hours.

Not quite. After nearly an hour and a half of standing in silence, he had grown attuned to the slightest nuance of sound. He could hear the occasional car horns and plastic trumpets from passing cars traveling along the side street on their way to the big party on Front. And then, just after 1:30, he heard light steps slowly approach the outside door. A moment later its hinges groaned gently and there was the tick of steel touching brick. The footsteps followed his path—along the wall, out of sight of the cameras. Unlike Greene's slow, cautious movement, this person was walking quickly. Confidently. Like someone who knew the way very well. He heard the steps pass his hiding spot and go over to the stairway door.

Greene yearned to lean over and catch a glimpse, but he didn't dare. Instead he waited. Listening. He heard the stairway door close, and then waited again, listening hard. He could hear the fading footfalls climbing the concrete stairs, the pace slowing as they ascended.

He emerged from his hiding spot, lilacs in hand, and walked to the elevator. He pushed the Up button, and the white light came on. At this time of night he expected the elevators to run quickly. But after thirty seconds, one hadn't yet come. He resisted the temptation to push the button again.

A few seconds later the door slid open. Just before he stepped in, Greene took out his cell phone, pushed a preset number, and said just one word: "Go."

Inside the elevator he pushed the number 12 and the Close button. When it opened on the twelfth floor, he pushed two buttons—Basement and Close—before he stepped out. He walked to his right, to the point in the hall where it turned toward 12B, and took a quick look around the corner to confirm that the hallway was still empty. Then he waited.

It didn't take much longer. In a few seconds he heard the approach of footsteps in the far stairwell. The metal door at the end of the hall opened, and a moment later he heard another door open, closer to where he was standing. That would be the door of 12B, Greene thought. Perfect.

He walked around the corner, moving quickly. He took half a dozen long strides before the two people in the hallway realized he was there. Approaching them. They both turned simultaneously. Surprised.

Greene put on his best smile, lilacs in hand.

"Good morning, ladies," he said when he got to the doorway of 12B. Edna Wingate was a few steps out into the hall. She wore a simple white T-shirt and a pair of gray slacks. On her feet were plain white sandals. Not exactly sleepwear, he thought. More like something you'd wear late at night when you were waiting for a visitor.

Wingate turned toward him, her usual calm rattled. Greene turned toward the other woman, who'd just come up the stairs. She was harder to read. No shock there. What was it? Anger, defiance, resignation?

She paused only for an instant and then strode right up to him.

"Good morning, Detective Greene," Sarah McGill said.

"I come bearing flowers," he said, holding out one of the lilac twigs.

"If I'd known, I'd have brought you some of my homemade bread."

"Looks like I'll have to make another trip up to the café," he said.

"You're welcome anytime," McGill said, taking the flowers. Her hands, he noticed, shook ever so slightly.

Keeping his eyes fixed on McGill, he tilted his head toward Wingate, who still seemed to be reeling from his sudden appearance in the hallway. He lifted the remaining lilac twig in his hand.

"It's Mother's Day on Sunday," he said to McGill. Then he turned to Wingate and handed her the second twig. "So I brought one for your mother."

He looked back at McGill.

She held his eyes for a long moment. "You don't miss much, do you, Detective Greene?" she said at last.

53

This is not a dream this time, Nancy Parish told herself as she wheeled her unsteady cart stacked with evidence boxes onto the creaky elevator at Old City Hall. Even if it's almost ten in the morning and for some reason the whole damn courthouse is empty, and there's not one person around, this is *not* a dream.

With so much stuff to carry, she'd decided to take the elevator instead of the broad stone staircase. She really had no choice—even though the old elevator was notoriously slow—because she was hauling around three boxes of evidence. Where was everyone? She checked her watch. Yep. Ten to ten. She was cutting it close for Summers's court, but she'd make it. Just.

It took forever for the old metal elevator doors to rattle open. She looked at her watch. It was 9:55. She'd better hurry. She wheeled her cart carefully over the bumpy metal grating onto the filthy carpet and hammered at button number 2. The doors closed halfway, then stopped.

I can't believe this, Parish thought as she banged away at the Close button. The doors wouldn't move. She tried the Open button. No luck. "Come on, come on," she said, smacking the Open button, then the Close button. Nothing. She was stuck.

There was only one thing to do. She turned her body sideways and squeezed into the narrow space between the doors. She looked down the hallway. Strange. There was still no one around to help. Grimacing, she leaned against the door with all her might. The sweat began to accumulate on the back of her neck. At last she felt a gear engage, and the doors rumbled open.

She wheeled her cart back over the bumpy grating to the bottom of the stairs and unhooked the bungee cord keeping the boxes in place. Then, like a one-person fireman's brigade, she walked each box first to the landing, then up to the second floor, stacking them outside the door of courtroom 121.

There was still no one around. Not even Horace and his bell. She checked her watch. It was just after ten. This couldn't be a dream. This was real, and she was late. There was no time to go back downstairs to get her cart. Everyone else was already in court. She turned the door handle. It was locked. She could hear the murmurs of people inside. She knocked on the door, but no one came. She knocked louder. Nothing.

She started to scream. "This is my case! Let me in. It's not my fault!"

"It *is* your fault, Nancy Gail," a voice down the hall said. She looked up. It was one of the small, sculpted faces on top of a round granite pillar. Its stone mouth had turned as flexible as a child's hand puppet. "It's *all* your fault, Nancy," the stone mouth said.

Parish felt her body give a jerk. She grabbed again for the door handle of 121 and realized she was holding on to the edge of her bedsheets. Her eyes flew open. She clutched her clock radio and turned the lighted dial toward her. The red digital display read WED 1:40 AM.

She flopped back onto her pillow. Her bulky cotton T-shirt was soaked. Last week, when the courtroom nightmares started, she'd sweated through all four of her nightgowns. Now she was working her way through her T-shirt collection.

Sitting up in bed, she pulled the shirt over her head. I'll just add this to the laundry pile, she thought, turning the shirt back from inside out and tossing it into the bulging bin in the corner.

Her mouth was dry. She hauled herself off the bed and to the bathroom. She'd left her glass downstairs, so she ran the cold water over her hands, letting the cool settle in before she cupped her fingers and brought the water to her mouth.

These court nightmares were getting worse. In the first one she opened her boxes in court and found that the papers were all for the wrong case. The next night, she had the right boxes, but for some reason she'd driven to a suburban court out in Scarborough and no one had heard of the case. Or of Brace. She woke up when she'd started screaming at some confused-looking Somalis in the hallway, "Kevin Brace, the Voice of Canada, and you've never heard of him?" The third night, she'd made it to the right court, but she'd missed a week of the trial, and Judge Summers ordered that no one was allowed to tell her what had happened. Two nights ago she'd finally started cross-examining a witness. It was the Iranian concierge, Rasheed, and he was speaking some foreign language. Parish couldn't understand a word he was saying, but no one seemed to notice. Finally, Summers peered down at her over his reading glasses and said, "Ms. Parish, didn't you take your Farsi classes?"

She took a facecloth, soaked it in the cold water, squeezed it, and ran it over the back of her neck, her forehead, and the rest of her face. She clicked off the bathroom light and felt her way to her clothes cupboard. There were just two T-shirts left. After that she'd have to do the laundry. Unless she pulled some T-shirts out of the bin and hung them over a chair.

Parish folded the covers back on the side of the bed where she hadn't been sleeping. All week she'd been alternating sides, letting the sweat-soaked side dry out while she switched to the dry one. This is not why they invented queen-size beds, Parish thought as she bulked up the pillows on her new side and flicked on the reading lamp.

It was always like this once she started a big trial. The rolling nightmares, the slow descent of her personal life into a slovenly mess. When she was in court all day and running to the jail at night, there was no time for anything. Forget cooking or cleaning, just managing to eat was an accomplishment.

Before a long trial she tried to plan ahead. Stock up on provisions, like those people on the Gulf Coast battening down before a storm. She'd get money from the cash machine, boxes of pens and paper, piles of frozen meals, fresh stockings and underwear. Inevitably she forgot some vital cog in the wheel of her life, and disaster loomed. The printer for her computer would run out of toner, she'd be out of shampoo, her period would hit and she'd be down to her last Tampax.

Maybe I should strip the bed and do the laundry, she thought, knowing there was no way she was going back to sleep. Maybe, she thought, yeah maybe. Instead, like a rejected lover rereading a Dear John letter, she picked up her trial binder and turned to the notes she'd made to herself about her visit with Kevin Brace last night.

As she looked at the page, the fog of her sleep cleared immediately. She remembered exactly how it had happened. She'd decided to write out what she wanted to say to him, so she took his notebook and printed:

Mr. Brace, the Crown has just told me that within the next 24 hours they may have some new evidence. At this stage they won't tell me what it is. They'll probably want to adjourn the hearing tomorrow and let you out on bail.

Parish watched Brace's eyes as he carefully read her note. For once, he showed some emotion. He seemed alarmed by this news. He wrote back:

No adjournment. No bail. Please proceed.

Well, you couldn't call the man verbose. That would make a good cartoon, she thought. A lawyer is at the counsel table with her client, who passes over a piece of paper just as the trial is about to begin. He's written, "I hate to tell you this now, but I did it."

She took Brace's book, doing a little tit for tat, and wrote back:

I understand you don't want bail. But why not adjourn this?

He looked her straight in the eye and held her gaze for a long moment before he wrote back to her. The joke she'd just told herself was playing in her brain, and she'd just allowed herself a little smile when she read his reply:

I am going to plead guilty.

She couldn't shake the look she'd seen in his eyes. To her amazement, he had looked relieved.

Parish got out of bed and walked to the little bay window in her front room. Even though she lived four blocks south of the Danforth, one of Toronto's busiest streets, she could hear car horns blaring up and down the big street. I should feel relieved too, she thought. Be out celebrating because the Leafs have won the cup and I'm going to get my life back.

Yay. Celebrate losing my first murder trial. Lucky me. I'll be able to go home for Mother's Day.

She looked back at her rumpled sheets, the pile of laundry, unread books and magazines stacked high beside the bed. And a box marked BRACE beside them.

There was no way she'd get back to sleep. Instead she sat down cross-legged on the floor next to the box and pulled it open. My last night on this case, she thought as she hauled out her trial binder marked "Witness Statements." What is it, Kevin Brace, that I'm missing here? she wondered for the thousandth time. What is it?

54

Ari Greene looked hard into Sarah McGill's eyes. He'd expected that she'd be shocked to see him here in the empty hallway of the Market Place Tower in the middle of the night, but her eyes were calm. Waiting. Refusing to be surprised by anything. The eyes of someone who'd been through enough torment in her life that there was nothing left to shock her. He recognized those eyes. They were the eyes of the survivors. Of his parents and their friends.

Greene turned to Edna Wingate. She still looked stunned. He nodded his head back toward McGill.

"Sorry to interrupt your mother-and-daughter reunion."

Wingate looked at McGill, then back at Greene. Her face was flushed.

Greene reached into the pocket of his sport coat and pulled out an official-looking envelope. "You know, I can organize a big criminal file perfectly, every page in the right spot. But when it comes to my own paperwork, I'm a disaster. The other day I got this in the mail."

The envelope made a crinkling sound as he extracted a single sheet of paper. "Damn parking tickets. I get a ton of them, especially when I'm on a big case. Always forget to pay them on time, so I get one of these: Notice of Trial. It always takes months for the paperwork to come through. This ticket is for December 17, Market Lane. The street beside this building. Officer Kennicott used my car and parked it there the day

Katherine Torn was killed. He didn't have my badge, and we both forgot about the meter. Yesterday when I got this in the mail, I thought back to that first morning and the pickup truck that was parked in front of me. The one piled with snow on it. From up north somewhere."

Greene reached into the envelope again and pulled out a second piece of paper. He took a moment and looked at it, as if he were reading it for the first time.

"Ms. McGill, I got your license plate and ran it to see if you'd gotten any tickets. Only one." He held up the piece of paper for her to see. "Your truck was parked on the side street beside the building on the night of the murder. I parked behind it when I came in that morning." He looked McGill full in the face. "Usually you'd leave before six so you wouldn't get a ticket. But with everything that was going on, you were delayed. Needed a place to hide for a while until the coast was clear. Then I thought, Where did you go? Must have stayed with someone you knew in the building. But, I thought, how would you know someone on another floor?

"Tonight I was at my dad's house watching the game. You could smell the lilacs out back. Mother's Day is coming up. It's the first one since my mother died. I used to pick those lilacs for her as a present. And I thought about you, Ms. McGill. You're a botanist. What, I wondered, did your girls give you for Mother's Day? Amanda and Beatrice. My father commented a while back about how you gave them very British names. And it came to me. Edna Wingate's your mother. The night Katherine was murdered, you stayed right here with your mom until the coast was clear."

He turned back to Edna Wingate. "And, Ms. Wingate, that morning you had to get to your yoga? I called the place. Your class didn't start until nine. You invited me to come back the next morning, so it gave your daughter time to make good her escape."

Both women were stone silent. Greene was doing more talking than he usually did with witnesses. But in a situation like this, their silence spoke volumes. He was guessing a lot here, and their lack of response was all the confirmation he needed.

Greene looked back to McGill. He reached into the inside pocket of his sport jacket and, feeling a bit like a magician now, pulled out a plastic bag. There was a thin metal spoon inside. A big green label taped across it read R.V. BRACE: SPOON FROM HARDSCRABBLE CAFÉ, DECEMBER 20.

"Ms. McGill, I'm afraid I owe you a spoon," Greene said. "The first time I visited your café back in December, I picked this up on my way out. Bad habit of mine, collecting things." He waved the spoon back and forth slowly, like a snake charmer's flute. Really, this was just a prop, not evidence. Officer Kennicott had found her prints on file months ago, and McGill would realize this if he gave her time to think about it. The idea was to throw her off gaurd. Get her talking. "We found some fingerprints on the inside front-door handle of apartment 12A and matched them with this spoon. They're your prints."

Greene had rehearsed in his head many times what he'd say to McGill at this moment. Should he say, "Kevin Brace's apartment" or even "your ex-husband's apartment"? He'd decided to be strictly legal about it. The Braces had never gotten divorced, and Greene wanted McGill to know he knew that. Besides, in her mind, maybe Brace still was her husband.

Looking at the spoon, McGill's eyes widened. Greene wasn't sure if she was surprised that he'd found her prints in Brace's place or if she was just glad to recover her lost spoon. Greene had the feeling that not one piece of cutlery went missing from the Hardscrabble Café without Sarah's knowing about it. She didn't say a word.

"If your prints were on, say, a jar in the back of a kitchen cupboard or an ice-cube tray buried in the freezer, it wouldn't mean much. Those are places where a print could remain for weeks, months. But prints in a high-traffic area like the inside front-door handle are presumed to be very recent."

McGill flicked her eyes toward Wingate, then back at Greene.

Greene had no grounds to arrest McGill. He had a subpoena in his pocket and could force her to testify at the prelim, but the questions she could be asked there were limited. Right now was the time to get her to talk. He needed to get her out of the hallway. He took a step closer—not too close, but close enough to let her know he wasn't going away.

"It gets worse," he said, lowering his voice. "We found another of your prints on the metal bracket behind the door." Greene still had the plastic evidence bag in his hand. "Mr. Singh, the newspaper delivery fellow? We've established that he never looked behind the door when he walked into the apartment. Kevin pushed it all the way over to the wall to let him in. When Officer Kennicott arrived a few minutes later, the door was halfway open again. That could only mean one thing. Someone was behind the door when Singh first walked in."

McGill was staring at the plastic bag with the spoon inside. For a moment Greene thought she might try to grab it and run.

Just then he heard footsteps in the stairwell, coming up quickly. A moment later the door behind McGill swung open. Officer Kennicott, gulping air yet remaining very calm, stood in the doorway. He wore a business suit and tie, just as Greene had instructed, and carried a small briefcase under his arm. Kennicott had effectively—and, more important, psychologically—cut off any means of escape.

"This is Officer Kennicott," Greene said calmly, as if it were an everyday occurrence for the four of them to meet in the hallway of the Market Place Tower in the middle of the night.

He turned back to Edna Wingate. "May we come inside for some tea?"

Wingate simply nodded.

Without being asked, McGill led the way in.

Wingate followed her daughter, and Greene let Kennicott go in before him.

Everyone sat around the circular glass-topped kitchen table. No one spoke.

McGill pulled out a package of cigarettes. It was already open. She tapped hard on the bottom of the pack, trying to get out a smoke. It wouldn't come.

"I fell off the wagon, Detective," she said to Greene, who was sitting across the table from her. "Tried to quit. No dice." She smacked the pack again until a filter finally emerged.

Greene smiled. McGill was playing for time. He tried to track the emotions he saw running through her cool exterior. Shock, anger, denial, bargaining, acceptance. What was it? The key thing was that she was talking. She hadn't denied the fingerprints or that she'd been in 12A on the morning Torn was killed. That was a good thing because the fingerprint evidence in and of itself was not as open-and-shut as he'd presented it to her.

He decided to completely change the topic. Take them by surprise and put them at ease a bit. "Ms. McGill, I saw your daughter Amanda a few months ago. Before the baby was born. I heard she had a girl. Your first grandchild. And, Ms. Wingate, your first great-grandchild. Congratulations."

This seemed to transform McGill. She slid the cigarette pack onto the table. The cellophane made a squeaking sound. Her face broke out into a magnificent smile.

"Shannon is four months tomorrow, and little Gareth out in Calgary is six weeks," she said. "It's funny. You have kids, and you think they'll never grow up. All of a sudden they have jobs, spouses, mortgages. And now babies."

Greene nodded. "You deserve it, Ms. McGill, especially after your son."

Her mood change was instant. She clawed back at her cigarettes. "Read my whole damn file, I bet, didn't you, Detective? All those fucking social workers." For the first time she seemed to lose her composure.

Wingate looked over at McGill. Mother, daughter. A look of seasoned pain on her face.

"Things were very different back then," Greene said, watching her intently. "They treated you terribly, that much I understand."

"Understand?" Her face reddened. "How could you ever understand what it's like for a parent to have her child taken away?"

Greene curled his hands, digging his fingernails into his palms. For a moment he thought of Hannah, his father's lost daughter. He feared he'd never know what else his father had lost.

"Back then, as you call it, they thought nothing of just grabbing your children. Taking them away." McGill tapped the back of her cigarette again. "They labeled you a bad mother, and that was it."

Greene nodded. "I've read the reports. Kevin junior was severely autistic, and from the age of two—"

"Refrigerator mom, they called me. Preoccupied with myself because I left Kevin in the crib for half an hour," McGill said, the bitterness barely below the surface, like a rocky outcrop covered with a thin layer of moss. "Those books and articles by that ass Bruno Bettelheim. Children's Aid made me read them all. Their favorite was one called "Joey: A Mechanical Boy," all about how the child was saved from his evil, neglectful parents by his warm and loving therapist. A goddamn fairy tale."

Greene nodded. McGill was dead right. When he'd come across this in the file, he'd done some reading about the controversial psychologist Bruno Bettelheim. In the 1950s Dr. B, as he liked to be called, developed a theory of treatment for a then-new field of study—childhood autism. Bettelheim, who claimed to have studied with Freud, blamed the parents, mostly the mothers, who he said had subconscious death wishes for their children. Especially boys. Even the most conscientious mother was suspect.

"Those social workers would come and sit in our kitchen and write down everything I did on their damn little yellow charts. Every word I said. Every gesture I made. They didn't care that Amanda and Beatrice were perfect children. Oh no. They said I didn't even realize that I wanted Kevin junior dead. I was a threat to my own son. Even to my daughters. Whatever I did, I was guilty."

Tears jumped from her eyes. A bit of a surprise to Greene, like her swearing and her smoking. They slid down her cheeks, and she didn't move to wipe them off.

Wingate put her hand out across the table and held McGill's arm. "It was worse than losing my parents in the war," Wingate said. "Seeing my daughter blamed. Then the threat that we'd lose the girls."

Kennicott had passed Greene a beige file folder from the briefcase he was carrying. Greene opened it. "That's why, Ms. McGill, you quietly signed over custody of the girls to Kevin," he said.

McGill looked at Greene, still not wiping away the tears. "It was the only way to keep from losing them. Kevin left me, and the girls went to live with him. I had to sign over full custody to him. No access." Suddenly she laughed. A loud, strong laugh. "You should have seen those Children's Aid people when they heard that Kevin had my girls. They were desperate to get their hands on them. What could they do? And poor Kevin. Everyone thought he was the bastard who'd dumped his helpless wife, left her and took their kids. The press hated him for it. Kevin just took it. Never said a word."

Now the tears were streaming down her face. Greene reached into his pocket, pulled out a freshly pressed handkerchief, and passed it across to her. She clutched it, but still made no move to wipe her face.

"The day I heard that Bettleheim committed suicide was the best day of my life, after the birth of my children and my wedding day," McGill said. She looked at the handkerchief in her hand as if she was uncertain how it got there. No one moved.

"After they took my son, I lost it. Poor Kevin," she said, taking up her pack of cigarettes, crushing it, and tossing it back onto the glass table. "He loved two women in his life, and we were both crazy."

"You weren't crazy, Ms. McGill," Greene said. "Your child was stolen from you."

McGill finally put the handkerchief to her face. "Stolen," she said.

She picked up her crushed cigarette pack. She dug into it and managed to get out a slightly mangled cigarette. She lit it and calmly blew the smoke away from the table. "Now you know our little secret, Detective. Kevin would bring the girls to Sunday figure skating, Sunday soccer, Sunday gymnastics. I was a master of disguise. All those years when the kids were growing up, I snuck down. Never missed a week. By the time the social workers finally backed off, the girls were teenagers with a million friends each." She eyed the beige file on the table. "That my Children's Aid file?"

Greene shook his head and tapped the closed file. "No. I have your recent bank records in here. Tough times for the Hardscrabble Café."

She met his eyes. "I told you that the first time you came. It's a difficult business."

"Every month, you get a cash injection of two thousand dollars. Seems to be keeping you going."

McGill twirled the cigarette in her hand.

"And I've got your husband's bank statement," Greene said, deliberately choosing the word "husband." "For the last year, two thousand dollars in cash has come out of his account at the beginning of each month." Keeping his hand on the unopened file, he met her eyes. "As you told me, the mail takes only two days to get up to Haliburton. In a homicide investigation, sometimes it's the most obvious things you overlook. Yesterday it all fell into place for me. You came down to Toronto the night before Katherine Torn was killed. The concierge, Rasheed, told me that Kevin had asked him to put a brick in the basement door on Sunday. You came in unnoticed. Never caught on video."

McGill began to twist the handkerchief. She didn't speak.

"Your truck, which still had snow on it from the drive down, got the parking ticket because you got delayed, didn't you?"

The silence in the room was palpable. All eyes were on McGill.

"I was in 12A that night, Detective," McGill said at last.

"And that morning too," Greene said. "When Mr. Singh came, you were right behind the front door."

Like hikers cresting a high ridge, they'd just crossed over into new territory. And they both knew it.

55

Fernandez checked his watch as he pulled open the gray steel door of Vesta Lunch. It was 1:59 a.m. Stacks of freshly printed newspapers blared out headlines declaring THE LEAFS WIN THE CUP, LORD STANLEY IS OURS, and LEAF NATION CELEBRATES. The counter was packed with customers, most of them wearing blue-and-white Leafs hockey shirts. The big stand-up fridge behind the counter was plastered with GO LEAFS GO bumper stickers, and blue-and-white flags sprouted on all sides of the old-fashioned cash register. Even the picture of Mother Teresa above the door was adorned with the team's flags.

The Vesta Lunch had been a low-rent Toronto tradition since it opened in 1955. Serving breakfast twenty-four hours a day—and preparing take-out meals for the prisoners housed at nearby 14 Division, often with a little bonus for the police officers who picked up the brown bags—the diner was a natural late-night hangout for prostitutes between gigs, students wired on coffee, and the assorted detritus of the city's midnight hours.

Fernandez had driven by the place many times and never thought to go inside. But earlier that evening, as he was crossing Queen Street, Phil Cutter, the loudmouthed Crown Attorney, had come up behind him.

"Fernandez, I need to talk to you," Cutter said, getting close, so that his booming voice sounded all the louder.

Fernandez looked to his left and saw a streetcar coming toward them. He quickened his pace. Cutter followed in step.

"You know the Vesta Lunch? An all-night diner at Bathurst and Dupont?"

"I've seen it," Fernandez said as he reached the far curb. As usual, the sidewalk was packed with people.

"Good. Meet us there at two a.m. sharp," Cutter said.

"Two a.m.?"

"Two a.m. Don't be late."

"What's this about?"

"Just be there. The Vesta." Cutter turned and vanished into the crowded sidewalk traffic. That was it. Nothing in writing. No cell phone calls. No e-mail.

Fernandez looked around the diner. The window side had a number of booths with high-backed bench chairs. Phil Cutter, Barb Gild, and the chief of police, Hap Charlton, were in the last one. There was a space open for Fernandez beside Charlton.

Fernandez took the empty seat. In his hand he had a folded notebook and a new, thick pen that he put in front of him on the table.

"Coffee?" Charlton asked. He was as affable as ever. There was a steaming mug in front of each of the other three.

"No, I'm fine," Fernandez said.

"Our distinguished colleague doesn't deign to drink watery Canadian coffee," Cutter said. Even when he tried to whisper, his voice was a growling bark. There was a napkin on the table, and he was flipping it over and over. A substitute for not being able to pace back and forth, Fernandez thought.

Charlton chuckled. "This stuff *is* pretty darn watery," he said. "Drank it for decades. Night shift—Vesta Lunch—one and the same for a copper. Getting spoiled by the fancy lattes at headquarters."

Fernandez gave Charlton a forced grin. Everyone grew quiet. It was time to end the chitchat.

"So," Fernandez said, opening the notebook and picking up his pen, "what've you got?"

"Put down your fancy pen, Albert," Cutter said. He kept flipping his napkin back and forth, faster now.

Fernandez looked him in the eye as he slowly closed his notebook and put his pen on top. He looked around, unsure who was going to speak.

"Brace wants to plead guilty." To Fernandez's surprise, it was Barb Gild who was talking.

Fernandez gave her a slight nod and waited for an explanation. No one said anything.

It took a few moments until it sank in. So this is how they want to play it, he thought. They're going to tell me only what they think I need to know. If I want more information, I have to ask for it.

"What's he want to plead guilty to?" Fernandez asked.

"First," Gild said.

Fernandez felt a spasm in his stomach. "When?"

"This morning."

His stomach started to churn. "Who told you this?" he asked Gild. He could think of only one thing. The pages Marissa had found in the photocopier outside her office.

"Do you really need to know?" It was Cutter speaking. For once, his voice actually was quiet, and he'd even stopped playing with his napkin. He looked at Gild, then at Charlton, and flipped his napkin very slowly.

"Do I?" Fernandez asked.

"Look," Cutter said. Remarkably, he was still keeping his voice down. "This plea needs to go through without a hitch. Got it?"

"Well, I'm not going to stand in the way of his pleading."

"Yeah, but Summers might."

"Summers? Why?" Fernandez asked.

Cutter gave his colleagues another look. "There might be complications."

"Such as?" Fernandez looked around. Silence. "Do I have to keep guessing?"

Charlton finally spoke. "Such as Brace's lawyer."

"Parish?" Fernandez had not expected this. "She'll be upset, sure.

She's worked her tail off, and she's got a good shot at beating the first degree at least. How's that a complication?"

Again he looked around. No one moved. He'd never seen Cutter so still.

Then he saw it all. So clearly.

"Wait," he said. "How do you know what he's told his lawyer? That's solicitor-client privilege."

Silence again.

"No judge in this province would authorize a wiretap on her phone."

"True," Charlton said. "No judge would authorize it."

Again the silence. Fernandez understood. They were telling him that just because it wasn't authorized doesn't mean they'd never do it. No one would ever know. The image flashed through his mind of a bunch of police officers sitting in a room listening in on Nancy Parish's personal phone calls. The ache in his stomach seemed to rise in his gut. He thought of the photocopied pages again. About Brace's silence; his writing out of instructions.

"But I thought Brace wasn't talking," Fernandez said.

Cutter leaned in real close, his voice as near to a whisper as he could get it, but still loud enough to hear clearly. "We got the information from the best possible source. Brace's own handwriting." Then he began to laugh—that piercing, annoying laugh, which seemed even more sinister at half volume.

Thank you, Cutter, Fernandez said to himself, moving his pen a bit farther toward the other side of the table. "You had someone in the jail looking at that notebook Brace carried everywhere with him?"

Cutter could barely contain his glee. "Most people forget, but I started out as a defense lawyer. Long time ago. Let's just say that I'm still on good terms with an unnamed veteran guard at the Don."

Fernandez nodded his head slowly. "And that's why Detective Greene isn't here," he said.

"Listen, Fernandez," Cutter said. He was playing with the napkin again. "This city is going to rat shit. You know that. We see it every day in court. All the guns. The gangbangers. You want to prosecute homicides? This is what you're going to be up against. Don't give me any of your Boy Scout bullshit: 'Crowns don't care about winning or losing.' Up here in homicide prosecutions, we play to win. Besides, don't worry about your pal Nancy Parish. Brace never calls her. Period."

"Okay," Fernandez said. "What do you want me to do?"

Cutter started to laugh. "Easy. Win the case. If Brace tries to fire Parish, object. Parish tries to get off the case, object. Don't give Summers any wiggle room."

Gild jumped in. "The law is clear. Absent evidence of mental incapacity, which she doesn't have, Parish has no right to prevent her client from pleading guilty. Worst-case scenario, she steps down as counsel, Brace enters his plea. He should be off doing twenty-five years by ten thirty this morning."

"And, Albert," Cutter said, "you'll be undefeated in your murder prosecutions. Perfect start to your new career." Cutter had never called Fernandez by his first name before. "We're thin on talent at the top, buddy. There's going to be a lot of work for you."

Fernandez nodded. Then he smiled. The tension in their little booth seemed to ease. Cutter ripped up his napkin.

"I assume this meeting never happened," Fernandez said.

Charlton gave a big laugh. "We're paying cash. Nick behind the counter there, he's known me since I was a beat cop. We'd come here on slow nights and drink coffee for a few hours, and every fifteen minutes one of us would go outside and report in a new position. Nick never said a word. Anyone comes snooping, he'll tell them he hasn't seen me in months."

Fernandez looked back at the counter. A tall man with a graying mustache was wiping it down with long, relaxed strokes. His white uniform and apron had a night's worth of stains on them. The black-and-white clock on the wall said it was 2:30.

"Looks like I've got an interesting day ahead of me," Fernandez said, picking up his notebook and pen. "I'll see all of you in court."

And Marissa, I'll be home early for a change, he thought. It should be a very nice evening. With something special to celebrate.

56

We lose ten, sometimes fifteen pieces of cutlery a month, mostly knives," Sarah McGill said, raising the plastic bag with the spoon in it and waving it accusingly at Ari Greene. "It adds up."

"I'm sure it does," he said.

Greene had seen this over and over again with witnesses. And it never ceased to amaze him. Faced with the biggest crisis of their lives, people would focus on alarmingly trivial matters. Losing everything else, they grasped at the small things they could control. And clung to them hard.

During the last murder trial he worked on, the prisoner was more concerned about what he got for lunch than the evidence that kept piling up around him. The worse the case got, the louder his mealtime complaints became.

Still holding the bag in front of her, McGill began to worry the edges of the plastic, like a little girl holding the corner of her favorite blanket.

"I won't go to court," she said at last.

Greene had expected this. He tapped the inside of his jacket pocket. "I have a subpoena for you right here," he said. "I'd hate to force you to go, but your husband is looking at a possible twenty-five-year sentence. Clearly you have material evidence."

"Children's Aid will be there."

Greene hadn't expected this. Never underestimate the deep currents that run through people's lives, or their unseen motivations, he thought. "Ms. McGill, this is a murder trial. I can't imagine Children's Aid would have any interest in it."

McGill brought her fist down on the table. *Bang.* She hit it with such force that he was afraid the glass would break. "Can't imagine. No, you can't imagine, can you?"

Greene met her eyes squarely without saying a word.

"These people just don't give up," she said. "Never. If they hear I was in the apartment when Katherine died, they'll never let me see my children again."

"But, Ms. McGill, your daughters are grown," he said. Greene glanced at Kennicott. He seemed equally bewildered. "The Children's Aid Society has nothing to do with them anymore."

McGill tightened her lips in anger. "You don't get it, do you?"

Suddenly he understood. Despite all her appearance of well-adjusted normalcy, McGill was paranoid beyond reach. And with just cause. Like his parents and all their survivor friends. He, of all people, should have seen this coming.

"Your grandchildren," he whispered.

McGill stared straight ahead. No eye contact. She was shutting down.

"Those bastards," McGill said at last. "I'm not going to let them keep me from my babies again." She shook her head hard, in a way that said, "I don't want to talk about it anymore."

"We know that Katherine had problems with alcohol," Greene said. Using "we" made it seem more authoritative, and more comforting. He needed to kick-start the conversation. Get her talking. "Officer Kennicott here has spoken to a number of people about Ms. Torn. The people she injured."

McGill nodded. That was a start.

Greene kept going. "We know that Katherine was a penny-pincher. Officer Kennicott found a whole stack of food coupons in her wallet. Her Visa bill shows very modest spending. How did she feel about Kevin giving you two thousand a month?"

McGill flashed a look at Wingate, then turned back to Greene. She didn't say a word, but at least she wasn't refusing to talk.

Greene jumped into the silence. "Did she know about the money?"

"She found out."

Good, Greene thought, relieved to hear McGill's voice again.

"I imagine she wasn't very happy," he said.

"Nothing made Katherine *very* happy, Detective. Not having my husband, not having my girls, the apartment, the travel, the media attention. None of it. She was angry from the day she found out about her father."

Greene glanced over at Kennicott, then back at McGill. "You mean Dr. Torn?"

McGill snorted loudly. "You don't know, Detective?"

Greene shook his head.

"I mean her *real* father. Some horseback rider down in California her mother hooked up with on one of her riding competitions. Katherine found out when she was thirteen. Never got over it."

Greene nodded at Kennicott. So that explained Dr. Torn, he thought. "Kate was *her* only child," Dr. Torn had told Greene and Fernandez when they first met at Old City Hall.

"Why were you in your husband's apartment the morning Katherine died?" he asked, echoing her phrase "Katherine died"—not "Katherine was killed."

"I needed more money. The highway construction. They said it would take nine months. It's killing the café. Even two thousand wasn't enough."

"So you came early in the morning?"

McGill didn't say a word.

"And your husband was awake."

"My husband never slept much. Katherine, she slept all the time."

"Except that morning."

"I thought she'd be asleep. It was five in the morning."

"But you were wrong, she was in the bath."

"Katherine? You must be kidding." McGill started to laugh. It was her loud, real laugh. "You think Katherine Torn would ever take a bath in the hallway tub instead of in her five-thousand-dollar Jacuzzi?"

Greene remembered all the receipts Kennicott had found in Torn's wallet for expensive toiletries. And Detective Ho remarking that the hallway bathtub didn't even have a soap dish. He thought of his house. How he preferred his own bathroom, the one where Raglan had joined him to soap his back, instead of the ratty one in the basement. And he knew that Sarah McGill was telling the truth.

"My husband's a creature of habit. He's taken a cold bath every morning of his life. When I got there, he was still in his bathrobe. He'd only just filled the tub."

"Then how did Katherine end up in the bathtub, Ms. McGill? The one in the hallway."

"Kevin put her there," she said, as calmly as if she were telling a customer about the restaurant's daily specials. "After she died."

"Died" again. Not "was killed" or "was murdered," but "died." As if death were something that just happened to Katherine Torn, like night sweats or a migraine headache.

"And how did that happen? Katherine dying?"

McGill picked up the plastic bag with the spoon and rubbed it. "It's amazing how fleeting life is. But I guess you know that from your job. My husband and I were in the kitchen, whispering like two teenagers who think their parents are asleep. He was just cutting up his morning oranges. Suddenly Katherine was standing behind us. Stone naked. I don't know what woke her up. She grabbed Kevin by the neck. It happened so fast. She started yelling, 'Bastard, bastard . . . you'll never be on the radio again.' Don't feel bad for Katherine, Detective. She got everything she wanted out of this."

No one in the room seemed to move or even breathe. Greene scanned back in his mind through all he knew about the case: Brace cutting up his oranges every morning; his hoarse, barely audible voice the one time he talked to Dent in his cell; the scratch marks Torn had inflicted with her bare hands on the two men who had tried to help her, Howard Peel, her AA sponsor, and Donald Dundas, her radio teacher; the unsigned million-dollar contract; Torn and Brace not holding hands when they came back through the lobby after their meeting with Peel.

McGill's eyes had lost focus. "It took forever to pry her hands off him." She was looking vaguely over Greene's shoulder. He could tell she was no longer seeing the apartment. She was staring into the past.

"Then what happened?" Greene asked softly.

McGill nodded as if in a trance.

"Kevin was saying, 'Katherine, Katherine.' He was making a gurgling sound. His face was turning red. I screamed something, I can't remember what, and I grabbed her hands. She finally let go of Kevin and spun on me. Her eyes—they were so, so angry."

Greene nodded. Once a witness started really talking, the best thing to do was to keep your mouth shut.

"Kevin was gasping for air. Katherine broke her hands free from my grasp and turned back to him. She grabbed his hand that was holding the knife and yelled, 'Now you're both fucked!' I'll never forget those words."

McGill's eyes turned back to Greene like a camera lens coming into focus.

"That's what she wanted," McGill said, her voice down to a faint whisper.

"What was that?" Greene asked, finally breaking his silence.

"To keep us apart. To fuck us over. She knew about the grandchildren and Children's Aid and that, because I was there when this happened, I'd be screwed. She plunged Kevin's knife right into her stomach. Kevin tried to stop her. My first thought was that this was another one of Katherine's drama queen acts. I figured one stab wound, she'd be all right. But she slipped, fell somehow."

Greene glanced at Kennicott. He was looking down.

"I slipped on that floor too," Kennicott said.

McGill turned to him. She seemed to have forgotten he was there. "The knife must have hit an artery or something. She died so fast. In seconds."

Greene remembered Dr. McKilty showing them the thin slice of her aorta. All it took to kill her in seconds.

"I couldn't believe it. Kevin couldn't speak. We heard the elevator down the hall. He barely whispered 'Hide' and pointed behind the front door. I was so stunned. It's a wide hallway, so there was lots of room. When I got behind the door, someone was walking down the hall, humming away. I looked back into the apartment, and Kevin was carrying Katherine's body into the bathroom. I wanted to call out, tell him to stop. But there was no time. The man was right at the door. I heard him shuffling his feet. He even dropped the newspaper on the floor. I just stood there, inches away, not moving."

Greene looked over at Kennicott. Their eyes met for a moment; then he turned back to McGill and nodded.

"Kevin came to the door. I heard him whisper to the man, 'I killed her, Mr. Singh.' He could barely speak. Kevin followed him into the apartment, down the main corridor, without looking back. He signaled with his hands behind his back for me to leave. There was nothing else I could do."

Greene replayed the scene in his head, trying to see how it had all unfolded. Katherine Torn, angry, crazed. Brace, shocked, panicked. Singh relentlessly punctual. And Sarah McGill, frozen behind the door.

McGill crossed her arms in front of her. She started to rock very slowly.

"Ms. McGill, your husband is charged with first-degree murder. Twenty-five years in jail if he's convicted. Why didn't you tell us this before?"

McGill looked over at Wingate. She rocked back and forth a few more times. "My husband wouldn't want me to."

"How do you know that?"

"He's my husband."

"Officer Kennicott and I are not in the business of convicting innocent people."

"Then don't call me as a witness," McGill said. "You try to put me on the stand, and Kevin will plead guilty in the blink of an eye."

"But what you've just told us would provide a complete defense. I can promise you we will deal with Children's Aid."

McGill looked over at Wingate. The daughter looking to her mother for something. What?

"If you testify, I can—"

"I won't testify," she said, slamming her hand down again. "I can't. I won't. I won't let them. Not again . . ." Her voice trailed off.

The tension in the room was almost unbearable. It was important at a time like this to change tack, give everyone a breather. But still make your presence more permanent, so the witness forgets that she always has the option to simply ask you to leave.

The lilacs Greene had given to Wingate and McGill sat in front of them like purple place decorations. It had been more than two hours since he'd picked them. They were wilting but not beyond saving.

Amazing how fast life can go out of something, he thought as he reached out for both twigs. "I'll put these in water," he said as he stood up from the table.

He opened a cupboard in the kitchen to the right of the sink. The bottom shelf was filled with clear glass cups. But it was the glasses on the second row that caught his eye.

The whole shelf was filled with a vast array of blue-and-white Toronto Maple Leafs glasses. He reached up and took two out, filled them with cold water, and scored the bottom of the lilac twigs with a sharp knife before he plunked one in each.

He turned to bring them back to the table in time to see McGill and Wingate exchange worried glances. They stared at the glasses in his hands.

Like a man digging for treasure whose spade had struck metal, Greene knew he was right.

How could I have missed this? he thought as he sat slowly back down in his seat, keeping the two glasses of drooping lilacs in front of him.

"You're wrong about me not missing much," he said to Sarah McGill.

She looked at Greene. Fire in her eyes.

"Your son. Kevin junior. The one they took away as a boy. He's been living here with your mother," Greene said. "His grandma's here, and his father's right down the hall to help out. He's tall, like his dad. That's why the Maple Leafs glasses are on the second shelf. And that's why these same glasses are over in 12A."

He turned to Edna Wingate. "That's the other reason you kept me out of your apartment that first morning. So your grandson could leave too."

No one spoke.

He turned back to McGill. "You're looking ahead. Your mom can't walk those stairs forever. You have your daughter renovating her basement so Kevin junior has a place to live. I'll bet he's there now. Where was he the morning Katherine Torn died?" Greene asked McGill.

"He needs us," she said.

"December seventeenth?"

"And his Maple Leafs glasses."

"In this apartment? Or was he with you and Kevin next door?"

"He won't let anyone else wash them."

"Was he with you in 12A?"

"He needs his things with him."

"Was he angry?"

"If they take him away, he'll die."

"Did he stab her?"

This seemed to snap McGill out of her mantra. "No," she said. "My son did not stab Katherine Torn. My son cries when a leaf falls off one of his tomato plants."

Greene turned to Wingate. "Where was your grandson that night?"

Wingate looked at him. Her eyes narrowed. There was steel behind those laughing eyes. The steel of a woman orphaned at nineteen, three times widowed, her only grandson severely disabled, but still carrying on. "The boy was not in 12A. You can do all the DNA and fingerprint tests you like. He's never walked in that door. Never even been as far as the elevator. The only times he goes out, we use the back stairs."

There are two things you think when a witness answers a question in absolutes, Greene always taught the young recruits at Police College. Words like "never" and "always" are very dangerous for a witness, and for an investigator. When someone tells you she's never done something, it is either the truth or a desperate, bold-faced lie. If you can contradict her, then you have her. But if the story holds up, she has you.

"I believe you," Greene said.

He turned back to McGill. "We really have no choice." He reached into his pocket and pulled out the subpoena and touched her hands with it. "I'm sorry, Ms. McGill. With all my heart, I wish there was another way."

"You don't understand about Kevin and his son," she said.

"I'm sure he loves him," Greene said.

McGill laughed. Her old, deep laugh. She shook her head. "Kevin loved Katherine. I had to accept that, and eventually I did. That she couldn't accept that he still loved me was her problem. But both of us didn't stand a chance next to Kevin junior. Don't you see that? Kevin hated his own father; his son is everything. Twenty-five years in jail. He'll do that without blinking an eye if it means saving Little Kevin one minute of fear. One more second of pain."

Greene looked back at Wingate. She was nodding her head. Her eyes closed.

"It's over, Detective," McGill said, turning the subpoena in her hand. "I know my husband. He'll have already figured this out." She looked over at Kennicott. "Amanda was in court when you testified the other day, Officer. She could see you piecing it together when you looked at the diagram of the apartment. It would be dead obvious to my husband."

Greene looked across the table at Kennicott. There comes a point in an investigation when there are simply no more questions to ask. When all the answers suddenly line up. He could tell by the look in Kennicott's eyes that they'd both seen the same thing. That they'd got to ground zero.

"You're wrong about just one thing." It was Wingate talking. She'd opened her eyes. "We're not moving because I can't do the stairs," she said.

Greene found himself smiling.

"Oh, Mother," McGill said. She was smiling too.

"The stairs are getting too hard for Kevin junior. That's the only reason. My yoga instructor says I've got the strongest quads he's ever seen in an eighty-three-year-old."

Greene nodded, about to tell Ms. Wingate that, yes, she'd told him that before. But he stopped. He sat back and caught Sarah McGill's eye. She'd heard it too. The repetition. He saw the perfect facade her mother wore to hide the early signs of decay.

Sarah McGill, he thought, you're the one who doesn't miss a thing.

He took one of the lilacs in front of him and passed it over to Edna Wingate. "I'd love to take a yoga class with you when this is all over," he said.

"Hot yoga," she said, putting the purple twig to her nose and inhaling deeply.

"Hot yoga it is," he said. And, as so often happens at times of extreme tension, everyone laughed.

57

Now, this is as good as it gets, Awotwe Amankwah thought as he lay in his small bedroom watching the lights of passing cars crisscross on the white ceiling, listening to the revelers outside on the street honking their car horns, blowing long plastic trumpets, and cheering and carrying on.

He couldn't care less about the Leafs. What made him so happy right now were his children, who lay asleep softly on his shoulders. The bedtime story he'd been telling them hours ago—about a town in a big valley, which one morning awoke to the rumbling of a volcano, and the two children who rushed from door to door waking up all the villagers, saving the old people—had lasted a long time. He could feel his kids struggling to stay awake, as the molten lava rushed down the hillside and the young heroes raced to get to the last cabin in the village along a winding, deserted path.

And now, in the early hours of the morning, he was still basking in the afterglow, the wonder of finally being alone with his children. Who would have thought, two years ago, that living in a stinking one-bedroom apartment on Gerrard Street—with the screeching sound of all-night streetcars passing by the flimsy window, his upright piano from home replaced by a used electric, the smell of cornstarch and garlic wafting up from the Chinese restaurant below—would ever feel like paradise.

From below on the street he heard a particularly loud whoop of revelers, and they began to chant, "We're number one, we're number one." No one ever gave Toronto hockey fans points for originality, Amankwah thought, shaking his head as he cradled his sleeping children.

What did it matter that his credit cards were maxed out? So what if he hadn't been with a woman for almost a year? Right now there were two hearts pounding next to his, the two chests rising and falling in the eternal rhythm of children's sleep. With all the overtime from covering the Brace trial, he'd finally saved up enough money to rent a place of his own.

"Enjoy your time with your children, Mr. Amankwah," Judge Heather the Leather had said to him last week when she gave the order allowing him overnight access.

Thank you, Kevin Brace, for stabbing Katherine Torn in the bathtub, he thought. Where would he have been without this lucky break? Amankwah shuddered to think. He'd have lost his overtime gig and fallen further behind on his support payments, and they'd have thrown his photo up on the Internet as a deadbeat dad.

The shouting outside grew particularly loud again. Someone kept blowing one of those blue plastic horns while a bunch of voices yelled out "Leafs! Leafs! Leafs!" and another set started singing an out-of-tune version of "We Are the Champions." He slipped over to the window. A few young Vietnamese kids, their black hair dyed Maple Leaf blue and white, were spilling out of the pool hall down the road, drunk.

He wondered what Nancy Parish would ask Detective Ho today. Yesterday after court everyone in the press corps was talking about her cross-examination of Mr. Singh. Amankwah smiled. If they only knew all the work he'd done through the *Star*'s India correspondent to get Mr. Singh's work history. It had been worthwhile.

He thought back again to when Officer Kennicott was on the stand. Amankwah picked up something he thought no one else saw. While he testified, Kennicott had kept his eyes on Fernandez, then Parish, with laserlike precision, except when Fernandez brought him to the floor plan of Brace's apartment. When Kennicott was back on the stand, Amankwah saw him sneak another look at the drawing. When he finished testifying and was walking out, Kennicott looked at the plan again. He'd seen something.

What was it? Amankwah said to himself, not quite sure if he'd said it out loud. He watched a near-empty streetcar roll by. The hockey fans seemed to have finally scattered.

Kennicott, what are you up to? he wondered as the car squealed its way down the street, curving at the end of the block.

He checked the time. It was just past six. He decided to send Nancy Parish an e-mail, but before he started typing, he saw that she'd just sent him one: "Call when you get up. How was the first night with the kids?"

He dialed her number.

"Hi, Awotwe," Parish said. "I thought you'd be asleep."

"Wide-awake," Amankwah said. "I was about to e-mail you."

"How was your night with the kids?"

"Fantastic. I can't even describe it," he said. "It's my name."

"What do you mean?"

"Awotwe. Means 'eighth.' I was the eighth child in my family. To live alone, for me, is torture."

"I'm so glad for you. Why were you e-mailing me?"

Amankwah told her about watching Kennicott on the stand and how, when he was leaving the court, he was looking at the floor plan. A thought occurred to him. "You weren't just e-mailing me about the kids, were you?" he asked.

There was a long pause on the line. "Just make sure you're there on time today," Parish said. "I can't tell you anything else."

After he hung up, Amankwah found himself looking at the phone in his hand, the way they do in the movies. Her message was unspoken but very clear: solicitor-client privilege—there was something happening, but she couldn't say what.

Back at the bookshelf beside his bed he pulled out a large notebook with BRACE written on it. He had extremely neat handwriting.

The teachers back home would slap the back of your hand with a ruler if you didn't hold your pencil properly. Not like these lax teachers his kids had in Canada. It amazed him how many Canadian journalists didn't know how to hold a pen.

This was his private diary of everything since the start of the Brace trial. He began to reread it page by page. Kennicott had seen something. What?

He finished the diary and, as he always did when he wanted to think, sat down at his keyboard. Slipping on some headphones, with the volume low, he began to play a gentle Chopin nocturne.

Through the sound of his music he heard another streetcar squeal its way down Gerrard, curving at the end of the block, until the sound faded and his own music took over again.

He thought back to the night he'd been at Brace's apartment with his ex-wife for their annual Christmas party. The place was exclusive, the only apartment on the whole half of the floor. The big front door and wide hallway. Brace had joked that it would be large enough to fit a wheelchair in there one day.

Amankwah's mind began to drift. He compared Brace's penthouse with his hovel over a store. He'd been so afraid of what his kids would think when they came here for the first time last night, but their resiliency amazed him. They just ran in and jumped on the bed in his little bedroom, and within minutes they were playing hide-and-seek.

The ability of little kids to hide, he thought, laughing to himself now at how they'd fooled him. When he was "it," he'd gone into the bedroom and counted to ten. Coming out, he searched the whole apartment, surprised that he couldn't find them. For an instant he had a flash of panic. Where had they gone? He yelled their names, and they came running out of his room. They'd slipped back in while he was counting and had sneaked behind the door. He, of course, had walked right past them.

It was the oldest trick in the book, he thought, laughing at himself.

His hands froze above the keyboard. Behind the door. Brace's wide hallway. Kennicott looking at the floor plan.

That was it. There had been someone else in Brace's apartment. Playing hide-and-seek, but not a child's game.

He banged down on the keyboard so hard it sent a jolt of sound into his headphones. He ripped them off and grabbed the phone.

"Nancy, he wasn't alone," Amankwah said when Parish answered the phone. "There was someone else in the apartment. Behind the door."

"Ahhh," Parish said, exhaling hard. "That's why—"

"Why what?"

Parish hesitated. "You know I can't tell you. But parade or no parade, don't be late."

58

Eight in the morning, and there was already a two-block lineup of cars outside Gryfe's Bagels. Along the east side of Bathurst Street, expensive foreign models were parked illegally, their emergency flashers blinking. Unshaven men dressed in sweatpants and running shorts rushed out of the store, clutching paper bags filled with warm bagels.

Ari Greene pulled his Oldsmobile up behind a Lexus. He got out slowly, tossed his badge on the dashboard, and didn't bother with his flashers. Gryfe's was a simple storefront, and the lineup of men stretched back out onto the street. Most of them were bent over, tapping at their BlackBerrys, talking to their wives on their cell phones, or reading portions of the sports pages, which blared headlines about the Leafs' victory.

The line progressed slowly inside. The bakery was a long, rectangular room. In the back were rows of tall metal racks filled with fresh-baked bagels. On the mostly bare walls there were scattered old black-and-white photos of the early days in the bakery, dating back to the early 1900s. The side of the old white refrigerator was plastered with cheaply made signs advertising everything from Jewish musical theater productions to hand-sewn religious wigs to travel agencies specializing in trips to Israel. There was a particularly colorful one that read "TORAH 4 TEENS: Earn Ministry-Approved High School and Pre-University Credits!" Incongruously, on top of this ad someone had stuck a black-and-white business card for Super Movers, with the name Steve S. and a phone number on it. An empty metal newspaper rack was behind the door. It looked like it had been there, unused, for years.

An older woman stood behind a linoleum counter dispensing the orders with practiced ease. The sweet smell of baking dough and warm sugar permeated the air. The combination of the ovens and the crowd of people in a confined space made it very warm. An old black fan over the front door and two white standing fans inside seemed to do no good at all. Greene undid the top button on his shirt and loosened his tie. The line moved fast.

"I'll have two dozen sesame and a dozen poppy seed," the man at the front of the line said.

With a swish the old woman opened a paper bag and filled the order. "What else?" she asked.

"Give me a dozen plain."

"A dozen poppy seed," the next man said.

"What else?" the old woman said, ringing the order up on an ancient cash register. A hand-scrawled sign on the front of the machine said CASH ONLY.

Greene fished out his wallet. Cash, he thought. For the last few months, as he'd ramped up the hours preparing for the trial, he'd practically lived off his Visa card. He liked using credit cards when he was on a big case. It made it much easier for him to tally up his expenses at the end of the day.

He pulled out his wallet and started to paw through it. I hope I have enough money, he thought as he reached inside. There was the familiar feel of cash, and then he touched a folded piece of paper. What's that? he wondered as he unfolded it.

It was a receipt for thirty dollars from City Hall parking lot. He shook his head. It didn't make sense. Whenever he parked in the big underground lot, he always used his credit card. Why would he have paid cash?

"What else?" the old woman behind the counter asked another customer. Greene moved up a step. He was getting closer.

He looked at the receipt again. It was dated back in mid-February. He shrugged. He'd been up all night, and he was tired. Needed his early-morning tea.

"What else?" he heard the woman ask the customer in front of him.

Greene had been coming to Gryfe's since he was a kid. In grade seven he went to a junior high school down the street, and he and his friends used to come here after school. The same woman was behind the counter, and she looked just as old way back then. She'd give them bagels right out of the oven. In the springtime they'd bring winter gloves to school with them so they could hold the bagels and eat them piping hot.

He'd been hearing this same old lady ask customers "What else?" for his whole life. Just now it occurred to him what a brilliant question it was. Classic witness interview technique. Always use an open, not a closed, question.

For example, don't ask a witness, "Did anything else happen?" That leaves a fifty-fifty chance that the witness will say no. Better to say, "What else happened?" It turns the mind to giving more information.

He held the receipt in his hand. What else can you tell me? he wondered.

"A dozen sesame, and what else?"

Greene looked up. Without even asking, the old lady had tossed thirteen sesame bagels into a brown bag. His usual order.

He smiled. "Some cream cheese," he said, pulling a plastic Loblaws bag from his pocket. "You won't tell my dad?"

"Of course not. How is he?"

"As difficult as ever."

"Good," she said. "What else?"

"That's all."

Greene grabbed his bag of bagels and took another look at the parking receipt on his way out of the store. The time stamp was for 10:15. That didn't make sense either. He always arrived early when he went to court, never later than nine o'clock.

He felt an elbow jab into his arm. "Oh, excuse me," a man said. "I was just loosening my tie. It's hot in here."

"Yeah, it's warm," Greene said, taking a quick look up at the man, then refocusing on the receipt. "Everyone loosens his tie in here."

He took another step. Then it hit him.

The receipt. The cost of parking. The overheated room. Now he remembered.

He looked back at the man loosening his tie. Of course. It was the natural thing to do in a warm room. On a warm day. Your neck is the first place you feel the heat. And the last thing you want to cover up, unless . . .

"Oh no, oh no," Greene muttered as he muscled his way out the door. He looked at his watch. "Oh no," he said again as he headed toward his car two blocks away. In a dead run.

59

There was a smell to the Toronto harbor that was foreign to the rest of the city. Pungent seagull guano, moist coiled rope, and a whiff of outboard motor oil. Sounds too. The squawking gulls, the flapping sails, and the rhythmic undertone of waves hitting the tall piers.

In fact, most of the city had precious little awareness of Lake Ontario, where it was strategically perched. Toronto seemed designed to ignore the fact that it was on the water at all. In the 1950s, highway-hungry politicians had slapped an elevated expressway right next to the shoreline, effectively creating a six-lane barrier along the lakefront. Twenty years later, when supposedly more enlightened politicians awoke to the fact that Toronto was a city on the water, they made a halfhearted attempt to resuscitate the moribund lakeshore. What followed was a quarter of a century of Keystone Kops–like grand plans, political promises, and—improbably in the name of "opening up the waterfront"—a Berlin-style wall of ugly high-rise condominiums.

Through it all, the one surviving piece of real on-the-water life was a community of small houses on the Islands at the far eastern side of the lagoon. Daniel Kennicott had fond memories of taking the ferryboat across to the Islands as a child, playing on the beaches with Michael and his parents. Now he was going back for the first time in many years because Jo Summers had called him on his cell. She said it was urgent, and clearly she didn't feel comfortable speaking about it on the phone.

The big white ferry chugged into view. There was something comforting and old-fashioned about the sight. It was a bit less than a fifteen-minute ride across the half-moon bay, then a pleasant five-minute walk along the south shore. There was a rich bank of trees along the path, and he drank in the heady smell of spring foliage.

When they'd left the Market Place Tower earlier this morning, Detective Greene had turned to him as they stepped onto Front Street, saying, "Get some rest, Kennicott."

"Nothing we can do?" he'd asked.

"Not unless we come up with some more evidence," Greene said. "Speaking of more evidence, this is for you." He gave Kennicott a large manila envelope with no writing on it. "This is not pleasant, I'm afraid. My father has this idea about your brother Michael's trip to that hill town in Italy."

"Gubbio," Kennicott said. His hands were shaking.

"He got this yesterday. I'm sorry. We'll talk about this after today. Now I've got to run. Get some sleep."

Kennicott had walked to a small park across the street from the condo and sat on an empty bench. He was stunned by what he read. For more than eight years now he'd believed that his parents were killed in a car accident. A drunk driver. Fifty-year-old guy who'd lived on welfare his whole adult life. Crossed the line on the two-lane highway five miles from their cottage. The same road they'd driven every Friday night for thirty years.

Over the years, Kennicott had tried not to think too much about the courtroom in Bracebridge, the small northern town where the driver, a pathetic alcoholic, stood with his head bowed and pleaded guilty. The judge, his robes looking tattered, which for some reason Kennicott focused on and felt angered by, sentenced him to two concurrent terms of six years in prison. He could remember only snatches of the judge's speech about the horrible loss to the community, how Daniel and Michael's parents had come to Canada on their own as a young couple. His father had built a successful business. His mother, such an accomplished academic. What a waste it was of two such productive lives. And then it was over. Standing on the narrow steps of the sad little courthouse with Michael, the police officer shaking their hands, feeling that there was really no logical place for them to go next.

Arthur Frank Rake. Kennicott had tried to forget the man's name. But it kept popping up in the infrequent letters he got from the Parole Board of Canada, telling him that Rake had been transferred to this or that institution, making his way down to minimum facilities, taking alcohol and addiction courses. And then one day telling him that Rake had been released and was living in some godforsaken halfway house in Huntsville, a town even farther north. And then the final letter— Rake had completed his parole. It was over.

But now he was reading a letter from the Italian consulate in Toronto, addressed to Mr. Yitzhak Greene. Rake had purchased a country home in Gubbio. The hill town in Italy where Michael was headed before he was murdered.

Michael had flown into Toronto from Calgary the night he was killed. They were going to have dinner together, and he was flying out the next day. Why Gubbio? Kennicott had never heard of the town. He'd assumed that Michael was going to Florence, where he went often to meet with bankers. There was a shop on the north bank of the Arno that their father had introduced them to years ago, where they both still went to buy handmade shoes. Kennicott had never heard of a shoemaker in Gubbio, and Michael had never mentioned going there. He'd been cryptic on the phone the night before and said there was something important they had to talk about over dinner. That was the last time they ever spoke.

Greene had attached a yellow sticky note to the letter: "My father had a hunch about this and followed it up. I checked. Arthur Rake never won a lottery. He just finished his parole and disappeared. I know this is tough for you to read. It looks like we might have a lead at last."

When they'd parted earlier that morning, Greene had told Kennicott to keep his cell phone on. "What are you going to do?" Kennicott had asked him.

Greene shrugged. "Buy my dad some bagels."

Just the thought of food made Kennicott's stomach churn. He'd been up all night and hadn't eaten for hours. Maybe Summers would have something at her place. He liked the idea of having breakfast with her.

The day was already warm. As he left the ferry, he took off his tie and slung his jacket over his shoulder. It wasn't hard to find Summers's place. As she'd described it, there was a row of small cottages facing the inner harbor. Hers was the one with the blue and green swirling colors on the door.

"They're the Mayan color symbol for 'west,' something I learned in Mexico," she'd said. "That's the direction my front door faces."

The floorboards creaked as he walked onto the small porch. Before he could reach the door, Summers opened it. She wore a pair of loose-fitting jeans and a white T-shirt. Her hair was up, but it didn't look neatly tied, the way it usually was. She looked exhausted.

"Thanks so much for coming, Daniel." She reached for his arm and practically pulled him inside.

Her cottage consisted of one large room, with a ramshackle kitchen to the left and a few old sofas facing a woodstove to the right. Early-morning light poured in from the window above the sink.

"I didn't know who else to call. I needed to talk to a criminal lawyer and, well, Daniel, I trust you."

Kennicott nodded. He found himself looking around her small place, wondering, a little guiltily, if there were signs of another man.

She reached up and fiddled with her hair and then, seeming frustrated with it, pulled out the clip. Her hair rained down in a great cascade, but she seemed oblivious to it. She rubbed the clip in her hands, as if it were some kind of good-luck charm.

"It's Cutter and that buddy of his, Barb Gild," she said at last.

"The Crowns? What about them?"

"I don't trust them."

"No one does . . ."

"I got stuck late again last night in bail court. I went into the office by the back door, and I don't think they heard me."

"And?"

"They were talking about the Brace case."

Kennicott stood absolutely still.

"Maybe I shouldn't tell you this." She gave him a wan smile.

They both knew their conversation had already gone too far. "You can't unring the bell," Kennicott used to tell juries when he was a lawyer and a witness had made a fatal admission on cross-examination.

Summers went into her little kitchen and poured herself some coffee into a handmade ceramic mug. She raised the pot toward him, asking if he wanted a cup.

He shook his head. "Just a glass of water?" he asked.

"I keep a cold pitcher of it," she said.

The light coming through the window backlit her hair.

She poured a glass and gave it to him.

"I didn't hear everything," she said. She was cradling the mug in both hands. "Cutter and Gild were talking about Fernandez. How he was such an eager beaver. Perfect Crown for this. And how if he didn't come through this morning, he'd be prosecuting impaired-driving cases for the next decade."

Kennicott took a sip of the cool water and nodded. "They're assholes. They think they run the office. Everyone hates Cutter."

"I know." She sounded nervous. "But then Cutter said, in that damn loud voice of his, 'That Spanish fucker better keep his mouth shut about this.' Gild said, 'Fernandez is Mr. Ambition. He knows this case is his big chance.' 'Yeah,' Cutter said, 'and he knows what Brace told his lawyer.'"

"What?" Kennicott said. "How would he know what Brace told his lawyer? That's privileged."

Summers scowled. "Of course it's privileged. That's why I called you. Grounds for a mistrial, at least. It stinks. They talked about some guard over at the Don—sounded like Mr. Bunt or something."

Kennicott put his glass down. "Mr. Buzz," he said.

"You know him?"

"You Crowns never go to the jails. Every defense counsel knows Mr. Buzz. He's a fixture at the Don."

"This just keeps getting worse," Summers said, biting her lip.

Kennicott looked out the front window. Along the sidewalk by the shore he saw well-dressed men and women carrying briefcases, walking quickly toward the ferry launch. That's what it would be like, he thought, if I lived here.

"You're right," he said. "Something about all this stinks."

60

Ari Greene grabbed the police flasher from his glove compartment and slapped it on the roof of the Olds. He pulled a fast U-turn and bulled his way through the rush-hour logjam to the entrance to the highway. Once on the open road, he gunned it, tearing his eyes away from the dashboard clock. It was 8:20.

By the time he got to the King City turnoff, it was after nine o'clock. As he crested the hill and came down toward the small town center, he jammed on the brakes. A school bus was stopped in front of a small wood house, and two girls in shorts and T-shirts, wearing backpacks, were crossing the street. When they got halfway across, the shorter girl threw up her arms and ran back toward the sidewalk where she'd come from. She hadn't looked back up the road. Greene had spotted her red-and-white lunch box on the curb and slowed down in anticipation of her doing just this.

He grinned as he watched her grab the box and scamper back toward the bus. Rule one, do no harm, Greene told himself as he watched her disappear into the bus.

Driving carefully to the main intersection, he swung north through the rolling hills until he found the Torn property. He kept the police siren off. A trailer was parked in the broad driveway, and as he drove up, Dr. Torn had a horse out of the barn and was leading it toward the trailer. He wore khaki shorts and a T-shirt.

Greene popped out of the car. Already the day was hot, and he began to sweat. "Dr. Torn," he said, extending his hand, "sorry to barge in on you."

Torn's hard blue eyes were icy cold. "I hope you're here to tell me this whole mess is over," he said after he shook hands. He turned back to adjust the bridle. "Allie and I are on our way to West Virginia."

"It's not over yet," Greene said. He could feel the tension in his system. "Sir, I need your help."

"We're not interested in playing the victim's family."

Greene focused his eyes on Torn. "Doctor, I know why you want to stay out of this."

Torn let go of the bridle and looked at Greene, meeting his gaze.

"I need to talk to Mrs. Torn," Greene said firmly.

Before Torn could say anything, the garage door opened. Mrs. Torn stood still as the two large dogs flew up the driveway, their big tails waving ecstatically. She wore shorts, sandals, and a blouse with a silk scarf tied around her neck.

"I want to talk to your wife, Doctor, but I know she can't talk to me. She can't talk to anyone, can she?"

Torn looked at his wife, who was walking toward them. Then back at Greene. His eyes were no longer defiant. But lost.

"You were right, Doctor," Greene said. "Too many people have been injured already." He looked over at Mrs. Torn, who'd come up beside her husband.

"Dr. Torn, I want to protect your wife, but I can only do that if you let me talk to her."

"I-I . . . ca—" It was Mrs. Torn, trying to speak.

"Please, Doctor. Don't make me force your wife to go to court," Greene said. "She'll have to take her scarf off and show the whole world how her daughter Kate crushed her vocal cords when she tried to strangle her to death."

61

"Wait!" Daniel Kennicott yelled as he ran along the sidewalk at the edge of the lake, making a beeline toward the ferry dock. "Wait!" His legs were churning full speed, his quads straining under the tension, his black oxfords slapping on the wooden slats.

It was futile. He had at least two hundred yards to go to the ferry dock and he could see the steel door closing behind the last of the morning commuters. In desperation he stopped, cupped his hands around his mouth, and screamed, "Stop! Urgent police business."

But just as he yelled, the ferry gave a loud blast, drowning out his voice and all hope he had of catching the boat across the harbor. He looked at his watch. It was 9:30. The ferry ride took just under fifteen minutes. Even if he'd made the boat, it was going to be touch and go to run up to Old City Hall and get to court by ten o'clock.

After Jo Summers told him about the conversation between Cutter and Gild, she'd insisted on making him some Mexican-style eggs. As he'd started eating, his cell phone had rung. That was just five minutes ago. It was Detective Greene.

"Kennicott," Greene said, his voice sounding tense, "you've got to get to the Hall by ten. This is urgent."

"What?" Kennicott said, gulping down his first mouthful of eggs. They were spicy and delicious.

"I've just left the Torn farm up here in King City," Greene said.

"Katherine Torn had a thing for choking people. Two years ago she crushed her mother's vocal cords. That's why Mrs. Torn never said a word. Because she can't talk."

"Just like Brace," Kennicott said as he wiped his face clean with a red napkin. The pieces were falling into place like the final entries in a crossword.

"McGill's story holds up. Her testimony will completely exonerate Brace," Greene said. "And Brace is going to walk into court this morning and plead guilty to protect his wife and son."

"There's something else you need to know," Kennicott said. He quickly told Greene everything Jo Summers had overheard Cutter say.

"Shit," Greene said.

It was the first time in all the years he'd known him that Kennicott had heard the detective swear.

"Kennicott, you've got to get there."

"I'm over here on the Toronto Island."

"Just get there somehow. And keep your tie on. Summers won't let you speak in his court if you're there as a cop. Maybe he'll listen to you as a lawyer."

He won't listen to me at all unless I get into his court somehow, Kennicott thought as he watched helplessly while the ferry chugged away into the harbor. Looking around in desperation at the boats moored along the shore, he remembered what Jo Summers had said on Valentine's Day about what she did if she missed the ferry: "You're stuck for half an hour, unless you steal a boat or find Walter, the water-taxi guy who's been there for a hundred years."

Steal one on police business, Kennicott thought as he looked over the boats moored there. Or find Walter. Just then he heard a honking sound coming from the end of the pier where the ferryboat had been.

It was the water taxi. Walter must do a good business picking up the stragglers who miss the ferry, Kennicott thought as he ran toward the end of the pier, waving his arms crazily.

"Thank goodness," Kennicott said as he lowered himself into the narrow skiff. "I've got to get across fast."

The driver swivelled in his seat. He wore a battered blue sailor's cap with the words WALTER'S WATER TAXI sewn on in faded red thread. A big handlebar mustache and long muttonchop sideburns dominated his narrow face. He was easily in his sixties. The wooden seat he was nestled in looked as if its contours had molded to the shape of his body over many years, like a groove carved into a rock in a river. He looked at Kennicott with the languid ease of a man who'd spent a lifetime dealing with people in a hurry.

"I wait five minutes for the other latecomers," he said, then turned slowly back and picked up a newspaper from a large stack beside his chair.

Kennicott was breathing hard. "Officer Daniel Kennicott," he said, pulling out his badge. "This is urgent police business, sir."

Walter turned back reluctantly and looked at Kennicott's badge. He seemed to be totally unimpressed. "Is Hap Charlton going to pay me for the four fares I'd probably get if I waited?"

"Even better, I'll pay you for eight right now," Kennicott said. He took out his wallet. "But we have to go."

Walter took his time. "I don't *have* to do anything," he said, turning back to the front of the boat.

Kennicott clenched his fists. He was considering his options. Raise his voice. Pull his gun. Then he heard the engine rev.

"But you might want to sit," Walter said. The boat took off, slamming Kennicott into a hard wooden seat. He looked at his watch. It was 9:35.

Walter's Water Taxi rolled through the harbor at full throttle. As it bumped across the waves, Kennicott reached into his pocket and pulled out his tie. Walter took a look at him in his rearview mirror.

"You dress well for a cop," he said.

Kennicott nodded at him, but didn't say a word.

"Daniel Kennicott," Walter said, pondering the name. "How come you look familiar?"

Kennicott looked across at the approaching city as he began to do up his tie. He knew what was coming. It happened about once a month.

"I got it. You're the lawyer turned cop. Right?"

Kennicott pulled hard on the knot of his tie. "Yeah," he said with no enthusiasm. "How'd you know?"

Walter kicked his nearby stack of newspapers. "I'm a news junkie," he said. "Never forget a face."

Kennicott nodded. "I didn't want any of that publicity," he said.

Walter gave his usual sluggish nod. "I lost a brother too," he said. For the first time since Kennicott had gotten into the boat, Walter turned to meet his eyes. "Twenty years ago," he said. "Still hurts."

Kennicott nodded. "How much longer?" he asked after a long moment of silence, pointing toward the approaching towers of downtown. They'd just cruised past the ferryboat.

"Bit more than five minutes."

They landed just before a quarter to ten. The moment the boat touched the quay, Kennicott jumped out. "Thanks, Walter," he said as he began to run. He'd tried to give him a hundred bucks, but Walter had refused any payment.

There was a crowd of people at the ferry docks. "Excuse me, excuse me," Kennicott called out as he pushed his way through. He ran up to Queen's Quay, the wide street that bordered the lake. Without waiting for the light to change, he barreled onto the road, dancing through the east–west drivers, their horns blaring. Ahead lay the tunnel below the Gardiner Expressway. The narrow sidewalk on the right side, which had a protective concrete barrier running between it and the road, was plugged solid with pedestrians funneled into it.

Kennicott couldn't risk getting stuck. He crossed over to the other side of the road and ran head-on toward the traffic. It was safer if he could see the cars coming. Most drivers were so surprised to see a man in a suit running toward them in the low-lit tunnel that they jammed on their brakes.

Emerging from the darkness at the north end, he squinted into the sunlight as he rushed up the hill to Front Street. To his left was Union Station, the city's enormous central train station. On the broad sidewalk in front he spotted an ornate standing clock. It read 9:48. There was a group of Somali cabdrivers huddled near one of their cars. A particularly tall man noticed Kennicott running up the street.

"Taxi, sir? Taxi?"

Kennicott looked up Bay Street. It was wall-to-wall cars. And people. Madly waving blue-and-white Maple Leafs flags.

"Thanks," he said. He was huffing. "No time."

He pressed on across Front Street. Looking up Bay Street, he could see in the distance the big Old City Hall clock tower hovering over the middle of the road. The minute hand was approaching the number 10.

The Leafs' victory parade had begun. People were screaming. A few strategically positioned television trucks had their satellite dishes reaching up into the air, like the heads of giraffes raised above a stampeding herd.

But this crowd wasn't stampeding. Just the opposite. Kennicott could hardly move through the crush of people. Dodging and weaving and pushing, he finally made his way north. But two blocks south of Queen, he was stuck. The big clock, closer, yet still too far away, showed that it was 9:55.

To his right there was a big construction site. Donald Trump's new building was finally going up. He shimmied his way over to the chain-link fence, then hoisted himself up, digging his oxfords into the diamond-shaped spaces. He landed on the other side with a hard thump.

"Sorry, sir," a burly off-duty policeman said, rushing up to him. "This site is closed."

Kennicott gasped for breath as he reached inside his coat pocket. He pulled out his badge holder and flicked it open.

"Oh, I thought you were a lawyer," the cop said.

Lawyer, cop. Cop, lawyer, Kennicott thought. "I got to get to the Hall," he said, finally catching his breath.

"Follow me," the officer said.

They rushed north to the other end of the site. The cop swung open a metal gate.

"Thanks," Kennicott said as he rushed across the street. The side door of the Bay was right in front of him, and an employee was going in. Kennicott grabbed the door just as it was swinging shut.

"I'm sorry, sir, we're closed," a security guard said to Kennicott as he rushed up an old set of marble stairs.

"Police business," Kennicott said, flashing his badge. He didn't stop.

The ground floor of the Bay was filled with cosmetics counters and huge posters of gorgeous models advertising the world's most famous cosmetics. Kennicott whiffed the smell of perfume as he ran past perfectly made-up women getting ready for the day. High above him a poster caught his eye. It was Andrea, his old girlfriend, wearing a remarkably skimpy negligee.

I think I can put you in the former girlfriend category permanently, Kennicott told himself as he crashed through the north fire door onto Queen Street. The street and sidewalk were packed with pedestrians. This time he was totally stuck. He looked at the big clock tower and heard the sound he most dreaded. The clock began to chime. The clock would play its four-part tune, and then he'd have ten dongs to get into Summers's court.

62

Nancy Parish knew exactly what was going to happen next. In about ten minutes Kevin Brace, the Voice of Canada, Captain Canada, the Radio Guy, the Bathtub Guy, Mr. Dawn Treader—take your pick of names—would be led into court. She'd stand up and tell Judge Summers that she had new instructions from her client. Brace would then plead guilty to first-degree murder, and Summers would automatically sentence him to twenty-five years in jail. It would all be over by 10:30, tops.

Great result for my first murder trial, she thought as she opened her binder for the last time. The fact that Brace refused to speak to her, and that she'd discovered he was pleading guilty to protect someone else, was something she'd never be able to tell anyone. Solicitor-client privilege was a one-way street. She was gagged forever. Brace's secrets were safe with her.

She turned and looked around the near-empty courtroom. There was only one person in the public gallery, which just yesterday was full. In the back row sat a dark-skinned guy with salt-and-pepper hair, probably in his late fifties, and wearing a beat-up leather jacket with a union logo sewn on the front. Obviously he'd stumbled into the wrong courtroom.

There was a smattering of reporters in the press section of the first row, only a few young journalists, sent to cover what was expected to be a nothing day while the real reporters were at the parade. Awotwe

Amankwah was sitting closest to the door. Positioned to make the quickest getaway. Parish gave him the slightest nod.

Well, this is my one lucky break, Parish thought. Even with the guilty plea, this story will be buried by the avalanche of Leafs coverage.

It was ten to ten. Fernandez and Greene weren't there yet, which was unusual for them. The damn parade had made a mess of the city.

Parish walked up to the clerk's desk. The man's head was buried in a crossword puzzle. "I assume that despite the traffic, His Honor is here and ready to go," she said.

"Right about that," the clerk said without lifting his pen. "Before we left court yesterday, he told the staff that parade or no parade, there was no excuse for being late. Captain's orders."

"My client's downstairs," Parish said.

"I know. I've already got a call to bring him up."

Parish wandered over to her counsel table and thought back to her visit with Brace downstairs half an hour ago. At the cell door, she'd asked a favor of the shift supervisor. He'd agreed to let her meet Brace in the P.C. interview room so she could talk to him in private, not through the glass with other prisoners listening.

The supervisor led Brace to the little room. He was handcuffed.

"Good morning, counsel," the officer said, and Brace turned, without being asked, to have his handcuffs removed.

"Thanks for doing this," she said to the supervisor as Brace, his hands free, moved inside the small room and took the seat opposite her.

"No problem," he said. "It's busy today. Lots of arrests last night, drunk kids celebrating, breaking windows. I can't spare a guard for the door, so I'm going to have to lock you two in. Just bang hard on the door when you want out. Kick it if you have to."

Brace looked surprised to see her. Which made sense after his instructions to her last night. He was pleading guilty. What else was there to say?

"Good morning, Mr. Brace," she said once the door was shut. She pulled out a fresh pad of paper and a brand-new pen and passed it across the table toward him. He didn't move. Just stared back at her.

She looked away. My turn to play the averted-eyes game, she thought.

"I figured out why you're pleading guilty," she said. "I couldn't sleep last night, so I pulled out the file and took another look at the floor plan of your apartment. The one that Officer Kennicott was staring at in court."

There was no need to tell Brace about her call from Amankwah.

Brace was watching her, his arms crossed in front of him. She took back her pad and started to draw.

"Here's the apartment," she said, quickly sketching the floor plan. "This is the main hallway. It's pretty wide, isn't it? Here's the front door. I've drawn it touching the wall. Lots of room behind it."

She looked up at Brace. He glanced down at the page for a moment.

"You led Mr. Singh into the apartment, all the way to here," she said, drawing a line to the kitchen. "And he sat back in this chair, with no view of the front hall. Right?"

She didn't bother to look up, but she could feel his eyes on her.

She put a big X behind the front door. "But you could see the hallway. There was someone hiding behind that door. And whoever it was, you're protecting them, right? Kennicott couldn't take his eyes off the floor plan. He figured it out. And you saw it, didn't you?"

Finally she looked back up at Brace. She wasn't sure how he'd react to this. His eyes were wide-open. Filled with emotion.

"Want to tell me who it was?"

Brace stood up so fast that for a brief moment Parish felt a flash of fear. But it passed instantly when she saw what he was doing. He was on his feet, his back to her, banging as hard as he could on the door and kicking it with his foot in a worn-down spot where it looked like hundreds of other prisoners had kicked.

Great last meeting with my client, she thought now as Horace came over and put his brass bell on the table beside her.

"I see you're here nice and early," he said.

"Thought I'd surprise you," she said.

"Well, dear. Judge just sent word, we might be delayed a bit."

"Summers delayed. What's the world coming to?"

"Family business, apparently."

What did a few minutes matter? she thought. An hour from now she'd be back in her office, her five minutes of fame a thing of the past. The stack of unfiled papers, legal memorandums to write, unanswered e-mails and voice mails, her dreary future.

The comedown after a big trial was always the same. A big burst of energy, the excitement of suddenly having your life handed back to you. Just great. Time at last to catch up on all your other files, straighten out your banking, get the Law Society off your back, see all those friends you'd ignored for months and read those *New Yorker* magazines piling up on the floor beside the bed, radiating guilt.

None of it would happen. A few years earlier Parish had dated a defenseman on the Maple Leafs, and she'd been warned by some of the other players' wives that there was no one lazier than a professional athlete in the off-season. It was true. Once the play-offs were over, he spent about six weeks barely getting out of the house. Then he got traded to Pittsburgh, and that was that.

She pulled out the sports page of the *Star*. At least she could read about the great Leafs victory and the amazing save by the old goaltender at the end of the game.

The courtroom door opened. Two Crown Attorneys every defense lawyer hated—Phil Cutter and Barb Gild—sauntered in along with Hap Charlton, the Chief of Police. The axis of evil, Parish thought to herself as they sat in the front row.

Fernandez finally came in just before ten. Neat and trim as ever. He approached the counsel table without even looking around the room.

Parish put down her newspaper and walked up to him.

"Albert, I got here before you," she said, shaking his hand. "That's a first."

He just nodded. None of his usual banter. Did he have any kind of hint of what was coming? As ever, Fernandez was impossible to read.

She was tempted to tell him that something was afoot. The only other case they'd had together, when she'd won it, he'd taken it well. He insisted that he hadn't lost anything. That it wasn't his job to win or lose.

Parish had laughed when he said that. It was the oldest line in the book for Crown Attorneys.

Maybe he was a good loser. Let's see if he's a bad winner.

63

Follow me," a deep voice called out behind Daniel Kennicott. It was the burly off-duty cop from the construction site. Kennicott hadn't realized that the man was behind him. He barreled into the crowd, and Kennicott tucked in behind him. They squeezed their way across Queen Street as the chimes of the bell tower finished their four-part introduction.

Bong, it rang out. Nine more to go, Kennicott thought. I'm not going to make it.

The plaza in front of Old City Hall was packed. The off-duty cop kept moving people aside, like a plow cutting through virgin snow.

Bong. Bong. Bong.

They got to the broad steps leading to the front door, and there was an opening. Kennicott took the steps three at a time. A group of hookers were standing in front of the cenotaph smoking, sending out clouds of smoke as he brushed by them.

The clock was up to its eighth bong.

Kennicott kept moving. He had to break through the waiting line. He spotted two bewildered-looking businessmen in suits. Must be a tax-evasion case, he said to himself as he rushed up to them. He could hear the clock bong again.

"Police. Let me through."

The men looked up, startled, and instinctively parted.

Bong, the clock rang out for the tenth and last time, silence filling the space where the next beat should have been.

Damn, Kennicott thought as he grabbed the big oak door and yanked it open. Inside, he cut his way to the front of the line, grabbed his badge, and waved it at the stunned-looking guard.

"Police, urgent business," Kennicott yelled as he rushed through the security check and ran into the big main rotunda. It was packed with cops, lawyers, clients, and even a few judges, accompanied by their clerks, rushing to court. Everyone seemed to be talking at once, creating a buzzlike hum.

He charged up the stairs, cut around the corner to his left, and ran headlong toward courtroom 121. The old constable with the bell was still outside. Kennicott waved his badge as he ran up.

"You haven't started yet?" he practically screamed at the man.

"His Honor was delayed. Had an important phone call. Family business."

"What luck," Kennicott said as he rushed inside and stopped. His heart was pounding. His forehead broke out in sweat.

The court was about to begin. Kevin Brace was standing in the prisoners' box. Fernandez and Parish were on their feet. Up in his chair, Judge Summers was uncapping his old fountain pen. Next to him in the witness-box, Detective Ho was opening his police notebook.

The rest of the courtroom was almost empty. Phil Cutter and Barb Gild were in the front row with Police Chief Charlton. Aside from a handful of reporters, there was only one other person in the audience, an olive-skinned man in an old leather jacket.

Kennicott looked at Phil Cutter. The guy had a smug smile on his face. He thought about Jo Summers and what she'd overheard Cutter say to Gild. The Crown's office was a place where careers could rise and fall on the whim of whoever was in charge. Just like prisoners who never wanted to rat out their fellow felons, or doctors who'd never point out the mistakes of their colleagues, or cops who'd cover for each other, there weren't too many Crowns willing to stick their necks out to criticize an office mate.

Kennicott thought about his last moments in Jo Summers's cottage. He'd hung up the cell phone after talking to Greene, looked at her, and said, "I've got to run. You know your father. He's never late for court."

"Believe me," she'd answered, "I know."

He looked at his plate full of freshly cooked food. "Sorry," he said. Instinctively he started toward the kitchen with it.

"Just go," she said, stepping forward and taking the plate from his hands.

For just a moment they stood very close to each other. He reached out for her elbow, and she grasped his biceps. He kissed her and her hand tightened on his arm. It was only a second or two, but it seemed like much longer.

She was the only person who knew he was desperately trying to get to court on time. Her father's court. And the constable had just told him that Summers was delayed by an important phone call, family business.

"Thanks, Jo," Kennicott whispered to himself under his breath.

"Oyez, oyez, oyez," the clerk said, pulling his robes lavishly forward on his shoulders. "All persons having business in this court, please attend and ye shall be heard."

No one seemed to have noticed Kennicott come in.

The moment the clerk sat down, Nancy Parish said, "Your Honor, I wish to address the court immediately on an urgent matter. I have new instructions from my client. I'm going to be making an application to be removed as counsel, and I believe my client then wishes to address this court."

Kennicott's heart was racing, from nerves now, not exertion. After all his running to get here, the next few steps were the toughest to take. He swallowed hard, pushed through the swinging wooden gate, and entered the lawyers' arena.

Suddenly noticing Kennicott, Summers glared down at him. Parish turned and stared. So did Fernandez.

"Officer Kennicott," Summers shouted, "what do you think you're doing?"

"I'm here not as a police officer," Kennicott said, instinctively straightening his tie, "but as a lawyer. In that capacity I wish to address this court on an urgent matter."

Summers looked stunned. Good, Kennicott thought. He needed to buy a few seconds to talk to Fernandez and make him adjourn the case before Parish got to speak.

"But you have no standing in this case," Summers said.

"Your Honor," Kennicott said, planting his feet firmly, "I could argue that I'm technically a part of the prosecution team. But of greater import, I'm a member in good standing of the Law Society of Upper Canada, and as such I am obliged to act at all times as an officer of the court. I'm making an extraordinary application for standing in your court in order to prevent what I believe could be a serious miscarriage of justice."

"In thirty years on the bench," Summers stammered, "I've never seen anything like this."

Kennicott moved up to Fernandez. "You need to adjourn for ten minutes," he whispered.

"Your Honor," Parish said, raising her voice, "it's not just extraordinary, it's improper. I need to address this court immediately."

Kennicott kept whispering to Fernandez. "Greene just saw Katherine Torn's mother. You need to hear this."

Fernandez's dark eyes widened as he stared at Kennicott. His look seemed odd. Hard to read.

"Mr. Fernandez, what do you say?" Summers said, shouting from the bench.

"If I could have a moment, Your Honor," Fernandez said. He was remarkably calm.

Kennicott kept talking quietly. "Katherine almost choked her mother to death two years ago. Like Brace, Allison Torn can't talk anymore."

"Mr. Fernandez!" Summers was screaming now.

Kennicott tried to read Fernandez's eyes, but they were expressionless. He kept whispering. "Greene told me to tell you that this is why Mrs. Torn never said a word when you met her in December. Why she always wears a scarf around her neck. The reason Dr. Torn kept her away from you."

Kennicott willed him to nod in agreement, but Fernandez's head didn't budge. He seemed to grow even calmer.

"Mr. Fernandez!" Summers shouted from the bench. He was turning red with anger. "Mr. Kennicott, stand forward."

"Your Honor, please," Parish called out.

"Look, Fernandez," Kennicott hissed. "You just heard Parish say she's resigning from the case. Brace wants to address the court. He's going to plead guilty to something he didn't do to protect his first wife, Sarah McGill. She was there, hiding behind the door. And their son. The autistic one. He lives down the hall. You've got to stop this now."

"I will have a court officer lead Mr. Kennicott out," Summers shouted from the bench. "And have him cited for contempt. Mr. Fernandez, what do you say?"

Fernandez broke his eye contact with Kennicott. He turned and looked to where Cutter, Gild, and Charlton were sitting. Fernandez nodded, and Kennicott felt a chill go down his spine.

Oh no, Kennicott thought. His heart sank. What have I done? I've just shown Fernandez how to win his first homicide case. All he has to do is let Brace plead guilty right now and he'll be a hero. Then he'll go after Sarah McGill.

This is it, Kennicott thought, expecting Fernandez to turn back to the front of the court. Instead, he shifted his gaze to the factory worker sitting in the audience. Kennicott took a second look at the olive-skinned man and then studied Fernandez. The resemblance was obvious.

Fernandez's stone face broke out in the smallest of grins. He reached into his lapel pocket and pulled out a large pen, and he seemed to tip it to the man, who could only be his father, before he turned back to face Judge Summers on the bench.

"Your Honor," Fernandez said. He placed the pen carefully on the desk. "The Crown has many concerns about the continuation of this prosecution. Unfortunately, certain members of my office have taken actions that compromise the integrity of not just this case, but their higher duty to this court. Moreover, Mr. Kennicott has just confirmed information that would provide Mr. Brace with a complete defense. I thank him for that. There can no longer be said to be a reasonable prospect of conviction in this matter. Nor is it in the interest of the administration of justice to continue with this prosecution. I wish to remind this court, and everyone in this courtroom, that the role of the Crown Attorney is not to win or lose a case, but to ensure that the integrity of the system is upheld. Therefore, Your Honor, the Crown withdraws the charge of first-degree murder against Mr. Kevin Brace."

For a moment there was total silence in the court. Like the pause between the flash of lightning and the crack of thunder when a storm is overhead.

Summers's jaw dropped. Parish turned to Fernandez and let out a loud sigh.

Kennicott could hear the reporters scrambling to their feet.

Suddenly a voice came booming in from the audience. It was Phil Cutter up on his feet. "Wait a minute, Your Honor!" he shouted, his words blasting through the silence.

"That's against Crown policy." It was Barb Gild, on her feet now too.

The clerk rose, tugging his robes forward, and said, "Silence in the court."

"Thank you," Summers said, recovering his cool.

Kennicott looked over at Fernandez.

Fernandez sat down and calmly straightened the edges of his papers. He put the pen carefully back in his pocket. Kennicott wheeled around and looked at the prisoners' box.

Brace was on his feet, his eyes a whirl of confusion. He lifted his head. Kennicott could see that he was straining to speak. "No . . . I'm . . . I'm . . ." he said, trying to squeeze the words out.

"Silence!" It was Summers. "Officer," he said, addressing a young court officer who stood beside Brace just outside the prisoners' box, "is Mr. Brace being held on any further warrants?"

The officer fiddled in his breast pocket, pulled out a narrow piece of paper, and read it for a moment. "No, Your Honor."

"Any outstanding charges?"

"No, Your Honor."

"Any other detention orders pending trial?"

"No, Your Honor."

"Officer, do you have any cause to continue the detention of this man?"

The officer scanned his piece of paper one last time. "No, Your Honor."

"Release the prisoner. Mr. Brace, you're free to go. This court stands adjourned. God save the Queen."

Brace seemed utterly baffled. The police officer opened the door to the prisoners' dock, but Brace didn't seem to know what to do. Instead of walking out, he turned his back to the officer, his hands still behind him, waiting for the handcuffs to come on.

Out of the corner of his eye Kennicott saw the reporters scrambling to get out of their seats.

He turned to Fernandez, who was calmly packing up his briefcase. For a moment he glanced over at Kennicott and nodded. Kennicott looked at Nancy Parish. She was sitting at her desk, her head in her hands, her shoulders heaving. He looked back at the judge's bench. Summers gave him a slight smile before he bolted out of his chair.

Then Kennicott felt it. The cleansing wave of it all washing over him. The coursing of clean blood rushing through his veins. The feeling that he so wanted to savor for just one moment of one day for his lost brother. The thing Michael deserved more than everything else. Justice.

PART IV: JUNE

64

I made you some tea," Jennifer Raglan said as she opened the door to Ari Greene's room and slipped into bed beside him.

Greene took a pillow and propped himself up.

"Didn't boil the oxygen out of the water," she said, laughing a bit as she put a tray between them. There was a teapot, one mug, and a plate of sliced oranges, neatly arranged.

"Thanks," he said, reaching over for the teapot.

"I'll do it," she said.

Greene waited. She filled the mug and passed it over to him.

"Nothing for you?" he asked.

Raglan shook her head. She was wearing one of his black T-shirts. The sleeves were halfway down her forearms.

"I gave notice at the Crown's office yesterday," she said, looking straight ahead. "Taking the summer off. When I come back, I'm stepping down as head Crown. I want to go back to prosecuting cases one at a time."

The mug Greene was holding was very thick. He held it tight, but there was no warmth in it yet.

"The kids are a mess," she said, shaking her head. "Simon's talking about quitting hockey, and William left his science project at my house when it was his dad's week and I was up north on a conference and Dana can't stand . . ."

Greene reached down and took her hand.

She finally turned her head to him. Her bottom lip was quivering.

"It's okay," he said.

"It's just—just—" She started to cry. The way someone who doesn't cry very often cries. "The kids just hate this. And I'm afraid they're going to start to hate me." She shook her head again. "He's not a bad man."

"It's fine," Greene said.

"I need to give it one more try. I'm so sorry." She buried her head in his shoulder.

He lifted her back up. "Nothing to be sorry about," he said.

She wiped her eyes on the sleeve of his shirt. "Don't worry," she said, laughing. "I'm not Ingrid Bergman about to get on a plane."

He laughed back. "And I'm not Humphrey Bogart walking away into the mist."

"What are you going to do?" she asked.

Greene shrugged. The answer was obvious. But he was afraid he'd hurt her if he said it. "There's always another murder," he said instead.

"And always another woman," she said, jabbing him playfully in the ribs.

"Now, now," he said. "You can't have it both ways."

She touched his cheek and let out a long sigh. "I don't have to pick up the kids for another hour and a half."

He took her hand away from him and held it. "I'm going back up to the Hardscrabble Café for breakfast," he said. "It's a long drive."

She squeezed his hand and nodded. "Never give up, do you?"

"There's always something I missed," he said.

She leaned over and kissed him and snuggled into him. "I lied," she said. "I am Ingrid Bergman. Just hold me, Ari."

65

Ari Greene is always the detective, Daniel Kennicott thought as he looked out the front windows of his flat and saw the big Oldsmobile drift past his front door. Even though there was plenty of space right in front of the house, Greene parked farther up the street and walked back.

It was a real cop move, probably so instinctive that it was second nature—drive past the scene and take a look at it before you make your entry. And he was ten minutes early. Another cop move.

Kennicott zipped his carry-on suitcase. It took him a few minutes to close up everything in the apartment. He had a note for Mr. Federico about watering his plants for the two weeks he'd be gone.

By the time he got down to the front lawn, Greene was engrossed in conversation with Kennicott's landlord. The topic, of course, was Mr. Federico's tomatoes, which were already in full bloom thanks to the unusually hot spring.

"Is full moon today," Mr. Federico said, pointing to the horizon, where a round early-morning moon hovered over the housetops. "Best day for planting."

Greene nodded solemnly as he caught Kennicott's eye.

"My landlord is very proud of his plants," Kennicott said as he slid into the passenger seat of Greene's car. "My flight leaves at seven thirty tonight."

"Plenty of time. It's just a few hours' drive," Greene said as he put the big vehicle in gear.

The traffic was light. They drove in silence through the city and onto the highway north, and soon they were on scenic two-lane highways that were dotted with farms and freshly planted crops of corn.

Greene had phoned him late last night and offered to take him to the airport by way of this six-hour detour. Kennicott had readily agreed. Like Greene, he was curious about what they'd find at the end of their drive. Besides, his flight didn't leave until tonight.

They both knew his upcoming trip to Italy was the best lead they had in his brother's case. The ride would give Kennicott uninterrupted time with the detective to talk it over. But instead of talking, Kennicott found himself simply staring out the window. Thinking.

Thinking was somewhat of a lost art, Lloyd Granwell, Kennicott's mentor at his old Bay Street law firm, used to say. Granwell, the senior partner who'd personally recruited him, had a system for lawyers before they went to court. He'd ask them to come to his office with all of their trial notes, greet them in his usual courtly manner, and then gently take everything out of the hands of the nervous young advocates. Next he'd take away their laptop computers and their ubiquitous BlackBerrys.

"Now," he'd say, leading each lawyer to a door off to the side, "please have a seat in this room." He'd open the door to a small, comfortable room furnished with one chair and nothing else. The only thing on the walls was an old IBM sign from the 1950s, with just one word on it: THINK.

"Spend the next hour with no cell phone, no laptop, no binders, no pads of paper, no sticky notes," he'd say. "Just the brain that God gave you. Do something most people have forgotten how to do: think."

The lawyers always went into the Granwell Box with a look of terror on their faces. Inevitably they came out relaxed and confident. Thankful.

The countryside grew wilder and rougher as they traveled north, the deciduous trees and lush farms slowly giving way to the coniferous forest and rock of the Canadian Shield.

"It's nine o'clock," Greene said as they passed an abandoned farmhouse. "Listen to this." He reached down and turned on his old car radio.

"Good morning," a familiar-sounding voice said. *"I'm Howard Peel. The owner of Parallel Broadcasting. Today I'm very pleased to announce that we have a new morning show and a new morning-show host."*

Kennicott looked. Greene nodded, a sardonic smile on his face.

"Hi. This is Donald Dundas, and I'm thrilled to join the Parallel Broadcasting team. Welcome to our new show—Sunny Side Up.*"*

Greene and Kennicott both laughed.

"It gets better," Greene said. "Listen to who his first guest is."

"This morning we'll be talking to Toronto's chief of police, Hap Charlton. He's going to tell us all about the new domestic policing unit the force has just set up to—"

Greene reached over and clicked the radio off. *"Plus ça change,"* he said.

"Charlton has nine lives," Kennicott said.

"At least. When Fernandez met Cutter, Gild, and the chief at the Vesta Lunch, he brought a special pen his dad had given him. It's got a micro-recorder in it. His father's the leader of a union local, and he uses it whenever he meets with management. I listened to it a dozen times. Cutter and Gild put their feet right in it, but Charlton, he's a sly fox."

"Nothing incriminating?"

"He brags a bit about the owner of the Vesta Lunch covering for him as a beat cop decades ago. But the meat and potatoes, he stays right out of it."

After almost two hours the road dipped downward and the brilliant blue of a big lake jumped into view. It was fronted by an old-fashioned wood-framed building with a wide sand beach and a big square dock stretching out into the water. Groups of children played in the sand, swam in the water, and jumped off a tall diving tower. It was as if someone flashed a postcard of a perfect summer scene before Kennicott's eyes.

The road turned and rose quickly through a big rock cut. Straight slabs of sheared granite sandwiched the two-lane highway on both sides, instantly replacing the bucolic summer scene.

Kennicott had tried to find out more about the elusive detective, but could only get the bare bones. Greene had grown up in Toronto, joined the force when he was close to thirty years old, and rose quickly in the ranks. A number of years ago, something happened—Kennicott couldn't discover what it was—and Greene took an extended leave of absence. His parents were Holocaust survivors. Greene's father, who once ran a shoe repair shop downtown, was helping out with the investigation of Daniel's murder, which was Greene's only unsolved case. Was Greene single, married, divorced? Did he have kids? Siblings? All a mystery.

"My parents sent me to camp one summer up here," Greene said. It was very rare for him to ever talk about himself.

"Did you like it?" Kennicott asked.

Greene shrugged his shoulders. "Here, take a look at these," he said, handing over some pages from his briefcase.

The first was a printout of the driving record of Jared Cody, 55 Pine Street, in Haliburton, Ontario. No criminal record. No outstanding charges. Just a couple of speeding tickets.

"Who is this?" Kennicott asked.

"A guy who was always at the café when I was there. Another bad habit of mine. I write down license-plate numbers. When I was up here last time, I'd put his on the back of a receipt for some denture cream I'd bought for my dad. I called the number in yesterday and got the readout. Look at the other pages."

Kennicott looked at the next sheet of paper. There were two police occurrence reports. The first one was dated March 15, 1988. It said:

A number of citizens gathered outside the office of the Children's Aid Society in Toronto. They carried protest signs and bullhorns and were shouting: "Give us back our children." The leader of the group, Jared Cody, d.o.b. May 1, 1950, identified himself as a child advocate lawyer. He and the group were cautioned with respect to causing a disturbance and trespassing. No arrests were made at this time.

The second was dated 1989.

A number of citizens gathered on the main street in the town of Haliburton. They carried protest signs and bullhorns and were shouting: "Give us back our children." The leader of the group, Jared Cody, d.o.b. May 1, 1950, identified himself as a child advocate lawyer. Police officers attended, and a scuffle broke out. One officer was pushed from behind through the front window of a store named Stedmans. Ms. Sarah Brace, d.o.b. December 21, 1947, was arrested with respect to this occurrence and released. Charges were eventually withdrawn.

"Sounds like she pushed that cop pretty hard," Kennicott said.
"From behind," Greene said.
They drove on for quite a while.
"The road construction was really bad the first two times I came up here," Greene said as they climbed higher. A folksy highway sign declared WELCOME TO THE HALIBURTON HIGHLANDS. "This extra passing lane here's all new."
"McGill said it was killing her business," Kennicott said.
"It probably was. It went on for miles," Greene said. "You know, it's another bad habit. Once a case is over, I like to go back for one last look. There's always something I overlooked. Usually it's real obvious."
About twenty minutes later they pulled into the driveway of the Hardscrabble Café. It was before twelve, and the parking lot was filled with a collection of cars, mostly pickup trucks.
Inside the café, Kennicott, smelling the fresh bread, was instantly hungry. The restaurant was packed. An overhead fan was rotating at

full force, but the room was warm. Beautiful flowers hung from the ceiling over every table. They took the last open table near the back window, and in a few minutes a thin waitress came up to take their order.

"Sorry to keep yous waitin'," she said. She turned her little yellow pad over.

"Hi, Charlene," Greene said. "What's the fresh special today?"

Charlene looked at Greene. Clearly she didn't recognize him. "Tomato and cucumber salad," she said, looking at the back of her pad and reading. "All homegrown right here."

Greene ordered the salad. Kennicott ordered homemade lasagna. As Charlene was about to leave, Greene leaned toward her, a conspiratorial look on his face. "Could you do me a favor?" he said, pulling out a spoon wrapped in a plastic bag. "Tell Ms. McGill that Mr. Greene is here and I've got some cutlery to return to her."

The waitress's eyes widened as she watched Greene put the bag on the table beside his plate.

They ate slowly. Greene was right, the food was good. Greene ordered raspberry pie for both of them. Just as they were finishing, Kevin Brace walked out of the swinging kitchen doors. Kennicott looked at Greene. Greene didn't seem at all surprised.

Brace carried a rectangular orange plastic container and moved at an unhurried pace from table to table, piling up dirty plates and cutlery. He was methodical in his work. Plodding. In no hurry. Like someone on prison time, Kennicott thought as Brace approached their table.

Up close, Kennicott could see that Brace's hair had been cut. A blunt, inexpensive haircut. Despite the heat in the room, he wore a white turtleneck. When he saw Kennicott and Greene, his sober face cracked into a bemused smile. He stacked their dishes slowly.

When he reached for the spoon in the plastic bag, Greene's hand shot out and covered it.

"The fingerprints on this spoon are the reason you're a free man today," Greene said. His voice was neither angry nor conciliatory. Just factual.

Brace looked Greene right in the eye and then nodded. The smile remained. Not a hint of celebration in it.

Kennicott remembered what Howard Peel had said about Brace: "The whole damn country sucked the guy dry." He was probably happy to be in jail.

Grinning widely, Sarah McGill emerged from the kitchen, a dish towel slung over her shoulder, and sat in the chair beside Greene.

"Hello, *Mr.* Greene," she said, a glint in her eye. Brace kept stacking the dishes, like any other employee getting paid minimum wage.

"I've got something to return to you," Greene said, pushing the sealed bag toward her.

"Maybe I should call the police, report a theft." McGill laughed. So did Greene.

Kennicott watched Brace. His eyes gave away nothing. He just reached for the spoon, pulled it out of the bag, and dropped it into his plastic container. There was a layer of soapy water on the bottom, and Kennicott watched the spoon gradually submerge.

"How's your garden this year?" Greene asked McGill.

"Good. It's been hot."

"Food is delicious," Greene said.

"Thanks," McGill said. She put her hand on Greene's arm. Brace stopped stacking the dishes, and the table grew silent. No one said a word. Clearly McGill was thanking Greene for more than complimenting her food and returning her spoon.

"'Scuse me. Sorry, Ms. McGill," a voice from behind Kennicott said. He turned and saw the young waitress, Charlene. "We've got a spill at table four," she said.

McGill took one last look at Greene. Kennicott saw her squeeze his arm. "I'm coming," she said, reaching for her towel.

"I don't see Mr. Cody here today," Greene said. "The fellow who always complains that you close on Mondays."

McGill eyed Greene, then laughed. "Jared's gone fishing," she said. "Besides, now we're open seven days a week."

Greene stood quickly, held his arm out to McGill, and shook her hand. "The best of luck to you and your husband," he said.

Back in the parking lot, Greene tilted his head at Kennicott. "Let's go look at her garden," he said. "It's out back."

They walked around to the far side of the building. A rectangular plot of land was under cultivation, the whole thing fenced in by high chicken wire. There were a number of elevated rows of plants in straight vertical lines, with all kinds of vegetables and herbs growing in labeled, neatly ordered batches.

"My landlord would be envious of all this land they have up here," Kennicott said.

The back door of the café opened, and an awkward-looking man wearing a Toronto Maple Leafs hockey jersey walked out carrying a yellow pail and a pair of scissors. He looked over at Kennicott and Greene for an instant, then looked away as he unlatched the back gate and let himself into the garden.

Greene stood motionless beside Kennicott. The man was almost the spitting image of his father. The same deep brown eyes. He was tall too, but hunched over.

Stepping precisely between the rows of plants, Kevin junior carefully snipped a handful of lettuce and herbs, all the while humming slightly off-key. Then, putting his pail on a wooden side table, he bent down over a newly hoed row, reached into his back pocket, and pulled out a tomato-seed packet. He shook his head. Seemingly upset.

He looked over in their direction again, not making eye contact. He looked at the sky, then shrugged his shoulders, as if resigned to some terrible fate. Kennicott looked up and saw the full moon, visible well above the horizon.

Kennicott looked back just in time to see Kevin junior gently tap the seeds into the virgin soil, take out a marker, and slowly, precisely, write out a label.

Mr. Federico would approve, Kennicott thought, looking at Kevin junior so at home amid his plants.

Back in the car, Greene was silent. The road was empty and they made good time. As they descended through the granite rock cut, Greene turned to Kennicott. "Any thoughts?"

"Food's good, just like you said. And fresh. I remember when I was a kid, my mother had a garden at our cottage and—" It hit Kennicott with a jolt. "That's it."

"What?" Greene said. His eyes darted over toward Kennicott, then back to the narrow road. "What?"

"The Leafs," Kennicott said. "The Toronto Maple Leafs."

66

I can't believe I'm back here again, Nancy Parish thought as she slid into the hard plastic chair in interview room 301 at the Don Jail. The same chair she'd spent half the winter sitting in, across from the inscrutable Kevin Brace.

She wasn't supposed to be here this afternoon. But this morning Ted DiPaulo, her partner, had slipped into her office.

"Nancy," he said, "you won't believe this." He tossed a square envelope of fancy stationery across her crowded desk. The envelope was already opened. Inside was a finely embossed, thick piece of paper.

Mr. Philip Cutter and Ms. Barbara Gild, Barristers and Solicitors, are pleased to announce the opening of their new offices. Please attend our opening celebration on July 10.

Parish laughed as she tossed it back at him. "Ted, you can go for the firm."

"Not in a million years," he said, not even cracking a smile.

DiPaulo was still fuming at the treatment Cutter and Gild had received from the Crown's office. Instead of being summarily fired, they'd been allowed to resign quietly and even keep their pensions intact. Now, without missing a beat, they were joining the defense bar. It offended him to the core.

He put the envelope down and reached for Parish's key chain, which she'd tossed among the piles of paper strewn about her desk. Without asking, he adeptly began to work one of the keys off the chain.

"This is what partners are for," he said.

Parish had picked up yet another Law Society form that she was supposed to have filled in months ago. She looked back up at him. "What are you doing?" she asked.

"Taking your office key."

"What?"

"You're banned from here for the rest of the week."

"You can't do that," she said, playfully grabbing at his hands.

"Too late," he said triumphantly, holding up her key in his hand.

"Ted—"

"Nancy, I'm serious," he said. "Those stacks of paper aren't going to get any smaller by you moving them around again. It takes a long time to get over a big trial. The weather's beautiful. Take the week."

"But it's only Monday."

"You've got four days. Go plant some petunias."

Parish frowned. "I tried that when I bought the house a few years ago. I spent five hundred bucks on annuals."

"Great."

"No. They all got leggy because I never pruned them."

"Go prune. Just go out into the sunlight."

Parish knew he was right. It had been six weeks since the Brace trial ended, and she'd gone through all the predictable withdrawal stages. The first week she did little but shuffle paper around her office and linger over lunches, reading her way through all four major daily newspapers. For fun, she deleted the perpetual voice-mail messages from reporters wanting to interview her about the case.

Her friend Zelda dragged her out for a night of vodka and talk about Zelda's favorite topic—her sex life. A guy at a bar had asked Parish for her number, and she'd actually given it to him. When he called a few days later, she told him she'd get back to him in a month or two. He sounded genuinely disappointed.

The next week she solemnly promised herself to be more productive and actually did a short trial, a few guilty pleas, and some JPTs. Her perceived "big win" in the Brace case had kicked up a host of potential new clients. Some were interesting, but many were losers. People with hopeless cases who wanted to switch lawyers in the vain expectation that she could pull a rabbit out of a hat.

At the end of the third week, she couldn't put it off anymore. She went home to her parents' house and actually managed not to get in a fight with her mother for two whole days. My Bridget Jones weekend, she thought as she found herself late on Saturday night sitting in her old bedroom, the window wide-open, smoking the first cigarette she'd had in years.

The last few weeks had been an indistinct blur. Ted was right to kick her out of the office. She'd gone straight to George's Garden Centre. George, a crusty old goat who seemed to wear the same pair of striped overalls all year round, greeted her in his usual irascible style.

"Good day, Counsel," he said as he picked the buds off some dangly-looking plants.

"Hi, George," she said. George's usually bountiful botanical supply looked thinned out, picked over. Clearly all the good plants had long since been snapped up by the conscientious, responsible gardeners.

"You're later than ever."

"I've had a busy year."

"I think I saw you in the paper once this spring. When I was wrapping up some perennials for clients who buy in season."

"Is there anything decent left?" she asked.

Just then her cell rang. George rolled his eyes as she answered it.

"Nancy Parish," she said, turning away.

"Ms. Parish," a male voice she didn't recognize said, "I was given your number by a former client of yours—"

"Can you call the office, please?" she said. "I'm taking the week off, and my partner—"

"I shared a cell with him all winter," the man said. "I think you'll want to see me."

She grabbed some plants that George recommended and rushed out.

Half an hour later, Kevin Brace's former cell mate walked into 301 and sat in what Parish had come to think of as Brace's seat.

"Fraser Dent," he said, reaching out to shake Parish's hand. The man was bald on top, with long hair on the sides, giving him a clown-like appearance. He had a broad, sarcastic smile on his face.

Parish realized that she'd gotten so accustomed to Brace's silence in this room that hearing someone else speak was surprising.

"What's up?" she said, pulling out a fresh sheet of paper and an only slightly chewed pen.

"Nothing, really," he said, rubbing his hands over his face. "I kicked in a window yesterday at the shelter."

"And . . ."

"Oh, with my record, there's no way I'll get bail. I want you to do me a favor. Call Detective Greene and tell him I'm in here."

"Detective Greene," Parish said cautiously. "Last time I looked, he was a homicide detective. Why would he care about a guy breaking a window?"

"Tell him that the air-conditioning broke at the shelter, so I'm resting here for a few days. Besides, the Jays are playing in Kansas City, and inside I can watch the games after curfew."

"You want me to tell him that?"

"You can tell him I'd like to get out, say, Friday. I looked at the weather map. This heat wave should be done by then."

Parish put her pen down and smiled.

"Sure," she said. "I'll call Greene for you."

"If you can't get ahold of Greene, then just call Albert Fernandez. I hear he's doing well these days at the Crown's office."

Parish laughed. "What a coincidence. He's prosecuting murder trials, so I'm sure he'd be very interested in your case too."

"Perfect," Dent said.

"Okay, Mr. Dent," Parish said, "I'll call them both if you answer one question."

"Shoot," he said.

"A guy like you has had his share of lawyers. Why call me?"

Dent broke out into a big grin, befitting his clownlike appearance. "Like I said on the phone, a former client of yours *told me* about you."

"What did he say?"

Dent laughed out loud. "He didn't *say* anything, Ms. Parish. He just gave me this note. And he told me anytime I'm in jail, you're the best lawyer in the whole damn country."

Dent handed over a folded piece of paper. Parish slowly unfolded it, her hands shaking. She opened it and instantly recognized Brace's handwriting.

May 7—Early Morning
Nancy

Whatever happens today, I want you to know that you are an extraordinary lawyer and very special person. I wish you all the happiness you deserve.

Please take care of Mr. Dent. He may need your services from time to time.

Kevin

For some reason the garbage smell in the metal elevator wasn't as bad as Parish remembered it when she took it back down to the ground floor. As the front door of the jail clanged behind her, she turned down the long ramp that ran off to the side, the same ramp she'd trudged up with her loaded briefcase all through those dark winter months.

There was a soft breeze, and the air was warm, moist. As she went down the ramp her footsteps sped up. She knew what she was going to do today.

When she had left the garden shop, George had foisted two potted plants on her.

"You're a bit late for these, Ms. Parish," he had said.

"What else is new?"

"Time you moved up to perennials. Give them a try."

"What are they?"

"Lavender."

"Lavender?"

"They smell great and don't even need fertilizer. Just keep them in the sun, Counsel. The only trick is, don't plant them too deep."

"I think I can handle that," she had said, taking the two pots as she slid her cell phone into her jeans pocket.

"Besides," George said, almost smiling, "lavender kind of reminds me of you, Ms. Parish."

"Why's that?" she said.

"Because they love the heat."

Lavender it is, Parish thought as she sped down the ramp—pen bouncing *rat-tat-tat* off the rails—and hit the street. Running.

67

What about the Leafs?" Ari Greene asked. He'd gunned the car to get through the rock cut and had pulled over at the side of the road in front of the old lakeside resort. Kennicott looked over Greene's shoulder and spotted a teenage girl alone on top of the tall wooden diving tower. She looked nervous.

"Kevin junior's a fan. Like his dad," Kennicott said, looking back at Greene. "Remember all the different Maple Leafs glasses in Brace's apartment? I noticed them the first time I rushed in there. I assumed they belonged to Brace."

Greene was listening intently, looking at Kennicott. "There was a collection in Wingate's apartment too," he said.

"That's my point," Kennicott said. "The son's autistic. Likes to have familiar things with him. It makes much more sense that all those glasses were his, not his father's."

Greene snapped his fingers. "Brace was alone in the apartment every afternoon during the week."

Kennicott shrugged his shoulders. "He stayed home to nap."

"He wasn't napping," Greene said. "McGill told us herself, Kevin didn't sleep much. He was taking care of his son."

Kennicott's eyes drifted back to the girl on the tower as she peered over the edge, steeling her courage to jump.

"But Wingate told us her grandson was never in Brace's apartment, and you believed her."

"I *said* I believed her," Greene said. "I had to keep her talking. When a witness makes a definitive statement like that, it's either entirely true or a desperate lie. At that point she and McGill were both desperate to keep the boy out of this."

"You think Kevin junior did it and they're all covering for him?"

Greene shrugged. "Why would he be in the apartment so early in the morning? More logical that Sarah McGill was there."

Kennicott was still watching the girl on the tower. By her body language he could see her confidence ebbing.

"Let's stand back," Greene said. "When a case is over, I like to ask, Who won and who lost?"

"Sarah McGill wins. Hands down," Kennicott said. "She's got her husband back, and her son too. Katherine Torn is dead. The café is saved, and Children's Aid will never bother her about the grandchildren. No one even knows she was in the apartment that morning except you, me, and Fernandez. You think she killed Torn?"

Greene just stared at Kennicott. "Torn's father and her riding instructor both said she had great balance. Made her a terrific rider. Why would she fall on the knife the way McGill says she did?"

"The floor was slippery," Kennicott said. "I fell on it."

"Yes," Greene said.

"McGill told us that Torn grabbed the knife out of Brace's hand," Kennicott said.

"She probably did. Torn was desperate for attention. Most suicide attempts are just that—attempts, cries for help, not meant to succeed. Given everything we know about Katherine, I have no doubt she was choking Brace. Probably pulled the knife toward her just like McGill told us."

"But?"

"Most turning points in people's lives happen in an instant, with little or no conscious thought. Torn was at the end of her rope. Drinking again. Her platelet level going through the floor. Sarah McGill was desperate too. Her restaurant failing. Her kids having children. Still paranoid about Children's Aid. Suddenly Torn comes running out of the bedroom. Naked. Crazed. Without warning she starts choking

Brace. McGill rips her hands off—remember, she has strong hands; she's made bread every day of her life for many years. Torn grabs Brace's knife and shoves it toward her stomach. The moment of un-planned opportunity presents itself. All those years of anger, all those years of loss; for McGill this is her one and only chance."

"You think she stabbed Torn?"

"Doubt it. Her prints weren't on the knife."

"She could have put her hands over Torn's hands."

"Or she could have pushed her. Imagine. Torn snatches the knife and points it at her stomach. Maybe even pierces her own skin. McGill grabs Torn by the upper arms." Greene squeezed both his hands hard around the steering wheel, demonstrating. Then he pushed his hands forward. "All McGill had to do was give her a shove."

Greene looked over his shoulder to see if the coast was clear on the busy highway as a trail of cars zoomed past. Kennicott saw that the girl on the diving tower had walked off the platform and was starting back down.

"Remember what McKilty, the pathologist, said about skin?" Greene said. "Once a knife penetrates the surface, there's nothing in the stomach to stop it. It's like going through a feather pillow. Back in the 1980s McGill pushed a cop through a window in a protest against Children's Aid. Just one hard push this time is all it would take."

Kennicott looked back at the tower. The girl had stopped when she was at eye level with the platform, clutching the rungs of the ladder. Even from a distance Kennicott could see that she was squeezing the wood hard. He imagined her knuckles turning white under the pressure.

Her fingers.

Kennicott looked back at Greene's hands, both still tight on the steering wheel.

The idea came to Kennicott so clearly he felt his eyes pop open. "The bruises on Torn's upper arms," he said.

"What bruises?" Greene asked, looking back at Kennicott.

"Remember the autopsy? When you came in with McKilty and I was looking at Torn's body."

"You were looking at her shoulders."

"And the top of her arms. There were prints. Ho said they were nothing. McKilty said the same thing. Could have been caused by almost anything."

"Especially with her low platelet level. Body bruises very easily. We see those kinds of marks all the time," Greene said. "Useless as evidence."

"Unless there's something unique about the marks," Kennicott said. He held up his hand, fingers spread. "The hand mark on Torn's right arm had a thumb and four fingers, but on her left arm, there were only impressions for three fingers."

"Three fingers," Greene echoed. "McGill is missing the ring finger on her left hand."

They stared at each other for a long moment.

"Maybe Sarah McGill was holding Katherine Torn and she pushed her into the knife," Greene said. "That explains why Brace put her in the bathtub. To wash away McGill's DNA. His voice box has been cracked and he can hardly talk. So he waives bail to keep his secret safe. He sees you testify, realizes that you figured out there was someone else in the apartment, and decides to plead guilty."

"To protect who? Sarah, his son, his grandchildren?" Kennicott asked.

"Remember what McGill said to us about Brace," Greene said. "'Poor Kevin, he loved two women, and they were both crazy.'"

"Where does that lead us?" Kennicott asked.

"December seventeenth wasn't the only time McGill was in Brace's apartment," Greene said.

"When else would she be there? Torn would know about it."

Greene shook his head. "Go back to your chart. Torn spent Sunday nights with her family. Brace didn't work Mondays. Even insisted on it as a condition of his contract with Parallel Broadcasting."

"Because?"

"Because he spent Sunday nights with his wife," Greene said. "Two women. Six nights with one, the seventh with the other."

Kennicott nodded. "But on December seventeenth Torn surprised him. Came home in the middle of the night."

"Remember Rasheed, the concierge," Greene said. "You caught him on video making a phone call just after Torn pulled into the underground parking. We assumed he was calling Brace to tell him Katherine was home."

"But he was calling to warn him. Because he knew Sarah McGill was there."

"McGill. The master of disguise. She closes the café at two o'clock on Sundays. Takes her an hour to clean up, then three hours to drive downtown. Free parking starts on Market Lane at six. And her daughter told me that nothing unusual happened on Sunday night—just the normal family dinner. Four generations. Edna Wingate; her daughter, Sarah McGill; her son-in-law, Kevin Brace; her granddaughter Amanda; and her grandson, Kevin junior. One big happy family. Like they'd been doing forever."

"And then Brace and McGill . . ."

"Had their regular night together. Wingate can look me straight in the eye and tell me the truth. She didn't see anything unusual that Sunday night. Rasheed understands smuggling people in and out of places. That's why we see him on the video going into the elevator. I'll bet he pushed the up button for number 12, to buy Brace some more time. Still, McGill would have been in a rush to get out."

"That's at two o'clock."

"Right. A few hours later McGill goes back to talk to Kevin. Maybe to get the extra money. Or just for one last kiss. She knows Kevin will be up, the door will be open for Mr. Singh. She assumes Torn is asleep. But Torn isn't asleep. A woman's intuition, maybe, or her own little trap to catch Brace fooling around with his wife."

"This all gives McGill motive to kill Torn, doesn't it?" Kennicott said. "Get rid of her once and for all. Especially if Torn's standing in the way of a million-dollar contract."

"Exactly." Greene put his arm on Kennicott's shoulder. Kennicott couldn't remember Greene doing something like that before.

A thick quiet descended on the car.

"But why did Brace tell Singh he killed her?" Kennicott asked.

"Maybe he didn't see what McGill did," Greene said.

"Or maybe Torn really did kill herself, and he felt responsible," Kennicott said.

"Or maybe the son did it, and they're all covering for him," Greene said.

Greene took his hand off Kennicott's shoulder and glanced back at the highway to see if he could pull into traffic. There was no gap in the oncoming cars.

"But we've got Sarah McGill's three-finger handprint on her arm," Kennicott said. "That's powerful evidence."

"Is it?" Greene said. "Maybe she was trying to pull Torn away. Save her. Maybe Torn fell back into her arms. McKilty said that with her platelet level that low, she'd bruise easily."

Kennicott turned back to the reluctant diver. The girl was motionless on the ladder. She seemed frozen in space.

"Where does that leave us?" he asked finally.

"Nowhere, really," Greene said. He looked at the highway again. There was still no break in the traffic. "McGill's hand mark on Torn's arm, three fingers or not, by itself isn't enough to prove anything. We need more. If we can show she was there every week, that she misled us about that, well, it might be something."

"What's our next step?"

"I take you to the airport, and you go to Italy. Tomorrow morning I'll drive down to Brace's old apartment. With luck, the new residents will let me in to snoop around. With even better luck, they'll still have all those Toronto Maple Leafs glasses. If McGill's prints come up on a bunch of them, we're one step closer."

"What if the glasses are gone?" Kennicott asked.

"Kennicott, sometimes you have to live with thinking you know something but not being able to prove it."

"We just forget about it?"

"If you and I have one thing in common, it's that we never forget. We'll drive back up here once in a while."

"And eat McGill's homemade bread," Kennicott said.

Greene looked over his shoulder. "The only thing we know for sure is that Brace never stopped loving McGill. Always thought she was beautiful."

"How do we know that?"

"Because he told Mr. Singh every day."

Kennicott smiled as he remembered the notes he had taken the very first day. "You mean: 'Mr. Kevin, how is your wife?' 'More beautiful than ever, Mr. Singh. Thank you so much for asking.'"

"That's the one. I bet she stood behind that door every Monday morning so she could hear him say it," Greene said. "You know, my father wondered why he never married Katherine Torn. Now we know."

"He did love two women."

"And he almost got away with it."

They both laughed.

Greene spotted a gap in the traffic. He gunned the Olds. There was a spray of gravel under the wheels as the car took off with surprising speed and they were quickly on the highway. Kennicott swiveled to take one last look at the diving tower. The girl began to shake on the ladder. Suddenly she grabbed the rung above her and yanked her body upward. Without hesitation she charged across the platform and flung herself over the edge. Greene's big car began to accelerate, and though Kennicott craned his neck to look, the lake was out of sight before he could see her hit the water.

68

Mr. Singh particularly enjoyed the long days of late spring and early summer in Canada. It reminded him of back home, where at this time of year he was accustomed to waking up to the light at 4:13 in the morning and then seeing that the sky was still bright well past 9:30 in the evening. It did make his work more pleasant.

And he had pleasant news this morning, Mr. Singh thought as he cut open his bundles in the lobby of the Market Place Tower with his penknife. He'd received notice that deliveries were to recommence at Suite 12A. Who, he wondered, would be his new client—the one to take his last delivery of the day?

After Mr. Kevin's trial, Ms. Wingate in 12B had put her condominium up for sale, and the new owners took the *Toronto Star*, not *The Globe*. It was only yesterday that Mr. Singh learned that the new residents of 12A were *Globe* subscribers, which meant that once again he had reason to return to the twelfth floor.

The Market Place Tower was a well-maintained building. The air-conditioning was most effective, so Mr. Singh felt quite cool as he exited the lift on the top floor. He turned to his right, taking his once familiar route again down to 12A.

He was not halfway down the hall when he saw that the door was open. A hopeful sign. As he approached, he heard a voice. It was male, quite young.

"Hon, I've loaded up the dishwasher with all those Toronto Maple Leafs glasses."

"Fantastic. Let's run it while we're out." This voice was female and young as well. Friendly-sounding. "We can give them all away to the Salvation Army."

Mr. Singh walked slowly. He could see the front door. The old metal numbers for 12A had been replaced by a white plaque with elaborate blue lettering.

Mr. Singh heard the man say, "I've just got to tie up my laces," and then he heard the swishing sound of the cycle changing in the dishwasher. A pair of footsteps approached the door, and suddenly it swung all the way open. In an instant a young-looking couple were in front of him. They wore matching thin aqua-blue T-shirts, black shorts, and bright white running shoes.

"Oh, hi," the young man said, stopping in his tracks. His hair was quite blond. He smiled and showed strong white teeth.

"Good morning, sir." Mr. Singh turned to the woman. "Good morning, ma'am." He had the last newspaper of the day in his hand.

The woman stepped forward. She had short black hair and most striking features. "*The Globe*'s started. Fantastic," she said, taking the newspaper from Mr. Singh with confident ease. "Cal, we can pick up some lattes after our run and read it on the porch."

"Great," the man named Cal said. He held out his hand to Mr. Singh. "Cal Whiteholme."

"Welcome," Mr. Singh said. "I am Mr. Gurdial Singh, your newspaper delivery person."

"This is my beautiful wife, Constance," the man named Cal said, touching her arm.

The woman named Constance, who was already reading the paper, looked up at Mr. Singh. She had remarkably blue eyes. "Hi," she said with a big smile.

"The bank just sent us back home after two years in Paris," the man said. "And I'll tell you, a fully furnished apartment, the little things like kitchen garbage disposals, getting a paper delivered, and being able to actually run on the grass in the parks are just wonderful."

"We jog every morning before work," the woman said, looking up again. Beaming. "It's fantastic that you come so early."

"I make my delivery to 12A each day at exactly five thirty a.m.," Mr. Singh said. "I am formerly a chief engineer for Indian Railways, so one becomes accustomed to punctuality."

"That's great," the man named Cal said.

Mr. Singh smiled.

There was an awkward silence.

For a moment Mr. Singh considered informing the young couple that Indian Railways was the largest transportation company in the world. Then he noticed the woman named Constance jiggling a set of keys in her hand, and he decided to forgo the conversation.

ACKNOWLEDGMENTS

It's a particularly warm day in Toronto, made all the warmer because I'm sitting in the lawyers' lounge at Old City Hall, a building with no central air conditioning and plenty of overheated people within its stone walls. It feels like an appropriate place for the daunting task of thanking some of those who've helped get this book into print.

During my magazine years, Robert Sarner brought me to Paris and taught me how to edit. Carey Diamond lived a lifetime with me as my partner in our own publishing venture. The talented writers David Bezmozgis, Michelle Berry, and Antanas Sileika have been of immeasurable assistance.

I can't imagine practicing criminal law without my associate of so many years, Alvin Shidlowski. Jacob Jesin, the newest member of our firm, has liberated me for this and new books to come. Dr. Jim Cairns and other physicians gave generously of their time and expertise. Tom Klatt, homicide detective turned private investigator, and Debra Klatt, fingerprint expert extraordinaire, were endlessly patient and resourceful.

My great friend and most insightful critic, the writer Douglas Preston, helped beyond measure.

All writers think their agent is the best, but none can compare with Victoria Skurnick. She's been my partner every step of the way, exceeding the call of duty on a daily basis. Lucky me.

When I chose Sarah Crichton as my editor, she told me, "My name will be on your book." I couldn't be happier.

Special mention, among so many who gave of their time, to Katherine McDonald, Howard Lichtman, Nancy Davis, Tina Urman, Lori Burak, Marvin Kurz, Selene Preston, Ricki Wortzman, Alan Bardikoff, Corinne LeBalme, Lee-Anne Boudreau, Alison McCabe, Valerie Hussey, Avrum Jacobson, Mark, Marsha and Bob Davis, Helen and Will Tator, Cheryl Goldhart, Glen Gaston, Ellen Kachuk, David Israelson, Denise Sawney, Kate Parkin, Susan Gleason, Kevin Hanson, Elizabeth Fischer, Alison Clarke, Cailey Hall, and my three tremendous brothers, Lawrence, David, and Matthew Rotenberg.

That my mother, Gertrude Rotenberg, isn't here to share this with all of us is the toughest part. When I held the hand of my eighty-seven-year-old father, Dr. Cyril Rotenberg, and said, "Dad, our family name will be known all over the world," that moment made it all worthwhile.

Seventeen years ago, when my wife and I started having children, I finally got down to writing in earnest. It's counterintuitive, of course. Time, always at a premium, became a scarcer resource with their arrival. Peter, Ethan, and Helen, this shows the depth to which you inspire me every day. I'm more thankful than you'll ever know. (My kids would never forgive me if I didn't also save a pat on the head for our little dog Fudge, my constant 5:00 a.m. companion.)

More than she will ever know, my wife, Vaune Davis, is the reason for this book. After almost twenty-five years together, she continues to amaze me. That this novel is dedicated to her, and her alone, says it all.

Toronto, September 2008

Ten days after he was called to the bar as a lawyer in Toronto, Robert Rotenberg was on a plane to France, where he'd talked his way into the job of managing editor of *Paris Passion,* the English-language magazine of Paris. Returning home to Toronto, he created, edited, and published his own city magazine, *T.O., The Magazine of Toronto.* He spent almost a decade in the magazine business, then worked as a film company executive and a current affairs radio producer before he opened his own criminal law practice. Eighteen years later, at his firm Rotenberg, Shidlowski & Jesin, he defends people charged with, as he likes to say, "everything from murder to shoplifting."

Rotenberg lives in Toronto with his wife, Vaune Davis, a television producer at CBC News, and their three children. He's played hockey on Monday nights in the winter with the same group of friends for more than twenty-five years and is currently at work on his next novel.